Colin P Brown

RUST

To my daughters, Amy and Laura.

1

Peter's bladder had grown steadily more impatient over the previous hour. Suggestive signals had been ignored, it having proven too much effort for him to get up and make his way the short distance across the landing to the bathroom. Discomfort had rapidly given way to pain such that his condition needed urgent remedy. Adding to his distress, the ambient temperature of the room had fallen well below that which the bare flesh of a British citizen found comfortable. He was cold, a steady breeze having blown across his semi-naked body since the early hours. His night attire - a pair of underpants and an extra-large 'Save the Whale' tee shirt - hardly compensated for the lack of duvet that his wife, Tessa, had unconsciously claimed for herself sometime during the night. It had been hot and close when they retired to bed, requiring that the windows and curtains be left wide open in a vain attempt to coax a little fresh air into the stifling confines of the bedroom. Conditions had changed, though. The temperature had cooled considerably during the night and only began to mellow through the actions of the sun that brought with it a third discomfort – daylight overwhelming Peter's retinas, its intensity barely subdued by his delicate eyelids.

Finally he gave in, begrudgingly swung his legs out of bed, lurched to his feet, closed the windows, drew the curtains, and staggered from the room, finding his icy limbs stiff, uncoordinated and uncooperative.

His mission complete, Peter slipped back into bed using the roll of his body to lever the duvet from his wife's clutches. She had warmed it to such a degree of perfection that he could not help but indulge himself in a long series of toe-curling, back-arching, fist-clenching stretches. The pleasure that resulted warranted a visit to the confessional, and a silent affirmation from Peter of his intent to remain exactly where he was for the rest of his life.

Despite the stealth with which Peter had handled the situation, his wife had woken.

'Let me guess, it must be an hour before the alarm goes off.'

Tessa's sarcasm was unwelcome at any time of day, but particularly so when the day had not yet started.

'I can't help it. You wait 'til you're my age.'

'Darling, I'm only two years younger than you. Perhaps if you drank cocoa before bed instead of beer... Besides, it's not the fact you need an old man's wee at the age of thirty-four; it's the fact you make so much noise – enough to wake the dead.'

'I aim for the porcelain,' Peter replied indignantly. 'What else do you want me to do?'

'I'm not complaining about the sound of you peeing - although I'd prefer it if you aimed for the porcelain *inside* the bowl - it's the noise you make going to and from the bathroom that bugs me.'

'Ha, ha, very funny. There's nothing wrong with my aim – straight as a die. If it was an Olympic sport, I'd hit the bull every time.'

'Poor bull.'

Tessa surprised herself that she had made a joke and smiled.

Their conversation having died, Peter allowed his head to sink into the pillow, his mind tasked with shutting down every muscle in his body, one set at a time – lips, eyebrows, shoulders – until he had achieved a state of near perfect relaxation.

Bliss reigned for no more than three minutes.

'Come on sleepy head,' his wife said, nudging him. 'Now we're both awake, we might as well get up. We've got lots to do today.'

All attempts to ignore this statement were futile; the sounds of one aerosol after another de-pressurising, and of a hair drier working on the highest setting, saw to that. Then there was the sound from the bedroom next door; of small feet dropping to the floor and padding heavily towards where he lay.

'Hello Daddy,' Emma said, cheerily, wearing a beaming smile across her face. 'I want my breakfast.'

Emma was nearly five, blonde, blue-eyed, and had a lovely temperament. Peter loved her and Tess more than anything on Earth, but right now he just wanted to sleep. Unfortunately, he knew full well that Emma would never let anyone else pour her cereal. So, for the second time in twenty minutes, he reluctantly got out of bed, this time making his way downstairs to the kitchen. Emma followed close behind, singing.

Father and daughter sat at the table. *She* was wide-awake and chatty; *he*, on the other hand, sat motionless, staring, accepting only shallow breaths. His mind was still in bed, his body still asleep.

'What are we doing today Daddy?' chirped Emma.

'I don't know. Why don't you run and ask Mummy?' he replied, in a low, weary tone, wishing to be left in peace, at least until he had had the chance to come round fully.

Not long afterwards, Tessa came downstairs to find Peter still sitting at the kitchen table in a trance-like state.

'You're not even dressed yet,' she said, rolling her eyes as she walked past, collecting a pile of laundry in her arms, destined for the rotary airer.

'No, sorry love. I was just about to put the kettle on, but then I got distracted.'

Peter flicked the switch and walked from the kitchen.

Having placed his hand on the newel post, he groaned theatrically before slowly climbing the stairs. At the top was the bedroom, and in the bedroom was the bed that looked so inviting, especially so because Tessa had worked her magic, plumping the duvet and the pillows in a way he had never been able to emulate, try as he might. However, as much as the bed called to him, he knew that even thinking about returning to its warm embrace was out of the question. It was far safer to have a cold shower, get dressed and let the anticipation of his return to unconsciousness tease him throughout the day.

By the time he made his way back downstairs, Peter's wife had already called up to him three times.

'How are you getting on?' was a warning she had closed the breech.

'Are you nearly ready?' translated to the target had been acquired.

'Hurry up, we're sitting here waiting' demanded evasive action if he was to avoid being blown out of the water.

His hands riding the bannister and handrail, Peter's feet barely kept up, touching only every second or third step.

A minute later, the front door shut with a thud, the knocker emitting an annoyed rattle.

Inside the house, the kettle had clicked off and the water had cooled to the extent it could no longer scald. Neither Peter nor Tessa had found time to pour, let alone drink their much-needed cup of coffee and for Peter it was worse, he having nothing in which to dunk his morning biscuit – the first biscuit of the day. In fact, his favoured Rich Tea remained within its packet, there to live another day.

All three members of the Allerton family had occupied their seats in the car - engine idling - before Peter had even had the chance to inquire as to the agenda for the day. His wife began to list the main events.

'First, we have to take Mum to the doctors to get her prescription. Then we've got to take her shopping; apparently she's run out of food for the dog. Besides, I've not seen her for over a week now. Would you be a love and stay at her house and mow the lawn for her?'

That was a good start, Peter thought. He had the unenviable choice of either cutting his mother-in-law's grass under the constant supervision of that damn dog, which would bark incessantly, or he could accompany his wife and Eileen to the shops. Considering the relationship he had with the latter, he thought that perhaps it would be better to opt for physical exhaustion. After all, his body would heal; his mind might not.

Tessa was not finished.

'Then we'll pop in to see your grandfather. He wanted some soap didn't he? Bless him. I know for a fact that he's got bars of the stuff in his underwear drawer. He does like to have an emergency supply of things though. You know how he is. It's probably something left over from the war - rationing and all that.

'I suppose we could take him into town, but that old wheelchair of his is so awkward. Besides, we really don't have time.'

Peter loved his wife dearly, but he was tired and grumpy and Tessa did not pause for breath.

'You've got all that stuff on the patio which needs to go to the tip. You can take Emma with you. That'll give me a chance to do the housework. You like helping Daddy don't you, Ems?'

Peter's rest day seemed to be going the way his rest days always went and yet his wife had more items on her seemingly endless to-do list.

'We must clean out this car. It's embarrassing. I'll do the inside if you mow the lawn. *You* can wash the car though because you know what you're doing.'

Peter began to suspect that even an all-day shift would have been less demanding. At least at the jail he would have enjoyed exchanging banter with his colleagues, giving as good as he got, unified against the common enemy – that being prisoners.

'Emma's got dance at four so I'll have to leave you to go into town to Jones' for that wallpaper I ordered. I don't know when we'll get time for tea. Maxine's expecting me at her house by seven. You can get Emma to bed, but don't keep her giggling all night.'

Seeing the glazed expression upon her husband's face, Tessa stopped issuing instructions for a moment, long enough to ask a simple question.

'What's wrong with you?'

'Nothing sweetheart,' replied Peter, failing to sound convincing.

'Oh come on Pete, I know you're tired, but if we don't get these jobs done today, they'll never get done.'

'I know. It's just that I was hoping for us to have a bit of quality time together – stop somewhere nice for lunch or something.'

To reassure her he was not in a mood, Peter placed his free hand upon Tessa's thigh and squeezed gently, only to be reminded of another reason he would like to have remained in bed.

His hand slid to her inner thigh, out of sight of their daughter who occupied a booster cushion on the back seat, singing without the merest hint of a tune. Tessa said nothing, but simply picked up his hand, placed it back on top of her leg and held it there, her face issuing a mock reprimand.

Peter continued driving.

Days like this were so wearing: in and out of the car every few minutes; Emma in the back complaining she was bored; completing one chore just as another reared its ugly head.

In truth, Peter felt sorry for himself, believing he had just cause. Sensibly, no one ever thought to highlight the career of a Prison Officer as an example of good work-life balance. Most worked alternate weekends, four out of five weekdays, two or three evenings per week, and the sets of nights came round all too often. It was difficult to get time off, the estate operating all day, every day, and the new staff just would not stop resigning, forcing the die-hards to plug the gaps. Peter was used to staying on beyond the end of his scheduled finish time. He was used to not knowing until the last minute whether his request for leave had been granted. And when it was not, he was equally used to pleading with his colleagues, hoping one of them would swap their shifts so that he might attend a wedding, a funeral, or some other major event, for pain or pleasure. Over eleven years this had become the status quo, but just because he was used to it did not mean he liked it. Mid-week rest days were his own. Between chores they provided an opportunity to engage in hobbies; to watch TV progammes that Tessa had no interest in. They also provided quality time with his daughter, walking Emma to and from school, engaging in conversation on an endless variety of subjects. However, they were also a lost opportunity to spend time as a family; to do the things families enjoyed doing together: going to the zoo; a day at the beach; and if money was tight, a free trip to the local aquatic centre, their stock meant for sale, but their fish tanks a delight for a little girl of five whose eyes saw wonderment in anything even mildly out of the ordinary.

Tessa knew her husband would leave his job were it not for the grip of the mortgage company on their lives. Their claws where unforgiving, having no sympathy for a customer who temporarily needed to draw a smaller salary as he attempted to forge an alternative career. Tessa knew what the job did to her husband, but dared not accept it.

'That's a lovely song, Em,' Tessa lied.

The list of chores was completed with only a little moaning from Peter's grandfather. He complained the soap was not his usual brand but accepted it nonetheless, adding it unceremoniously to a collection of half-a-dozen other bars that nestled in a drawer among his generously sized Y-fronts.

Emma and her parents even found time to ward off starvation, finding a few minutes to grab a bite to eat from an American-style fast food restaurant. Of all the family, Emma enjoyed the experience the most as she received with her meal another plastic toy to add to her partially completed set.

When finally they reached home, Peter immediately set about keeping his daughter from under her mother's feet while Tess got ready for her much deserved evening out. This being his intention, he decided he and Emma should bake a cake together.

Sometime later, Tess appeared at the doorway to the kitchen to find Peter and Emma at the sink, manually washing items that would not fit in the dishwasher. Every surface was covered with flour, including Emma, who stood on an upturned washing up bowl, a spare that she used whenever she wanted to reach the sink to wash her hands.

'You've used rather a lot of liquid haven't you,' Tessa said, laughing at seeing the dome of suds that pressed against the underside of the mixer tap, spreading across the draining board.

Peter, unashamedly wearing his wife's flowery apron, twisted round at the waist, his head looking back over his shoulder, his hands remaining buried in bubbles.

'Wow! You sure you're only going round to see Maxine?'

Tessa's appearance compelled her husband to abandon the washing up and turn round completely, affording him a better view.

'You're dressed a bit dead sexy for a girls' night in.'

Tessa smiled.

'We like to dress dead sexy for each other. Have you got a problem with that?'

Walking towards him, her hips swung seductively, teasing him mercilessly.

Threatening to daub her face with suds, Peter's outstretched hands halted her progress at the optimum distance to look her up and down, admiring her curves.

'Not at all. I just wish I was there to watch.

'Mummy, what does dead sexy mean?'

'Oops!' Peter said, giving his wife a cheeky grin.

This was one of those situations in which both parents were too embarrassed to explain and not in any position to admonish. The only solution was to ignore the question and rapidly change the subject, Peter instinctively closing his hands gently against Emma's soft, plump cheeks, before bending forward to receive a retaliatory deposit of foam, delivered by two smaller hands.

Tessa's smile waned a little as she realised her husband's child's play was not over. Reloaded, Peter's hands stretched forward, accompanied by his best zombie impersonation. Despite his wife's protestations, his fingers hooked behind her ears and pulled her forward.

Two squeamish expressions were uttered; the first from Tessa whose ear canals did not appreciate being filled with foam; the second from Emma who thought it all too soppy that Daddy should plant a kiss on Mummy's lips.

'Thanks for that,' Tessa chuckled. 'It's lucky I haven't applied my face paint yet.'

'You don't need any. You look lovely without it.'

Thankfully, Peter just managed to stop himself saying the words 'dead sexy' again. Had she heard it a third time, Emma would no doubt have started chanting it and Peter was all out of subject-changing material.

As promised, Tessa left the house at seven o'clock to enjoy her girls' night in. Emma had gone to bed shortly afterwards, sitting up against the padded headboard while Daddy read to her. Accepting she was fighting a losing battle to keep her eyes open, she deliberately chose a thin book with very few words on each page. Emma was prepared to keep the familiar custom short, but it was unthinkable she would ever forego the bedtime story completely.

Peter, equally aware just how tired his daughter was, spoke as quickly as possible, without making it sound as though he was reading the legalese, commonly added at the end of radio advertisements, especially those that involved any form of financial lending. With only a few pages to go, Peter noticed Emma still had a goodly deposit of flour in her ear. The thought crossed his mind to make her get out of bed and walk to the bathroom, but he soon dismissed the idea, recognising she would fall asleep on the bath mat long before he had time to wring out a flannel and apply it to her face.

With Emma's shoulders pinned beneath the duvet, father and daughter's lips touched. Her eyes shut.

'Night, Em. Love you.'

There was no reply, Emma already being fast asleep.

With his wife out on the tiles for the evening, Peter found himself at a loose end. His response, as always in these circumstances, was to go directly to the kitchen where he started a methodical search of the refrigerator, the freezer and the cupboards, hoping to find comfort food with which to lift his spirits. The weekly shopping delivery still being several days away, stocks of 'the good stuff' were sadly depleted. There was not a trace of chocolate to be had anywhere, not even a chocolate-coated biscuit. Nor were there any packets of crisps, individual trifles, or ice creams. The initial sweep left Peter feeling bitterly disappointed, but it was not in his nature to give up so easily. The cake he and Emma had baked together was not on the menu, he having promised her – hand on heart – that he would not touch their creation until they had iced it together the following day. With this in mind, the search area widened to include the dining room where he had known Emma to keep a supply of confectionery in the past. She was obviously aware of her father's total disregard for matters of ownership where sweets were concerned as she had either eaten or hidden her entire reserve. His philosophy was that if he could find it, he was entitled to eat it. It was amazing then that his body did not resemble that of a sumo wrestler.

Having failed in his primary objective, Peter considered alternatives. Spending the evening in the garage tinkering at his workbench was out of the question. The noise would irritate the neighbours and besides, with it being situated fifteen metres from the house, at the bottom of the garden, if Emma were to wake he would not hear her. Watching the television was not an option either, the many channels being filled with re-runs and second-rate imports.

Feeling fatigued and a little lonely, Peter would happily have elected for an early night, but he wanted to wait up for Tess whose return was anticipated at around eleven o'clock. Although she never expected him to stay up on occasions such as this, she was always grateful that he did, and they would usually relax with a drink together before bed.

In the end, he chose to settle on the settee with Podge – the oddly, but accurately named family cat – curled upon his lap, a book in his hand and a number of small bottles of chilled French lager by his side. However, it did not take long to realise that reading and alcohol do not make good bedfellows. By the fourth or fifth bottle, Peter's eyes were scanning the pages, but the words were not registering. By ten o'clock there was little point in continuing.

Putting the book down, he turned his attention towards the television, deciding to pass half an hour watching the news. Unfortunately, the remote controls were just out of reach and necessitated Peter lifting the cat off his lap and placing him gently on the seat cushion beside him. Podge took it as an affront, turning his back towards Peter's apologetic face as if to punish him.

Podge had been saved from an animal sanctuary and had been money well spent. Although he regularly persuaded Peter to get out of bed in the middle of the night to open the front door, and cost a small fortune to feed, Emma loved him and that was justification enough to keep him. Besides, Peter also had a soft spot for the creature and was grateful for every sign of affection it ever showed him, which was not often, it had to be said.

In the past, a single remote had been sufficient, but these days it required one to control the sound bar, another to operate the satellite box, and a third to switch on the television itself. Peter picked up each in turn, pressing the appropriate button before returning it to the coffee table and taking up the next. Three remotes, three presses, but still the television did not become active, Peter's aim or thumb control not being to one of the remotes' liking. Annoyed, he tried again. It worked but the unnecessary extra step, coupled with Podge's refusal to offer forgiveness, added to the irritation of being alone on a Saturday night, denied any creature comforts.

Angela Dearlove and Christopher Shawshank took it in turns to read a list of the top stories to come.

'The headlines on the hour...Up to fifty people are feared dead after a landslide hit a busy road in Southern Italy earlier today.'

Angela spoke first, using her well-rehearsed solemn voice, smoothly handing over to her colleague to read the next sentence.

'Following yesterday's decision by the Bank of England to increase the base rate, most of the high street money lenders have raised their mortgage rates by half of one percent.'

'Bugger,' thought Peter.

Angela continued, this time using her upbeat voice.

'The biggest ever National Lottery winner has come forward to tell us exclusively how he feels about his new found wealth.'

'It's all right for some,' added Peter, this time speaking aloud.

Christopher concluded the headlines with his curious-and-surprised tone.

'And a meteor shower has taken astronomers by surprise. We'll be talking to an expert and we'll being telling you how to get the best views.'

'But first the tragedy in Italy where falling rock has claimed the lives of up to fifty people. At least five of them are thought to be British,' announced Angela.

She seemed to have become confused and was using her upbeat voice again. It made Peter mad. The way these people read the news was disgraceful: matching the right voice to the right story; giving statistics on British casualties as though the other poor bastards were somehow less important. They seemed to be using an unofficial league table –

'In order of importance, the casualty list is as follows: two British, three American, one French, a small puppy and some other miscellaneous foreigners.' Or there would be the reassuring, 'There has been a terrible disaster but don't worry, none of them were ours.' Then there would be a film crew at the scene trying to find footage of a child's toy that might serve to tug the viewers' heartstrings.

By now, Peter had consumed his initial stock of lagers, had made several trips back to the fridge for more and was feeling comfortably drunk. Alcohol made him melancholy; news of interest rates rising made him worse.

He had just started to feel a little more financially secure with his latest pay rise. Another half a percent on his mortgage, the third such rise in as many months, would take him straight back to square one.

'Bugger.'

Again, he spoke aloud.

'It's all right for that lucky sod who's won the lottery,' he thought.

The trouble with lottery winners, so it seemed, was that they were either criminals, foreigners who took their vast fortunes out of the country, people who were too old to enjoy it, or people who could not cope with the sudden wealth.

Why, thought Peter, did the Gods never look favourably upon people like himself? *He* would keep the money in the country. *He* had never broken the law, save for the odd parking ticket, and even then it had been due to a genuine mistake on his part. *He* could most certainly deal with a sudden increase in his spending power and he was just the right age: any younger and he might fritter it away in a matter of months; any older and he would be buying top quality picnic blankets and going on holidays to Bournemouth, no expense spared. If the hand of fate were to be swung by good intentions, he would have won the lottery the very first time the balls had rolled from the machine.

This line of thought made Peter even more miserable, knowing it was unlikely he would ever be faced with the problem of what to do with such an enormous sum of money. What made matters worse was that the winner of the largest ever jackpot turned out to be totally deserving of his good fortune. He was forty years old, had been selflessly caring for his disabled daughter for the past seventeen years with the help of his wife, to whom he had been happily married to for twenty-two years. They intended to use the money to ensure their daughter had as fulfilling a life as possible and would be donating a large portion of their winnings to research into curing her disease.

Finally, the news reached the story about the unexpected meteor shower, Christopher Shawshank interviewing an expert in the field - Professor Ian Michaels.

It was inevitable that the Professor should have become a scientist. It was encoded in his DNA, his RNA and any other as-yet-undiscovered-NA that might, in future, be reported in one of the leading scientific journals. At the age of forty-five, he exhibited all the hallmarks. He wore a rather dated sporting jacket with leather patches at the elbows, and beneath this, a brown jumper. However, neither of these items of clothing could conceal the Professor's pear-shaped torso; one that barely understood the concept of regular exercise. His hair *had* seen a comb, but still managed to break free from all convention. A rambling beard covered the underside of his jaw, reaching for his ears at either side, but there was no moustache; that would have looked far too conventional. Peter was sure that if he could see the man's lower portions, he would prove to be wearing brown or mauve corduroy trousers and they would stop unfashionably short of his shoes.

The Professor did seem to know what he was talking about though.

'Tell us Professor,' inquired the news reader, 'what's all this about meteors that has taken the world of astronomy by surprise?'

'So,' Professor Michaels began, as apparently did all men of science these days, 'to give you an overview, a meteor is a streak of light seen in the night sky when a meteoroid - an interplanetary rock or dust particle - enters and burns up in the Earth's atmosphere, about eighty kilometres above the Earth's surface. Meteor showers can be observed, usually at the same time each year, two examples being the August Perseids and the December Geminids. Putting it succinctly, we were not expecting a shower at this time of year.'

'So, it's unexpected, but is there anything else that our viewers might find interesting?'

Christopher prayed there was.

'Yes. So this is where I get to my first point. Even the most prolific meteor shower achieves a peak Zenithal Hourly Rate of between eighty and one-hundred-and-seventy. That is to say, eighty to one-hundred-and-seventy streaks of light per hour. However, this current phenomenon breaks all the rules, giving us many times that number - nearly a thousand hits per hour and that figure appears to be rising.'

'Interesting.'

The way in which Christopher delivered his response suggested he might prefer discussing the manufacture of premium quality cardboard.

'Professor, you said that was your first point, suggesting there are others.'

The news presenter could only have asked another question if he had been prompted to do so by the producer, urging him to fill a gap.

'Yes indeed. So, meteor showers are caused by the Earth moving into a stream, or cloud, of particles, ejected by a comet, which stretches along the orbit of that comet. In the case of the Perseids, for example, this is the comet Swift-Tuttle. Although meteors can be seen all across the sky, because of the path of Swift-Tuttle's orbit, Perseids are primarily visible in the northern hemisphere. However, the current event can be seen simultaneously in both hemispheres. Normally the meteors are most noticeable in the pre-dawn hours, but on this occasion they can also be seen clearly throughout the day – quite unusual.'

At least the professor was talking in layman's terms.

'Strangest of all is the nature of the strikes. I have repeatedly referred to a meteor shower as being a series of streaks of light in the night sky. In the case of this current phenomenon, this is not so. The particles do not streak. They merely twinkle, as though iron filings have been cast into a flame.

Again, this is most unusual.'

Christopher Shawshank would like to have left it there but was receiving further prompts from the gallery, via his ear piece, instructing him to fill a few more seconds of airtime, until the Chancellor of the Exchequer could be made ready to discuss the interest rate rise from studio 6. Consequently, there was nothing more to do than fish for a more interesting story.

'So, Professor, is it dangerous?'

'No. The only risk would be to the many sensitive and valuable satellites that orbit our planet, but there have been no reports of any of them being affected. The astronauts currently inhabiting the International Space Station have reported seeing the flashes from space, but also that the station has not been struck and they have not sustained any damage.'

'What would happen if one of these rocks hit the Earth?'

'Well, now we are talking a different kettle of fish; a whole new ball game; a salad rather than a Sunday roast. The sizes of the particles I am describing are anywhere from a grain of sand up to ten kilograms in weight and are quite harmless. A meteorite on the other hand, a large piece of interplanetary debris that falls to the Earth's surface, usually weighs more than one hundred kilograms. However, they normally break up into smaller pieces on entering the atmosphere. If one of these were to hit a populated area then some damage, or even loss of life could occur, but it is very unlikely.'

Here was the story.

'So Professor,' Christopher said, almost drooling. 'You are saying there is a danger that one of these huge rocks could crash down on, say, London, claiming many lives and wreaking untold damage?'

'No,' the Professor replied simply, but then, on seeing the cynical look on the newsreader's face, felt the need to expand. 'A meteorite in the magnitude of at least one hundred kilograms might cause such damage, but the planet is relatively sparsely inhabited and it is statistically unlikely to hit anyone. Do not forget that seven tenths of the Earth's surface is covered by water.'

'And who was it who said there are lies, damned lies and statistics?' replied the newsreader, raising an eyebrow to camera. 'Remember the skies over Russia?'

Before the Professor had a chance to reply, Christopher brought the interview to a swift close.

'Thank you Professor. That is all we have time for.'

Christopher Shawshank had confirmed everything Peter Allerton had ever thought about everyone who worked in the media, causing him to take up all three remote controls, killing all three devices by applying unnecessary pressure to the off buttons of each.

With half an hour to kill before Tessa was expected home, Peter took the opportunity to look for meteors. Easing himself up so as to maintain his balance, he made his way to the window. Pulling back the curtains, he peered up at the night sky and sure enough could see lights twinkling as each particle of harmless dust gave up its life for the pleasure of mankind – a gentle firework display without the oohs and ahs.

He was still at the window as Tessa walked into the living room.

'Have you seen the lights in the sky?' she asked. 'They're really pretty.'

'It's been on the news', Peter replied, slurring his words.

Tessa noticed a collection of empty bottles on the small table, Peter having arranged them into a neat line stretching from one side to the other. A second line was making the return journey.

'You've been having a good time then,' she said.

'I've been having a great time,' her husband replied sarcastically.

'I'll put some coffee on,' Tessa said, moving through to the kitchen.

The couple took their mugs with them outside to look up at the light-polluted sky. Every second, a dozen silent flashes appeared and vanished in an instant.

'Pretty isn't it?' Peter said, pausing for a moment before adding. 'Hey, do you think we'll all wake up tomorrow, blind and surrounded by triffids?'

'Let's hope not, but maybe we should prepare a bucket of seawater just in case.'

'Good thinking,' Peter replied, taking Tess' free hand in his.

The conversation paused, both Tessa and her husband having become mesmerised by the twinkling sky.

Tessa broke the silence.

'We're lucky. Normally when they tell you to stay up until all hours because a comet's arriving, or there's some sort of an eclipse, we never get to see them because it's always too cloudy or something. The fact we actually get to see the lights probably means it's a good omen.'

'Omens? Next you'll be telling me you believe in your horoscope.'

Finishing their coffee, the couple made their way upstairs to check on Emma.

By the time Peter had finished in the bathroom, Tess was to be found sitting up in bed, her legs beneath the duvet, smart phone in hand, amending her on-line shopping.

Peter walked up to her side of the bed, completely naked.

'I've washed him. I don't suppose...'

Tess took her eyes from the small screen and looked to one side. Without a change of expression she rolled towards her husband and lifted an inebriated appendage between her fingertips and dropped it.

'Put your pants on and come to bed, Casanova. Your mind may be willing, but our little friend has clearly had too much to drink.'

'You're probably right. He does feel a bit numb,' Peter sniggered, his words ever so slightly slurred.

Having pulled his favourite, faded and thinning, World Wildlife Fund tee-shirt over his head and secured his second best friend inside a pair of underpants, selected for comfort, Peter slipped beneath the duvet, his face quickly sinking into the soft, plump pillow. Tess heard a muffled, 'Night'.

'Don't I get a kiss?'

A mumble and some heavy breathing indicated that she would not.

Having turned out the bedside lamp, Tessa made herself comfortable and was pleased to feel a near lifeless arm drop across her shoulders.

'Good night sweetie.'

'Mmm.'

2

Peter was a light sleeper. The slightest noise or trickle of light was usually enough to keep him awake, or wake him from sleep. During the winter months, he often went to the extraordinary lengths of applying black electrical tape to every stand-by light in the bedroom, and refused to have the clock-radio on his side of the bed. Even so, despite the display being dimmable, Peter often claimed the light still penetrated his eyelids. On more than one occasion, Tessa had taken drastic measures in order to keep the peace, reaching into a bedside draw to select a pair of her black knickers with which to hide the faintly illuminated digits. As he then suggested other ways she could help him to sleep, she began to suspect her husband derived some perverted pleasure from her practical solution.

The summer months were far more problematic. Given that Peter had tried and failed to get on with the wearing of an eye mask, and that the master bedroom was not equipped with a fan, or air conditioning unit, the couple were often forced to leave the windows and curtains open. On these occasions he could only expect to benefit from some sort of sleep between the hours of eleven at night and four in the morning.

Three days after first sighting the meteor shower, the alarm had been set to go off at six o'clock in the morning, giving Peter an hour to shower, eat and pull on his uniform, ready for another day at the big house. Setting the alarm had not been necessary. On this particular day, the sun officially rose at eleven minutes to five, but acted upon Peter's sleep long before then. Inwardly cursing his bladder for being too weak, his eyes for being too sensitive and his wife for once again stealing the duvet, Peter finally accepted defeat and opened his eyes, immediately becoming aware of a strange hue bathing the room. Curious, he swung his legs over the edge of the bed and stood up. Delaying his trip to the bathroom, Peter leant his hands on the narrow window sill and allowed his upper body to dip forward so that his nose almost touched the glass. Such was the sight that met his eyes, he repositioned immediately to lean his head through the open casement, affording a better view – what could only be described as the most awe-inspiring sunrise he had ever seen in his entire life; so astonishing, he felt it worth the risk of evoking his wife's wrath by waking her more than an hour ahead of schedule. In fact, his amazement was such that he found himself dragging her to the window. Her displeasure at having been woken from sound slumber, in such a fashion, quickly faded as her eyes became accustomed to the colours she was seeing. The sky was a painting - a work of art - brushed by an old master. It might even have passed for the sky from another planet.

A minute later, Tessa was rifling through the drawers in a frantic search for the camera, or at the very least her mobile phone, eager to capture the moment before the colours faded.

'It's a sad fact that the best skies are caused by the pollution we pump into the atmosphere,' Peter commented. 'I wonder what sort of pollution has caused this one. The light has got a sort of magical quality to it. I've never seen anything like it.'

***

Scientists on the evening news were happy to provide the answer to what had caused the spectacular morning display. They also had an opinion with regard to the more interesting question, being asked in many languages across the globe - why it was that the 'sunrise' had continued throughout the day, getting more and more vivid by the hour.

Apparently it was due to the meteor shower. The unprecedented number of particles entering the upper atmosphere had caused very much the same effect as was normal with the aftermath of a large volcanic eruption. In 1883, Krakatoa spewed huge quantities of dust into the sky. The resulting clouds had circled the Earth for weeks. Then, London had reported having experienced wonderful skies, persisting for many nights.

Now, around the world, the skies refused to fade, and every country that boasted so much as a test tube directed their experiments upwards: balloons soared to the upper atmosphere; aeroplanes, equipped with every monitoring device known to man, flew through it; satellites analysed the atmosphere from space; visual observations were made and samples were taken. The results were mixed. The good news was that nothing toxic had been detected and whatever the particles were, they were not going to ground commercial flights. The bad news was that, globally, despite the wealth of data scientists had at their fingertips, governments were reluctant to expand on their findings. At first it all seemed rather sinister, but in the end most people came to believe the powers that be were simply unable to comment on something of which they knew nothing about; they were just too embarrassed to admit it.

As the days passed the hue remained as bright as ever, but the initial interest shown by the media began to dull. The tabloid press relegated their coverage of the astronomical anomaly to page four, devoting instead the first three pages to revelations on the subject of the extra marital activities of minor television celebrities. The very real threat of World War Three breaking out - the result of an East Asian country playing with nuclear weapons, demonstrating total disregard for international law - managed only a single column on page nine, the choice and position of stories being determined by the ability of the editorial staff to come up with the most humorous headline. Had the prospect of a nuclear winter conjured up a suitable pun, it would surely have been given pride of place on the front page.

Professor Ian Michaels was invited back to the television studio.

'Tell us Professor, where are all these meteors coming from?' Angela Dearlove asked, adopting her *interested* tone.

Ian shifted in his chair.

'So, I am unable to say exactly where the current material originates from, but I can explain the general principle. As a comet travels its orbit, it ejects a cloud of particles. The Earth, on its own orbit, enters the cloud at the same time each year and at the same place, giving the impression the shooting stars originate from a certain constellation. For example, the Perseids shower appears to originate in the constellation of Perseus, who was the son of the Greek God, Zeus.'

With the mention of Zeus, Angela immediately feared her guest was about to head off at tangents so diverse, only a theoretical mathematician could explain them using a chalk board and a very long equation. Thankfully, the professor was in the mood for keeping matters concise.

'The particles from the comet's cloud burn up in Earth's upper atmosphere, causing multiple shooting stars - peaking, as I stated on my previous visit to these studios, at close to two hundred per hour.'

The fact he not only paused for breath, but stop completely, was a blessing.

'Now Professor, you and your colleagues weren't expecting this one were you?'

'No, I have to admit, this one is something of a mystery. We haven't discovered any new comets. Also, given that the Earth normally enters a cloud, one hemisphere or the other tends to see them but not the other. The field must be very wide. The Quadrantis shower peaks for as little as an hour;

the Perseids over five days. In contrast, with regard to the current anomaly, we are witnessing several thousand meteors per hour, in both hemispheres simultaneously, and the shower has persisted for several weeks now.'

'Do you still maintain these meteors are of no danger to this planet?'

'So, from the analysis of all the evidence gathered across the world, I can see no harm being done to our planet, or to its inhabitants. In my opinion, the things potentially most at risk are the satellites, but we, in the scientific community have received no reports of any of them being destroyed, or damaged as a result of coming into contact with the source of the meteors.'

'Thank you Professor.'

The camera cut to a new shot. One that spliced Professor Ian Michaels from the left of the screen, replacing him with Christopher Shawshank to the right.

'Chris, I believe there's been some goings on in the world of footballers' wives and girlfriends.'

***

Professor Michaels' voice was not the only one to be heard on the subject of the meteor shower. New theories were pronounced at intervals. Some commentators had scientific backing and, like the Professor, were given airtime; others made their ideas known through social media and the use of more traditional methods - the sandwich board and a powerful voice. Speakers' Corner, in London's Hyde Park, was awash with them. They were not so much theories as declarations that the end of the world was nigh. These harbingers of doom did have their followers though. Many a news story showed candle-lit midnight vigils begging forgiveness and praying for deliverance. Some waited for what they imagined to be the Second Coming of Christ, or saw it as the precursor to an alien invasion. Most people, however, got on with their everyday lives as usual.

The end came as quickly as it had started. Observers who had been monitoring the skies saw a rapid decrease in the frequency of meteors penetrating the atmosphere until, after only a few days, sightings were back to normal for the time of year. Within two more days there was a noticeable watering down of the 'sunset effect'; a sound bite invented by the media.

There was no one day when it could be said that things had returned to normal, but over the period of a couple of weeks, Britain started to experience overcast, grey skies once more. This brought another indication everything was as it should be. Women could once more be found in the street, engaged in idle conversation about the weather, with friends they had bumped into while out shopping.

'This is supposed to be summer,' said one old lady, bathed in the cool, damp daylight.

'It's not like it was when we were young and that's for sure,' replied the other.

***

Peter had kept abreast of events in the news and, in particular, the items about, as he saw it, the meteor pollution. He felt the weight of the world upon his shoulders when he thought of all that dust from outer space being deposited in the Earth's atmosphere. It worried him to think of what effect it might have on global warming. After all, it was not long previously that scientists had been concerned by the amount of methane produced by cattle and its effect on the planet's temperature. This new threat had to be of more significance than that. However, despite all his unease with the state of the skies, Peter had become far more concerned with his financial position. All the bills seemed to have gone up at once and with no corresponding increase in his salary it meant cutbacks had to be made; but where? As a family they had already cut their budget to the bone. Either they would have to give up eating, his daughter would have to go up the chimneys as in the Victorian days, or his wife would have to bring in a little extra money by standing on street corners wearing fish-net stockings and swinging her hips. None of these options being practical, Peter decided to place more faith in the National Lottery, and hope for the best. Tessa, being of a more practical nature, suggested she could take on more hours and was confident she could spend less at the supermarket, or even shop at independent local stores and farmers' markets.

Her view of the passing of the sunset skies was restricted merely to the opinion the world seemed blander; rather like the house did after the Christmas decorations had been taken down on Twelfth Night, or New Year's Day, which was more usual in the Allerton household.

Emma was much more interested in her new bicycle with its pink paintwork, white shopping basket, tassels on the handlebars, and stabilisers. Whatever the colour of the sky, be it pink, grey, blue or green, she just wanted to ride her bike, sitting astride the white vinyl saddle and holding the matching grips tightly in her hands.

Worldwide, groups of followers blew out their candles, packed away their sandwich boards and returned to the grind of everyday life, filling social media with negativity and videos of fluffy animals behaving badly.

3

Fine drizzle fell silently upon Hillcrest farm. So fine that Joseph Dugdale could hardly feel its impact upon his skin, although it made him every bit as wet as if he were experiencing a torrential downpour. Despite the weather, Joseph continued at his work, his spirits undampened. A lifetime living in the hills had made him almost oblivious to the elements, and besides, experience told him the shower would soon pass and the warmth of the sun would not delay in drying his sodden clothes.

Maggie stood patiently beside her master, beads of water forming at the ends of her eyebrows where they hesitated for a few seconds before dropping to the ground. She did not mind the rain either. Her coat was thick and the water found difficulty penetrating to her skin.

'Ayup girl,' Joe said, with a quiet but purposeful manner.

Maggie immediately sprang into action and trotted to the side of the herd, coaxing a stray cow back onto the lane heading towards the milking sheds. A quick nip was all that was needed. Joe walked at a slow pace behind, every so often issuing gentle guidance to a straggler with his long staff. His eyes were focussed on the cattle, paying little attention to what his dog was doing. Maggie knew what to do and rarely needed reminding, the two of them having followed the same routine together more times than either of them cared to remember.

The dairy farmer and his faithful canine had a symbiotic relationship similar to that of a couple who had been happily married for many years. They each knew what the other was thinking, shared an undying loyalty towards each other and each held a deep affection for the other which did not need to be expressed openly. Each other's company was more than enough.

The herd reached the end of the lane and wheeled left, avoiding the closed gate standing before them. On the other side of the gate a car stood in the farmyard, its engine ticking over. Two occupants sat inside, studying an unfolded ordnance survey map. There was little else they could do until the bovine traffic had passed. With Joe and Maggie bringing up the rear, the last of the cows disappeared into the milking parlour, leaving the route to the main road clear once more.

Joe's wife, Ann, was a sturdy woman; not attractive in the conventional sense. Over the years, her cheeks had taken on a rosy hue, thanks to the wind that regularly whipped across the exposed hillside. For the same reason, her hair most often appeared untamed, despite the one hundred sweeps of the brush she counted every morning, without fail. He figure had suffered too - the composite of the ravages of time and a married life of hearty home cooking. Nevertheless, Joe still found her as attractive as the day they first met. Ann, who thought the ageing process had actually improved her husband's looks, reciprocated these feelings. She cherished the wrinkles that adorned his face, as they catalogued their many years together.

Ann was aware of just how hard Joe worked to provide for his family. Because of this, she could never be so hurtful as to criticise their way of life. Not that she would want to change a great deal in any event. But milking cows every day did have its drawbacks. It had been many years since the family had taken a holiday together and they would certainly never be rich. The children *had* been away with the school on a couple of occasions, and she had taken them on trips to the beach; though this was hardly a satisfactory alternative to the four of them spending two weeks being pampered in a hotel in somewhat warmer climes - a week would be nice; even if it was not that warm, and they were not pampered.

Ann had not burdened her husband with these thoughts as he did not deserve to be. He worked very hard to keep food on the table and a roof over their heads. Besides, the only way in which she could get her wish was by changing their lifestyle completely and it was unthinkable that they might sell the farm. The land, a little over one hundred acres, had been passed down from father to eldest son for generations and she was not about to break with tradition for the sake of a few days' vacation. For all the drawbacks, Ann was quite content with her life, especially now she was doing something for herself.

It had been two years since she used their savings to convert an old barn into four holiday cottages. The business was entirely her own project and she derived great pleasure from running it. She had approved the plans, chosen the furnishings and arranged the advertising. It was her desire to make the country experience as pleasant for her guests as possible, partly for financial reasons - happy holiday makers tended to come back - but also because she was proud of the country and wanted to present it in the best possible light. To this end she always greeted the new arrivals with a plate of home-made cakes, some complementary tea bags, and a small jug of fresh milk. She also offered to provide home-cooked country meals on request. So far, the formula had worked and all four cottages were fully booked throughout much of the year.

Joe approved of his wife's endeavours, benefiting from them in a number of ways. Firstly, it made her happy, which in turn made him happy; secondly, it provided a useful additional income. However, it was not all a bed of roses. Joe was a man well known for keeping himself to himself and his wife's business was at odds with this. He could understand why folks who suffered town life on a daily basis would want to invade the countryside for part of their year, but that did not alter the fact he preferred to tend to his cattle without being interrupted by a bunch of impatient guests who talked too much and wore inappropriate shoes. Nevertheless, he was prepared to tolerate the odd tourist infringing upon his privacy for the sake of the love of his life.

Neither Joseph nor Ann were totally without assistance. Their two children, Alice and Nathan, both teenagers, had been raised on the farm and were no strangers to doing their share of the work. Not for sexist reasons, but Alice had gravitated towards helping her mother, while Nathan had steered clear of the holiday business, preferring to get his boots muddy in the fields with his father. This may have been because Nathan knew the farm would one day be his and Alice knew it would not be hers. Joe also employed the assistance of a cowhand who cycled up from the village early every weekday morning.

Once the cows were safely secured in the milking shed, they could be heard through the creosoted walls, protesting at the indignity of having suction cups attached to their udders. It was not the noise of animals in distress, more that of old women expressing displeasure. They had long forgotten that their offspring had been taken from them so that the calfless mothers might perform the task the farmer had set them.

The Cubits, Norah and George, put away their map and prepared to move off. They chose to shun the use of satellite navigation because the phone signal was poor among the hills, and because neither liked technology. They might have liked it more had they known how to use it. To them, a mobile phone was considered a Godsend, but a smart phone was the work of the devil.

Norah got out of the car and picked her way across the yard to open the gate. The car moved forward slowly and rumbled across the cattle grid before coming to a halt once more. The Cubits were better than most other holidaymakers, thinking to shut the gates they had opened. It was just a shame the same could not be said of all the guests that stayed on Hillcrest Farm.

Norah got back into the car, carefully placing her feet on the newspaper that her husband had lain in the foot well to protect the carpets.

'We're going to have to give this car a good spring clean when we get home and that's for sure. This mud gets everywhere. And the smell!' she said, peering down at her shoes which now oozed a pungent sticky substance from beneath the soles. 'You'd think they'd do something about it wouldn't you?'

'If you ask me, this country lark isn't all it's cracked up to be,' replied George, checking his wife's feet were indeed firmly on the paper, his nose screwed up in disgust. 'Never mind, we'll just have to make the most of things.'

'So what's on the menu for today?' asked Norah.

'Well, I think we should head off for the beach, hire a couple of deckchairs and a wind-break and get some fresh air into our lungs.'

'What about this rain though?'

'It won't last long. Just look at that sun trying to break through. Anyway, we've got blankets and our umbrellas in the boot, so we're covered for all eventualities.'

'I hope they do a nice cream tea,' Norah said, thoughtfully.

'Sure to.'

The other families were not nearly so early to rise, but as they did so, they each took it in turns to run the gauntlet that was the lane down to the main road. It was long, single track and had a ninety-degree bend in it. Some strategically positioned hedges, and the steepness of the road, restricted visibility to a matter of metres. It meant there was always the possibility that half way down the lane, a holidaymaker's car would be confronted by another vehicle coming in the opposite direction, or worse still, the cows. With nowhere to pass, someone would have to give way and reverse back along the lane, the onus for doing so always seeming to fall upon the townsfolk. It was difficult to argue with a herd of cows, just as it was with a man driving a large lorry whose language consists entirely of a series of grunts. Besides, a man with a job to do rarely gives way to a tourist.

The Smiths were by far the youngest family staying on the farm. Susan and Tom and their two children, Becky and James, were more appreciative of the qualities that country life had to offer. The smell of the cow shed next door to their accommodation went unnoticed after the first night. The parents found the views that met them in the morning just breath-taking - rounded hills interlocked along the valley like a zip fastener with light playing upon the distant fields, rendering the whole scene truly three-dimensional. They became aware that whole minutes could pass without hearing the rumble of traffic and, at night, in stark contrast to their own county, the huge, unobstructed sky was actually dark. The children, however, were more taken with the residents of the paddock opposite their front door: three donkeys destined for a working life on the beaches giving rides to children. The animals were very docile and seemed quite content for Becky and James to stroke their foreheads and were, in fact, the highlight of James' holiday.

Becky, on the other hand, quickly developed a special fondness for the farmer's dog that would climb the steps to the threshold of the Smiths' first floor apartment and sit waiting patiently for the appearance of her new friend, her coat damp from the rain and matted with mud. In return for their kindness, she would escort their car across the farmyard, wagging her tail frantically behind her.

'I hope that dog isn't bothering you,' the farmer's wife commented as Susan went to open the gate.

'Not at all. I think Becky here wants to take her home.'

'Where are you off to today?'

'We passed a village yesterday with the most wonderful baker's shop, so we're going back there. Apart from that, a lot depends on what the weather does. It doesn't really matter though; it's just nice to be away from home.'

'Well, I hope it clears up for you.'

Like the Cubits, the Smiths were delayed in setting off. This time it was the farmer backing up a lorry, laden with cattle feed. Had the Smiths not known this was a working farm, they might otherwise have been fooled into thinking it was a museum. It was a marvel to see such an ancient piece of machinery still running. Indeed, with the noise that emanated from beneath the bonnet, it was nothing short of a *miracle* to see it still running.

When Mr Dugdale emerged from the cab, it could be seen that his clothes matched the surroundings perfectly. The children were particularly amused that he was wearing an odd pair of wellington boots, one green, and the other black; evidence the farmer cared not for appearance; functionality was everything. If further evidence was needed, it came by way of unsightly piles of scrap, lying about the farm, kept in case they proved to be of use some day. Tom thought it strange that, for a farmer with two sources of income, he did not appear to have much to show for his efforts. There were no clues as to how his family spent their money. They had a relatively new but rather ordinary family car, and their house was small. It was a puzzle.

Mr Dugdale indicated his apologies for having held them up by raising an arm, his back turned towards them, and mumbled something that might be taken as a thank you. He came across as being someone who was more shy than rude, and appeared incapable of establishing eye contact.

Their path clear, the Smiths drove off with sufficient speed to get to the end of the narrow lane as quickly as possible, and so reduce the possibility of meeting anything that might be coming the other way. At the same time, they drove slowly enough that if they *were* to meet any surprises, they could stop before colliding with it, or them.

Joseph continued about his business.

Twenty-five minutes later, the first of the two remaining families - Gill and Simon Robertson - left the farm for the day. Gill was in her late thirties and held down a well-paid job as a personal assistant to a managing director of a city bank. Simon, her common-law husband, and two years her junior, fitted plastic guttering for a living. His could not be described as a glamorous occupation by any stretch of the imagination, but it did pay well. Gill had adopted Simon's surname. Although they had never been legally married, they had lived together for more than fifteen years. Their only financial commitments were a modest mortgage on their house and the monthly repayments on their large, four-wheel drive vehicle. It was not, however, the kind to impress farmers, being far too showy, and Joseph could never understand the reasoning behind paying good money for the privilege of having a personalised number plate.

Gill and Simon's combined income could comfortably have accommodated an expensive holiday abroad. However, they chose to remain in Britain for two very good reasons. The first was Simon's absolute distrust of aeroplanes. He had read of the statistics that flying was safer than crossing the road, but he had also read of aircraft falling out of the sky; of them crashing into hillsides; of them being blown up by terrorists. If travelling abroad were to be undertaken at all, it would have to be done in a manner that avoided flying. The second reason was Gill's fear of water. She was content to sit on a riverbank, throwing bread to the ducks, but refused point blank to set foot in any vessel that floated upon it, or travelled beneath it. This prohibited them from taking cruises, travelling by ferry and even hiring rowing boats. It also denied them use of the channel tunnel through fear that water overhead might suddenly come cascading through, drowning all inside.

For a couple living on an island, these limitations on their mode of transport posed a real problem. The simple solution was to stay within the boundaries of their own country. It was fortunate that Gill and Simon happened to prefer the activities that could be found at home. They enjoyed long walks, visiting mediaeval castles and discovering what each county had to offer. What they did not like was the thought of lazing in the sun beside a Spanish swimming pool. It was almost too awful to contemplate. Furthermore, neither of them were great consumers of alcohol, so the bars would be of little interest either. Instead, their plans for the day involved a visit to a working steam museum, finding somewhere nice to eat and perhaps taking in a late movie if they were able to find a cinema in the sparsely populated land surrounding the farm.

The Malones were the last to set off. Graham, the father, had spoken to Tom Smith on the first day of the holiday, as they unloaded their respective cars. A brief exchange of pleasantries led to Tom being invited in for a cup of tea. Tom could hardly refuse such hospitality, especially as he needed to get on the right side of them, knowing his children would be thundering about on the floor above their heads all week.

Graham turned out to be a very amiable man; one who smiled unceasingly. The whole time he wore an expression on his face of sublime amazement. His wife, Linda, and their teenage son, Robert, were both formed of the same mould and were very happy people.

It transpired the Malones had relatives in the area and it was their intention to spend most of the week visiting them. Apparently, the relatives did not have room to put them up so Graham had hit upon the idea of renting a holiday cottage nearby. It was a cheaper alternative to bed and breakfast, with the added bonus of having more space. Tom could not help but wonder if the relatives truly had a small house, or if it was a subtle hint for the Malones to stay well away. For his part, Tom could not bear the thought of having perpetually happy people hanging around him for seven hours, let alone seven days.

Graham, Linda and Robert pulled away from the entrance to the farm anticipating a very good day.

It had been nearly two months since the brilliant colours, caused by the meteor shower, had left the skies above the farm. Joseph had more opportunities than most to study them, as the majority of his life was spent outdoors, providing him plenty of time to be alone with his thoughts. It was a hard life but the air was pure and the views were stunning. The landscape, his workplace, changed moods with the weather: sometimes mysterious with mist hanging on the hilltops; sometimes satanic with black clouds promising a storm; sometimes, simply beautiful. Joseph particularly liked the way the shadows of the clouds dappled the rolling meadows below and the way the distant trees served to enhance the grand scale of the hills. There was always the danger that any man might take for granted the magnificence of the countryside when exposed to it every day. At least, in this respect, tourists served a purpose other than merely injecting money into the local economy. Their enthusiasm for what they experienced was a reminder to those who lived in the countryside of just how lucky they were. This was a gift that Joseph could bestow upon his children, something of far greater value than the usual family heirloom.

Joseph was a philosophical man. Although he worked land that deeds legally stated to be his own, he felt it was conceited to believe it belonged to him in any wider sense. In this respect he had much in common with the Aborigines of Australia who pointed out that no man can truly own a mountain that has been around for millions of years before his birth and will remain in being for millions of years after his death.

This feeling of continuity brought him an inner strength and contentment. This is not to say he was immune to the pressures of everyday life. He had a sick cow to tend to and this made him very troubled indeed.

The vet was a good man. Joseph had known him in a professional capacity for years and in a social one for nearly as long. His bills, although fair, still made an unwelcome dent in Joe's bank balance, but he did not begrudge paying the money as his stock were not merely a financial concern; he cared for them as if they were his family. He always found time throughout the day to pay a visit to the sick. In fact, he could often be seen entering the barn during the hours of darkness with an oil lamp in his hand, a scene reminiscent of Florence Nightingale during the Crimean war.

At half past five in the late afternoon, the Smiths returned to the farm to freshen up before they went out for the evening in search of a somewhere to eat. The wheels of their car rolled slowly over the coarse stone chippings that formed the parking area. Chippings might not be the best way to describe these miniature boulders. They presented little concern to farmers who drove Land Rovers, but they did cause concern to Tom Smith. Until now, the roughest terrain to which his car had been subjected was the car park at the local shops, the tarmac surface of which had been sadly neglected, despite many letters to the council, all signed by an angry Mr T. Smith.

Stepping from the car, Tom's family were presented with a stunning panorama, bereft of noise, other than the sound of the occasional curlew, the harsh tones of the farmer's geese, and the munching of grazing cattle.

Throughout the day the weather had improved and so too had the visibility. The veil of mist that had descended upon the surrounding countryside during the night, restricting views to a mere half a mile, had lifted again by lunchtime. However, among the hills it failed to dissipate completely, remaining as a thick layer of cloud sitting just clear of the hilltops, supported on columns of vapour that rose from distant ridges; columns that gave the impression the clouds were not shedding rain but actively sucking moisture from the ground. It was a very calming experience and seemed to Tom to be the justification for having brought his family to the spot, several hundreds of miles from home. To his way of thinking it was an experience that any father would want their children to have – to witness such natural beauty, as desirable as could be found anywhere else on the planet. The only moot point being the Forestry Commission's decision to plant thousands of coniferous trees along the ridges; firstly, because they were all of the same species and looked out of place next to the wide variety of native deciduous trees that lay dotted about the valley; secondly, because they had been planted in square blocks, hardly sympathetic to the random nature of the surrounding countryside.

The Smiths' home for the week was an upstairs apartment in the very old stone barn that had been tastefully converted by the owners. It was a substantial building with walls measuring at least a metre thick, more than could be said of the adjacent cowsheds with their corrugated iron roofs. The upstairs rooms had two main advantages over the accommodation below them. One was the view afforded by the higher windows. The other was that the first floor residents were raised above the smell of the cows. The Smiths enjoyed the country experience, but the odour that permeated the flat downstairs was just too close to nature for their liking.

There was time for a leisurely cup of tea before they journeyed out again. Susan used up the remains of the milk provided by the farmer's wife, despite Tom's conviction it had been obtained directly from one of the farmer's cows.

'It can't be, it's all got to be pasteurised nowadays. I'm sure there's a law.'

Tom was not convinced by her argument. He had seen Mr Dugdale cross the yard that morning with an empty plastic four-pint milk bottle, returning a few minutes later with it full to the brim. Three scraggy farm cats tailing the farmer, licking their whiskers, provided further evidence.

On the subject of the cats, they were obviously being kept as working animals and not as family pets. All three of them lived in the hay loft of one of the outbuildings, gaining access to their living quarters by means of three ladders that leant at a steep angle against an opening high in one wall. The cats seemed to be reasonably healthy, if lacking a little tender loving care.

The time came for what Tom and Susan considered to be the best part of their holiday - eating out. The children enjoyed the experience too, but were far more excited by the prospect of being let loose in the play areas after they had eaten their meal. It was easy to find a local pub that provided good quality food. There were many in the area. Providing meals seemed to constitute the main part of their trade while the serving of alcoholic beverages had taken on a secondary role. The Smiths had already tried out two local hostelries and were keen to try out a third, but first they had to negotiate the lane to the main road and this time the cows were out in force. In fact, as Tom sat in his stationary car half way down the lane, trying to out-stare one of the creatures, he was convinced they had sent for reinforcements. As each of the beasts came into view, it would look straight into the eyes of the occupants of the car, pause for some considerable time, and then move ever so slowly off the hard surface of the road and onto the soft grass that lay on either side. Tom could then ease his foot off the brake and permit the car to roll forward a short distance, only to be confronted by yet another side of beef. What they were all doing on his side of the barbed-wire fencing, Tom could only speculate, but one thing he was sure of was the cows had a real attitude problem.

Susan could stand it no more and, after some prompting from her husband, got out of the vehicle with a view to reaching some amicable agreement with these formidable adversaries. Remaining close to the passenger side door at all times, lest she suddenly felt the need to claim sanctuary, she began waving her arms about, quickly and successfully bringing negotiations to a satisfactory conclusion. The herd began to disperse and it was not long before the holidaymakers were free, Susan buoyed up by a sense of achievement, but much in need of a drink.

Thankfully the Smiths' efforts were rewarded by a splendid meal. It was just a shame that having the two young children with them meant they had to leave so early. However, even on holiday, the kids needed their sleep, and it had been a very long day.

When they reached the entrance to Hillcrest Farm, Tom was relieved to see the demonic cows were no longer to be seen.

Rounding the corner of the converted barn where his family were staying, Tom could see the parked car belonging to the older couple who had rented one of the odorous, but otherwise pleasant, apartments on the ground floor. The occupants of the two other flats were apparently still out enjoying some evening's entertainment.

Inside their accommodation, the Cubits, having returned from a wind-swept day on the beach, were about to enjoy a well-earned cup of tea. Despite their earlier reservations, it had turned out to be quite a nice day. Norah had managed to find a cafe that served an acceptable cream tea, although the scone had been a bit on the crumbly side; and away from the hills, the weather had cleared nicely so there had been no need to unsheathe the umbrellas.

For George, the day had been marred slightly when a gull had decided to spread its droppings across the polished paintwork of his cherished car; a vehicle he had bought with the retirement cheque, received at the end of a distinguished forty-year career in the personnel department of a large manufacturing company; a car he had looked after lovingly - almost obsessively - for the last three years. In this respect, seagulls were currently the least of his problems – a bottle of mineral water and a soft cloth had easily dealt with their waste products without any lasting damage being done. However, had he known the parking facilities on the farm were going to be so demanding on the tyres, he would probably have booked alternative lodgings; something he had been meaning to bring to the attention of the farmer's wife since their arrival.

As the couple sat back enjoying their steaming hot cups of tea, one question was on their minds. What *was* that terrible smell? George resolved to mention it to Mrs Dugdale the following morning; that and the noise of the cows being milked so early in the day, acting as an unwelcome alarm clock. Their list of complaints was growing daily.

The Malone family stayed at their relatives' house well into the evening, enjoying several well-cooked meals and an abundance of good-humoured conversation. It was the first time they had paid a visit to Graham's cousin's new house and it turned out to be far more spacious than they had been given to believe.

The two families had a lot of catching up to do. They had only been round each other's houses on one previous occasion and that had been nearly ten years previously. Soon afterwards, Graham's cousin and his clan had been relocated to the north of England by the company he worked for. Since then they had completely lost touch, except for an exchange of cards at Christmas. Graham, Linda and their son, Robert, who had been a lad of only seven years when the two families last met, all thoroughly enjoyed the reunion and vowed not to leave it so long before their next visit. Graham's cousin concurred.

The hour grew late and it was time for the two families to bid each other goodnight.

'It's been a wonderful day and we'll see you all again bright and early in the morning,' Graham said cheerily as he and his family walked to their car.

Graham's cousin looked surprised.

Driving off, Graham turned to his wife.

'Nice house they have there,' he commented brightly. 'I expect you heard Ian telling me they're a bit embarrassed about putting anyone up in the guest room. By all accounts it's in desperate need of redecoration.'

'I thought it must be something like that,' Linda replied. 'Although I had a peek at their rooms when I popped upstairs to use their toilet and they shouldn't worry; they all seemed lovely to me.'

The Robertsons too had enjoyed a thoroughly good day out. The steam museum had exceeded Gill and Simon's expectations and had kept them both occupied until late in the afternoon. They came out with just enough time to call in at the Tourist Information Centre before it closed for the night. A badge gave a name to the man who sat behind the counter – Eric - who was extremely helpful and proudly revealed the town boasted its very own cinema. This came as a great surprise to both Simon and Gill, who, when driving around earlier in the day, had been unable to find even the most basic of facilities, such as a petrol station, or a general store. Eric informed them there was a choice of one film, showing once a week, at seven p.m. As luck would have it, they had visited the information centre on the very day of the next screening. Eric was also able to furnish them with a guide to the best places to eat.

The cinema was actually an old village hall and was delightfully quaint. Simon and Gill agreed the film was incidental to the experience of seeing such a high-tech production in such low-tech surroundings. They had half expected the feature to be in black and white, preceded by a reel from Pathe News. It was almost a shame when the screen came to life with the vibrant colours of the latest Hollywood action movie.

Their chosen restaurant took the couple further from the farm, but it was worth the extra miles.

It was getting late by the time they got back. Even so, they noticed a light coming from one of the barns.

'Who'd be a farmer?' Gill remarked.

Joseph was oblivious to the couple's return, being rather more concerned with the welfare of one of his cattle. Despite the vet's best efforts, the cow had failed to make a full recovery. There being nothing more he could do for the time being, the farmer determined to look in on her the following morning.

4

Accompanying the completion of the extension to the premises of G.J.K. Whitley (Financial Services Ltd.), a corresponding increase in the size of the workforce brought additional vehicles to be shoehorned into an already overcrowded car park. The situation had become something of a headache for the security staff who had been forced to take on the role of event marshals, directing cars to available spaces. The problems the lower ranks endured daily were of no consequence to Alistair Whyte though, a placard on the wall reserving his spot, only a few spaces from of the man himself – Mr Appleford-Gray.

As usual, the barrier rose immediately upon Alistair's arrival, enabling his company car to sweep past the gatehouse without stopping; a privilege enjoyed by only the few - those in middle management and above. Everyone else had first to submit their passes for interrogation. The gatekeeper's overt display of reverence towards him made Alistair feel very important indeed.

Having parked, Alistair stepped from his car, picked up his briefcase from the passenger seat, took his jacket from a hanger in the rear, closed the door, activated the alarm, and stroked his fingertips along the car's silky smooth metallic-painted bodywork. It felt like an executive car; it filled the space as an executive car should; its curves painted a thousand word curriculum vitae, declaring to the world his place in the company – a successful thirty-two year old with the potential to rise all the way to the top. The badge emblazoning the boot lid declared his status and was the envy of many a sales rep that had seen it. With it, he had earned the right to travel in the fast lane and had the confidence to flash other drivers out of his way as he glided along the motorway, well in excess of the seventy miles per hour speed limit.

Alistair had a high opinion of himself. He had every right to. Leaving school at the age of sixteen with only minimal qualifications, he had managed to get his foot on the first rung of the ladder within a week. Admittedly, it had only been as an assistant in the mailroom, but it avoided him the indignity of having to claim state benefits.

He was fortunate in that he did not have to wait long before his foot stepped up onto the second rung. One Tuesday morning, Charlie, Alistair's immediate boss, had unexpectedly clutched at his chest and died, slumped over the franking machine. He was a strange little man and had been with the company since before most of the other staff were born. His demise shocked everybody in the building except for Alistair. After all, he had not known the man for very long and had certainly not formed an emotional attachment to him.

Charlie's passing meant that full responsibility for the smooth running of the mail room transferred to Alistair's shoulders. Still only a lad of seventeen, he found himself in charge of a junior assistant, bringing his first taste of power, and a desire for more.

Accepting as Gospel the adage, it is not what you know but who you know, Alistair set about making himself known to the right people. It was easy. Delivering the post gave him the necessary vehicle. It was just a matter of talking to people and showing an interest in what they were doing, while always providing them a good service. Working additional un-paid hours and taking on extra tasks outside his official job specification also helped to get him noticed. The basic plan was a sound one. Whenever a vacancy in the company arose, Alistair was the first to know about it, and when he applied for a post, he was already at an advantage, being well liked and trusted by those in charge of recruitment.

Rung after rung followed in quick succession; so fast it was as though he had traded in the ladder for an escalator. Instead of having to apply for new positions, members of the senior management team began to approach him with offers of advancement.

Alistair had evolved, not so much by luck and natural selection, but through conscious planning. He did not dress or act in the way his colleagues did. Instead, he dressed and acted as he saw those one step above him - a visible indication he considered himself ready for promotion. His decision to manipulate his environment in this way could be traced back to the beginning; to that first interview. He had been the only post room applicant not to wear denim. He had been the only office junior to wear shirts that required cufflinks. He had been the only first-line manager to opt for golfing lessons.

Walking across the car park, the doors to the monumental mirrored-glass building opened before him as if to acknowledge his importance. Stepping into the marble-floored foyer he was greeted by the receptionist who wore the sort of smile normally associated with a travel agent.

'Good morning Mr Whyte.'

'Morning Pippa,' he replied with an air of superiority.

Once in his office, Alistair rang through to his secretary, next door.

Shirley was in fact shared between himself and Ralph Hurley, a constant source of annoyance that would be relieved only when he achieved promotion to the fourth floor. Besides, she was old; efficient and trustworthy, but old. He deserved a younger model who would set his heart racing whenever she bent down to retrieve files that Alistair would make sure were always on the lower shelves.

'Good morning Shirley. A cup of my usual please.'

The rest of the staff shared a vending machine on the floor below, fed by tokens allocated to them on a weekly basis, but this was not for Alistair. He had requisitioned the latest machine, capable of producing a wide variety of coffees from a range of expensive capsules: espresso; lungo; cappuccino; latte macchiato. No one needed reminding the capsules were expensive, and that was the way Alistair Whyte liked it.

He also liked his mobile – always the latest model. When not in his hand, it invariably lay on the mahogany effect desk before him, glowing every so often, attracting the attention of visitors who would undoubtedly be impressed by the number of people keen to communicate with him. It helped that he subscribed to cricket updates; not a sport he cared for, but the frequent messages caused his phone to illuminate on a regular basis.

It was all about image.

'The image makes the man,' he had once heard someone say. Never a truer word spoken, he thought.

With this in mind, he no longer ate in the canteen with the lower echelons. Instead, he would have the ever-faithful Shirley bring up a salver of salmon sandwiches for lunch. Far more appropriate.

Having finished his coffee – one that required two pods – Alistair commenced his rounds.

At the door to the main office, he paused to take a deep breath, exhaling as he pushed through in what he considered to be a purposeful manner. First impressions being all important, Alistair felt it was always worth taking a moment to compose himself before confronting those beneath him. To him, opening doors had much in common with exchanging handshakes. Nobody respected a man with a grip like a limp lettuce. Few of his colleagues shared this belief, but then, none had risen so far and so fast as he.

The fire door sprung shut behind him with a resounding bang. Despite this, none of the staff looked up from their desks. Had he been paranoid, Alistair would have taken this to mean they were deliberately trying to ignore him. Instead, he assumed they were working so hard to please him that all external distractions had been blocked from their minds.

Slowly making his way along the length of the open-plan office, Alistair stopped at each section in turn, requesting an update on the figures. They were duly presented and found to be pleasantly favourable. However, having furnished the manager with their statistics, the section heads immediately returned to their job in hand without uttering another word.

Reaching the door at the far end of the office, Alistair paused to take another deep breath. Exiting a room was equally important as entering it.

'Now,' he said loudly, clapping his hands together.

The door swung open and he was gone.

Nobody thought his behaviour in any way unusual, because it was not. Mr Whyte always made his exit in the same fashion. The office staff assumed it was meant to give the impression he had pressing business to attend to, but judged it was actually the habit of a man who had developed the practice as a means of escape from moments of awkward silence.

Back in his office, his mobile placed on the desk in front of him, pulsing every few minutes, it began to play on Alistair's mind just how disrespectful his staff had been. Perhaps it would be appropriate for him to circulate a memorandum instructing them in future to greet him with the words, 'Good Morning'. The idea needed some thought.

In the main office, the staff suddenly found their work not nearly as engrossing as it had been during Mr Whyte's brief visit.

This had been the first time the new girl, Karen, had seen her boss since the interview. She was curious to know what type of man he was. Mark, who had been given the task of training his new colleague, was more than happy to share his opinions.

'What, Mr Charisma-by-pass? He's a bit, how can I put it, anally retentive.'

Karen, a naive girl of only seventeen, looked bemused.

'You know, full of shit,' he explained. 'Before he got this promotion, he worked in planning and was a bit of a pervert by all accounts. One of the secretaries down there made an accusation of sexual harassment against him. She's never been seen since. You ask Vicki what he's like, she'll tell you.'

Vicki, who was sitting close by on the next section, overheard the conversation and was quick to add the details.

'I had a cold one day and he came up to me and said, how are you feeling today? I'd like to find out, but I guess you'd hit me. What a creep.'

Karen was left wondering what kind of organisation she had come to work for.

Half an hour passed before there was a call from the Managing Director's office, requesting Alistair's presence. As no hint was given as to the purpose of the summons, the young executive's mind immediately began working overtime, trying to guess what the reason might be. His thoughts ranged from instant dismissal - a result of some unfounded, malicious allegation of sexual harassment - to him being awarded a higher status company car, or even getting his own secretary at last. However, it was a pointless exercise, there being not a scrap of evidence to support any of these hypotheses. There was nothing else to do but put on a brave face, go upstairs, and meet his fate.

Mrs Trimble guarded the hallowed room.

'Take a seat please, Mr Whyte,' she said, efficiently.

Mrs Trimble was married and as old as Shirley, but she was groomed; more attractive than a women of her years deserved to be.

Five minutes passed before Alistair was allowed to enter. The wait reminded him of his schooldays, when he was made to sit outside the office of the head mistress at Cobblestone Secondary, sixteen or more years before. While he waited, flicking through some industry magazines, Mrs Trimble continued about her business without saying a word.

Her phone rang discretely. She answered, spoke briefly, and then replaced the receiver.

'You may go in now, Mr Whyte.'

He paused, breathed in, breathed out and entered.

'Alistair. Please, take a seat,' Mr Appleford-Gray said in a welcoming tone, beckoning him forward.

Alistair did so, trying to maintain his composure.

'I don't know if you are aware, but Geoffrey has broken his leg skiing. Rather nasty by all accounts.'

'No, I wasn't,' Alistair replied, fighting the compulsion to end every sentence with 'Sir'.

'He was just about to fly out to the States to represent us at the International Financial Services Fair. I'd like you to go in his place.'

'Thank you,' Alistair responded, his face and tone revealing his surprised delight.

'No thanks needed. This is your chance to shine, Alistair. Make the most of it. I'm sure your secretary - what's her name - Shirley? I'm sure she can make all the necessary arrangements. I'll have Mrs Trimble contact her.'

Having spoken, Mr Appleford-Gray smiled, looked down at his desk and began shuffling miscellaneous sheets of seemingly important paperwork; a not so subtle indication the meeting was at an end and it would be appropriate for Alistair to leave.

'Thank you again, sir. I won't let you down.'

'Sir!?' He could have kicked himself. In that single word his all-important image had crumbled, winding back sixteen years to the age of Alistair as a subservient schoolboy. Still, it did not alter the fact his career had just ratchetted up another notch. Up to this point, the only occasion on which the company had paid for his flight was to send Alistair to Scotland for three days. America was in a whole different league – a long haul flight, not just a quick hop up the backbone of the British Isles.

Returning to the familiar surroundings of his own office, Alistair felt back in control.

'Shirley, I'm flying out to the States tomorrow on business. Make the arrangements please. Mrs Trimble will furnish you with the details.'

Alistair arrived home late in the afternoon to find his wife, Diane, in the lounge, reaching up on tip toes to adjust the hang of some new pictures she had recently purchased. She wore a simple, pale blue cotton dress - the hem of which stopped fifteen centimetres above her knees - and very little else. His eyes rapidly scanned the aesthetically pleasing contours of her body, fixing for a moment upon her shapely calves. Her awkward pose gave definition to her smooth, tanned legs; an effect normally only achieved by the wearing of high heeled shoes. It was a pleasing sight, but Alistair's eyes were not satisfied. His visual exploration turned towards his wife's buttocks where he could just make out a pair of white cotton briefs beneath her dress. He would happily have spent the remainder of the evening studying his wife's form. Even four years of marriage - of seeing her naked each and every day - had not dulled the experience. The fact she remained unaware of his gaze made it all the more exciting.

The moment of voyeuristic pleasure ended for Alistair as Diane turned round to greet him, stepping forward to give him a peck on the cheek. She smelled good. However much that perfume was costing him, it was worth every penny.

Diane could tell by the smug expression on her husband's face it had been a better than average day and that he was itching to tell her something.

'How was your day?' she asked, her recently whitened, perfect teeth flashing from within a smile that would cause even the heart of a monk to flutter.

Alistair tried to sound nonchalant as he related to Diane how he had been called up to see the boss, William Appleford-Gray, in his office, and how Bill had expressed an interest in him. He painted a slightly different picture of the circumstances of the meeting; having by now convinced himself he had behaved at all times as one would expect a confident young executive to; certainly not like an overawed schoolboy.

She took the news well, being genuinely pleased for her husband, and perhaps more so for herself.

Diane too was a social climber. Any advancement Alistair achieved - she never abbreviated his name to Al - was a reflection upon her.

Diane did love her husband in her own way and she did find him attractive. He had money - quite a lot of it if the truth be known - and he had the potential to earn a great deal more. She found that attractive too. He looked after his body, paying a visit to the gym three times a week; he dressed well and he had access to the right circle of friends.

Alistair was by no means perfect though. He was a bit lacking in the trouser department, although she never said so, and his topic of conversation always seemed to work its way back to financial matters. The only financial matter Diane was interested in was the state of their bank balance. And then there was his obsession with playing golf. Like a lot of other things Alistair did, he was very accomplished at the game and when he played, he played competitively. The problem was it had become the second most important thing in his life, after financial services. She rated herself number three, just above his precious company car. He had even wanted to play eighteen holes on the morning of their wedding.

If they ever decided to start a family, Diane wondered when they would find time to do the necessary. She imagined it would all be very clinical, with entries in his day planner, reserving slots when he could fit her in.

While Alistair went upstairs to shower and change, Diane was left to prepare their evening meal. Twenty minutes later, he came back down and arranged himself carefully in front of the television. It was important to be seated in just the right position to take full advantage of the surround-sound system. The TV itself was a large, slender, expensive, wide-screen, all singing, all dancing affair; a bit unnecessary for one who only watched the news and the occasional sporting event, but it met Alistair's needs, one of which was to demonstrate to the world just how much money he made.

Over the previous days, he had seen the televised coverage of the meteor anomaly, dismissing the on-going story out of hand. Little bits of rock falling from space were not a real issue, however much they stained the skies. News of the largest ever-British lottery jackpot was another matter though, and his mind had allocated many days to the worthy problem of how best to invest the man's winnings.

The business of the meteor shower had begun to irritate him as the papers had been full of nothing else. Even the answers to the crosswords started making references to the event and so, when the skies had cleared and the world's economy was once more on the centre stage - where it should be - it was not a moment too soon.

The evening meal was superb as usual and so too was the bottle of red that accompanied it. Diane was an exceptional cook and had a very good taste in wines. This talent alone made her indispensable when it came to entertaining Alistair's clients. What is more, she also possessed a body that looked ravishing in an evening dress and an ability to charm the pants off the most loathsome but important people. In short, Diane was worth her weight in gold, although she would probably be content with her Gold card instead.

The rest of the evening was spent making meticulous preparations to ensure nothing could go wrong for Alistair's trip the following day.

'What time have you got to get up in the morning?'

Alistair found his tickets, noted the time of his flight and began working backwards.

'Let's see. I take off at half past eight and I have to check in three hours before that. I'm driving myself to the airport, so that should take another hour. Make it ninety minutes to be safe, and I'll need an hour to get ready. Which means I should set the alarm for three.'

His last task then was to disappear upstairs briefly in order to set his alarm clock, never trusting the alarm on his phone.

Finally, when all was ready, the couple settled down into their leather settee to watch the news together. Diane had dutifully poured him a tumbler half filled with whisky. He was an executive and drank like one. It bothered neither of them.

Diane sat sideways at one end of the settee, legs curled up next to her. Her left arm, bent at the elbow, lay along the top of the backrest, her hand giving support to her head. Cupped in the fingers of her right hand she held a glass of wine. The hem of her short dress had risen up, revealing the tops of her slender thighs and Diane was aware of just how good they looked. She felt sexy, her feelings enhanced by the effects of alcohol. Sipping at her wine, she carefully studied the contours of her husband's face as he sat listening to the headlines. Reflecting on his latest success made him seem that much more attractive and maybe he deserved a treat for all his efforts. A seductive smile crept across her face. Placing her glass on a copy of 'House and Home' that lay on the marble-topped coffee table in front of them, she slid down off the settee so that she knelt before him and proceeded to undo the fly of his trousers. Alistair smiled a contented smile, took another sip of his whisky and reflected on what an exceptionally good day it had turned out to be.

5

Lynn Connor arrived home from the dental surgery where she had worked as a receptionist for more years than she cared to remember. A bundle of old magazines, bound with string, lay on the front door step. Tucked beneath the knot was a hand written note indicating they were from her best friend and confidante, Brenda. She thought Lynn might find some use for them in the waiting room at work. It was a typically thoughtful thing for Brenda to do and it brought a smile to Lynn's face as she dragged the bundle inside.

The donation could not have come at a better time. There was nothing worth watching on the television and her husband, Gerald, would be at his club all evening. Having something to read was an unexpected treat.

It was still only seven o'clock in the evening. Nevertheless, Lynn decided to change out of her work clothes, straight into her winceyette pyjamas. There seemed little point in changing twice as she did not anticipate staying up late.

Curled up on the sofa, Lynn began flicking through some of the more recent publications and soon came across an article entitled, 'How faithful is your man?' Already having her suspicions about Gerald, she read on with interest. The item was less an article, more a questionnaire, compiled by an ex-marriage guidance counsellor, purporting to be able to judge a partner's faithfulness on the strength of the answers given to twenty multiple-choice questions. The three possible answers given in each case covered an enormously wide spectrum and could not possibly be applied to genuine circumstances. For example, question one: Which statement best describes your partner's routine for changing his underwear?

a, He doesn't.

b, He sniffs them before making any decision.

c, He has started changing his underwear far more frequently since the new secretary started at the office.

This, the other nineteen questions, and the conclusions that were drawn in the closing paragraphs of the article, were designed to fill space in the magazine and were never meant as a genuine attempt to explore man's complex psyche. However, Lynn, blinded by a general distrust of her husband's virtue, took the findings at face value.

Without knowing it, Lynn's husband had scored thirty-eight points out of a possible forty. This placed him in the compiler's third category, describing Gerald thus: 'A complete and utter cad. This man plays away from home more times than the England national football team...'

It was several hours before Gerald returned home from the working men's club where he had been an active member since his bachelor days. This provided Lynn a dangerously long time to mull over the results of the questionnaire before he made an appearance at the door to the lounge, completely unaware he was about to be bombarded by a tirade of accusations. So taken aback was he by his wife's reaction to his arrival, it took several minutes before he began to understand the thrust of her grievance. On him raising his hands in submission, Lynn noticed the gold wedding ring, that to her knowledge he had not removed in more than nine years of marriage, was no longer on his finger. This was confirmation, if confirmation was needed, that he was indeed guilty of infidelity.

'You bastard!' she screamed, moments before the floodgates that held back her tears suddenly burst open.

'What are you on about?' Gerald said defensively, wondering how much his wife knew.

Lynn made her position clear.

'You've been having an affair haven't you?'

'What?'

Not a very strong counter attack on Gerald's part, but taken by surprise it was the best he could manage.

'Don't try to deny it. You couldn't even be bothered to put your ring back on when you'd finished whatever you were doing with your whore,' Lynn's harsh words emerged through a distorted mouth; dribble and tears merging, spluttering from her lips.

At this point, Gerald looked at his left hand and was genuinely surprised to find his wedding band was missing. He had not removed it. He never removed it. After all, there had been no need. Nicole knew he was married. For her it was part of the excitement. Besides, it was on so tight that, even soaped, it would be almost impossible to remove without a scalpel and a pair of pliers.

Gerald's only remaining course of action was to bluff it out.

'What makes you think I'm having an affair anyway?' he asked.

'For a start, you haven't shown any interest in me for weeks now,' she said, using the fingers on her left hand as a tally.

Gerald was quick to counter her first point with a thrust of his own.

'That's rubbish. Anyway, you know I've been under an incredible amount of pressure at work and it's all so that you can have your damned foreign holidays. So don't blame me when I'm so tired I can't get it up.'

Lynn skilfully parried his remarks.

'How do I know you've even been at work and not off sunning it with your tart?'

It was not easy for Gerald to defend his position. He had been living a lie for the past six months and he had finally, and if he had thought about it, inevitably, been caught.

'Okay, I admit it, but it was only a couple of times and it didn't mean anything. I promise,' he spoke quietly, his head hung low.

His admission brought stunned silence; so silent and so prolonged that Gerald found himself quite unable to cope. He would far rather have been on the receiving end of a few swift blows dealt by Lynn's clenched fists.

'How did you find out?' he asked incredulously. 'I was so careful. I didn't want you to know. I knew it would hurt you.'

'I didn't know. I just had my insecurities. Then a crummy questionnaire in a crummy magazine made me think that perhaps I wasn't being so stupid. Then I had time to think it over in my head and I lashed out hoping you were going to prove me wrong. And then, when I saw you weren't wearing the ring, I knew.'

No longer crying, her bitter words poured forth.

The taxi, with Gerald on the back seat and his suitcase in the boot, drew away from the marital home less than an hour later. Lynn was not the forgiving kind. She was pleased with herself for having not caved in and for not having let him off his infidelity on the strength of an apology. If there was to be any future in their marriage, he would have to suffer first.

The episode had left her feeling bitter, angry, dirtied, but most of all, confused. For one thing, Lynn could not grasp the fact that someone else might find her husband attractive. He was balding, his body was in no great shape, and his conversation was, to say the least, limited.

Throwing her husband out of the house had put Lynn in control of the situation and lifted her spirits a little, but she needed someone to talk to and a shoulder to cry on. That someone was Brenda; it was always Brenda. Their itemised telephone bills were punctuated at regular intervals with each other's numbers. The log of their calls was a reminder of the good and the bad times they had shared together. Now, another entry was to be made.

'Hello, it's me. Sorry it's so late.'

'Lynn? Don't worry about it. I was only watching the news channel. Anyway, I was going to call you and tell you about what happened at work today.'

'Bren, I've thrown Gerald out.'

'What? Hang on Lynn, let me mute the TV and get myself sorted out.'

There was a short pause while Brenda made herself comfortable in preparation for what promised to be another long session.

'Right, I'm all yours. What's happened?'

As Lynn related the events of the evening she felt a weight lifting from her chest. Brenda said few words, judging it was more important for her friend to do the talking. After the best part of an hour, Lynn had finished.

'That's enough about me. What was it you were going to tell me about?'

'It doesn't seem so important anymore.'

'Tell me anyway, it might take my mind of things.'

'Well, okay. It was my turn to open the hairdressers this morning. When I got there, I opened the front door, switched on the lights and I was just taking my jacket off when I realised none of the mirrors on the walls were reflecting anymore.'

'That's odd. What caused that then?'

'I don't know. That's what's so strange. We had to remain closed all day because none of the customers would be able to see what we had done to them. Andy, the bloke who owns the place, was furious and he took it out on me as though it was in some way my fault. Men.

'Anyway, we got some glaziers in to replace them all and the chap said he'd never seen anything like it before. All the silvering had come off the backs. He could only imagine it was something to do with the chemicals we use for the perms.'

'Blimey, it makes you wonder what that stuff is...'

'Hang on a minute, Lynn,' Brenda interrupted. 'There's something on the news about the Eiffel Tower. It looks like someone's been killed.'

Brenda restored the sound to her television. A reporter was speaking to camera from in front of a cordon surrounding the Parisian tower.

'...Yes, Eamonn, a spokesman for the Eiffel Tower has told me it will remain closed to the public until a full safety check can be carried out and that will not be completed until tomorrow afternoon at the earliest.

'Up until now, the safety record has been good, but this episode in its history brings into question whether the tower, built in 1889 for the Centennial Exposition, is now showing its age.'

'Thank you, John. That was our reporter, John Phipps at the Eiffel Tower in Paris, France, where an hour ago, three tourists were killed when girders which had become detached from the structure, fell on them. The victims were two Austrian students and a forty-three year old Belgian woman. We will bring you an update when we have more information.'

Lynn could not hear properly what was being said at Brenda's end of the telephone. She sat in eager anticipation for a short time until she heard the television being muted once more.

'Well, what about that then?' Brenda said.

'What's happened?'

Brenda explained as Lynn listened solemnly. She was very sensitive to the news of anyone dying under whatever circumstances. It did not matter to her whether they were young or old, died at the hands of a murderer or from starvation, or whether they had been famous or had lived their lives in complete anonymity.

'It puts my problems into perspective doesn't it?' Lynn said.

She found she did not want to talk anymore. It was time to be alone with her thoughts, however sad they were. Thanking Brenda for her patience and understanding, she said goodbye and retired to bed.

***

The advent of a new day brought Lynn a new sense of hope and to her surprise she found it possible to put the events of the previous evening to the back of her mind. There was a timetable to keep and if it were not adhered to she would be late for work.

Grabbing her handbag and the bundle of donated magazines, Lynn went out to her car. Christine, the next door neighbour, was already out there and was just about to lower herself into the driving seat of her own vehicle when she spotted Lynn. Wearing an ill-tempered expression on her face, Christine stood behind the half-open driver's door. Lynn could only assume her neighbour intended to complain about the noise made by her and her husband the previous evening. Instead, the source of Christine's displeasure was an entirely different matter.

'Have you seen what some mindless vandals have done?'

Lynn had to confess she had not.

Her neighbour was quick to elaborate.

'Only last week, Frank and I bought two very expensive brass numbers to go on the front of the house, and last night some little bastards made off with them. You wait 'til I catch them. I'll ring their bleedin' necks.'

Lynn did not particularly like the woman, or her husband for that matter, but she was sympathetic towards her plight all the same. Vandalism was becoming a real menace in the neighbourhood and it seemed so utterly pointless. She could not imagine there was a thriving black market in stolen house numbers, so the motive for the attack could only have been a malicious desire to cause others suffering.

At least there was some good to come from her neighbour's news. Lynn was an intelligent woman, but still she lived her life believing in superstition. Bad fortune always fell in threes, she told herself. First, there were her husband's revelations; then there was Brenda's trouble at work, and now Christine's house had been vandalised. The tragedy in France did not come into the equation as things happened globally all the time. With three events out of the way, Lynn could begin to get her life back into some semblance of order.

Having positioned herself behind the wheel, Lynn shifted the donated bundle of magazines to the passenger foot well and placed her handbag beside her on the passenger seat. The engine sprung into life at the first turn of the key, but all was not well. To the sound of the engine purring was quickly added another - a mysterious hissing. The source of the noise became apparent almost immediately. Hair spray was venting from a damaged aerosol can inside Lynn's handbag, taking only a matter of seconds to fill the interior of the car with a choking cloud of lacquer.

The old adage would have to be revised - bad things come in fours.

Lynn, coping extremely well under the circumstances, retrieved a slightly sticky purse from an even stickier handbag, secured the doors of the car and calmly walked off in the direction of the bus stop.

6

'Shit! The bloody alarm didn't go off.'

Alistair's cries permeated Diane's thoughts as she lay sleeping, but she was not about to abandon her dream so readily.

A police officer, having pulled her vehicle over for infringing some unspecified traffic offence, had Diane bent over the bonnet of his patrol car and was about to administer a rather unorthodox form of punishment. Her husband's words came as an unwelcome interruption to the proceedings and her mind tried desperately to incorporate them into the scenario in order that the dream might continue. Suddenly her husband was in the car, impatiently tapping on his watch glass, urging her to get on with it. But it was too late. The ruse was discovered; the damage had been done.

Diane woke with a start, finally realising what her husband had said, by which time he was up and showering in the en suite bathroom.

'Don't panic. What time is it?' she said blearily, her eyes darting first towards the clock radio which lay on Alistair's bedside cabinet and then, when she realised it was not working, to the ornate gilded timepiece standing on a table at the end of the bed.

'You're not that late. You still have plenty of time to catch your plane,' she said reassuringly, raising her voice so as to be heard over the sound of running water.

'Not that late! I was supposed to be at the airport fifteen minutes ago. I'm not even dressed and I've got an hour's drive ahead of me,' he responded angrily.

Ignoring her husband's outburst, Diane continued with an air of confidence and optimism.

'Calm yourself down. Remember, panic never cured anything. You'll be ready in fifteen minutes, even if it means skipping breakfast, and the plane doesn't leave for hours.'

It was a good estimate. Within the next quarter of an hour Alistair had dried, seen to his other ablutions, and dressed. Diane stood at the foot of the stairs with the front door open, holding out his briefcase, containing among other things his passport, ticket and a banana; in the other, his car keys.

'I've put your suitcase in the boot.'

Alistair threw on his coat, took the keys and bag from his wife and paused just long enough to pass inspection.

'Well, how do I look?' Alistair asked, clearly flustered.

'Like an international jet-setter,' Diana replied calmly, leaning forward to give her husband a quick peck on the cheek. 'Go do your thing. I'll be waiting for you when you get back.'

Her raised eyebrows promised a very pleasant home coming.

Diane had thoughtfully opened the door of the double-width garage. From the doorstep, she witnessed her husband enter, only to re-emerge a few moments later in even more of a fluster.

'Is someone having a fucking laugh? The fucking steering wheel just fell off in my fucking hands. I mean, when does that fucking happen? I am so going to sue the fucking manufacturer. That could have happened while I was on the fucking motorway. I could have been fucking killed. It's not fucking acceptable. Anyway, what the fuck am I supposed to do now?'

Diane had never seen her husband in such a state before.

'Don't worry, I'll call a taxi.'

It was an agonising wait for the cab to arrive, but arrive it did and at least Alistair was under way. There was still time to catch the plane, although it was clear he would be late checking-in.

Already the motorway traffic was building rapidly in preparation for the morning rush hour. Despite this, the taxi made good progress and before long was turning south for the last ten miles of the journey. The situation appeared to be improving by the minute. With the pressure upon him subsiding steadily, Alistair began to relax, easing his grip on the cab's upholstery.

However, his muscles and tendons had slackened too soon.

Firmly established on the road between two junctions, with nowhere to go but forward, the vehicles in front slowed abruptly to a crawl; then to a halt. Three columns of brake lights snaked into the distance. The driver of the taxi spat profanities. Having been speeding dangerously close to the BMW directly in his path, while paying no attention to the conditions beyond it, he was forced to stamp hard on the centre pedal to avoid a collision; so hard the cab's hazard warning lights activated automatically, the tyres locking and unlocking several times a seconds until the speedo registered nought. To Alistair's relief, they were soon under way again, but then only in sporadic bursts.

Alistair sat in the rear of the cab, staring at his knees, trying to convince himself this latest setback was of little or no consequence and that he still had time to catch his flight.

Unaccustomed to being in situations out of his control, the anxious passenger felt under increasing pressure to do something – anything - even if only to create the illusion his actions might promote a better outcome. His only tool was the phone in his pocket, but Alistair was reluctant to contact anyone with it, fearing it might alert his bosses to the fact he had overslept. However, the device was capable of so much more. Swift work with his index finger brought a map to the screen, further taps revealing three vital pieces of information: the vehicle had progressed to within just three miles of the airport's drop-off point; the red line indicating very slow moving traffic had an end; and a trustworthy estimated time of arrival he could live with – just. It also put to bed the fanciful idea he had briefly entertained, that he might get out and walk - a man laden with luggage might only achieve two or three miles per hour on foot, while the taxi was predicted to reach average speeds of four times that. Feeling slightly more at ease, Alistair slid the phone back into his pocket, making every effort to leave it there.

A local traffic announcement overrode the volume at which the driver had set the car's radio. There were road works, minor bumps and broken down vehicles to report across the county, but none of these were as significant, in terms of the sheer chaos they caused, as the event in which Alistair and many others around him found themselves ensnared.

The traffic announcement was not read in calming tones; rather, it would have been more suited to the reporting of a terrorist bomb, detonating in a heavily populated neighbourhood. Seemingly convinced in his own mind he was bringing news of war torn Syria, the man spoke of an earlier accident involving a vehicle breaching the central reservation's Armco barrier, separating the north-bound from the south-bound flow. The small family saloon had careered into the path of oncoming traffic, killing the driver and injuring three others. Of greater importance, so far as Alistair was concerned, the announcer revealed the scene had been cleared – hence the taxi's continuing progress towards its destination, albeit at a snail's pace.

The minutes ticked by until finally they were at the scene of the accident and witnessed, first-hand, the neat hole punched in the galvanised steel barrier, described earlier by the would-be war correspondent. As each vehicle drove slowly by, all heads craned round to absorb as much detail as possible. Thankfully, once clear, the traffic then took no time in accelerating to a comfortable, if illegal, ninety miles per hour, with the cab being no exception. Seemingly, Alistair Whyte was not the only person who needed to catch a flight.

'Strange,' the driver remarked.

'What is?'

'That there hole.'

'What about it?'

'Well, those barriers are designed to give way, aren't they - to absorb the impact. It's not the first time I've seen a vehicle go through one, you know. I mean, I've seen an artic hit it head on. God knows how - but it made a right old mess of the barrier for at least a hundred metres. I don't know about you, but I couldn't see any twisted metal. I think someone's made an enormous cock up, removed a section and then forgotten to replace it. There'll be all hell to pay, mark my words. Mind you, how unlucky were they to choose to go off just where there's a bit of barrier missing? On the other hand, it wouldn't surprise me if the driver had missed his turning and took the opportunity of a gap in the reservation to do a U-turn. There are some crazy people out there.'

Alistair was not listening to the driver's extended monologue. He was far more interested in trying to spot the turn off for the airport.

At long last the taxi arrived at the drop-off point for the airport's south terminal. As the vehicle came to a halt, Alistair burst from the car onto the pavement, wrenched open the boot, retrieved his luggage, thrust a fistful of sterling into the taxi-driver's hands, and without uttering a single word, scurried off to find a trolley.

His next task was to push his load up a seemingly endless spiralling slope, only to then be confronted by a long, wide corridor housing a moving walkway, measuring approximately one hundred metres in length. Unfortunately, the moving walkway was, in fact, quite stationary. Alistair cursed and broke into a slow trot, running alongside the non-moving, moving travellator.

It was sod's law he had chosen a trolley possessed with a mind of its own. For every metre he progressed forward, he would veer left by another, it being all he could do to stop it colliding with the wall. With his head down like a charging bull, teeth gritted, his face sporting a rather worrying purple complexion, Alistair lunged towards the automatic doors at the far end of the corridor, but they refused stubbornly to open.

Gripping the trolley's handle tightly in both hands, inhaling deeply through flared nostrils, he straightened his back, raising his face heavenward, prepared to offer up his soul to whoever or whatever it was that had chosen to punish him. What confronted his eyes were two glaringly obvious illuminated 'no entry' signs, positioned over the door. To his feelings of anger and frustration, which caused such a pounding in his chest his heart was on the brink of bursting, he added another - utter humiliation.

There being no time to consider potential witnesses, Alistair fought the will of the trolley, swinging the evil contraption towards the adjacent pair of doors. They opened, revealing the departure hall, brightly lit and boasting a bewildering number of check-in desks to his left, to his right and straight ahead. Monitors hung down, helpfully indicating in which zone each airline's desk could be found. Adrenalin caused Alistair to experience tunnel vision, making the normally simple task of finding the name on the left of the screen and relating it to a letter in a column on the right, almost impossible. He stared at the symbols that his eyes could register but his brain could not translate.

At that moment, an unsuspecting member of airport staff wandered into view, to be leapt upon by a half-crazed young executive who was very close to losing control of his bodily functions. The neatly uniformed lady seemed more concerned by his profuse sweating than with his desperate pleas for directions. At last she pointed, Alistair having reassured her for the tenth time he was not about to die.

Only a matter of metres now stretched between him and the winning post, but then, as if some divine being wished to test his mettle that tiny bit more, Alistair's briefcase slid from its position on top of the suitcase, plummeting to the floor. The impact caused it to break open, spilling the contents therein across the polished tiled surface. Frantically, Alistair ran to the crash site, stooped to gather up his papers and banana, stuffed them into the two open halves of his briefcase, and slammed them shut.

'What the fuck!'

Although his profanity caused heads to turn, it was most certainly justifiable.

Against all logic and reason, Alistair immediately discovered the catches were not only broken, but missing, presumably the impact having dislodged them and caused them to scud across the floor to who knew where.

'Damn, I paid a lot of money for this thing. You wait, I'll be writing you a letter.'

He spoke aloud, his narrowed eyes directing his frustration towards an imaginary chairman of the company that produced the case he was force to clutch to his chest, leaving only one arm free with which to push the uncooperative trolley to its final destination. More than one witness to his manic outburst hoped he was not to share their flight, some wondering whether it would be better to have him arrested, just to be safe.

The woman at the check-in desk greeted Alistair's purple, sweating body with a smile so insensitive, it seemed she was keen for someone to punch her lights out. As she processed Alistair's luggage, she reminded him he was supposed to have booked in three hours before the flight was due to take off. As if her admonishment were not enough – a mere girl, junior in years and pay grade, treating him like a child - a television screen set in the wall behind her informed him impassively the boarding gates would be closed fifteen minutes before take-off.

Alistair struggled to let the woman's rebuke wash over him, if only to prevent further delay. At least, having committed his luggage to the hold, both his arms were then free to hug his carry-on briefcase.

Perhaps marking the end of his string of misfortune, the next hurdles over which he had to jump, crawl beneath, and tunnel under, went without further hitch. Although, to a man running so desperately late, every minute's delay was magnified out of all proportion. First came passport control, and then the x-ray machine – why on earth did they require him to take off his shoes? If he had known beforehand, he would have worn slip-ons. Then there was the portal. Of course, it went off. The culprit was a single coin that once cast into the x-ray tray allowed him to pass through without triggering any sound. However, that single coin was sufficient to single him out for a thorough rub-down search.

Next came duty free; an area full of people who, en masse, had one intention in mind – to get in his way.

'Who allows children in an airport anyway?' he thought.

The screens refreshed slowly, causing him a delay of an additional few microseconds before he was able to establish he should head for hub 31-38. A slope; a tunnel to match that which lay beneath the English Channel, and then a button to call a driverless transit train.

The carriages took so long to arrive, Alistair began to suspect it was actually a normal train, complete with driver, and that he or she had gone on strike, or was taking a breakfast break. Another portal; another x-ray machine, and finally the boarding lounge. The information screen had gone to DEFCON 2, a yellow bar indicating - almost shouting - that his plane was boarding.

Alistair suspected the gate receptionist had been trained by the same person as the woman at the check-in desk. Having examined his boarding pass and passport, she ushered him into the telescopic boarding tunnel, which was empty – it would be; everyone else already seated on the plane, waiting for the final passenger. His was the walk of shame.

The stewardess took the boarding pass, made some rather unamusing comment about Alistair being just in the nick of time, and guided him safely to his seat. It was only then he discovered it looked out over the starboard wing; hardly appropriate for an up-and-coming executive such as himself, but under the circumstances it was something he felt able to tolerate.

All about him there sat excited passengers, and judging by their tone, for the majority of them, this appeared to be a once-in-a-lifetime trip. In contrast, if all went well, this giant ark of the skies would be ferrying Alistair backwards and forwards across the pond on regular business trips. Who knew, maybe next time he would be travelling business class.

The noise of the massive aero engines rose as the aircraft began to taxi. Staring out of the cabin window, casually watching the forward motion, Alistair thought of his wife waiting for him back home. Remembering her parting gift from the night before, and a veiled promise of more to come, a smile crept across his face, accompanied by a warm, tingling sensation in his silk boxer shorts. The morning had brought two extremes - overwhelming stress and then a sense of peace and wellbeing.

Three rows ahead of Alistair sat a young, apparently unmarried couple. The chemistry that existed between them would not have been so evident had they been joined in holy matrimony; else this was their honeymoon.

Sharon had a pressing matter to discuss with Martin and leant closer to whisper in his ear.

'As soon as the seatbelts go out I want you in the toilets.'

Martin simultaneously dropped his hands to his lap, still clutching a what-to-do-in-an-emergency instruction card, and whipped his head round to confront his girlfriend. His expression was that of someone who had just had his bottom pinched by his mother-in-law.

'What, you really want to go through with it then?' he responded, nervously.

'Yes I do,' Sharon said firmly. 'I'm not too bothered what height we're at.

It doesn't have to be a mile, but the sooner we do it, the less chance there is a queue will form outside the door.'

'What if we're caught though?' Martin responded, trying not to move his lips, or raise the level of his voice.

'We can't get caught. No one will know for sure what we're doing; they can only suspect. Besides, that's what makes it exciting.'

'It's a bit early in the morning isn't it?'

'I'm a morning person – you should know that by now. Besides, that's all the more reason for people not to suspect.'

There was a short pause while a member of the cabin crew walked past. As soon as he had gone, Sharon continued.

'It'll be easy. I've dressed for the occasion. Anyway, I'm only talking about having a quickie and that shouldn't be a problem for you, my little express train.'

'Charming.'

Alistair was sucking hard on a boiled sweet when the seat belt warning light went out. Immediately, the young couple rose from their seats and made their way towards the rear of the aircraft. The girl said something to her partner about not feeling well, speaking at a volume guaranteed to be overheard by the other passengers. Her actions distracted Alistair sufficiently that he neglected to remove his lap belt. Instead he turned his attention back to the limited view of the sky afforded by his seating position.

The wing was white, very large and exceedingly uninteresting. However, something caught his eye. A small flap of paint was fluttering in the three-hundred-miles-an-hour wind that swept across the wing surface. The flap was tiny; perhaps a centimetre in length. It could even be an edge of a sticker that was losing its grip. Either way, it was reminiscent of a hangnail, and caused a similar degree of alarm. Alistair found it mesmerizing and could not help but wonder how long it might last in such conditions before being ripped off. As he looked on, the small tab began to grow, peeling back ever so slowly, centimetre by centimetre. This was getting exciting. How much punishment could one small strip of loose paint take? It was clearly not a sticker. Alistair held his breath in anticipation. Then it was gone, leaving a bare patch of metal marring the otherwise perfect, gleaming white surface.

'Well, that's the entertainment over and done with,' he thought to himself. 'I wonder how often that happens? Can't be normal, that's for sure.'

It was not. Nor was the fresh tab of paint that began fluttering in the air stream. Nor any of the myriad flakes of paint that joined it. Within seconds, over the majority of the wing surface, ragged strips of paint were being torn away by the wind, leaving swathes of bare aluminium sheeting beneath, exposed to the elements. As Alistair looked on in amazement, the metal took on the appearance of a surface coated in a powdery white substance, being continually cleaned in the path of a sandblaster.

Turning to his left, Alistair reached over with his right hand to shake the shoulder of the man who sat beside him, then used the same right hand to point through the window at the wing.

'Stewardess!' he called out, frantically, rising as far out of his seat as the lap belt would allow, raising his arm and clicking his fingers as he did so, trying to attract the flight attendant's urgent attention.

'Yes sir,' she said, coming over, having already formed the opinion this man was going to be a nuisance all the way to America.

'Take a look out of the window; you can't tell me that's normal,' Alistair said hurriedly.

His was not the only voice of concern. Everyone sitting within sight of either of the wings was asking the same question, and an excited babble had begun to fill the cabin.

The flight attendant leant forward, peering through the small aperture before her. For a moment her face fixed with an uncomprehending gaze, her pulse rate responding to a sudden injection of adrenalin.

'I'll tell the Captain,' she said abruptly, and then hastened off.

Sharon and Martin stood facing each other in the confines of the aircraft's toilet; his arms wrapped round behind her, hands sliding down over her buttocks, reaching for the hem of her short, red, clinging dress. As he did so, he made a mental note to seek out and personally thank the inventor of Lycra as soon as they landed.

Tugging the material upwards, Martin's knuckles slid over bare flesh, revealing the meaning of Sharon's remark with regard to having dressed for the occasion.

Sharon, meanwhile, fumbled with the button of Martin's denim jeans; undoing it was proving to be more difficult than she had anticipated.

'Breathe in,' she said, impatiently.

The couple parted slightly so she could have clear sight of what she was doing. Moments later, his trousers dropped to the floor, revealing a bulging pair of black cotton briefs. Sharon bit her upper lip gently and with one quick downward motion, freed the whole package, only to be faced with the disappointing sight of something only partially interested in the proceedings. Her body was perfect. She was firm and well proportioned. Her skin was as smooth and unblemished as that of a baby, and above all, everything was very neat, clean and well presented. Despite this, Martin's part in the venture seemed to have an involuntary reluctance to perform its duty.

Alistair Whyte remained seated, his eyes transfixed by the developments taking place outside. The amount of dust was increasing at an alarming rate and the whole wing was beginning to discolour. His mind tried to analyse the situation in as calm a fashion as it would a financial report. He knew paint flaking from the wing of an aeroplane, and the exposed fabric of the craft disintegrating before his very eyes, was neither normal nor desirable. He was also aware the flight attendant had run off in the direction of the cockpit without uttering any reassuring phrases like, 'I'm sure it's nothing to worry about'.

A numbing sensation spread through his entire body as the first stages of panic set in. Before he had a chance to proceed to the more advanced stages, the co-pilot arrived, understandably wishing to view the problem for himself.

His lips managed to pass just three words before he too ran back towards the front of the plane.

'Oh my God!'

'What's wrong big boy? That thing's usually up like a flick-knife,' Sharon asked, concerned by the set back.

Martin failed to answer, being too busy trying to overcome nerves.

'Here, let me,' Sharon said, applying some well-practiced manipulation, relieved to find it was having the desired effect.

'That'll do,' she said, sitting awkwardly on the edge of the semi-recessed sink unit.

Martin's fingers fumbled a little between her legs, trying to acquire his target. With co-ordinates established, he advanced forward, felt contact, pushed home, and missed. It felt rather like jousting with a brick wall and sent him recoiling backwards in some pain.

'Give it here,' Sharon said, by now sounding quite irritable.

Taking hold with a firm grip, she guided him forward once more.

'There.'

He pushed forward.

'You're too high, I'm on tip toes,' Martin complained.

With a huff, Sharon slid down to the floor, this time leaning the small of her back against the sink with her legs spread wide apart.

'Let's try again,' she said, guiding him towards her for another attempt.

This time he eased himself in, paused to get comfortable, and then began rocking his pelvis.

Annette Bishop, the chief member of the cabin crew, needed information. She entered the cockpit and found the Captain speaking into the radio microphone.

'I repeat, I am declaring an emergency...' and then, cursing to himself, 'now this damn thing's not working.'

The co-pilot turned towards Annette.

'Get everyone to fasten their seatbelts and fasten everything down for an emergency landing.'

Hurriedly returning to the cabin, Annette found groups of passengers gathered at the windows on both sides of the aircraft, straining to see for themselves what had caused such a commotion. Others, having already seen the disintegration of the flight surfaces for themselves, sat among the crowd in stunned silence, or cradled in their loved-ones' arms, crying uncontrollably. One or two were making themselves busy scribing their last words to friends and relatives whom they never expected to see again. Many, with flagrant disregard for the rules of the skies, began texting, and calling using their mobiles.

'For your safety, the Captain has activated the seat-belt sign. I must ask everyone to return to their seats immediately, and fasten your belts,' Annette announced as loudly as she could, trying to project her own voice above a rapidly growing chorus of panic stricken passengers. She continued, desperately trying to regain control of the situation.

'Please remain calm, we will be landing shortly.'

Her efforts might have brought about some semblance of order were it not for several rows of empty seats spontaneously becoming detached from their mountings, only moments after she had spoken, followed immediately afterwards by a number of overhead lockers dropping open. It was becoming obvious for all to see that the aeroplane was falling to pieces and no words, however carefully they might be chosen, could challenge that fact.

Shirley, another member of the cabin staff, had been despatched to check the toilets. Finding one of them was engaged, she called through the door without receiving any response. Banging on the door proved to be no more effective. Any further action she might have taken at this point was abandoned when a sudden increase in the volume of voices drew her attention back towards the cabin area where the passengers were becoming hysterical. The aircraft had banked heavily to port, adopting a course it was hoped would facilitate an emergency landing. The sudden, violent movement would have been unsettling at the best of times, but under these circumstances proved for many to be the last straw.

'This is outrageous,' Alistair said. 'I have an important financial services fair to attend in New York and I have to be there by tomorrow morning. What do you intend to do?'

The attendant stared into his eyes for a moment as she searched for an appropriate answer, but as she settled on the torrent of abuse she intended to unleash, she was knocked unconscious by a falling overhead storage bin, hitting her hard across her temple.

The crotch of Alistair's best suit trousers darkened, the wet patch spreading down his left leg. He stood amid a scene of chaos and began to cry.

With the radio out, the flight crew had not been able to contact air traffic control to declare their emergency, nor had they been able to warn them that they were diverting towards Manchester, due to reluctance on the part of the aircraft to respond to directional inputs. All the crew could do was hope that radar would indicate their height and position and that someone on the ground would realise they were in difficulties and make the appropriate arrangements. Unfortunately, this was not the case. At around the same time as the radio ceased to operate, so too did the transponder. The sudden apparent disappearance of the aircraft brought confusion in the control room who were now frantically trying to raise them by radio.

Back on board, the compass had given up, followed closely by the failure of the starboard outer engine. The captain now relied solely on his eyes for navigation. Manchester airport was no longer their goal, anywhere flat would do.

At that moment, had it been possible to view the aeroplane from a remote point outside, this enormous feat of human engineering, with a steady stream of dust trailing from its surfaces, and aviation fuel being dumped from its tanks, would have resembled a crop duster plying its trade, rather than a passenger liner filled to capacity.

After several minutes of strenuous exercise, Martin's legs were tiring, the muscles in his buttocks were beginning to burn and yet there was nothing happening.

'It's not going to work, I'm too uncomfortable.'

'Keep going,' Sharon demanded.

Martin tried desperately to put his mind elsewhere in an attempt to fool himself what he was engaged in was an everyday occurrence. He felt something. No it was gone again. His legs were tiring with every thrust, pushing him to the limits of endurance. Only the forceful encouragement of his sexually demanding partner gave him the necessary impetus to carry on. There it was again, a distant welling in his loin. He put it to the back of his mind along with the pain in his legs and buttocks, afraid he might scare away the sensation.

Martin continued with renewed vigour, encouraged by this pleasant feeling that was creeping up on him, getting stronger by the second. His movements became steadier; more rhythmic. Sharon could feel they were at the threshold between being members and non-members of the mile high club. The fact there was probably a queue of a dozen irate passengers just outside the door, waiting with crossed legs to use the facilities, did not matter. In fact, it made the experience that much more pleasurable, convincing her that recollections of the event would act as a catalyst for some fantastic future performances in the bedroom, eligible for an entry in her personal diary.

'Almost there, almost there,' Martin said to himself, relieved the end of his ordeal was in sight.

The banging on the door, and the muffled voices accompanying it, hardly penetrated his thoughts. Neither did the violent movements of the aircraft as it banked. Whatever was waiting for them when they stepped outside the toilet, they would face the music together.

Sharon stifled a moan.

'Yes!'

As Martin's body stiffened, his moment of triumph upon him, his final act was accompanied by the strangest sensation that the floor was giving way beneath his feet. Then there was sudden and total confusion, intense cold and a rush of wind that deafened his ears and robbed his lungs of air. As he tumbled, Martin could see a shower of other bodies scattering in all directions.

7

Rain fell with a purpose upon the roof of the barn; the galvanised corrugated steel sheets doing well to preserve the warm, dry atmosphere beneath; something for which the farmer, and more importantly, his ailing dairy cow, were most grateful.

'Aye girl, we're in for another wet one,' Joseph Dugdale said, speaking quietly to the beast as though half expecting an answer.

They were alone together. Having assisted his father milking the herd, Nathan had gone back to bed. Alice had not even got up yet. Ann was busy in the kitchen preparing a steak and kidney pudding, filling an order placed by the Robertsons, later to provide their evening meal. As for the holidaymakers, there was little sign, other than a light coming from the window of the toilet in the apartment occupied by the retired couple.

Joseph wore a concerned expression upon his face as he rose to his feet, turned his back on his patient, and headed for the door where Maggie stood, wide-eyed, waiting. The sound of the rain beating down upon the roof increased, rising to a crescendo, like the drum roll preceding a circus performance, sufficient to evoke a sense of excitement and anticipation within him; a feeling of expectation he knew to be wholly unjustified, but yet a natural reaction to such a display of the forces of nature. On this occasion though, he was quite wrong. On this occasion, the drum roll was building to an event that would influence the rest of his life and the lives of those he held dear.

As the drumming reached its zenith, the peace of the byre was suddenly shattered by an almighty crashing sound, followed immediately by a dull thud which had Joseph spinning in his tracks, losing his balance, and falling backwards against the wall.

There, among the debris of the barn roof, being soaked in its own personal shower of rain, lay the mutilated, semi-naked body of a man who, up until a few minutes ago, had been experiencing exquisite pleasure in the arms of his fiancé. To add to the initial shock, Joseph could hear the sound of other heavy impacts outside, and the clattering of smaller, lighter objects raining down upon the farm buildings, accompanied by the pungent smell of unburned fuel.

George Cubit had been unable to sleep for most of the night. Like the cow next door, he too was feeling rather poorly and had entered his second hour sitting on the toilet when the bombardment commenced. A brief, deafening sound, usually heard only in the yards of scrap metal dealers, broke the silence with such vehemence it acted upon George's bowels with great effect. The sudden relief he felt was more than offset by the shock the cure for his constipation had given him, leaving him trembling uncontrollably.

Hastily making himself decent, George emerged from 'the smallest room', to join his wife who was, by that time, standing at the window overlooking the parking area. Both were eager to discover the cause of the commotion. The sight that met their eyes realised one of George's worst nightmares. Although quite distressing in itself, it was not so much the unexpected appearance of the dead body that elicited such great upset, more the spot where it had landed.

Since retiring, George had searched for a sense of meaning in his life and had found it by replacing his working schedule with a regime of devotion towards his car; a vehicle purchased with a view to seeing him through to the end of his driving days. Devotion had quickly turned to obsession, evoking a desire to protect it from any threat, genuine or perceived, by any means, stopping just short of murder. To this end, he had long held the belief that all bird life should be exterminated as a preventative measure to stop their unpleasant and corrosive deposits being splattered across the paintwork of his most cherished possession. So, to see the upper portion of the second greatest love in his life - his wife narrowly coming first - compressed to half its normal height, was more than he could bear. Ignoring repeated pleas from Norah not to do so, George ran outside, clutching his bathrobe about him.

From the windows of each of the four holiday apartments, many bleary-eyed faces locked on to George's movements as he scampered through the 'rain', dodging a flurry of small items that fell lazily to the ground. He pulled up short of the wreckage that had once been a fully taxed and tested car, complete with comprehensive service history. There he stood, staring in disbelief at the tortured and twisted metal before him. The faces in the windows of the converted barn continued to look on as he slowly extended one arm forward and began caressing the unaffected areas of bodywork, made softer and smoother by the film of fuel that coated every surface. He stopped for a moment to pick off a few shattered fragments of safety glass from the distorted window openings, inspecting them closely as though they might reveal answers to a mystery, or that, given time, he might be able to piece them back together.

The downpour ceased as abruptly as it had begun.

Each of the four families that remained indoors took this to be the 'all clear' and, having chosen representatives, sent them out into the open air to assess the situation.

Simon and Gill Robertson, and Tom Smith, from the two upstairs apartments, along with Graham Malone from the other ground floor flat, formed a neat semi-circular line around George and his car. All wore the same expression of disgust upon their faces, responding to the overwhelming aroma of aviation fuel that assaulted their nostrils. George, soaked in the stuff, appeared oblivious to the smell.

Despite a fall of many thousands of feet onto the roof of the car, superficially, the well-tailored deceased man did not look too much the worse for wear. His motionless body gave the appearance of someone sleeping serenely, belying the truth that below his skin every bone had been shattered, his vital organs so traumatised they now shared the same consistency of pureed baby food. The prognosis for a full recovery was not good.

Tom stepped forward.

'I wonder who he was?' he said choking, trying to avoid breathing in the fumes.

Nobody offered any suggestions.

Rummaging in the man's jacket pockets, Tom was surprised to find a wallet that had somehow stayed with him throughout his fall.

'Let's see. His name's Alistair Whyte. He looks pretty well off if all this money and plastic are anything to go by.'

'Looked,' Simon interrupted, emphasising the past tense.

'Looked,' Tom conceded.

Simon could not have guessed what had led to the disaster, but it was patently obvious this man had come from the sky; a fact that added credence to his conviction that flying was inherently unsafe and a justification for his many years insisting his feet remained on terra firma.

Joseph crouched down inside the door of the barn, holding Maggie close to his side by the scruff of her neck, fearful she might bolt into the open at any time. Breathing shallow and fast, he waited anxiously for the fallout to subside, his eyes darting in all directions in reaction to the smallest of noises.

Even after the sounds had finally ceased, he remained rooted to the spot until he was absolutely certain all was safe. Then, rising to his full height, shoulders shrugged, Joseph made his first tentative steps out into the farmyard, his gaze directed towards the heavens. There was not a trace of any further bombardment, or any clue as to where the body or the debris had originated. He might have remained fixed in this position for longer was it not for the voice of his wife calling frantically from the farmhouse.

'Joe, come quick!' she said, her tone being one of utter desperation.

Ann stood in the doorway of the farmhouse just long enough to attract her husband's attention, before running back inside. Without hesitation, Joe ran after her. It took only a matter of seconds to cover the ground between them, despite his ill-fitting wellington boots, but this was more than enough time for him to discover what was causing her such concern. The slate roof above the children's bedrooms had received a direct hit from something large enough to cave in the entire structure.

'Oh my God!' he said softly, but with the emotion of someone who was shouting at the top of their lungs.

Inside was a mess. Dust filled the air; debris filled the stairwell.

'Alice, Nathan, are you all right?'

Joseph's words emerged from his mouth, forced from the very pit of his stomach, able to penetrate the thickest of barriers. Until that moment, having only ever issued quiet instructions to the herd and to Maggie, he had been unaware the ability existed within him.

The pause might have lived for only a fraction of a second, but it seemed to last the life of an octogenarian.

'Daddy!'

Alice was crying. For a girl of thirteen to use such an expression meant she was scared; very scared.

'Are you okay sweetheart?' Joseph asked, his voice trembling.

'What's happening?'

Alice was shouting and crying at the same time, making her words difficult to understand.

'Hang on. I'm coming to get you. Where's Nathan?'

Alice composed herself just long enough to answer, but her voice was broken, choking, scared.

'I don't know. I think he's in his bedroom.'

Nathan did not answer directly, but instead made his feelings clear.

'Get me out! I can't breathe in here.'

His voice possessed the quality of a man constrained within a straitjacket.

'Thank God,' Joseph said beneath his breath. 'Don't worry boy, I'll have you out of there just as soon as I can.'

The main obstacle between the farmer and his children was a wooden beam of oak that had come down through the ceiling at the top of the stairs, bringing with it several tea chests that had been used for storage in the roof space. The fallen lath-and-plaster ceiling, the chests and their contents, all restricted access, but it was the beam alone that made it impossible to reach the children's bedrooms via the stairs.

The shouting brought the holidaymakers to the scene. Even George responded, although, having difficulty in coming to terms with what had happened to his beloved car, he held back for a few moments longer than the rest. Seeing their arrival, the farmer assumed they were there to help.

'We're going to need ropes and tackle. I've got some in the garage,' he said, firmly in control of his emotions; suddenly a leader of men.

The response he got was unexpected.

'Don't you think we should leave it to the emergency services,' George suggested, calling from the back of the gathering, feeling their efforts might risk further danger to themselves and the children.

Being close to seventy years of age, *his* call for inaction was both understandable and forgivable, but several others in the party agreed with him, their excuses being harder to see, or accept.

'I've tried ringing the fire service but the phone's dead,' the farmer's wife explained. 'I expect the line was damaged when the roof was hit.'

'That's no problem,' Simon replied, trying to be helpful. 'I'll get my mobile from the apartment.'

Joseph was not having any of it.

'Look! By all means go and phone the police, the fire service, the ambulance, mountain rescue, and the coast guard for all I care, but I'm not waiting for them to turn up - they're miles away and my kids are trapped and need our help now!'

He spoke aggressively for the first time in his life. His passion could not - would not - be ignored.

'Okay, okay,' Simon said, seeing there was little point in trying to change the farmer's mind. 'But at least rethink our options. If we remove that beam, there's no telling what might fall on top of us. I suspect it would be far quicker and safer to climb in through the upstairs windows.'

Joseph could see merit in Simon's argument.

'There's a ladder leaning against the hayloft. We'll use that.'

Ann waited anxiously as Joseph and Simon scaled the ladder to Alice's bedroom. Both disappeared through the open window, emerging from it a short while later with Alice, still wearing her pyjamas, slung over the farmer's shoulder; a technique frequently used by firemen for carrying humans to safety, and by farmers for carrying sacks of feed to the barn.

The exit from Alice's room to the landing being impassable, farmer and holidaymaker were forced to reposition the ladder, leaning it against the windowsill of Nathan's bedroom, and from there making a second assault.

The farmer's wife comforted her daughter while they awaited news of Nathan. This time the window was fastened, but the glass yielded easily to a hefty blow from Joseph's elbow, protected by the sleeve of his thick jacket.

Having popped back to the Cubit's apartment, Norah appeared at Alice's side, wrapped a blanket round her shoulders and dropped a pair of backless slippers to the ground for the young girl to step her bare feet into.

'Thank you,' Ann said on behalf of her daughter, pulling the blanket tight.

Norah smiled, demanding nothing more, understanding the farmer's wife had greater things on her mind than to engage in distracting conversation.

Ann positioned herself behind her daughter, holding the blanket in place.

While Alice's eyes remained fixed on the ground in front of her, her mother's eyes looked upwards, searching for any sign of her husband, her son, and their holiday tenant.

The delay began to feel unbearable, bringing Ann to the verge of climbing the ladder herself, but just in time, movement was at last seen at the window. First Simon stepped out onto the ladder, followed closely by a very dusty Nathan, and finally, Joseph.

'The boy's okay. Just a bit shook up,' Joseph called down, even before he had placed a single foot on the ladder, keen for his wife to be reassured at the first opportunity.

'What took so long? I was so worried.'

'He was trapped in the far corner of the room and it took a while for us to get him clear.'

With her son back on the ground, Ann gathered both her children to her, almost squeezing the air from their lungs. Under normal circumstances, Nathan would have pulled away, unwilling to submit to such signs of affection, as would the majority of boys his age, but not on this occasion.

Thankfully, having helped his father early in the morning, Nathan had returned to his bed fully clothed, all but his boots which he had left just inside the front door. Fortunately for the boy, his trainers remained next to his bed and he had been able to retrieve them and put them on before being rescued.

Joseph turned to Simon.

'Thanks.'

'Think nothing of it. I'll get my phone.'

'Is it wise to use the phone with all this fuel about?' Susan Smith asked, her arms pulling her two children close to her. 'Doesn't it create a spark?'

All were suddenly reminded of the aviation fuel that dampened every surface.

'That's an old wives' tale,' Graham Malone responded confidently. 'They used to think it was responsible for a series of explosions at the gas pumps in America, but now they think it was caused by static from the nozzle.'

Simon looked about the group, ready to listen to any opinion. Nothing more having being said, he ascended the stone steps to the Smith family's upstairs apartment, emerging a few moments later, phone in hand. At the bottom of the steps, he held the device up, displaying it to the group. His face bore a look of uncertainty. Seeing the device fail to prompt further opinion, Simon was left with the sole responsibility for their combined safety.

His hand closed about the phone, his arms dropped to his side. Then, having decided upon a course of action, and without a word having being spoken, he moved away to the far side of the farmyard, to a patch that appeared to be dry.

Only then did his wife, Gill, realise that what her husband was about to do might kill them all, engulfing them in a giant ball of fire. She raised her hand, begging him to pause what he was doing. In response, Simon shrugged his shoulders and dialled. To everyone's relief, there was no explosion; only the sound of the phone ringing at the other end, audible even at this distance, the entire surrounding area now devoid of any other noise.

The group stood in a semi-circle, waiting. Simon's voice was raised as he repeatedly twisted his upper body this way and that in an attempt to secure a better signal.

Having pressed the screen to terminate the call, he quickly returned to the rest of the party with an update. The emergency services had received many such calls and, as a result, resources were stretched to their limit. As everyone on the farm was either uninjured, or confirmed dead, they had been classified as a level two priority. As the woman on the other end had explained, level one was reserved for those who needed immediate medical assistance; were trapped; or whose property was on fire - that sort of thing. Level three was for those who had been least affected. She did not go into too much detail. Obviously the woman had not the time to explain everything if she was as busy as she claimed.

Gill and Simon invited Joseph, his family, and the rest of the holidaymakers back to their apartment while they waited for the emergency services to appear.

George declined, his priority being to change out of his fuel soaked clothing and take a shower.

Joseph joined them, but not before he had made one sortie into the ground floor of the farmhouse in order to retrieve clothes for his daughter that had been hanging on an airer, dry but un-ironed.

Once indoors, Susan immediately occupied one of two, two-seater settees, her children squeezed next to her on either side, her arms pulling them close. Likewise, the farmer's wife held Alice and Nathan captive on the matching settee. None of the children made any effort to free themselves, all four remaining motionless and silent.

There being no more seats, Robert Malone, despite being a young man of seventeen, stood next to his mother, their arms wrapped round each other's waists.

'So, what do you think's happened?'

And so the conversation continued among the adults; a discussion that lacked input from Tom Smith who stood at the window throughout, gazing up at the sky, searching for clues that were not there.

After a short while, the stronger members of the group decided each of the four holidaying families should return to their respective apartments to pack, believing it was best they all be kept occupied while they waited for the emergency services to arrive. There were no gainsayers. Having suffered such trauma, the families now wanted nothing more than to be home and saw packing their bags as a positive step to reaching their goal.

Joseph had nothing to pack and no reason to do so. If necessary, he was prepared for his family to decant into one of the holiday lets until the insurance company effected repairs to the farmhouse. He still had a herd of cattle to work and tend, and that meant being on hand, night and day. Instead, Joseph made it his first task to find a tarpaulin with which to cover the Cubit's car and the body that nestled within its crumpled bodywork; a second to cover the body of the naked man who lay on the floor of the barn, taking the opportunity to check and calm his ailing cow, which lay close by, evidently stressed by the events of the morning. He was then free to check on the remainder of the herd.

All this and more had been done, but still there was no sign of rescue. On invitation, all five families returned to the Smith's apartment, but thankfully, they did not have much longer to wait.

When the cavalry finally arrived they were not what had been expected. Nathan had been keeping a lone vigil by the cattle grid and was the first to spot the trucks making their way up the long, winding drive. He ran across the yard, up the stone steps and into the Smiths' apartment, where, by now, everyone else was waiting. Until then, news had been frustratingly scant. Both the radio and the television reported there had been an air accident and the loss of life was expected to be total. Other than providing a telephone number for concerned relatives, that was it.

With none of the windows overlooking the entrance to the farm, all fifteen men, women and children immediately made their way outside.

'Army trucks,' Joseph said, thoughtfully. 'This thing must be big if they've run out of regular ambulances and the like.'

As soon as the vehicles stopped, their tailgates dropped and several dozen soldiers, all wearing chemical warfare suits, jumped down and deployed among the various outbuildings.

A man approached, similarly dressed, but clearly in charge.

'We have instructions to transport you all to a temporary holding facility.'

The man's voice was muffled but firm; his words spoken with conviction.

'Why?' Joseph asked.

'For your own safety.'

The answers were efficient but hardly satisfactory. Joseph was not about to leave his cattle without good reason. The cows needed milking regularly. There were repairs to the buildings to be got underway, and so far, no mention had been made of how long they would be gone for, or where they would be taken. It was all very suspicious; especially as it was coming from a man wearing an all-in-one black suit, his face disguised by mask and respirator.

'Why all this?' Joseph asked, directing an open hand, indicating the soldier's mode of dress.

'Just precautions. There's a lot of aviation fuel around. Best not to breathe it in. That's why you must come with us.'

Joseph was sure he had just provided the soldier with an excuse.

'And why do you need guns?'

Unintentionally, Joseph had become the spokesperson for the group, instinctively asking all the questions that hung on the lips of those who stood gathered behind him.

'Just part of the uniform.'

The holidaymakers were more easily placated than the head of the Dugdale family and, having heard what the soldier had to say, were not nearly so reluctant to leave. In fact, it had become their first desire.

'I'll just go and get our bags,' George said, leading his wife towards their accommodation.

The soldier raised one hand.

'That won't be necessary sir.'

George turned and walked towards the suited man who lowered his hand to his side.

'What do you mean, that won't be necessary? What about all our things? We're all packed you know. It won't take a minute.'

'Everything you need will be provided. The experts need to carry out a thorough investigation and that means leaving everything just the way it is. Please allow us to do our job and maybe this type of thing will never happen again.'

It was a clever ploy. If George or anyone else refused to comply, they would be showing their contempt for those who had fallen from the sky – that they were prepared to let more innocent people die in preventable accidents in future, just so they could protect a few bags of clothes that would be worn out, or out of fashion, before the families of the deceased had come out of mourning.

Each member of the group took it in turn to be helped up into one of the trucks, fitted with bench seats down either side, with a further, removable row of back-to-back seating running down the centre of the floor. Alice held Maggie close to her chest. Joseph was the last, hesitating, needing further reassurance.

'What about the herd?'

'Don't worry. They'll be well taken care of.'

Joseph looked as deep into the soldier's eyes as the man's mask would allow, looking for signs of dishonesty.

'Okay, I believe you; but if this is an ordinary plane crash, where's the wreckage? I haven't seen a single piece of fuselage.'

'In my experience, when we get a sudden loss of a pressurised aircraft at high altitude, the wreckage can be spread over areas of up to six hundred square miles. It's just a matter of time before we find it.'

Joseph paused to consider the situation, stroked the stubble on his chin, and then relaxed.

'Okay.'

He was not the last man into the truck. That honour fell upon two armed, protectively suited soldiers, each man taking up position sitting at the ends of the internal benches, next to the opening. Neither uttered a single word.

As the vehicles moved off, Joseph studied the visible features of one of the soldiers, trying to gauge the nature of his expression and that of his body language. There was something about the man's manner – about the manner of both soldiers – he could not quite put his finger on. Why were they not talking? Was it simply because it was difficult to hold a conversation while wearing a mask? Were they remaining silent to avoid having to answer awkward questions? Was this just the military way? After all, they were men trained to fight. They were not the emergency services.

Joseph considered these options, but none seemed to fit. What he was seeing was two men who looked scared; two men that did not want to be there; two men that did not want any interaction, but did want to maintain their distance. They appeared uncomfortable, as though being around someone they knew was about to die – the guards looking after the condemned man prior to his execution.

Whatever the case, the soldiers turned in unison, concentrating on the landscape visible from the open back of the truck.

The trucks were heavy and made slow progress to the sports field of the local school where they parked up for a short time, awaiting the arrival of other trucks. By the time they were on the move again, the convoy numbered at least twenty and had an escort. A few miles further down the road, the convoy slowed as it passed through a military roadblock. Yet another sign this was no ordinary air crash investigation.

Their destination turned out to be a disused airfield, complete with hangers, various permanent buildings, and row upon row of large tents, set out in regimented lines. The perimeter was under the guard of regularly dressed soldiers, while others, wearing chemical warfare suits, worked among the refugees within the camp.

The convoy pulled up outside a building that had been set up as a reception area. Here, each truck in turn was emptied, the passengers being allocated a tent and provided with essential clothing, bedding, toiletries and a leaflet setting out the general rules and running of the facility. It was undeniably a slick operation, but being several trucks back, it was still some time before the vehicle in which the party from Hillcrest Farm sat was ready to be received. By then, several on board were in dire need of a toilet, but despite numerous requests for the families to be allowed to get off and use the bathroom, the soldiers met them each time with a slow and expressionless shake of the head.

Finally their turn came. Personal details were taken, the clothes they wore were removed and sealed in yellow plastic bags and Maggie was taken away to be quarantined, much to the upset of the teenage Dugdales who did not feel at all reassured by the receipt handed to their father.

The rest of the day passed with hardly a moment to reflect on events: there were beds to be made; queues for meals; queues for the latrines; queues for just about everything. The only thing that was not available, having queued or not, was news. There were no televisions; radios and mobile phones had been confiscated; and the military guards were saying nothing other than that needed to enforce the compliance of those in their charge.

As night drew in, high intensity floodlights replaced the sun's rays. It made sense; there were a lot of guy ropes fanning out in all directions, any one of which could cause a nasty accident if someone were to trip over them. None of the adults in tent G17, allocated to the Dugdale and Smith families, believed this was the primary reason for having them though. It was far more likely the lighting was an aid to the armed guards who continually patrolled the perimeter with their Alsatians; nasty beasts who strained at their leashes every time they observed movement, and with close on a thousand civilian 'guests', that was a frequent occurrence.

The Malone family - Graham, Linda and their teenage son, Robert - and the Robertsons, Gill and Simon, had been allocated G18 with George and Norah Cubit.

Despite the day having been long, none of the occupants of G17 or G18 were in any mood to go to sleep – even the young Smiths. Instead, they all gathered, squeezing into one tent to hold counsel.

'So what do we make of all this then?' Tom asked as soon as everyone was settled, putting the first question to the floor.

His wife, Susan, was quick to respond.

'Something's not right and that's for sure. I can understand why the authorities would not want us in the way. After all, they have to carry out their investigations on the farm and make the place safe. What I don't see though, is any reason for them taking all our belongings from us, not allowing us to use the phone, and for all this security. And why are all the soldiers who enter the camp wearing those suits?'

'And I don't see why they had to take Maggie,' Alice snapped, clearly still upset at being separated from the fifth member of their family.

Simply saying the name brought another tear to her eye, prompting her father to wrap a comforting arm around her shoulders.

'It all points to some sort of outbreak. Perhaps the plane was blown up by terrorists and the government thinks there may have been chemical agents planted on board,' Simon suggested.

'Or it was a military plane transporting a chemical warfare agent and it was attacked, or simply was destroyed in an accident,' Graham added.

'Accident, my arse,' George said, much to the surprise of his wife who had never heard him speak so crudely in all the fifty years she had known him. 'When have you ever heard of a plane *accidentally* breaking up in mid-air so completely? Even the 747 brought down over Lockerbie left dirty great pieces in tact – poor bastards. You can't tell me they haven't found parts of the fuselage, or the wings. All I saw were bodies and nothing else bigger than a seat tray.'

Everyone began chipping in with a hastily concocted theory.

'Then it must have been a deliberate explosion, and a big one - big enough to atomise it.'

'If it was atomised, why were our unexpected guests in such good shape? I didn't see any burn marks.'

'Maybe they *have* found the fuselage. Maybe it broke in two, dumped the bodies and the rest fell somewhere else and has already been recovered. They wouldn't tell us.'

'Maybe not, but they lied, and in my book you only lie like that if there's something serious to cover up.'

'I don't think the event was as unexpected as we might think. First off, I know we had to wait a while but the army still turned up pretty damned quick. Disasters like this are bound to overwhelm normal rescue services, but the army can't be expected to mobilise that soon. I mean to say, do you really think they could have got the call and set up this camp all in the space of a few hours? No, there's something else going on.'

The farmer's wife, sensing the emerging conspiracy theories were not helping matters, tried her hardest to keep the situation in perspective.

'Let's not overreact. In all likelihood there's a more simple explanation. The plane probably broke up in mid-air. It may well have been as a result of a terrorist attack, but the only way they could think there was a chemical on board is through prior intelligence, or having received a message from the terrorists claiming responsibility. Remember, it only happened this morning. Between everything falling on the farm and the time the army turned up, they didn't have time to take samples and analyse them. Let's face it, they would have to take the threat seriously and they would have to do whatever they could to prevent the spread of panic. Unfortunately, people who go to work with a gun strapped to their shoulders are not the best people to ask. They only know one way. I say there's probably nothing wrong with us, and if there is, they'll be able to treat it. We'll know soon enough.'

'All right Mum, but what about Maggie?'

'Like the man said, they don't want dogs running all over the place; it's as simple as that.'

The occupants of the tent fell silent. Becky yawned, causing her brother to do the same. It came as a reminder that it was getting late and prompted everyone to suddenly realise they were tired.

'Now, may I suggest we all get to bed,' Joseph said. 'I don't know about you, but I'm all in.'

8

A pleasant morning greeted the occupants of G17 and G18, but that did not stop the women moaning that none of them had been able to sleep, and just how much they disliked sharing toilets and queuing. To be fair to both sides, there were substantial queues for the toilets, the washing facilities and for breakfast, but in general things seemed to have improved since the previous day. Obviously the army was settling into a routine.

With nothing to do after they had eaten, the children were permitted to explore their new environment. Robert Malone from G18 was old enough and sensible enough to ensure the others did not get into too much mischief and, in any event, they could not wander too far because of the security.

An hour or so passed before they returned, excitedly bursting into the tent where all the adults of G17 and G18 had gathered.

'Dad!'

Nathan had some news he could not contain.

'Whoa Boy! First things first. Where did you get those,' Joseph asked, pointing to a pair of binoculars carried in his son's hands.

'That doesn't matter right now. Dad, we've just been over the far side of the camp and they've got some really big buildings - like the barns - only bigger.'

'They'd be hangers then,' Joe said, calmly.

Nathan's excitement was in no way dulled by his father's reception.

'Anyway, one of them is all sealed up, except for one door.'

'It's an airlock,' Robert butted in, every bit as animated as his recently discovered new best friend.

'Yeah, and these men keep going in and coming out wearing these white suits.'

'Tell him about the other bit,' Robert prompted, impatient to break the real news.

'Dad, the other building has got a container outside the door with a really big silver pipe going inside.'

'Looks like a refrigeration unit to me,' Robert added.

'Yeah, and the biggest thing is we saw a load of lorries pull up outside and these forklift trucks were unloading dead cattle - loads of them.'

At this, Joe's ears pricked and he was instantly filled with a feeling of dread and anger.

'Where son? Show me.'

Nathan and Robert took the lead, followed closely by Joseph. Realising the significance of the children's discovery, everyone else from tents G17 and G18 followed.

The group massed at the inner perimeter fence that bordered the civilian enclosure. Beyond lay no man's land, then another fence topped with razor wire, and beyond that, a number of medium sized buildings, and the two enormous hangers described by the boys. At least half a dozen cattle trucks were parked outside, devoid of any sign of life.

Without once taking his eyes off the trucks, Joseph fumbled for the binoculars his son had acquired. The magnification was good, enabling him to see in through the open doors of the building that the boys had speculated was a gigantic refrigerator.

'I can see them. There's a mountain of carcasses in there,' Joseph spoke in disbelief. 'What the hell are they doing?'

'Calm down Joseph,' Ann said, placing one hand on her husband's upper arm. 'There's nothing to say any of those cattle have anything to do with us. There's probably a perfectly good reason behind all this.'

Joseph appreciated his wife trying to soothe him, but remained rigidly sceptical all the same.

'I'm going to find someone and start asking questions.'

The group moved off towards the buildings within the civilian encampment where they had been registered the previous day. Someone in there was sure to have some answers, or know someone else who did.

One hundred metres from their destination, Joseph stopped abruptly and craned his neck forward, squinting.

'What the…That looks like Maggie.'

It was indeed Maggie, muzzled and leashed and being walked from one outbuilding towards another by an armed guard dressed in his protective suit.

'What is it with all these soldiers dressed up as though there's been a nuclear war?' Graham asked rhetorically.

'Ayup Girl!' Joseph called, as if it were work as usual for his dog.

Maggie responded immediately, straining on the leash until she broke free and ran towards her master's location. Her route was not clear. A second soldier, wearing only the uniform of a serving member of the British Army, stood in her path, lunging at her, desperately trying to effect a recapture. The dog was terrified by his action and turned at right angles, heading off in the direction of the outer perimeter fence. The first soldier did not hesitate. He raised his rifle, took aim through his visor and despite vehement protestations from Joseph and the entire group, fired. Maggie somersaulted once and lay motionless.

The crack of the rifle rent the air, but the sound was not as lasting as the high pitched screams of Alice and Becky, the former bringing her chin to her chest, her elbows to her sides and her clenched hands to her eyes. Two mothers threw themselves into the line of sight, gathering their daughters to their chests, Ann and Susan themselves being unable to contain their tears.

Outraged, the men all began shouting at the two soldiers, the most vocal of them being the normally placid Joseph.

'You damn fools, why did you have to kill the dog? What's she ever done wrong?'

At that moment, Joseph would gladly have used the soldier's own rifle to seek vengeance, but the wire was impenetrable.

The soldier who had fired the shot was already on the radio asking for transport to remove the body. He seemed unmoved by the incident but it was hard, if not impossible, to judge a person's feelings when they were wearing such a heavy disguise.

The soldier closest to the party raised his voice in response to Joseph's question, and to the unintelligible cacophony of unpleasant words being hurled at him. He was not well versed in the art of tact and diplomacy.

'If you have an official complaint, then I suggest you take it up with the camp's commander. We are only following orders. Now move away or you will be placed under close arrest.'

Seeing a crowd was gathering behind Joseph's party and that a mini riot looked likely, more soldiers ran to the scene, weapons at the ready. None of the civilians believed the army would fire upon them with live rounds - that was the stuff of Middle Eastern revolts. However, those that remembered the troubles of Northern Ireland were quite prepared to believe they would fire baton rounds and smoke grenades into their midst.

There was nothing for it but for the unarmed detainees to retreat reluctantly back to their tents and take stock.

The mood was low as the occupants of G17 and G18 once more crowded into the one tent.

'Why did they shoot Maggie?' Ann asked, tearfully, having lost all ability to look on the bright side.

No one had a definite answer, but Tom at least had an observation to make.

'I don't know about the rest of you, but to me that soldier who threatened us looked scared.'

'Well, you would too if you were facing an angry mob on your own,' Graham responded.

'Maybe, but it makes me question how a man can be so quick to gun down a pet, unless he was really scared it might escape, and that raises the question, why?'

A chill suddenly ran down the spine of every one of the refugees who was listening.

Tom made a further observation.

'Did any of you notice? Just before your dog was scared off by that oaf in the suit, I caught a glimpse of its coat. There was definitely a shaven patch around the neck area.'

'Why would they do that?'

Tom suggested an explanation.

'We had a dog once which had to go to the vet. He tried to get blood from the leg, but in the end, the only place he could get it from was the neck and that meant shaving off a small area of fur.'

By now, Ann was utterly incapable of comprehending anything that was going on.

'Why would they need to take blood?'

Joseph looked thoughtful for a while and then spoke quietly.

'After what we have seen today, I think we can only expect the worst.'

9

Peter's phone vibrated against the bedside cabinet, the ringer on silent so as not to disturb his wife's sleep. The subtle purr was all that was needed to start his day, Peter having already been awake for at least an hour, thanks to his impatient bladder, the light that penetrated the lined curtains, and a lack of duvet, his half having once again been robbed by Tessa during the early hours of the morning.

Peter moved round the bedroom, gathering together items of uniform as quietly as the creaking floorboards would allow. The task was easier during these summer months, the sun being already above the horizon. Winter, on the other hand, was a different matter, when the dark and cold made it harder to prise himself from the bed, and finding his clothes had to be done by the reflected light from the bathroom. Then it was not unknown for Peter to land up wearing two odd socks; something his work colleagues never failed to notice. The day he wore a pair of novelty socks, marked 'L' and 'R', on the wrong feet, not only provided a source of amusement, but for many months afterwards became the benchmark by which all other acts of stupidity were measured. This episode would have remained in the top spot had it not been for another officer parking his car in the back of a furniture removal lorry, much to the surprise of the man who was unloading a potted aspidistra at the time.

To the sound of the electric toothbrush whirring was added a sigh; Peter's reaction to his brain randomly reminding him he was detailed to work an 'A' shift – more than twelve hours trapped within the four walls, surrounded by the dregs of society whose smell and self-centred attitude pervaded every nook and cranny. He often wondered, if the walls could talk, what they would say. He imagined they would ask why they could not have been something nicer, like a hospital, or a school.

Peter dressed in the bathroom, looked in on Emma from her bedroom door, ate his breakfast in silence in the kitchen, tied his shoes in silence in the hall, and clicked the front door shut behind him as gently as the spring bolt would allow.

Seven years before, having moved house, the new journey to work had been unfamiliar. Peter had only ever desired to work his contracted hours - not a minute more - and always aimed to pull into the car park at precisely two minutes before his start time. To this end, he deemed it vital to know, at any stage of his journey, whether he was a minute behind, or a minute ahead of schedule, so he might adjust his speed accordingly. Within the first week, he had identified and memorised a dozen waypoint markers, but it took a further month for him to make a mental note of when he should pass each, depending on his shift and on the day of the week.

Seven years on, each marker remained hard-wired, but his conscious mind no longer paid them attention. The journey had become so routine he drove on autopilot to and from the jail, often failing to stop for petrol when prompted to do so by the dashboard warning light. In fact, such was Peter a creature of habit, it was often three days before he finally released the fuel cap to find himself embarrassed by the hiss of air rushing into fill the vacuum, clearly audible to other customers on the forecourt.

Driving on autopilot was not wholly a bad thing. It left the conscious part of his mind free to take in the surroundings, and this particular Sunday was a good opportunity for doing just that. The wind that blew through the open window was already warm, even at such an early hour. The sight of wild rabbits sitting upright on the grass verges, their ears pricked to the sound of danger, added to his pleasure. However, it took the addition of a soundtrack provided by Antonio Vivaldi to complete the experience.

The journey had been timed to perfection, Peter pulling open the outer door to the jail at exactly half past eight – his start time.

The four main wings, located in the Georgian half of the prison, extended from a central hub. Peter arrived on C wing with a contented smile on his face, much to the puzzlement of his colleagues who were sitting in the office, waiting to receive the morning briefing, to be delivered as soon as the last man – Peter - arrived. Jumping the gun, they were already discussing something that had happened during the night.

'What's up?' Peter asked, realising he had missed something juicy.

'That guy we bent up yesterday, he's shit up down the block,' Frank replied, never one for pleasantries.

'Wiggins?'

'Yeh. Stan says he's done a good job. Caught him with a huge turd in his hand, using it like a bar of soap all over his body. Dirty, fuckin' animal.'

'Nice. It's at times like this I'm glad I don't work down the seg. Who wants to get kitted up every time you open the door. Mind you, at least the staff get paid a bit extra for it.'

'What you do to upset him anyway?' Mikala asked.

'Nothing, really,' Peter responded, nonchalantly. 'I went in his cell after lunch yesterday. Found him wacked out on Spice, with a phone on his chest – on charge, no less. Cheeky fuck. Of course I'm gonna take it. When he came round and found it was me, he smashed the cell to pieces. Tosser.'

At this point, the Supervising Officer, sitting behind his desk with the handover book open before him, chose to interject, offering the newer officer an insight to the way things worked.

'I think the problem was that the phone wasn't his. He probably owes someone six hundred quid for it. Probably shitting up so he's kept down the block. If he comes back on here, someone's going to want to get paid, and that could be ugly.'

'Yeh, we've got some right violent cunts on here.'

Frank clearly agreed with his boss, but lacked the subtlety to express himself without resorting to base language.

'Watch it, Frank - ladies present.'

This was the first time the S.O. deemed his staff had overstepped the mark. Those further up the food chain were less forgiving, thinking nothing of pulling someone up for failing to use the prefix, Mister, or their first name, when talking to and about prisoners. Some went further. Many officers remembered with outrage the day Josh was taken to one side for not wearing a tie, just after he had been punched in the face for telling someone he could not have a shower. Respect was hard won and easily lost. Such an error by management set relations back years.

'Anything else?' Peter asked, seeing a page full of entries in the handover book.

'Andrews on the 'twos' cut up last night,' Jeff replied, 'There's a bed watch out if you're interested.'

'No, not really. It was a good one then?'

'Was it? You should see his cell - there's claret everywhere. It stinks.'

'Have we got any bio-trained cleaners on here?'

'No, they're all on G Wing.'

'That's a pain. When are we going to get the chance to fetch them? Maybe someone from G Wing could drop them here when they go to the gate to get the papers.'

Peter looked as though he was trying to remember something.

'Andrews – he's the short, fat ginger fella, isn't he?'

'That's him.'

'Yes, I know him. Likes to give it the big'n. He threatened me on the exercise yard the other day, just because I wouldn't drop everything to get his clothes from reception. It was quite bizarre really. Kept on saying you wait 'til you unlock my cell. I mean, why wait when he could have done it then and there.'

The S.O. saw an opportunity to rib his colleague.

'So, it's your fault Wiggins is shitting up and that Andrews cut himself, is it?'

'That's not fair. I've done a lot for that kid lately. They're all right until you say no for the first time. Then they show their true colours. Some are better than others, but I've never met one whose life didn't revolve round them.'

With all his staff present and up-to-date, the Supervising Officer decided it was time to get the day started.

'Okay, let's get going, and Pete, try not to upset anyone.'

C Wing held a variety of prisoners: convicted and unconvicted; first time and prolific offenders; fines dodgers, murders and those who had broken every law along the spectrum.

Peter had worked with prisoners of all ages, from eighteen to ninety plus. The youngsters were the most trying as they had not yet learned to play the system. Adults at least pretended to comply with the regime, keeping their dodgy deals a guarded secret.

Remand prisoners had been accused of committing various crimes, but had not yet had their day in court. This could make them awkward to deal with as they could always claim, and invariably did, they were innocent men and should not be treated as prisoners. Technically this was true, but many of them, although guilty, elected to plead otherwise until the last possible moment in order to reap the benefits of their unconvicted status.

Over the years, having seen the same faces return to jail time after time, Peter had formed the opinion that most of them were probably guilty. He had seen them grow from young boys into men and worried he might still be looking after the same people until his retirement. He supposed they would all be using walking aids by then, him included, especially as he was now expected to continue working until his late sixties.

Fielding was a good example. Peter first had him in his charge when the career thief was a lad of eighteen; a boy of slight build with a wispy fur covering his top lip, his sleeves pulled high to disguise underdeveloped biceps. Over the years, sentence after sentence, Peter had seen the young man fill out, developing a well-toned physique, courtesy of the prison's gym. He was one of those who always claimed his innocence until the last possible moment, but over the years he had come to say it with a wry smile. He had also become well-read – violent, but well-read.

Whenever anyone not connected with the prison asked about Peter's clientele, they were always shocked by the revelation he worked with murders, but killers rarely caused trouble. Peter maintained he would rather work on a landing full of murders than with a bunch of wife batterers and twenty-something gang members.

Peter was pleased to find himself working with Brian – an old school 'screw'. The two men had a lot in common and often met outside work. They were now both family men and openly talked on such subjects as do-it-yourself and touring holidays in Britain, provoking mystified looks from prisoners who overheard them. It was all such a far cry from a life of raves, drugs and crime. If they were not committing it, they were planning it, or bragging about it, greatly overstating their success.

The first order of the day was to unlock a handful of prisoners who had family and friends visiting them; a dozen more, employed in the kitchen, or on the yards party, making fifteen-hundred meals a day and keeping the establishment clean and tidy; and a small number of prisoners on the basic regime, being let out for half an hour to shower and clean their cells. The basic boys had breached a number of minor rules and ignored calls for their behaviour to improve. Being denied an in-cell TV, most were keen to show improvement, hoping to return to the standard regime at the first opportunity. However, because their time out of cell was severely limited, there were always some who failed to return to their cells at the first time of asking. Peter targeted one of them; a youngster by the name of Smith.

'Let's have you away, you're making my landing look untidy.'

The seasoned officer spoke in good humour, but at the same time meant what he said.

At nine o'clock, a handful of characters, with not a moral fibre between them, left the wing to attend the chapel service. It was at their own request, being more a way of seeing their friends located on other wings than seeking forgiveness from the Almighty.

With the chapel party clear, it was time to release the wing for exercise. It being a nice day, more than a hundred prisoners walked in circles around the yard – always, for some inexplicable reason, in an anti-clockwise direction. Throughout, a couple of officers – Peter choosing to be one of them – stood watching and chatting, ready to respond to fights and assaults, and the mad rush to retrieve packages thrown over the wall by young accomplices who often bunked school to make a little extra cash. It was not long before the first alarm sounded, but not on the yard. A call for all available staff to attend the chapel was announced over the radio, representatives from three different wings having decided to settle a score, imported from the outside.

The routine situation and exercise were soon over, making it time for association to begin. The call to come in from the yard brought about a stampede for the pool tables, of which there was one on each landing.

On this occasion, the jostling for position got a little out of hand. Peter, following the main crowd up the stairs to the landing, heard the first signs of trouble.

'I'm gerna up you so 'ard...'

This vivid description was delivered by an unknown voice. However, the reply came from someone Peter could identify instantly.

'You plum!'

It was Wilkins. Peter knew it was Wilkins. He knew because experience had shown that in times of conflict, the pitch of his voice rose steadily higher the angrier he got, and this was just such an occasion. It was unfortunate that at those moments in life when Wilkins needed to sound most ferocious, he actually sounded like a eunuch.

Brian, receiving the bodies onto the landing, was first to intervene. His calm nature persuaded them to reach an amicable agreement, pointing out that one of them wrapping the weighted end of a pool cue round the other's head would not be good for either of them in the long term. A fight at this stage would have meant everyone being banged away behind their doors and a loss of their association. That would have upset everyone, which in turn would have made the rest of the day much more difficult. On the other hand, hearing someone screaming in agony as they were dragged down to the segregation unit would serve as a reminder of what the prisoners could expect if they did not behave themselves. All things considered, Brian's solution was the least dangerous and the prisoners got their play time.

It was noisy. In addition to the general chatter, numerous stereo systems, the pool table, and a game of table tennis, all added to the din.

A group of grown men sat together in one cell, watching children's cartoons and seemed to be really enjoying them. Peter wondered what their wives and girlfriends would say if they knew.

Brian made both officers a cup of tea which they drank while they talked about stud wall partitions and plumbing, and before they knew it, the morning was over.

The prisoners filed downstairs to collect their dinners, giving the two officers the opportunity to exchange a few more thoughts as they waited for their flock to return in dribs and drabs.

'So, why do we do this?' Brian asked thoughtfully.

'I don't know,' Peter replied. 'The job's boring; our money never seems to go up; we work unsociable hours; and it's always a fight to get Christmas off with the family.'

After a moment's consideration, Brian felt able to suggest a more positive aspect of the job.

'On the plus side,' he said, 'when this lot misbehaves, we get to inflict pain on the dross of society with impunity.'

'Impunity - that's a big word for you isn't it?'

'Impressed eh? Actually, I saw it in a magazine the other day and I've been looking for an excuse to use it ever since.'

'Brian, you are sad. Besides, I think you left it ten years too late to use the word impunity. You can't even look at them these days without there being an investigation, especially with all these cameras around.'

Conversation continued while the prisoners ate their lunch, the majority seated at tables on the landing, in the company of friends. In another half an hour, it was time to herd them back to their cells. Even though they had been out all morning, it was customary for inmates to dart about from this door to that, doing last minute deals before being locked away again. It reminded Peter of the numerous occasions when he had lost a bar of soap in the bath. No sooner did he think he had a prisoner, he had slipped through his fingers. The analogy failed in one key respect - a bar of soap did what it did; a prisoner, on the other hand, felt the need to issue a limp defence, usually quoting a phrase taken straight from the book of standard prisoners' excuses - 'I'm just getting some sugar guv,' or some similar remark.

As was always the case, for a few minutes it appeared there was no control at all, but gradually, one by one, each door shut with a heavy metallic clunk.

In truth, the whole process took two or three minutes, but it always seemed much longer.

Peter went to shut Mattam's door.

'All done?' he enquired.

'Yes thanks Guv. What do you think of this, I've done it for my girlfriend?' Mattam held up a piece of paper decorated with a love heart and roses.

'Very good,' Peter said, encouragingly, adding with a smile, 'Enjoy your meal.'

He shut the door and was struck by the similarity between his job and that of an inner city school teacher. They too had their approval sought and were cheeked by the children they taught. Maybe that was why he often treated the younger prisoners as children. During a cell search, he had discovered some Spice – synthetic cannabis; a nasty substance that often caused the user to fit, and one to gouge out his own eyes. On confronting the occupant he had challenged him.

'You've been a naughty boy haven't you?'

The prisoner had looked rather sheepish, but had not commented about the way he was being talked down to.

Peace once again descended upon the wing. Securing the cell doors brought a pleasing order to the landing. Everything was in its place.

As the two officers walked downstairs to sign for their numbers, Peter remarked how strange he sometimes felt their job was, storing men in little boxes, with hardly any regard as to whether or not they had any moral right to do so. Brian agreed their occupation was different than most, but clearly did not suffer any form of moral dilemma.

'As far as I'm concerned,' he said, 'it makes no odds to me. We could be dealing with sacks of potatoes for all I care.'

'I'd rather deal with prisoners,' Peter added, continuing the analogy. 'They're more mobile. Imagine having to drag sacks of spuds around all day.'

'Yes, but at least potatoes wouldn't answer back, or punch you in the face.'

Most of the staff went to dinner, leaving a patrol on each wing. A few went home, it being the end of their shifts. Peter stayed, letting the C Wing lunch patrol go, giving himself time alone with his packed lunch and a crossword.

All too soon it was time to start work again. A few cell searches were the first order of the afternoon. Peter and Brian paired up and spun Williams - a young man who had a cell to himself because the standard risk assessment deemed him too dangerous to share; a bit of a nuisance, but at least he kept his cell neat and tidy. The bed was made, his clothing was folded, and his knife, fork and spoon were lined up on the cupboard top. The officers tried not to create too much mess, while still carrying out a thorough search. The job done, they brought Williams back to his cell.

'Just a few excess towels,' Brian said. 'Other than that, very good.'

Williams did not make a fuss, but did have something to say on the subject.

'You know how it is Guv, you get things just the way you want them and now I've got to start all over again. It's not nice having you lot go through all my things.'

'What are you in here for?' Peter asked out of idle curiosity.

'Burglary,' Williams answered.

'Commercial or domestic?'

'Domestic,' Williams replied openly. 'I did this big house and got caught by the owner. He was all right about it though. Held me until the police arrived. Didn't hurt me or anything.'

'Don't you think there's a lesson to be learnt here?' suggested Peter. 'It's not nice to have others rifle through your possessions is it?'

'No, but you know how it is Guv, you get things just the way you like them and then you lot come and mess it all up.'

It was no good; the young lad just could not make the connection. Brian and Peter smiled at each other and left Williams to get things back just as he liked them.

The remainder of the afternoon was a mad dash to exchange all the prisoners' dirty kit for clean. If going home marked the highlight of an officer's day, then the kit change was the complete antithesis. Despite the dirty work being carried out by the wing cleaners - prisoners employed on a meager salary, but allowed out of their cells more than most - the staff could not avoid the unpleasant aroma that rose from piles of over used laundry. At least the afternoon passed quickly.

The evening meal went almost without a hitch. The diets officer, having been taken ill quite suddenly, Peter stepped up to the plate – or more accurately, up to the entrance to the servery - calling out the corresponding letter that indicated which meal each prisoner had ordered. Davies swore 'on his baby's eyes' he had not chosen the meal assigned to him.

'Can't I have something else?' he pleaded.

'No', Peter replied firmly. 'All the other meals are spoken for.'

'I aint eatin' dis shit.' Davies replied in a deep, nasal tone, throwing his plastic plate down in protest. 'I'm goin' back to my cell an 'ave a pot noodle, innit.'

Peter should have been angry at such an outburst, but could see only the funny side. Yes, it was obviously food produced on a large scale, to a miniscule budget, and as such, could not compare with that served up in a posh restaurant. On the other hand, in his own opinion, it was better than his own experiences of school dinners, and *had* to be preferable to a pot of reconstituted noodles.

The prison roll was checked and once it was confirmed no one had escaped, most of the staff were allowed to make their way out of the main gate.

It was disheartening for Peter to see staff, having finished their shift, being able to go home to their families, while he had to remain for another four hours.

Peter remained on C wing, choosing to forego his half-hour break so the tea patrol could get away early. Brian was also staying, having been detailed an evening on B wing.

'Well, if I don't see you before you go home, I'll see you in the morning. We're both on the 'threes' again.'

'Sweet.'

10

Kim Oxfoot opened the front door of her four-bed semi and stepped out onto the driveway, carrying a mug of hot tea in each hand.

'Andy, take a break for a minute, I've made us a drink,' she said, talking to the pair of legs that protruded out from beneath the family's ailing car.

'Hang on a minute, I'm just doing up a bolt,' Andy said, his reply muffled by the close proximity of his face to vehicle's floor pan.

'I don't like you working under there; it frightens me.'

'Don't fret woman; it's perfectly safe. The car's up on stands and they're good for two tonnes a piece. The whole car only weighs one and a bit.'

Although grateful to his wife for having provided refreshments, Andy was nonetheless irritated by what he considered to be yet another example of her constant and unwarranted fussing. However, less than thirty seconds later, he was forced to eat his own words as the supports for the car spontaneously oxidised, crumbled and sent the full weight of the vehicle crashing down upon his chest.

There was no question of time standing still. So quickly did events unfold that even if a second were stretched to fill a lifetime, this brief moment would be but a day. Nevertheless, it was sufficient time for the car to suffer the same fate as the axle stands, reducing the impact from what one would have expected, to a sensation of having a barrow load of talcum powder dumped across the body. The analogy was good, the reddish dust having much the same effect upon his eyes and lungs.

Instinctively, Andy rolled onto his side, coughing so violently his knees drew up tight to his chest. His greasy fingers began clawing at his face, encouraging the worst of the deposits to fall to the ground. However, the pain did not abate, but instead grew with every passing second. He rolled onto his front, spitting and spluttering, and then onto all fours, his head bowed, his diaphragm working hard, trying desperately to force fine particles of rust from his lungs. His mouth remained open, the stricken man allowing saliva to flow freely, hoping to wash away the dust that coated his tongue. Every so often he blocked his throat, diverting his breath through his nostrils, ejecting copious quantities of discoloured mucus which hung, dripping, from the tip of his nose. All the while, his eyes remained wide open – unnaturally wide - as he fought the desire to blink. Blinking caused an intense, sharp, stabbing pain; incentive enough to keep staring downwards. Not blinking also caused pain; pain that brought with it tears that tried their hardest to moisten the drying surfaces of his eyeballs.

Kim stood motionless; dumbfounded; amazed. Under the circumstances, this was not an unnatural reaction. She had just been witness to the near silent disintegration of the family saloon, the burying of her husband beneath a layer of debris, and his subsequent blood-curdling screams, sufficient to strike fear into the most level headed person.

On hearing the commotion, neighbours began to emerge from their houses. Kim was to be found, still frozen to the spot, with a steaming mug of hot tea in each hand. Tessa Allerton, who lived in the adjoining semi, came rushing over.

'That was my car,' Kim spoke softly; her body rigid; her eyes fixed.

Linda and Dave Cunningham, the residents of the house next-door-but-one to Tessa's, also ran to the scene of the incident. Seeing that Kim was being taken care of, they immediately focused their attention on the apparently forgotten figure of Andy who remained on all fours amid a pile of glass, plastic and cloth, and covered across his back and shoulders by a stiff grey carpet, flakes of green paint, and a coating of fine, reddish dust.

Linda was well qualified to administer first aid, being trained to do so as part of her duties at the factory where she was employed. Day one of the course had taught her to assess the area for potential hazards before rushing in, possibly making herself a casualty – and on her neighbour's drive she discovered a big one.

The patient was not the sort of man to let the petrol gauge fall below a quarter full. Indeed, he had filled it to the second click of the pump only that morning. The disintegration of the tank had therefore spilled upwards of forty-five litres of highly flammable liquid onto the drive, the majority of it forming a shallow river, washing down a gentle slope into the rain gully. Some of it had combined with the rust deposits to form a wet, highly aromatic paste in which Andy knelt. One spark would set it off, engulfing the injured party in a fireball, the consequence of which was too horrifying to imagine.

Ironically, Andy had kept a fire extinguisher in the boot of his car. The bright red aluminium-alloy cylinder had survived the phenomenon, but the valve had not, discharging the vessel's contents impotently, failing to make the scene in any way safer.

Linda's instruction was concise, her tone bearing authority and a sense of immediacy.

'Get back. Right back.'

Her palms repeatedly swept from her shoulders to the full extent of their reach.

Tessa understood immediately, but Kim was incapable, her eyes fixed upon her husband. Tessa's arm wrapped around her neighbour's shoulders, guiding her with force to a safer place. Despite losing half their content, Kim maintained her grip on the mugs until her minder eased them from her grip, placing them on the Cunningham's doorstep. Even then, the Good Samaritan had to lower her neighbour's forearms to her side, Kim being incapable of anything but autonomous function.

Linda and her husband exchanged a look, their eyes wide. Both hesitated, clear in their minds what was at stake – not just Andy's life, but their own. Dave's will was the first to break, his hands sweeping away the vehicle's carpet before falling on the victims shoulders, urging him to overcome his pain and step away from the wreckage. Andy complied, but remained bent forward at the waist. When clear, he dropped back to the ground where he made further effort to eject the dust from his lungs.

Linda was by his side in a moment, her voice switched to silk mode.

'Come on, let's get you inside. We need to wash all that muck out of your eyes.'

'I can't move; it hurts too much,' Andy replied with a quivering voice, fearful the movement of a single muscle might aggravate his condition still further.

Linda spoke calmly.

'I know it must be very painful, but you must try to be brave. Let me take you indoors. I can bathe your eyes in there - they'll feel a lot better. And we need to get you out of these clothes. They're covered in petrol.'

'No! No, it hurts too much to move.'

Realising that by forcing the issue she might be making matters worse, Linda quickly relented, choosing instead to treat her neighbour in situ.

A group of onlookers gathered along the boundaries of the Oxfoot's property. They babbled and pointed, but none came forward with any practical assistance, or advice. In their defence, none of them had ever experienced this type of drama before and as a consequence *had* no advice to offer; practical or otherwise. Those at the front felt far from relaxed about what they were seeing – what they were smelling - and tried to retreat as one would from a raging fire that appeared to be getting closer. However, they were prevented from doing so by the numbers of residents building up behind them, craning their necks to see for themselves what was happening, phones on the end of outstretched arms, ready to capture the scene and share to social media.

Some of the older generation, who had been in the process of retiring for the evening, emerged from their homes wearing dressing gowns and slippers. Conscious of their attire, they remained close to their front doors, but this in no way dampened their desire to know what was going on. For those whose need to know became too great, they padded across the road, their arms wrapping their gowns tightly about them.

Following instructions from his wife, Dave re-entered his house at number twenty, emerging a few minutes later carrying a mixing bowl, half filled with tepid water; also a china cup and a bag of cotton wool balls. On his return, Linda immediately set to work irrigating her patient's eyes and gently wiping the foreign matter from his face. Her task was made more difficult by the violent cough her patient had developed as a result of inhaling at least as much of the dust as had fallen into his eyes.

Dave, unlike the developing crowd, was capable of independent thought and disappeared again in order to fetch a glass of water to soothe his neighbour's throat.

Meanwhile, Tessa had succeeded in persuading Kim to sit down on a chair she had dragged from the hallway of number twenty-two.

'Has anyone called an ambulance?' Linda asked, turning to the crowd.

Her enquiring eyes were met by a bank of phones and a wall blank faces.

'Never mind, I'll run them both to casualty myself,' she said, getting up off the floor.

At that moment, though, her plans developed a major flaw. Her own car, standing on the drive just a few metres away, collapsed suddenly, releasing yet more petrol, and producing a cloud of dust that was immediately picked up and scattered by a strengthening breeze. There were many analogies to be made, such as the separating of wheat from chaff, or the release of spores from a puffball, kicked by an adventurous child, but they were lost to Linda who found herself reacting in much the same way as her neighbour had.

In unison, the crowd startled, their heads and phones turning to watch and record this fresh development. Until then, only Kim and her husband had seen how there came to be a pile of plastics, glass and cloth strewn across their drive; what had happened to cause Andy to cry and splutter like a baby with whooping cough. With the disappearance of Linda's car, everyone was brought up to speed. The response differed with the individual. Some screamed, their hands springing to their face, cupping their nose and mouth, eyes wide with terror. Others stood in silence; heads twisting this way and that as car after car suffered the same fate, on either side of the road, and as far as their eyes could see. Within minutes, only Tessa's vehicle remained untouched, its recently polished bodywork still gleaming in the post-sunset light.

The sudden clearance of every driveway in the avenue, under such extraordinary circumstances, prompted the crowd to withdraw hastily to the middle of the road, among their numbers, Kim, who held a wet flannel to her husband's eyes, and their neighbours who had come to their aid. In the road, there seemed little else to do but scream. But not everyone, or everything, had been witness to the disaster.

Podge, who was a particularly curious specimen of a cat, strolled through the open side gate from the back garden at number twenty-four, and jumped up onto the one remaining, pristine bonnet, oblivious to the events unfolding. He judged his landing to perfection, not wasting energy by rising in the air even a centimetre higher than was necessary. It should have been a textbook landing, putting the greatest gymnast to shame, but it was not. Within a second of his paws touching paintwork, he found himself back on the driveway, the car's bodywork and engine block providing no more resistance than a handful of confetti. Given the circumstances, it was impressive that Podge maintained his balance throughout, landing as he did on all four paws. However, he did not wait for applause, but sped off as though a teenage thug had tied a firework to his tail; not so much through fear as embarrassment.

The screaming stopped. Everyone stood in stunned silence, wives clinging to their husbands' arms, mothers instinctively pulling their children close to them, arms protecting their heads from harm.

Like Podge, Emma had also been in the back garden of number twenty-four. Despite the hour, she had been riding her bicycle, oblivious to the turmoil occurring just a few metres away at the front of her family's house. She too emerged through the side gate, her knees rising and falling like pistons, powering her onto and along the pavement, to the T-shaped cul-de-sac at the end of the avenue. So focussed was she that neither the crowd, nor the vestiges of many deconstructed cars diverted her from her course, or slowed her progress. At the furthest reaches of the hammerhead, she reached a lamppost that stood at the entrance to a pedestrian alleyway – a cut-through to the next road – and stopped. This was as far as her mother would allow her to stray on her bicycle, and only then when one of her parents were out the front to supervise. Only then did she notice the crowd, but nothing else. Her mother, having moved to join them, was calling at the top of her voice, her arm beckoning wildly. Emma was used to this – although not from the middle of the road - and responded obediently by turning the bike round and heading back, a tuneless song passing her lips, her head tilted slightly, her young mind wondering why the neighbours were standing in the road and why they held each other so close. Her thoughts, however, were transient, much of her mind given to the task of steering, the front wheel being easily led by the undulations of each drop kerb.

Her knees knew only two speeds – full ahead and idle. She had been taught to use the brake to come to a stop, and to put her feet to the floor at the very last minute, to provide stability without rubbing away the soles of her shoes. Nearing her house, she did as her parents had instructed, slowing to a crawl, fully in control, her face demonstrating the utmost concentration. It was unexpected, then, that moments later she found herself falling forward, landing on the pavement, flat on her face, with grazed knuckles and knees. She still held tightly the white rubber grips, multi-coloured tassels protruding from their ends. The white plastic shopping basket lay squashed beneath her chest.

Emma remained in the prone position for several seconds before picking herself up off the floor and running towards her mother, crying uncontrollably. Two white rubber tyres, the remains of a saddle, a pair of white rubber pedals, and some flakes of pink paint marked the spot where she had fallen.

Tessa received Emma into her arms and pulled her into the road, but had no opportunity to check her daughter's wounds, or to comfort her.

Not all the houses behaved in the same manner, each falling generally into one of two categories. In the first, the nails securing the batons to the roof trusses failed, allowing the thousands of concrete interlocking tiles they supported to slide away from the properties, crashing to the ground, causing a cacophony of sound, loud enough to overwhelm the senses. The trusses then parted, falling inwards upon themselves, neatly separating the two materials; wood from concrete. Houses and bungalows in the other category behaved quite differently. In those cases, the trusses collapsed first, bringing the entire weight of the roof – tiles, batons, felt and rafters - down inside the properties, smashing through the ceiling joists below.

Not only was it the roofs that suffered. The lampposts that lined the street were also affected. Some turned to dust so rapidly the glass lamp units were momentarily suspended in mid-air, seemingly tethered to the ground by electric cables. Gravity then took hold, pulling the glass bowls downwards to the pavement below, where they exploded on contact with the hard surface, sending a spray of tiny shards in all directions. Other lampposts acted differently, falling like sawn trees, there being no man with a chainsaw and a hard hat to issue fair warning.

With nowhere to run, the crowd dropped to the ground in unison, their eyes tight shut or directed at the road surface. None saw the lamppost that fell upon Ken Rickman's head, shattering bone, spattering his wife and several of his neighbours with the contents of his skull. Then the cause of his death was gone.

Old Mr Sutton, who lived directly opposite the Allerton's, had been as curious as everyone to discover the cause of the initial commotion, but being in his dressing gown, he had remained close to his front door. Ultimately, the widower's decision not to mingle reunited him with his wife sooner than he had imagined, a flying tile causing an instantly fatal wound to his head.

Mr and Mrs Parkinson, a childless couple from number twenty-one, were buried as their neighbour's roof collapsed onto them. More bizarrely, Mr Cuthbert, a retired bachelor, who had the habit of plying Emma with sweets whenever he saw her, was standing on an inspection cover when it simply disappeared beneath him. This resulted in Mr Cuthbert plunging two metres into the uncapped hole. He might have survived were it not for him catching his jaw on the side of the opening as he fell, breaking his neck, leaving his lifeless body damming the sewage gulley at the bottom of the pit.

Tessa and Emma remained with the pack, both sitting on their haunches, daughter shielded beneath mother. From this position, Tessa's ears witnessed destruction, near and far. Terror prolonged the experience, but in reality, the total destruction of the neighbourhood was achieved in no more than ten minutes.

Even once the sounds of the apocalypse had subsided, Tessa and others held their position. What brought Tessa to her senses was the sudden release of her breasts from the confines of her bra, the metal elements having gone the way of sanity. Her hand reached beneath her tee-shirt and removed the now useless article, folding it neatly with the intention of returning it to the shop as faulty. She wondered if she still had the receipt.

The immediate danger having apparently past, amid cries of anguish, Tessa stood up, encouraging her daughter to follow suit, reassuring hands never once breaking contact. They were not the first to stand erect. All around, survivors scanned the environment from fixed positions, wondering at the devastation that met their eyes.

Tessa's lingerie was not the only item of clothing to be affected. Men and women who wore denim jeans clutched their waistbands, the zips and metal buttons having succumbed to whatever had caused this nightmare. Those who relied on belts found themselves in a similar situation. Other women – particularly those with larger chests – held their forearms close to their body, their hands clutching the opposite shoulder. Expressions of shock and indignation indicated failure of their undergarments.

With regard to their general attire, Tessa and her daughter had ridden the storm well. Emma's clothing - Wellington boots, pull-up shorts and a top - were entirely unaffected. Her mother wore elasticated leggings, a smock top and slippers, none of which relied on steel for strength or fastening.

Silence fell. Even those who could not stop themselves crying, did so without making a noise.

'It's the metal. All the metal.'

The words were whispered by a mountain of a man, positioned close by, whose dusted cheeks were striped with the tracks of unstoppable tears.

Testing the theory, another survivor stooped to pick up a length of cable, its end pointing in the direction of Ken Rickman's body and his bloodied widow whose face was buried in her husband's chest, her hands gripping his shoulders, trying to shake him back to life. The cable was flexible but stiff, suggesting the copper core had survived.

'Not all metal,' the second man clarified.

His voice was flat. It carried no sense of relief at discovering the phenomenon had some limits.

He then noticed a sign lying on the floor. The metal posts that had set it a metre above the pavement were gone, but the plaque itself seemed untouched, the name of the avenue picked out in black, embossed, letters on a background of reflective white paint.

He nodded in the direction of his find – a subtle movement of his head.

'Not aluminium either. Looks like it's just the steel then.

The evidence all about them gave weight to his conclusion. Every garage in the neighbourhood lacked an up-and-over door and there were signs the disaster spread much further afield. The skyline had changed as far as the eye could see. The lines of neat rooftops had gone, leaving the neighbourhood looking like a 1960s experiment in open-plan design. There were no vehicles or street furniture to obstruct the view, and the ugly radio mast that had towered over the children's playground had gone. Even the sky itself had changed. Being close to a regional airport, it was normally criss-crossed with vapour trails, horizon to horizon. The trails were still visible in the fading light, but it was telling that they had been snipped short, each ending in a scattered puff of white.

Tessa remained glued to the spot, pinning Emma to her thighs.

'What the hell is going on?'

She kept the question as a thought, trying desperately to insulate her daughter from the fear they both shared. Tessa's legs weakened, forcing her to the ground, pulling Emma with her. She tried not to cry, but tears came anyway.

Still hugging her daughter tightly, she began rocking them both gently back and forth.

'Why isn't your daddy here?'

People began wandering around, seemingly with no purpose in mind. It was a scene from the living dead. One man, badly cut on his forearm, began picking small pieces of litter from his flowerbeds. Another sat on the kerb, his head buried in his hands, blood oozing through his fingers. A woman's legs jutted out from beneath a pile of broken tiles. A small girl stood in the middle of the road calling for her parents, sobbing, her eyes tightly shut. They were close by, but preoccupied with discovering the fate of an immediate neighbour.

Some survivors were brought to their senses by the thought that members of their families were now trapped inside their houses. They began to dig feverishly with their hands, every so often stopping to call for assistance. In turn, these cries for help brought others back to reality, and soon parties up and down the avenue were working together to free their friends and neighbours.

Every so often, the sound of wailing could be heard as another victim was dragged from the wreckage of a fallen building.

The light was beginning to fade, accelerated by the formation of low level cloud cover, and so far there had been no sign the rescue services were on their way.

None of this was of interest to Tessa who continued to hold Emma close to her as they sat in the middle of the road, treating it as a place of safety. Thoughts were not registering in her mind. It was as though her eyes were following the words in a book, but were not attempting to make sense of them. Then, as quickly as her mind had switched off, it suddenly came back to life. Instinct for self-preservation, and for that of her daughter, took over. She was a survivor, not a victim.

'Don't worry darling. I'm sure Daddy will be home from work as soon as he can. He'll make everything all right, you'll see.'

Emma was no longer crying, but in truth, this was because her throat hurt too much to continue.

11

For the prisoners, the long night began a little before five o'clock in the afternoon - when most of the staff went home – with the prospect of the doors remaining locked and bolted until eight the following morning. The cells, whether occupied by one inmate or two, measured the same - approximately four metres by three. Each was fitted with bunk beds, bolted to the wall. In recent years, the old metal beds of tubular steel and woven slats had been torn out and sold for scrap in favour of MDF replacements. The new furniture had arrived in boxes, flat-packed, and easily returned to such a condition; either by prisoners choosing to break things in preference to breaking people, or by those wanting to render their room fit for single occupancy use only.

Ricky Lewis, an arsonist, had a cell of his own, but not by any act of prison vandalism. It being in the character of an arsonist to set fire to properties, paying scant regard to who might be trapped within, the authorities did not trust them to share with anyone.

Ricky had chosen to sleep on the bottom bunk, reserving the top as a platform from which he could shout to his friends through the small, barred window, set high in the back wall. On this occasion, though, he preferred to watch a film on Freeview, via his in-cell TV, rented to him by the Governor for the sum of £1 per week. As relaxed as he felt at the prospect of settling down to a two-hour children's comedy, he could not help but think how much more pleasurable it would have been had he had a hot, sweet cup of coffee in one hand, and a roll-up in the other. Prisoners were all supposed to have a kettle, but Ricky did not, having sold it for Spice the previous week. Knowing this, the staff had refused to replace it – an unofficial punishment that would continue until a day-tripping officer, unaware of the circumstances, did his job and provided a new one. Since making the unwise trade, Ricky had tried alternative sources of hot water. Drawing it from the hot tap at his sink had proven less than successful as it tasted funny and he was sure it had given him diarrhoea. He then tried getting his neighbour to boil some water just before they were banged up for the evening, keeping it warm in a spare cup, wrapped in the many folds of a towel, using it as a make-shift tea cosy. This approach was not terribly effective either, and at best kept the drink lukewarm. Thankfully, an old lag, who remembered the age before in-cell kettles, had provided a solution.

Removing the power lead from the back of his radio, Ricky inserted two small screws - smuggled from the workshops - into the end. He then dropped the two-pronged lead into a cup of fresh water and flicked the wall switch. With this, the television screen died in an instant, prompting angry yells to spew forth from the seven other cells that shared a common electrical circuit.

Ricky knew the noise would be investigated. He also knew the consequences for him the next day if he were found to be the cause of more than a dozen fellow criminals being unable to watch their TVs, boil water for their hot drinks and, for some, use their games console. Having thrown the incriminating screws from the window, Ricky quickly returned the slightly charred end of the power lead to the back of his radio before joining his peers in calling through the cracks between door and frame, kicking the metal surface violently, causing others to follow suit, despite them not knowing why.

Peter climbed the stairs wearily, checked that everyone was still alive and gave a lecture to all concerned that someone had obviously been tampering with the electricity, that he was not an electrician, that they would have to wait until the morning for it to be restored, and that they should be grateful for having an emergency light to piss by.

Locked behind a windowed door outside Ricky's cell, a tripped switch indicated who was to blame. Peter suspected the arsonist would be advised by his peers not to do it again.

Over time, the kicking and banging subsided, after which a number of voices could be heard at the cell windows, informing whoever was responsible of the exact nature of the advice to be given as soon as the doors were opened.

Ricky returned to his bunk, still without a hot drink. Far from making his evening that little bit more comfortable, it had clearly taken a turn for the worse – no film, no TV and no radio to keep him company into the early hours. And because of that dirty screw – Allerton - he had a whole lot of hurt to look forward to in the morning. Everyone knew a plastic prison knife, slipped behind the locked fuse box door, would restore the supply, but he had chosen deliberately not to. At that moment, Ricky determined if he was to receive a good pasting, so would Allerton.

Putting that thought aside, Ricky considered his options. There were ways he might be moved from the wing to avoid facing the music, or at least give him breathing space. The same technique, taken to the next level, would ensure he never had to face the music at all – no retribution administered in the showers, no time behind bars, no shitty life on the streets. Ricky had contemplated doing something to himself on a number of occasions, but had never mustered the courage to draw a blade over his wrist – or up the length of his forearm, as some of the less caring staff advised, if he was serious.

The worst thing about prison was the boredom. Ricky had never learned to read or write so, without entertainment, it looked as though it was going to be a very long night. He could talk to his neighbours at the window, but that entailed a lot of shouting which made him go hoarse after a while. Besides, there was not a great deal to talk about. Conversations usually centred on the inmates' criminal exploits and most of what was said was wildly exaggerated, or simply untrue – claims that made their years in captivity sound like a worthwhile trade.

Having exhausted all other avenues, Ricky chose to fall back on the small quantity of mixed weed and tobacco he had obtained from Roy - in number thirteen - earlier that afternoon. Bearing in mind the possession of tobacco in one of Her Majesty's prisons had become a criminal offence – not to mention the cannabis – it was far more expensive than would be the case 'on the out'. He paid for it with the promise of some vape juice and other commodities, purchased from the canteen – the prison's virtual corner shop – delivered on Friday, after lunch. Unfortunately, Ricky had already promised the very same items to Steve, in a deal he had struck the day before. It had to be said, neither Roy nor Steve were reasonable men, but Ricky was a young man who lived for the moment and decided he would not worry about the consequences until he was forced to.

Apart from drug abuse, Ricky was not entirely without things to do. The entire landing was one big lending library for pornographic magazines. Like everyone else, he had his own selection and thought about helping himself get off to sleep a bit later. Apparently, picking a hole through the vinyl covering into the foam mattress, then lubricating it with prison margarine, made a good substitute for a real woman; a theory Ricky intended putting to the test, having put aside an individual portion of the spread for the purpose. After all, he had not even seen his girlfriend in a fortnight, let alone slept with her.

Planning ahead, Ricky placed a stiffened and wrinkled issue of Reader's Wives upon an upturned cardboard box; a fine substitute for a bedside cabinet. On top of this he placed the small carton of margarine, a blade - freed from a disposable razor, with which to slit the vinyl - and a toilet roll.

Having gathered together the makings of the evening's finale, the lone prisoner returned his attention to the green substance, wrapped in a small piece of cling film, nestled at the bottom of his jeans' pocket. Since the smoking ban's introduction, the prison's population had been forced to find new ways of ingesting drugs. It had not taken long for one prisoner to adapt his vape pen and soon after the rest had followed, word of mouth passing faster than the speed of light through the prison's stale atmosphere. Unfortunately for Ricky, the battery in his was flat and he had no way of recharging it until power was restored to the cell in the morning, forcing him to go 'old school.'

In the absence of cigarette papers, Ricky used a page of the Bible – the best use of the thin pages an illiterate man could make. One thing he had retained, post-ban, was a lighter, and was glad he had. Under normal circumstances he would have pulled the switch wires from his kettle and rubbed the live ends together, creating a spark, but with no kettle and no power this was not an option either. In the circumstances he found himself in, the risk of being caught with a lighter and adjudicated upon had been worth it.

Having rolled a spliff from half a page of Genesis, he settled down on his bunk, staring out at the brick vaulted ceiling, knowing that soon things would not seem so bad. A short while later the focus of his slightly glazed eyes was drawn to the door. Regardless of the other fixtures and fittings, it was the main feature of the cell. Most noticeably, there was no handle on the inside. Other than that, it was plain, green and had a rectangular observation window, centred towards the top, covered on the outside by means of a hinged metal flap. The door was adorned with a picture of a naked woman in a compromising position; one that Ricky had stuck up using toothpaste. Glue, drawing pins and sticky tape were not allowed.

There was not a lot else in his room: a steel table-and-chairs unit bolted to the floor, with names scratched into the paintwork, supporting the aforementioned TV; a stainless steel sink-and-toilet unit which smelled awful, partially hidden from view by a metre-square 'modesty screen'; and a wooden cupboard with the door hanging off, no shelves and the back missing. There were also personal possessions: a set of plastics (plate, bowl, cup and cutlery) all of which needed washing up; a tea making kit; prison issue towels, clothing and toiletries; some old car magazines his grandma had ordered for him; and some letters from his girlfriend that he was unable to read without help. There was not a lot else. Not much of an inventory.

With the cares of the world fading away in a drug-induced stupor, Ricky turned his attention back to the door. It looked different. It had been glossy, green and smooth. Now it was matt and the paint had formed fine bubbles – as though subject to damp, humid conditions. So strange was the development, Ricky commented aloud – albeit it nasal tones; unnaturally slow and low; with a peculiar rhythm.

'This must be good stuff.'

Ricky studied the half-consumed spliff before rising unsteadily to his feet, and shuffled the short distance to the door. His fingers rubbed at the painted surface which, to his surprise, flaked off, baring large areas of exposed metal. Patches of the welded sheet steel then fell away, revealing a layer of mineral wool insulation beneath, the decomposing metal pieces shattering as they hit the floor. Pressing his hand forward, Ricky's fingers penetrated the door, closing round the solid metal fire hose inundation plug, plucking it from its home as an Aztec priest might pull the still beating heart from the chest of his sacrifice. The cylindrical lump of steel was the perfect weight for a cosh; useful for warding off debt collectors. Ricky dropped it into a sock, quickly tied several knots to reduce the elasticity of the material, and began swinging it about his head, testing its effectiveness. The first blow made a satisfying thud against his mattress; the second was mis-aimed and shattered the TV; the third impacted with the wall, but rather than mimic the sound of sledge hammer against brick, it produced a muffled sound, reminiscent of a bag of flour falling to the kitchen floor. Confused, Ricky held the limp sock up before him. Dust escaped through newly-formed holes, trickling like the sands of an hour glass, but less pure. The sock and its degraded contents dropped from Ricky's fingers.

Whether this was the weirdest trip ever, or the weirdest event ever, Ricky thought nothing of the consequences – he never did. All he cared for was that he had craved entertainment and that is what had been provided; in spades.

Being too good to keep to himself, the lone prisoner clambered onto the top bunk, positioning his face against the window bars, gripping them tightly to steady his position. Without warning, the bar, onto which his right hand clung, sheared off flush with the brick and stone aperture into which its ends had been embedded for generations. For a prolonged moment, Ricky stared

106

in amazement at the freed length of metal that lay across his palm, before instinct caused him to drop it as one would a hot potato. It held its shape until it hit the floor, but then exploded in a puff of dust, having no more solidity than the contents of an upturned pot of powder paint.

There was no time to ponder what had happened, for at that instant, the bar, gripped between the fingers of his left hand, lost its integrity, transforming into a quantity of orange dust. Gravity did the rest. Ricky, his arm no longer under tension, fell back on the upper bunk, landing face down on the hard wooden mattress base. Despite the effects of cannabis on his body, he still experienced a burst of pain. However, this was nothing compared to that caused by the total collapse of the bed, each of the bolts degrading with the speed of a burning fuse. The mattresses, sandwiched between two boards, acted as a shock absorber, helping to lessen the blow. Nevertheless, as the prisoner's downward motion was arrested by the cell floor for the second time, his nose was driven against the hard surface, flattening it. When Ricky was able to stand, blood trickled across his lips, falling from his chin to stain his light blue prison-issue tee-shirt. Fighting the pain in the only way he knew, he kicked out at the sink unit, only for his foot to pass without resistance through the metal sides, sending up clouds of dust. Satisfaction trumped fear; illicit drugs and pain banished rational thought; his body, not his mind, was in control, autonomously demanding further retribution for its suffering. Like a twister, destroying everything in its path, Ricky kicked and thumped the fitted furniture, thrilled to see it disappearing under his blows.

The sink taps, rapidly disintegrating, parted from the copper pipes beneath, the water pressure projecting them upwards, like small comets, their tails of rust. The spillage of water mixed with the dust upon the floor, forming a sludge, but the jets soon became impotent, suggesting to those who might consider it, that further back along the supply, copper must have joined with something ferrous; a tap, or a component of a pump.

Then the emergency light failed, strengthening the gloom within the cell, but soon after, a new emergency source of light appeared as the remains of the cell door fell inwards, allowing natural light to flood in from the 'Threes' landing, in turn supplied via great skylights in the roof. Although the light of the day was dwindling, a great deal more of it found its way to the interior of the wing than through the barely adequate cell windows.

Ricky could not help but walk towards the light, there to find other prisoners venturing onto the landings too, covered from head to foot in dust and flakes of paint, looking at each other in utter disbelief, spluttering in an attempt to clear their mouths and throats. When it dawned on them they were free, many forgot their breathing difficulties, cheering excitedly, filling the wing with a deafening cacophony of sound.

***

Down on the 'Ones', Peter Allerton had been sitting reading a magazine while drinking yet another cup of tea. In that respect he was no better than the inmates he locked up as he had only made himself a hot drink to pass the time. Brian had already gone off duty. He had wandered over from B wing for someone to talk to, but soon left in response to an announcement over the radio that his relief was in. Peter had looked at his friend whose face was a picture of smug satisfaction, and then to his own wristwatch.

'Jesus, he must have shit the bed.'

'You win some, you lose some,' Brian responded, pivoting towards the gated exit.

Peter's last words to Brian were said to his back.

'Lucky bastard.'

A few minutes after Brian's departure from C Wing, Peter witnessed the night man, Operational Support Grade Malcolm Ragg, being escorted across the Centre and onto B wing.

Aware that Malcolm would be busy counting prisoners and getting his paperwork in order, Peter knew he would be too busy to chat, so instead sat down to read an article entitled 'The English holiday maker in Spain'.

Twenty minutes later, Peter's attention was torn from what he was doing by a sudden rise in the ambient noise, usually reserved for the arrival of a New Year, or perhaps the England football team taking the lead in a World Cup match. On these occasions, the prisoners generally became more excited, banging and kicking their doors when a goal was scored, or in response to a knockout blow being delivered by a favoured heavy weight boxer. Sometimes it even marked a landmark moment in one of the nightly soap operas that dumbed down the TV schedule.

As his mind considered what might have triggered the commotion, his thought processes were rudely interrupted by his chair suddenly giving way, leaving him sprawled on the floor, nursing bruised buttocks. His immediate reaction was to be thankful no one had seen it, but his response changed in an instant on realising it had not merely been a leg collapsing under his weight, but the whole metal frame inexplicably turning to dust. The revelation caused him to jump up.

'What the f...?'

Peter rushed from the office onto the landing. Seeing prisoners emerging noisily from their cells, he had only two thoughts on his mind: to get off the wing, placing a door and a gate between him and danger; and then raise the alarm, very much in that order. In keeping with his hastily devised plan, the officer pulled his keys from his pocket. However, this served only to panic him further as the entire bunch – the tools of his trade - disintegrated in his hand. Peter's thumb instinctively felt for the transmit button, but the device let him down, the plastic components of his radio separating and falling in pieces to the floor. The alarm bell proved useless too, his finger penetrating the steel button, wiping the small green box from the wall. Even his whistle had perished.

Blind panic took hold, causing him to charge the heavy iron-barred gate at the entrance to the wing, all the while trying to raise the volume of his cries for help above the general din – one man's voice against those of one-hundred-and-forty-eight excited criminals, each and every one of them having something to shout about.

To his utter amazement, the gate offered no resistance to his passage. Passing through a curtain of falling powder, Peter stumbled out onto on the Centre, the residue sitting in his hair, on his shoulders and on the prominent features of his face – his ears, nose and cheeks. There he discovered he was not alone. Malcolm, the night man, stood several metres away, a changed man. The whites of his eyes were in contrast to the coating of dust surrounding them. Although visibly terrified, he was not lost for words.

'I don't know about you, but I'm getting the fuck outta here!'

Peter did not stop to discuss the matter and accelerated from the spot to run faster than he knew he was capable of. In the time it took both colleagues to clear the Centre, they were joined by the two staff from A and D wings. In all their minds, they ran from the phenomenon, but equally they ran from the hordes of prisoners, some of whom might be seeking revenge. Thankfully, none of the inmates had yet realised every form of control placed upon them had been removed by a force greater than the authority responsible for their incarceration, and remained on the landings busily shouting to each other in jubilant celebration.

So ingrained in them was it that they could beat an individual but not the system, most underestimated the hand dealt to them. Had they been brave enough to venture off the wings, more of them might have survived.

Peter and his colleagues emerged into the fresh air of the inner forecourt, clutching their trousers to their waists to prevent them falling about their ankles. Zips, clips and belt buckles had vanished. So too had their defensive metal batons.

Back on the wings, the railings lining the edges of the landings broke off at their bases. Those who had been leaning against them toppled forwards and fell, hitting the anti-suicide catch nets, sprung between the landings below. The wide steel mesh failed in its job, breaking free and disappearing before it had done anything to slow the fall of inmates, some of whom still clutched the hand rails. Those who had been on the 'Threes' fell ten metres, suffering terrible injuries as they landed on the 'Ones'. Some from the uppermost landing fared better than those who had been on the two lower levels. Those on the 'Twos' also fell, only to have their peers from the 'Threes' floor fall upon them. Those living on the 'Ones' had only their own height to fall, but suffered greatly from the impact of bodies landing on top of them. And it was not only people who fell upon each other, and not only those who had been leaning against the railings. The landings had been constructed of plywood and linoleum, supported on cast iron girders of the Victorian age. Without rules to abide by, some of the girders became harmless clouds of dust before impact, while others fell upon exposed, unprotected skulls, leaving their residue within deep gashes and fractures. In its death throes, the steel staircases that zig-zagged upwards, feeding all three landings, toppled and fell upon its victims, before disappearing with a whoosh. The roof then fell upon the survivors – more sheet materials, heavy lengths of timber, panes of glass and hundreds of slate tiles.

Only those who remained in their cells escaped serious injury and death.

Steve Trump had been on duty in the communications room since lunchtime - a mind-numbingly boring way to spend a Sunday afternoon. It was a post requiring only one officer at the weekend, leaving him with no one to talk to for hours on end - a strange thing to say of a member of staff in charge of the prison-wide radio network, but the limited weekend regime generated far less traffic than a weekday, when the task required an assistant to share the load. At the weekends, his shift could become so boring, he sometimes secretly hoped for an alarm to sound, just to relieve the monotony.

Being alone made it difficult to answer the call of nature, so it was inadvisable for him to pass the time by making endless hot drinks, unless he was then willing to run the network from a handset, held to his mouth as he aimed at the bowl. In such circumstances, the acoustics were a dead giveaway whenever he was forced to transmit. To reduce the likelihood of this scenario, Steve kept busy in other ways. He relied on a different kind of radio to keep him company, and he ate a lot, avoiding chewy food that might catch him out if he were suddenly required to speak clearly. He was also experienced enough to buy a Sunday newspaper on his way to work, the content of which could be pawed over for many hours, saving the supplements for emergency bouts of boredom, the articles contained within being only slightly more interesting than staring at a blank wall. And of course, there were the puzzle pages – quite extensive and varied, designed for the leisurely weekend reader who had no children.

A colleague had been detailed to relieve him for tea, once the prison population had all received their evening meal. Steve had seized the opportunity to use the toilet, but returned immediately afterwards so the other officer could go home, knowing the favour would be reciprocated at a future date.

A couple of hours passed with just enough telephone calls and radio messages to keep him comfortably occupied. The flat spots were spent playing with the cameras, but with all the prisoners safely locked behind their doors, there was not a lot to see. Steve had spent the last ten minutes panning left, right, up and down, zooming, focusing and even operating the wipers. The sum total of this activity was Officer Trump witnessing a pigeon's last moments on Earth, before being swooped upon by a bird of prey, pinning his victim to the floor of the inner forecourt, then plucking and spitting every one of dead bird's feathers all about. By the time the meal was sufficiently prepared, it looked as though several naughty children had held a pillow fight within the prison walls.

Steve turned his attention back to an unfinished two-speed crossword that lay on the desk beneath his elbows.

5 down: Condemns for a time this old book (8) D blank O blank S blank A blank.

Still the answer did not make itself apparent.

Being only an ambient noise, Steve had forgotten the stereo radio was even on, only being reminded when the transmitted voice of a sports commentator suddenly went dead.

The sudden quiet caused the lone officer to sit up and swing his chair round to face the cabinet behind him, on which the radio sat. His face wore a puzzled expression, deeper than that caused by the cryptic clue he had yet to solve. Before he could investigate the problem, though, his entire body jumped in response to a crashing sound coming from behind, caused by one of a bank of two dozen CCTV monitors falling from the wall to smash on the floor. In response, the officer's hand pushed against the cabinet, intending to redirect the chair to the front of the room. The chair obeyed, starting on its journey, only to collapse part way through the maneuver, casting Steve to the floor. From there he was further shocked to see the remaining monitors displaying evidence of Armageddon unfolding across the prison grounds: cell bars falling from their windows; internal mesh fencing seemingly breached by gusts of wind; roofs collapsing; pool cars shedding their bodywork; the residue of razor wire raining down; colleagues running from the buildings, clutching their waistbands.

A few seconds later, the remaining monitors fell from their mountings, followed shortly afterwards by the total collapse of the communications consul, bringing everything to the floor, including the folder of contingency plans which covered most eventualities, but not this.

Steve was unfortunate. The communications room was located upstairs in the gate lodge, a modern building which relied upon a substantial amount of steel for its structural integrity.

Fred Baker, one of Steve's closest friends, was perhaps even less fortunate, being downstairs at the time the phenomenon revealed itself. Fred was also bored, having nothing to do but control the main gates; vehicle and pedestrian. Like Steve, he had been passing the time as best he could, grateful for the occasional member of staff entering and leaving the establishment, but there were few on a Sunday evening once the main shift had departed.

His first introduction to the madness was through an expensive pen, given to him by his wife as a birthday present, just days before. Interested in calligraphy, he had identified an evening in the gate as a good opportunity to try his hand. The first flourishes were even and bold. He then took to writing out a nursery rhyme, chosen for no other reason than it came to mind when he wanted to test his ability beyond simply making patterns. The results were pleasing, but all went wrong with the addition of a simple full stop, the pressure of which caused the nib to crumble, providing a similar sensation to that of stubbing out a cigarette. Then the gates, for which he was the sole protector, fell from their openings. A pile of wood veneer and Perspex was all that remained of the vehicle gates; a slab of wood and several panes of laminated glass were all that survived of the pedestrian airlock.

Neither Steve nor Fred had time to panic.

The collapse of the gate lodge buried the two friends while creating a sizable breech in the perimeter wall, the pile of rubble that lay in the gulf being the only obstacle to freedom. Scrambling over it, the surviving skeleton staff made their escape.

Outside the walls, the officers came quickly to a halt, having nowhere to run. All about them the buildings that surrounded the jail were collapsing; and the vehicles in the staff car park were disappearing before their very eyes. Street furniture was vanishing too.

What the officers did not see were any signs of life, other than their own.

The prison being located in a less sought after part of town, the surrounding area was not so heavily populated. Even the council estates were several miles away. Most of the buildings, therefore, were shops and businesses, meaning few people had any reason to be there on a Sunday evening, unless they were passing through, going from somewhere to somewhere else. Nevertheless, it was beyond strange that no cars sped by and no lights illuminated any of the windows, near or far.

The small group stood alone, panting for breath. The air was filled with the sound of falling debris; some distant, some nearby. Officer Cluney was squinting. His spectacles had fallen apart, the plastic lenses having bounced away across the inner forecourt. He had not thought to stop to look for them and if he had it would have proven difficult, given his less than twenty-twenty vision. Living in a fuzzy world was unpleasant, but any thought he had that he would soon be reunited with his spare pair of spectacles was put into doubt by the sights he *could* see.

The first words spoken came from Dave Fielding's mouth.

'What the fuck's going on?' he asked, rhetorically, summing up the situation perfectly.

12

Tessa stood up slowly, coaxing her daughter to do the same. Together, they walked the few metres towards the entrance of what had been their home.

'It's going to be dark soon. I can't see the emergency services being able to get to everyone tonight. We must make up a bed somewhere and assume they won't be with us until tomorrow morning.'

Tessa was thinking more rationally.

She paused at the threshold, taking a moment to absorb the evidence of her demolished existence. The door was of a composite material and remained in one piece, although the locking mechanism and hinges were missing – so too the letter box and knocker. The uPVC doorframe survived, held in place by a bead of mastic that sealed it to the walls. It might have been possible to at least block the hole with the door, had it not been partially buried beneath a jumble of broken furniture, blockwork, wood, plasterboard and shattered tiles.

In the case of the Allerton's property, the roof had collapsed mainly inwards, the debris coming to land on the ceiling upstairs, spilling excess tiles over the sides.

The staircase had reverted to its component pieces – stringers, risers, treads, ballusters and the handrail - denying access to the upper parts of the building.

The spare bedroom had been situated directly above the hall, abutting the stairwell. There being no ground floor wall to support the stair-side first floor wall, a steel beam had been inserted during construction to support the bedroom floor. This disappeared at the very same moment Tessa and Emma were cowering in the road, listening to their roof and everything about them collapsing.

For such a house proud mother, the images that met Tessa's eyes were particularly upsetting. The effort of maintaining microscopically clean surfaces; of buying just the right scatter cushions to complement the theme; of purchasing expensive candles to fill the air with aromas designed to delight the senses; all of it had been for nothing. It was enough to make a woman cry and Tessa would have done just that had she not vowed to remain positive, if only for the sake of her daughter. On that note, she told herself, in time, the insurance would replace everything and when the cheque arrived she could build a new home for her family and it would be even better than before. Although it could wait until morning, Tessa knew her husband kept all their financial documents upstairs, including the house and contents insurance. She hoped Peter would be able to lay his hands on them, wondering what they would do if the documents were lost. Changing the insurance provider annually, she was not sure she even remembered which company they would need to contact.

Although the collapse at first appeared to have rendered entry to the property impossible beyond the width of the door mat, in fact the fallen floorboards had formed a lean-to structure against the downstairs toilet and cupboard. The void this created was dark, small and probably unsafe. Nevertheless, Tessa felt she needed to step inside; crawl if necessary.

'Stay here while I fetch some blankets. I won't be a moment.'

Tessa delivered her instruction, eye to eye, squatting on the doorstep, her hands cupping Emma's cheeks. Despite her efforts to placate her daughter, Emma was having none of it.

'No! I don't want you to go.'

Emma's expression made it clear there would be no negotiation, leaving Tessa three options: to temporarily abandon her daughter, exposing her to further trauma; to shelve her plan for entering the property; or succumb to her daughter's plea, risking her safety by keeping her in tow. Influencing her decision, the warmth of the day had already begun to ebb and promised to get even cooler during the course of the night. They needed blankets or additional clothing to avoid the worst of it. Secondly, the pile wood and rubble seemed stable, making no noise that might indicate further settling. To be sure, Tessa kicked at the structure which hardly shifted under the weight of the mixture of materials sitting upon it.

'All right, you can come too, but stay close and if I tell you to do something, you must do it straight away. No argument, right?'

Emma nodded, glad her mother had changed her mind, but upset by the way she was being spoken to; as though she was being told off for something she had not done.

The light indoors was poor and the dust that hung in the air reduced visibility still further. If there was any luck to be considered, it was that the event could have occurred during the winter, when the air would have been colder; the sky much darker, but it was of little comfort that they did not have to contend with snow.

Leading the way, Tessa crawled into the downstairs toilet, in which she could stand, the plasterboard ceiling having pivoted down to one side. The floor was awash with water, much of it dumped from the pressed-steel radiator as it disintegrated, but also from the plastic tank in the roof which had fallen from the structure that had held it off the ceiling joists. Thankfully, though, the quantity of water was finite, something having affected the mains supply to the house.

A toilet roll sat in the puddle, ruined, the chromed holder and the towel rail having vanished. Thankfully, she found a spare roll on the window sill and took it. The light switch plate had sprung from the wall, the steel screws that had held it firm having dissolved, while the copper wires within prevented it from falling to the floor. In such a condition it looked dangerous, especially with water dripping from overhead. Tessa was almost certain there could be no power, having already witnessed the disappearance of the electricity pylons, but still instinct caused her to keep her fingers well clear.

'Come on. There's nothing for us in here.'

Leading the way, Tessa got on all fours and crawled beneath the lean-to structure. She noticed immediately that what she could see of the new, very expensive fitted carpet had receded from the walls, the gripper having lost its nails, the hessian backing having lost its stretch.

The doors to the hall cupboard were held partially in place by the fallen floor, denying access to coats and shoes, but a gap at the bottom at least provided the means to recover a dozen plastic carrier bags, into which Tessa placed the toilet roll.

A metre further on brought mother and daughter into the living room, totally unrecognisable as the comfortable lounge Tessa had walked from less than an hour before. In places the plasterboard ceiling had pivoted downwards and stood leaning again the wall. In others it had fallen across what remained of the furniture. Although this hampered progress, at least the space was sufficiently intact as to allow them to stand. The joists to which the dozen sheets of plasterboard had been screwed remained stubbornly in place, fixed with mortar, not nails. On top of the joists, and running perpendicular to them, sat the floorboards of Emma's bedroom, and on top of these lay her underlay and carpet – layers that had prevented Emma's belongings and the remains of the roof from plummeting to the ground floor.

As noticeable as the downed ceiling, the far wall was missing in its entirety, having recently been fitted as a series of bi-fold doors, replacing an old fashioned window and side door combination. The Allertons had made the purchase following a prolonged pitch during which the salesman had promised they would be able to bring the garden into the lounge on summer evenings. Although Tessa and her husband had regretted paying too much, they did agree it was the best alteration they had ever made to the house, making it all the more upsetting the individual units had ended their life prematurely, laying shattered on the patio outside. In hindsight, the opening offered a much safer passage into the living room than had the front door and hallway.

Turning her attention to the matter in hand, Tessa quickly established that heaving sheets of plasterboard out of the way would need two pairs of adult arms. Her solution was instead to stamp down upon them, fracturing the sheeting easily, the shattered pieces, held together loosely by an outer layer of paper, moulding themselves roughly to the contours of whatever lay beneath. It was then easy for Tessa to discard the pieces into the garden, through the full-width opening, throwing them like Frisbees. Emma helped as best she could, picking up pieces as small as her hand, and throwing them, only for them to fall short of the threshold.

'Oh no,' Tessa said, sadly.

'What's the matter Mummy?'

'Oh, nothing really. Just some old ornament got broken.'

Tessa made light of it, but internally she felt a punch to her stomach. Her grandmother, with whom she had been very close, had been somewhat of an artist and had bequeathed in her will her one surviving sculpture she had fashioned from clay in her late teens. Unfired, it had survived the post-war era, the swinging sixties, a new millennium, and many years since, cherished and cared for by its creator and then by its custodian. Despite it not being metal, it had become a memory all the same, shattered into a dozen pieces by a fall, caused by the collapse of the cabinet in which it had rested. It was an example of those personal items the insurance company would not be able to replace.

With Emma clutching two cushions close to her chest - the only useful finds in the room - mother and daughter moved through to the kitchen, the ceiling of which had also collapsed. Here the damage was far greater. It was immediately evident the wall-mounted cupboards had fallen, but what remained of them, and their contents, would not be known until the plasterboard had been cleared away. Given the lateness of the hour, Tessa decided that would remain a task for the morning.

In the meantime, she made do with treading down the debris in order to reach the last unexplored room on the ground floor - the dining room. Here she hoped to find the basket full of ironing she had intended doing that evening, once Emma was in bed. If she could locate that, they would at least have warm clothing to see them through the night.

Standing at the threshold between kitchen and dining room, Tessa bent down, grabbed a piece of fallen ceiling and heaved it out of her way. Her effort was immediately rewarded as she revealed the red plastic basket beneath, piled high with material of all descriptions.

'Yes!'

Tessa produced a fist pump.

'There are some bath sheets among this lot; they'll do for blankets. Right, we'd best find somewhere to sleep. There doesn't seem anywhere in here. Anyway, I don't trust this building one bit.'

The missing living room wall offered the quickest and safest route to the garden. There, Tessa felt suddenly exposed, every wooden fence panel having suffered deconstruction. To one side she could see along the backs of a dozen houses. To the other, there lay a public path and road beyond. Only the view beyond the bottom of the garden was restricted, the Allerton's detached garage having been built across its width.

Emma was more concerned with the fate of her slide and swing-set, a few plastic components being all that remained.

'Don't worry, darling. We'll get you another one.'

In truth, Tessa was prepared to say whatever her daughter wanted to hear, if it kept her quiet until her daddy returned home from work. Until he did, Tessa felt she should make plans based on the assumption Peter was either going to arrive too late to help with the sleeping arrangements, or worse, she would not see him until the morning. The thought of spending the night in strange surroundings, without her husband, and in such unprecedented circumstances, was not a pleasant one, but it was something she knew she must accept.

The notion of Tessa seeking out her immediate neighbours was quickly dismissed. The Oxfoots and Allertons had been good to each other. Good in the sense they kept out of each other's way and did nothing to annoy one another. Other than that, they rarely spoke, even to pass the time of day. There was nothing sinister in their feelings - one family for the other - it was simply that they shared nothing in common – not even children. In fact, their only common ground had been established that very evening, with the sudden collapse or disappearance of their combined material wealth.

Going further afield, to the next-door-but-one neighbours - the Cunninghams - was even more out of the question. Unable to contact her husband, Tessa nevertheless knew he would be as concerned for his family as they were for him. Assuming the authorities had not cordoned off the area, she also knew Peter's anxiety would rise exponentially with each ruined house he past, especially if he saw evidence of fatalities. Whether he arrived by car or on foot, he would first see the general condition of number 24 when he was still several hundred metres away. Tessa could only guess what his reaction would be, not knowing whether his wife and daughter had survived or been buried beneath the rubble. Wherever they slept, Tessa new it must be within the boundaries of their property and they must be easily found.

The small summer house having been reduced to an even smaller pile of planks and tarred felt, the Allerton's brick-built garage offered the best and only alternative to sleeping in the ruined house. The steel up-and-over door had vanished, exposing the interior to the road. Miraculously, although the wooden side door had fallen inward, its glass panels had remained intact, and could be persuaded to sit in its intended position, propped there using a hoe that had become merely a long wooden handle.

Despite the missing door, the garage offered several advantages over its bigger brother across the lawn. Firstly, the flat felt roof remained more or less intact, held together by the pitch used to seal it. Secondly, being used more as a workshop and retreat for Peter than a place to store the car, the floor was carpeted and it remained dry, there being no radiators to spill their contents onto it. More importantly, it was not filled with unstable building materials that might fall on the occupants' heads as they slept. Lastly, the garage had been not only a refuge for Peter, but a dumping ground for everything the family no longer used, but was too sentimental to discard, some of which could be useful in an emergency.

Tessa, placed the ironing basket and carrier bags down just inside the side door.

'We'll sleep in here. It'll be an adventure.'

Tessa was well aware of the trauma her daughter had suffered. All she could hope to do was keep the drama as low key as possible and mask her own fears.

There had been many items within the garage that had been entirely fabricated from steel, or had steel components within them. The residue of this material could be found everywhere - over every surface of everything that remained. Having placed Emma within the laundry basket, her bottom seated on a folded bath sheet for comfort, another round her shoulders for warmth, Tessa made a sweep of the structure, on the lookout for anything that might prove useful. Instinctively, she tidied the space as she progressed. She could see no immediate use for many of the items, especially those that relied on metal to hold them together, or make them work. Nevertheless, the search provided quite a haul: a pair of large tarpaulins in perfect condition, save for missing eyelets; two mattresses from sun-loungers that had lost their sprung frames; a stack of white plastic garden chairs; a matching flat-packed plastic table; a cool box; a ball of garden twine; an industrial-sized roll of paper towel that Peter used for cleaning up his mess; and a cardboard box containing two dozen candles and a box of matches, kept 'Just in case'.

'I'm thirsty,' Emma said, in a pitiful voice.

'Will you be all right if I go back into the house and see what I can find?'

'Yes, but don't be long,' Emma said, quietly, too fatigued to make the return journey.

Before crossing the lawn, Tessa swung the laundry basket into the opening where the side door should have been. From there, Emma could see her mother's progress, at least until she dipped into the kitchen. Despite it being at her request, and despite her having given her mother permission to leave, Emma's eyes immediately filled with tears, but she was too tired to make a sound.

Aware she was on borrowed time, Tessa made swift work of breaking down the plasterboard sheets and moving them out of the way. The light being very poor, she gathered only those things that presented themselves to her: a bottle of lemonade; a multi-pack of crisps; a loaf of bread; a tub of margarine; and her entire plastic picnic set, complete with condiments.

Judging she had gathered enough for one night and her daughter's unspoken time limit had been exceeded, Tessa returned to the garage.

Inside the simple structure it was dark; dark enough that no amount of being accustomed to it was going to help. Lighting the candles was easy, but keeping them alight proved to be more difficult as the through-draught kept extinguishing the flame after only a few seconds. Propping the side door in its frame helped, but the better solution was achieved by retrieving several glass jars from the recycling bin at the side of the house.

Back inside the garage, Tessa shielded herself and lit one of the emergency candles. Having dripped wax into the bottom of one of the vessels, she pressed a second candle into the warm pool, holding it there for a few seconds until it held firm. Repeating this process two more times gave Tessa three usable lanterns and a surprisingly good amount of light – perhaps not enough to read or sew by, but ideal for making up camp beds.

The roll of paper towel provided the means for cleaning the picnic set to a reasonable standard, after which mother and daughter sat, eating crisp sandwiches, washed down with lemonade.

Needing to be alone for just a moment, having finished her small meal, Tessa rose to her feet and made her way over to stand in the unshielded main entrance. The outside world was in darkness, reflecting her mood. No chink of man-made light; no hints as to what had become of the other residents. The background noise that had accompanied everyday life up until a few hours before had been replaced by a deafening silence, periodically punctuated by individual sounds: a falling roof tile; a gust of wind; a sound of anguish, carried on the breeze from afar.

She did not have a headache in the normal sense. Instead her brain ached as would an overworked muscle. So much for needing to be alone with her thoughts; she found she was not capable of any.

After a few moments Tessa returned to her daughter. They lay, holding each other tightly, their cheeks pressed together, waiting for the return of Peter – of Daddy; waiting to be released from reality through much needed sleep.

From their makeshift beds the occasional sound of footsteps could be heard, each making Tessa startle, bringing hope for Peter's return, but also fear that looters might murder them where they lay. However, she suffered alone. Being so young, Emma could not hold out any longer and gradually fell asleep, occasionally letting out a whimper, met by a comforting squeeze from her mother's arm.

Tessa, exhausted both mentally and physically, pulled the tarpaulins over their shoulders for added warmth and security, and eventually succumbed to sleep.

13

A dozen uniformed officers made it to the forecourt outside the jail, dazed, bewildered, but thankfully still in one piece.   Inside the jail the dust was settling, revealing the extent of the casualties - the list was long.

Throughout the establishment, the surviving inmates who were still conscious began to realise the predicament they now faced. They were the lucky ones who had been inside the brick-vaulted cells at the time of the collapse. However, looking out through the doorway, it became apparent their ordeal was far from over.

Those on the ground floor - the 'Ones' landing - had the best opportunity to escape without injury, but many of the doorways were found to have become blocked by unshiftable debris – roof parts, landing floors and bodies. The only other route out of the building was via the window opening, high in the back wall. Making matters more difficult, the outer wall was particularly thick – at least sixty centimetres – with the window frame positioned mid-point towards the outside surface, the inside sloping upwards towards it to improve light distribution. At some point in history, these slopes had been rendered smooth with plaster, and over the years had received many coats of emulsion paint, causing there to be little or no grip. Had the windowsill been constructed with a more conventional ninety degree angle, the opening would have been a small square of light at the far end of a small-bore, rectangular tunnel – not good for everyday use, but would have provided a ledge to which desperate fingers could grip. As it was, the design denied all but the most athletic prisoner any purchase with which to pull himself up. However, necessity being the mother of invention, some of the survivors used their ingenuity to build platforms from the sheets of wood that had previously formed their beds and cupboards, finding ways to stack them without the use of fixings. Even then, those who managed to reach the opening were still faced with a pair of sliding windows - sheets of Perspex, set into aluminium frames - running in deep runners, also of aluminium. Fixing screws and catches had disappeared, but mastic and plaster held many firm. Moving both panels to one side provided a space big enough for a man to wriggle through, albeit only if they had been careful what they ate. Muscle bound prisoners had no hope of passing through, but on the other hand, they had no problem ripping the windows from the frames, widening the aperture. Whichever the circumstance, the only way out was head first as there was nothing to cling on to while legs were redirected downwards. Two metres, head first, onto tarmacadam being likely to end badly, those who got this far had the sense to first throw down whatever promised a softer landing – blankets, pillows and torn mattresses – rolling from the building to protect heads and necks.

Those who were trapped upstairs were in even more of a predicament, the drop being five to seven metres to the yard outside. A head first fall from these heights was not going to be solved with a small pile of inaccurately placed pieces of foam. Instead, their best route to freedom was through the cell doors, set high in the internal walls. For some of these men, though, the fear of being trapped in their cell, while the world collapsed about them, was all too much, forcing them to take the window option, the lucky ones only suffering broken bones. There were others who not only recognised the perils of diving from the window, but also possessed the intelligence to come up with a viable alternative. These few realised their best hope was to form their bedding into rudimentary rope. Tied at one end to a board, braced across the doorway, they were then able to lower themselves down onto the pile of debris below. Even then, for some, the wrong knot or the wrong choice of wood proved disastrous.

In addition to the dead and escapees, there existed a third category of prisoner. For a variety of reasons, not all in-cell survivors chose to make a break for freedom. Some feared they might get into trouble by leaving their cells without permission; some were so petrified by the events they had witnessed and endured, their minds demanded they adopt the fetal position; and some had been less fortunate than Ricky, being seriously injured when the beds collapsed, leaving them no choice but to stay put and await rescue.

Their prognosis was not good.

***

All twelve surviving members of staff looked on with disinterest as, one by one, the best part of two dozen inmates fled the prison, any hindrance to their progress being purely unintentional. The officers had reached the relative safety of the outer forecourt with little or no injury and had no plans to alter that fact by tackling escapees, or by returning to help the six hundred plus men who were still trapped inside the jail. For that they realised they would need additional support.

No one had spoken in minutes - not since Dave Fielding had posed his rhetorical question. Having had time to catch his thoughts, Jim Taylor repeated Dave's words, having no greater anticipation of an answer than had his colleague.

'What the fuck is going on?'

First to respond was Supervising Officer Paul Cluney, a middle-aged man with a great deal of experience in all things prison-related, but not so versed in scientific abnormalities.

'I'll tell you what's going on; all the metal's fucked. It's like someone's filmed a load of things rusting and played it back on fast forward. It's fucking crazy.'

'But how?' Malcolm responded, looking to Paul, as the senior man, for answers.

'How the fuck should I know?'

Malcolm did not like being spoken to in such a way and would have retaliated if it was not for Peter interrupting their exchange.

'It's not all metal; only ferrous,' he said, noticing his gold band still trapped in a groove on his wedding finger, and that loose change still lay at the bottom of his trouser pocket.

'Whatever,' Jim reacted crossly. 'I can't believe you're arguing the toss. All metal, or some metal! Who cares? We're in the middle of a fucking war zone and you're worried about Semitics.'

'Semantics,' Paul corrected. 'This has got fuck all to do with Hebrew.'

'Fuck you.'

Eleven of the twelve showed interest in the conversation; not so Gordon La Roche who remained confused, having received a blow to the head while escaping E Wing, at the far end of the jail. Without warning, he walked from the group in the direction of the staff car park, finding it no longer protected by a barrier, open to any member of the public who might care to steal a space they were not entitled to.

At first, Gordon struggled to remember even in which row he had left his vehicle, the fuzziness of his thought processes hampering his recollection; a state hindered further by the fact every one of the cars had been reduced to neatly parked piles of rubbish, each carefully maneuvered to sit within a three-sided box of white lines.

Before the event there had been a considerable difference between the values of the vehicles. That disparity had disappeared with the bodywork, a forensic search being required to determine whether the car had been an Audi or a Skoda, old or new, a prized possession, or a means of getting from A to

B.

Walking along the middle row, Gordon stopped, having recognised something that identified one particular collection of detritus as his own – a cardboard jelly bean air freshener, its elasticated loop still attached to the rear view mirror which, in turn, remained glued to the laminated windscreen. Bending at the knees to prevent himself losing his balance, Gordon flipped the windscreen on its back, carefully removed the fragrance, sniffed if, attached it to his wrist, and turned his attention to what remained of the driver's door. From its plastic pocket, he retrieved a packet of twenty Benson & Hedges and a lighter, the latter rendered useless by the absence of the roller against which, until recently, the flint had struck. Unflustered, the officer discarded the lighter also, placed the cigarette packet in his shirt pocket and moved his attention to the dash board, in particular its integrated glove box. From this he retrieved a book of matches - a souvenir from a foreign hotel.

Having retrieved all he wanted, Gordon retraced his footsteps from the car park, occasionally stopping to inhale the air freshener's sweet fragrance, before moving off in the direction of the main road.

Although waiting the opportunity to get a word in edgeways, Keith Jenkins was not so engrossed that he missed his colleague's actions, noticing Gordon appeared to be having problems with his ears, his fingers rubbing first his right, then his left; his index fingers trying to dig something from within both ear canals. Whatever concerned him, Gordon continued down the road, his trousers riding ever lower, being grabbed only at the last moment, preventing them binding his ankles; averting a fall.

Having allowed his colleague a head start, Keith could then not help but set off to catch the rogue officer – his friend of many years – to see if he was all right.

The remaining ten members of staff hardly registered the second departure - a chase that was conducted at a snail's pace - and continued to talk among themselves.

By now, tensions were running high.

'Nostradamus predicted this you know,' Mark Fletcher piped up – another surviving OSG - quoting the writings of this long dead fortune-teller as fact.

'What, that all the metal would suddenly and mysteriously turn to rust?'

Officer Gavin Smith made no attempt to hide his sarcasm.

'No, that the world would come to an end,' Jim responded, parrying sarcasm with contempt.

It was not enough to deter his adversary for one moment.

'When didn't he predict the world would come to an end?' Gavin responded, a note of derision in his voice.

'Well, he was right, wasn't he?' snapped Jim, satisfied he was keeping his own against his antagonist.

Peter was convinced the two men would continue indefinitely, until one killed the other, and was thankful, then, that Chelsea unwittingly killed the argument in its track, in a way only she could.

'It's all right for you cunts bickering with each other. I'm the only woman here. My bra's fucked and my tits are hanging round my fucking waist.'

Her words drew attention to the officer's sizeable chest, the bulk of which sat unnaturally low beneath her jumper.

Chelsea's predicament drew a line beneath Jim and Mark's unhelpful exchange, although Ted Shacklock felt obliged to address the antagonists directly, his eyes darting between them.

'Look, you pair of numpties, I don't know about you, but my priority right now is not worrying about what has happened, it's getting home to my the wife and kids and making sure they're all right; it's also about finding a way of getting there, bearing in mind none of us have cars anymore.'

'Fuck, you're right. What are we going to do?' Dave asked, incredulously.

'Walk,' Peter replied, simply. 'I live thirteen miles from here. At a steady pace I could probably make it in a little over four hours.'

'It's all right for you; I've got more than thirty-five fucking miles to go. It could take me days,' Chelsea responded, annoyed that Peter was thinking only of himself. 'My Barry's gonna go fucking ape when he finds out what's happened to the Beemer. The insurance better pay in full or I'll be down their office ripping their fucking throats out – and that's before Barry gets hold of them.'

Used to their colleague's formidable ways and colourful language, all knew it would take a brave man to consider using a get-out clause.

Chelsea's comments were not helpful, but raised a valid point, one which Malcolm hoped someone could answer.

'Do you think it's just the local area that's been affected then, or do you think it's happening all over?'

As he posed the question, his eyes scanned the horizon.

All about them, the prison roofs were shedding the last of their tiles; the rumble of falling masonry could be heard both near and far.

'You don't suppose it could be happening out as far as Pete's house do you?' Malcolm asked, 'or Chelsea's?'

Peter was becoming increasingly concerned with every passing minute; comments like this doing nothing to ease his anxiety.

'It's no good. I can't stand here any longer. I need to get home to my family and I suggest you all do the same.'

His advice was punctuated with a sudden, high-pitched screeching noise, emanating from a position somewhere beyond the borders of the car park. Startled, the group of ten could not guess the source, but whatever it was, it was too close for comfort.

One hundred metres down the road from the prison, Officer La Roche had stopped for a cigarette, having not had the chance since popping out at lunchtime. Then was to get his fix. Having stopped, it was to calm his nerves; to stop his head feeling the way it did. Despite standing closer to the source of the noise than anyone, Gordon failed to react to it. Even as he prepared to light his cigarette, his head tilted this way and that, attempting to dislodge whatever it might be that had made him so profoundly deaf.

Although he had closed the distance between himself and his troubled friend, Keith was still too far away to intervene, although, seeing the hazard, he was desperate to do so.

What worried Keith was the state of a stationary tanker, standing within metres of his friend. Myriad small holes had begun appearing in the surface of the cylindrical container, peppering the painted steel sides over its entire surface. Pressure within forced liquid petroleum gas through the breaches, at which point it immediately changed state, the process causing the ear-splitting noise that panicked everyone but Gordon.

The tone did not remain constant. As the holes increased in size, and merged, so the pressure within the tanker dropped, producing a corresponding fall in pitch. Like a bomb timer, inexorably ticking towards zero, the deepening note indicated the worst was about to happen.

Although, for the most part, their bodies remained standing in an untidy ring, Mark, Dave, Malcolm, Paul, Peter, Ted, Phil, Chelsea, Jim and Gavin's heads faced the same direction – towards the sound. Hence, none of them witnessed one of the Day brothers scrambling over the rubble of the gate lodge, two other offenders in tow. Joey Day was not a nice man. Of his brothers, all of whom had experienced life behind bars, this particular sibling was the most unpleasant of all and most deserving of the officers' efforts to prevent his escape, a fact he was all too aware of.

Coming face to face with ten uniforms, Joey instinctively flipped into survival mode, prompting him to select a suitable brick from the pile and raise it to shoulder level, defying anyone to stop him. He looked wild, intimidating, dangerous, but nobody noticed, their attention remaining fixed elsewhere. Taking further advantage of the situation, Joey cast the brick to one side and ran off in the direction of the noise, his two disciples following close behind.

For once, the prisoners had the upper hand. Wearing prison issue grey tracksuit bottoms with elasticated waist, each was free to run as fast as their legs and lungs would allow, unhindered by the need to hold their trousers up. At this speed, they quickly encountered two more uniforms in their path - a buffoon, who in stopping to smoke a cigarette, had allowed his trousers to fall about his ankles; and a second male officer, more animated than the rest of them put together, charging towards the escapees. Prepared to do battle, aware the odds where numerically and physically stacked against the rogue officer, Day came to a halt, mentally braced for a fight.

To his surprise, the approaching officer's eyes did not fix upon him, or his criminal associates, but looked past him. Confused, Day remained rooted to the spot. The officer continued towards him at speed but quickly passed by, showing no interest in any of the fugitives. Not one to push his luck, Day and his two allies continued away from the prison, in the direction from which the officer had just come. Over his shoulder, Day heard the officer shout.

'Run!'

The single word was bellowed from the very pit of his stomach, evidence of his previous career in the Military Police, barking orders across the parade ground. It was meant for no one but Keith's colleagues, not for the worthless Day or his peers who continued on their path to oblivion.

Such was the authority with which Keith's instruction was delivered, the entire group reacted without hesitation, accelerating away from the prison as fast as their legs would allow.

Even the least fit of the group made Roger Bannister's record-breaking four-minute mile look like a stroll in the park. They ran and ran, all the time their hands holding up their trousers.

Back at the stricken tanker, Gordon La Roche struck a single match, causing not a flame but a single spark. This was enough.

In an instant, twenty-three tonnes of liquid petroleum gas became a fireball, expanding rapidly to engulf an area at least twenty-five metres in all directions from the epicentre; from the spot where Gordon La Roche had been standing.

For the briefest moment, Gordon presented a silhouette against the boiling cauldron of burning gas behind him. Moments later, the expanding ball of flame engulfed him completely, then Joey Day and his followers, each in turn, micro seconds apart.

The exertions of the prison staff had not been in vain; nor had Keith's efforts to forewarn his colleagues about the peril they faced.

First came a brilliant flash of light, accompanied by a wave of intense heat; then, following in the blink of an eye, the sound of an explosion. An immense and powerful explosion that reverberated through the bones of every living thing standing in its path. It was a huge sound, but at the same time smooth, as if muffled by a gigantic feather duvet. Then came the ball of flame, rolling upward into the sky.

Even the fittest and heaviest of the group were blown off their feet and thrown to the ground. Peter came down heavily on both knees and his palms stung as the hands of his outstretched arms slapped the tarmac road surface; a particular pain he had not experienced since his days in the school playground many years before.

No one escaped the blast of hot air that overtook them, sufficient to curl the hairs on their forearms, causing pain that vanished almost before it could be registered, replaced by a cooling sensation as an artificial wind rushed in from all points of the compass towards the stricken vehicle, conscripted by the fire to replace the oxygen it had so greedily consumed.

Then all was silent and dark, the fuel having been exhausted.

The prison staff remained spread out on the ground, either too dazed to move, or unsure as to whether or not it was safe to stand.

Peter had reasons of his own to remain where he was: firstly, this particular section of road seemed as good a place as any to be at that precise moment; secondly, the thought that he might be seriously injured frightened him and he was not sure whether he could handle knowing the worst, at least not just yet; thirdly, and perhaps most importantly, he felt that if he stayed very, very still, with his eyes tight shut, allowing himself to feel nothing but the tingling sensation in his hands, the rest of this awful nightmare might simply go away.

'Is everybody okay?'

The voice that spoke was weary and without force.

No one answered directly. There was no roll call. Instead, the group replied by slowly stirring into activity. One by one each officer sat up, dusted themselves down, checked for injury and got to their feet.

Peter was the last to react. He had come down hard on both knees and although there were no visible signs of injury; no tears in his trousers; no grazing to his skin, his left knee in particular was throbbing.

'That's just what I need.'

Malcolm was close at hand to help him up, supporting Peter's weight until the weakness subsided.

The group looked back toward the tanker.

Four bodies lay on the floor, motionless and on fire.

'Poor bastards.'

There followed a moment of silent reflection, but the need for decisions soon brought its end.

'Now what?' Phil asked, putting his question to the floor.

'Now we go home,' Peter said earnestly, rubbing his limbs, the only form of treatment available to him.

There were no dissenters. There was no more bickering. In fact, the level of conversation was noticeably less than it had been before the explosion. Even Chelsea's usual colourful language was absent.

Before departing, something had to be done about their trousers. Zips, belt buckles and waist bands fasteners were all effected.

Peter had the idea of reinforcing his waistband using his clip-on tie that had been in his pocket throughout. It was not nearly long enough to circle his waist, but it was of sufficient length to tie two belt loops together. A few others, seeing his solution, followed suit, but many had no such tie as they were not obliged to wear them during the summer months; female staff did not wear them at all. The solution for them came by way of pollution. Despite the Government's drive to reduce consumers' reliance on single-use plastic carrier bags to transport their shopping home, there were still many about, stolen by the wind to be deposited in hedgerows and other vegetation, there to blight the landscape. Pulled taut, the bags became long and thin; easy to thread through belt loops; equally easy to tie in simple knots.

The only other matter arising was Paul's missing spectacles, without which he was almost totally blind. His eyesight had met the prison service's minimum requirements when he had joined, but that had been a very long time ago. In the short term, there was nothing that could be done. The plastic lenses had rolled away across the prison's inner forecourt and would doubtless never be seen again. Thankfully, Jim lived in the same road as Paul and vowed to see him safely to his door where he would hopefully be able to locate his spare pair. In the meantime, Paul's frustration at not being able to see clearly continued to shorten his temper.

Apart from their common problem with their trousers, and Paul's particular problem with his spectacles, the group's outer clothing had otherwise escaped the effects of the phenomenon. Their uniform shirts, all short sleeved, offered inadequate protection against the cooling evening air, but at least they remained serviceable. As for their shoes, not a trace of metal had been used in their manufacture, save for the eyelets, and their disappearance in no way affected performance. For the most part, underwear had suffered the least, with the notable exception of Chelsea's bra, the absence of which had already generated problems for her when she was forced to run for her life from the prison. Frustrating, uncomfortable, but not insurmountable.

With the last plastic bag having been tied, it was time for the small band of men, and woman, to part company, splitting into groups of those travelling in roughly the same direction. A final half-hearted wave and the small group were disbanded, not knowing whether they would ever see each other again.

'Come on Pete, I'm going your way. I'll keep you company.'

Malcolm was not somebody Peter would have previously considered a friend - more a colleague - but as the man said, at least it was company.

The two unlikely allies set off in the opposite direction to the main group, past the still burning bodies of four men, the smell of burning flesh attacking their senses.

14

When the fireball had extinguished, it appeared to the survivors the town had been suddenly plunged into darkness. In reality, this was simply the result of optics nerves being temporarily overwhelmed; restored by time Peter and his companion reached the point where Gordon had been standing. Artificially prolonging the day, flames had taken hold within a number of adjoining properties, threatening to engulf them; buildings that were likely to remain ablaze until all available fuel – wood and textiles - had been exhausted.

Turning their back on the renewed destruction, the pair continued on their way.

'Right, you and I part ways about ten miles from here. Let's hope we find normality before then.'

'Bound to,' Malcom replied, believing in the power of maintaining a positive mental attitude.

'Ok, so we both keep our eyes out for anything indicating the extent of the effected zone.'

'Should be easy enough. There's enough metal around. Cars, signposts, street lights.'

'True, but what do we do when we get to the edge?'

'That's a stupid question. We carry on going until we reach home with a story to tell, or we bump into the emergency services who are holding back, not knowing what the fuck to do.'

'I'm not being stupid. What if it's caused by some sort of infection? It might be on our clothing. We might be carriers. We don't want to go marching through the front door, running the risk of bringing this lot down on our families; our neighbourhoods.'

'Shit, I hadn't thought of that. So what do we do?'

'When we find the extent of this phenomenon, I'm thinking we should stay put. Hand ourselves over to the authorities as soon as we see them.'

'You mad? They'll experiment on us.'

'Maybe, but I'd rather put up with a military doctor shoving a finger up my arse and taking all my blood with a large syringe than inflicting this on Tess and Em.'

'Military?'

'Hell, yes. Haven't you seen the movies? This is way bigger than the normal emergency services can cope with. If the first sign of normality we seen is a check-point and a fella with a gun, I'm handing myself in for decontamination; isolation if needs be.'

'I can't think of anything worse.'

'I can. There may be not limit to area of destruction. Think about that.'

'I don't want to and I'm not going to either. It's going to be all right.'

The unlikely companions continued in silence, Peter absorbing the pain in his knee. For a while, all there was to do was take in the surroundings - the overall devastation and the finer details – noting what had gone; what was left.

It was not long before Malcolm noticed the wince upon Peters face.

'You all right?'

'Just my knee. Took a bit of a knock back there.'

Trying to put the pain to the back of his mind, Peter changed the subject.

'So, I wonder what caused it.'

'A weapon?'

'Maybe. In which case the first person we're likely to meet will definitely be military.'

'If it is a weapon it could either be an accident or war.'

Peter did not take kindly to his companion's suggestion, aware that if he was correct, several weapons might have been used to blanket the whole country, just like a nuclear exchange. Of course, if it was a weapon, it was far more sophisticated, being able to turn the enemy's arsenal to dust. The only comfort in that thought was that if a foreign power had used it, they must also have developed an antidote. The country might land up being under new ownership, but at least the population would enjoy some kind of future.

Unless there was another explanation.

'Maybe it's both.'

'Both?'

Malcolm was confused.

'Yes, accident and weapon. Our lot might have developed it as a weapon but then kept it under lock and key like they do all the worst nerve agents and weaponised diseases. A terrorist could have got hold of it and made some sort of dirty bomb.'

'In which case, our lot – or wherever it originated – might not have developed the antidote.'

'I hope they have.'

'If they haven't, it could be like the black death all over again, with half of Europe being wiped out before it dies out of its own accord.'

Once again, Peter and Malcolm fell silent, their heads filled with many more questions than answers.

They walked on, finding it almost impossible and unnecessary to keep to the pavements. Fallen debris narrowed the road in stretches of a hundred metres or more, but at least there were no moving vehicles to threaten their progress.

The buildings they past had mostly been small retail outlets, of brick and slate construction, with large, plate glass widows to their fronts. All provided living accommodation above, but in almost all cases the rooms upstairs had been turned over to storage areas and offices, long before disaster struck. Not one of the shops had survived intact. Most noticeably, the cycle shop had been worst hit, thousands of pounds worth of stock having been reduced to multiples of the few rubber and vinyl components that had made up each item for sale. Next door, the newsagent too was a mess. Its roof had collapsed inwards, but the upstairs floor joists had prevented it falling through to the shop. Nevertheless, ceiling tiles lay strewn across the floor, together with the remains of stock, fallen from shelves that no longer existed. Water and the contents of dozens of tinned products formed a sludge on the floor, but not everything had been affected or was beyond safe retrieval.

Despite both survivors being men of the law, neither had any qualms in becoming looters. The events of the evening had given both men a huge thirst; the adrenaline that had pulsed through their bodies and then dissipated had left them shaking and weak. Peter and Malcolm were in need of sustenance and the newsagent was as good a place as any to obtain it. Malcolm took the lead, quickly devouring a bar of chocolate, washed down with a bottle of carbonated water. Seeing the instant relief this brought, Peter grabbed for a packet of corn snacks. The fingers and thumb of his right hand plunged into the packet, delivering the entire contents to his mouth in as little as four portions. A bottle of coke washed away the salt; a bar of chocolate satiated his need for sugar; half a bottle of still water then restored a degree of freshness to his tongue. The other half was then poured into his free hand, used to wipe a layer of dust from his face, paying particular attention to the area around his eyes.

Both men felt at least partially restored.

Conscious of the night drawing ever closer, neither man wanted to waste what valuable time remained before the dark prevented further progress towards home. However, it seemed sensible to gather something for later, neither man having any sure knowledge when they might eat again. It took only a matter of minutes for each to find a carrier bag and fill them to the brim with sweets, nuts, crisps, biscuits and small bottles of mineral water. Small items, such as boxes of matches, were pushed into their pockets.

It then occurred to them they would have to carry their load for several hours. The solution was inspired by the tale of Dick Whittington. After a quick search, Peter and Malcolm left the shop, each with their bags tied to a broom handle, supported over one shoulder.

Having left the premises and walked only a few hundred metres further, the travelling companions were pleased to find the first signs of life, outside the prison population and staff - another row of shops. Unusually, the flats above them had been occupied by tenants - single men, couples and families. Survivors of the collapse were found huddled together, women comforting each other and their children; men scrabbling to free buried neighbours from the rubble. Even at a distance and with the light failing, many could be seen crying. None saw Malcolm or Peter. The unoccupied had instinctively moved further down the road, to a clear area, away from their unstable accommodation; the diggers were too busy to notice anything beyond the next length of timber blocking their path.

Malcolm did not like what he saw. Peter had not yet formed an opinion, his lace having come undone, causing him to walk unevenly, putting even greater strain of his knee. Under normal circumstances, he would have thought nothing of stopping, bending at the waist and re-tying the bow. However, his knee, being stiffer than was usually the case, prevented him. Instead, he needed to find something on which to rest his foot, bringing the unfastened lace to a more comfortable height.

'Hang on a mo, Malcolm. I've had a bit of a blow out.'

Malcolm paid no heed to his travelling companion, being pre-occupied with the group ahead and their situation. Without even the smallest hand gesture, he continued on down the road, quickening his pace towards the refugees.

'Charming.'

Peter concentrated on the job in hand, using both hands to raise his leg so that his foot rested on a low wall. When he had finished tying the knot, he raised himself to full height, ready to see how far his companion had travelled ahead of him.

Malcolm was further away than Peter might have imagined, having jogged over much of the ground. His arms were raised in the air, his hands waving frantically. Now alert to danger, Peter could see what was worrying him.

The survivors had chosen, as their refuge, an unadulterated area in the shadow of a tall building; a modern ten-storey block of flats that remained pristine, untouched and unimproved by the chaos surrounding it. Its inhabitants, unaffected by the phenomenon that had struck their neighbours, had taken advantage of their balconies to assess the unfolding mayhem from the safety and comfort of their expensive apartments. It was understandable that different buildings should react in different ways, but that such a building should have remained so much intact was beyond belief. Above all others, this particular edifice, with its exterior walls of mirrored glass, bolted onto a frame of steel and concrete, looked a prime candidate for spontaneous demolition.

'I don't like the look of that,' Peter said, frowning.

He could see Malcolm had the same concerns, and without thought for his own safety, had run towards danger in an effort to save others. Peter was of the same mind, hoping to catch his friend, if only to reinforce the warning Malcolm was trying to give, but his knee was having none of it. Having stopped to tie his lace, his body insisted he re-apply weight to his leg in incremental stages before he could hope to continue at anything like a normal walking pace, never mind running.

'Damn this thing,' Peter swore to himself through gritted his teeth, focusing all his attention on the road a few metres ahead, setting small goals. But before he had achieved the first, fear became reality, the disaster demonstrating the power of gravity. In an instant, the solidity of a large, modern building became nothing more than thousands of tonnes of formed concrete and glass thundering and crashing to the ground, so swiftly no one had time to react; no time to curl into a ball; not time to brace for impact. An invisible cordon contained much of the concrete but had no jurisdiction over the cloud of dust and flying shards of shattered glass that exploded outwards.

Peter fell behind a wall before the first fragments reached his position, but could see many scudding past. Malcolm could do nothing more than drop to the ground, witnessing the death of every other person within and around the defeated high rise.

The noise and the pain came so close together, Malcolm was unable to separate the two. Suddenly, his whole body seemed to be on fire, pierced by a thousand red-hot pokers. Instinctively, his hands covered his head, resulting in the backs of them being peppered with fragments, large and small.

Peter had no choice but to wait for silence to return, all the while unable to shake the vivid image from his mind's eye of Malcolm standing in the road, frantically waving his arms to the last. He knew there was no hope for any of the local residents – the women, the children, the brave men who had been working to free their friends and neighbours - but there seemed just a chance Malcom could have survived, being that little bit further away from the fall than they.

Peter rose to his feet and limped out from behind the shelter in the lee of the wall, his ailing knee having taken another unwelcome knock.

Malcolm was laying in the foetal position, his hands clutched to his throat. Peter hurried towards him, making best speed, a blanket of broken glass crunching under every step. On reaching his wounded colleague, he could see Malcolm was lacerated from head to foot; his clothes were torn; his white uniform shirt dyed crimson with blood, and he was gurgling loudly.

'Shit, Malcolm, you're in a right state.'

These were not the words of encouragement he had been taught to say in such circumstances. The first aid course had promoted words of reassurance.

Malcolm looked back at him, his eyes wide with fear.

This was not the first time Peter had experienced so much blood, but it was the first time the leak had been coming from one of the good guys – a colleague. On a number of occasions in the past he had been first on the scene when an inmate had slashed his wrists with a razor blade. It was because of this that Peter had since carried a pair of rubber gloves in his shirt pocket. Instinctively, and without fuss, he felt for them and put them on.

Prising Malcolm's hands away from his throat, Peter instantly realised his mistake as a jet of blood spurted from a nasty, ragged gash that extended from the side of his neck - a little below his left ear - round to the front and across his larynx.

'Keep the pressure on, I'll sit you up.'

Peter hoped this simple act of elevating the wound might help, but at the same time knew he was wasting his time, estimating there was by now more blood on the pavement and on Malcolm's clothing than there was circulating his body.

His diagnosis proved horribly accurate. No sooner had it been made, Malcolm's eyes relaxed, his hands slipped from his neck, and the upper part of his body slumped forward; lifeless.

There was nothing more that could be done.

Peter lowered the body gently to the ground, his senses overwhelmed by feelings of sadness and loss; of helplessness and hopelessness. Malcolm had been a husband, a father, probably a grandfather too. In all likelihood, his only crime in life had been stealing a handful of snacks from a condemned newsagent's only minutes earlier. Not least of all, Peter had lost a companion; a work colleague whom he had known for many years but only in the past hour had become a friend. The world had been robbed of a good man and all for the sake of Peter tying his lace.

Peter might have remained in a state of torpor for many hours had he not been brought to his senses by none other than the man whose death was causing him to grieve. Like smelling salts, wafted beneath the nose of a fainted woman, the nauseating metallic odour of copious quantities of fresh blood, registered within Peter's nostrils, bringing him to his senses. He was suddenly aware of the blood that coated his forearms between the tops of his gloves and his elbows, and how incredibly sticky it felt.

'Ah, Jesus, how much more of this shit can one man take?' he pleaded, staring up at the sky. 'I'm covered in the stuff.'

Peter stripped the gloves from his hands, flung them away in disgust and rose to his feet, wanting nothing more than to be gone from this place; to move on; to put this new horror out of his mind before it destroyed him.

'Sorry mate,' Peter said, looking down at the remains of Malcolm Ragg. 'Sorry, but I've got to get home to my family. You understand, don't you?'

Malcolm made no reply.

Peter's first steps sent spikes of pain shooting up his leg, causing him to limp heavily. After a few paces, he stopped; not because of the pain in his knee, but because of a sense of guilt – not only for leaving Malcolm behind, but also for dismissing the plight of all those in the prison who had perished, or had been left horribly injured. And while thinking solely of himself and his family, he had given no thought to the many hundreds of innocent residents of the town – and possibly beyond - who had lost loved ones that evening. And for what? So one man's ideology would triumph? So one country might claim a new empire?

'They better have an antidote for this shit…and a bloody good explanation.'

Peter closed his eyes, took a deep breath and exhaled hard before opening his eyes once more, steeling himself for the journey that lay before him. Having retrieved his travel pack, he then set off alone, no longer registering his surroundings, but focusing solely on the ground immediately ahead. With movement, the pain in his leg began to fade, allowing his pace to quicken to near normal. At no great distance past the fallen block of flats, Peter reached the river that cleaved the town in two, realising that, despite his years working there, he had no idea what it was called. Cambridge had the Cam - the clue was in the name, but what of Barrowfield. The Bar did not ring any bells.

Making his way to the water's edge, Peter bathed his forearms and face, frantically scrubbing both with his palms as best he could, with the ferocity of an axe murderer trying to cover his tracks. However, in the absence of soap and a flannel, or any scrap of material that could be used as such, he found it impossible to remove the last traces of Malcolm's blood from his exposed skin. As for the stains across the front of his shirt, Peter accepted they would have to stay until he could find civilian clothes to wear.

Feeling slightly less contaminated, Peter stood up, one arm pressing down on the corner of a low wall, easing the strain on his knee as it straightened. Bending at the waist, he then picked up his Whittington pole and held it vertically, one end pressed to the ground, his hands and chin resting on the other. From this position, he took a moment to further survey his surroundings.

This was the first time in all the years of routinely commuting over it that Peter had paid any attention to the river. It was at least ten metres wide; tamed within banks of poured concrete. Only the single, untroubled, mallard duck that floated upon it, and the occasional willow that reflected in its slow-moving water, connected it with nature. The tired, ageing road bridge was functional, but further detracted from what once had no doubt been an attractive feature – a place to water cattle; to fish; to bathe. Constructed of steel girder and riveted plate, decked with a tarmacadam surface, the crossing remained in one piece. Its sides had long been marred by unskilled graffiti – the product of anti-social youths wishing to make their mark on the world in the only way they ever would. It was also in need of a little routine maintenance - potholes had blighted the surface since winter - but visibly the bridge had escaped the ravages that seemingly every other structure had suffered. However, two things prevented Peter walking upon it: the knowledge it was no more likely to be immune to the phenomenon than had been the shattered tower block; and it was giving off a disconcerting pinking noise, as though the metal had become hot and was now cooling. He considered the worst case scenario. If it were to collapse with him on it, there was high probability of him drowning, some portion of it, no doubt, failing to become dust until after it had bludgeoned him to death, or pinned him to the river bed until the oxygen in his lungs was spent. On the other hand, he knew that finding an alternative way across would be difficult, and considered he would be very unlucky indeed if the bridge decided to fail in the time it would take him to hobble to the far side. The question of luck prompted Peter to look back over his shoulder, in the general direction of Malcolm's mutilated corpse – a stark reminder that luck, when tested, did not always favour the brave. In reality, luck was often granted to those who seized chance but who also assessed risk. In this instance, Peter made his own.

So silent and so rapid was the bridge's sudden death, it was not the sound of tearing beams, or plates of steel clashing together, that caused Peter's head to whip round to face the front; or his body to leap from his skin. The first sound was actually the result of the flat underside of the laid road surface slapping the water, the resulting displacement soaking Peter through to the skin. The enormous splash disguised the additional sound of huge quantities of oxidised material breaking the water's surface, fizzing on its way to the bottom, myriad tiny pockets of trapped air bubbling upwards from the deep.

Peter ducked in reaction to the weight of cold water coming down upon his head, his hands releasing the shaft upon which he had been resting. As the pack fell at his side, his outstretched arms adopted the pose of a man cuddling an enormously fat, invisible lady. Looking down at his sodden chest, legs and feet, Peter produced a prolonged, discontented groan.

So wet was he that Peter was forced to disrobe, to wring the worst of the water from his clothes. At least the process removed some traces of Malcom's blood, but the incident had caused him a delay he could ill afford and left him damp, cold and uncomfortable. It had also denied him the simplest means to cross the river. Not wishing to swim, especially as he wished to protect his travel pack, Peter looked about him for inspiration, quickly noticing the remains of a boat house belonging to the local canoeing club. Their fibreglass craft had been securely chained in racks outside the wooden building, until the phenomenon robbed the structures of their screws and nails. The clubhouse and boat racks had collapsed into an untidy heap, scattering canoes in all directions.

Standing next to the brightly coloured selection of craft, Peter realised he had never been this close to a canoe before, let alone used one. He was not even sure how to get in. Thankfully, he noticed there were two types: those with one or two holes in the top, requiring the wearing of a rubber skirt to keep the water out; and an open-topped type, the sort of which he had seen bear hunters use in the wilds of Alaska – at least, on the TV. He suspected one was a canoe, the other a kayak, but had no idea which was which. Whatever the case, for the novice, the latter looked far more suitable.

Having secured his craft, Peter selected a short plank as an improvised paddle.

Launching it, the novice found it was all he could do to hold the boat against the bank while he boarded nervously. However, once underway the river was kind to him, the slow rate at which it flowed doing little to deviate him from his course.

Alighting on the far side was executed with all the grace and dignity of a Canada goose taking flight. As Peter lunged from the boat onto shore, his action caused an equal and opposite reaction, propelling the now empty craft into mid-river. Two thirds of Peter's body landed safely, face down on terra firma. The other third - his legs - remained projecting out over the water, his toecaps dipping below the surface several times as he frantically hauled himself further inland, rolling onto his side to complete the manoeuvre.

The boat bobbed a little before setting off down river once more, free to explore on its own.

The roads that fed the 'Old Dog' roundabout, from its left and right, represented the border beyond which the town of Barrowfield had not encroached. However, it was not a border recognised by the phenomenon.

To keep the traffic flowing, a simple steel flyover had been erected, many years before, levelling off ten metres above the ground. To reach the road out of town, Peter was used to driving beneath it. However, it having met the same fate as the bridge over the river, the only way past was to walk across its width – the arc having flatten to form a carpet of buckled tarmac.

Far from reaching the edge of town being cause for celebration, Peter considered it a double blow, a feeling he could not help but express aloud.

'One mile! One fucking mile! All this and I'm only one fucking mile from the prison.'

Everything that had transpired since this whole awful affair began, had taken place in a distance of one mile. One mile in an estimated one hour and there were still twelve more to cover. Peter knew there was no hope of reaching home before the last vestiges of daylight failed, leaving him to navigate solely by whatever luminance the moon and stars could provide through breaks in the clouds. Worse, the road to be travelled showed no end to the affected area, the pressed steel crash barriers no longer a feature of the central reservation for as far as his eyes could see.

There was not a car in sight as Peter made his way down the dual carriageway, instinctively walking well over to one side, despite the total absence of vehicles. Dimly lit fields stretched away on either side of the road, unchanged, but in the immediate vicinity, evidence of disaster was everywhere: absent streetlights; missing signposts; evenly spaced holes in the carriageway where cats' eyes had once been installed; and something far more gruesome. The bodies must have been travelling in cars speeding along the road when the metal bodywork had disintegrated around them. The momentum of the passengers, now without vehicles, had carried them some distance, tumbling over and over, smashing bones and scraping flesh. A number were clearly dead. Others looked as though they soon would be. A family similar to his own had been driving at speed in the direction Peter was headed. He first came upon the father; alive but barely moving. The man lay on his side, his eyes trying to focus on the rest of his family. Peter read his thoughts and went to check on them. The mother had no face; their young daughter had fared no better; both were dead. Nevertheless, Peter searched for signs of life, knowing he could be seen by the one survivor. Having completed his examination, Peter returned to the badly injured man.

'They're okay. I told them not to move, just in case it makes things worse. I'll make them comfortable while we wait for the ambulance to arrive. They're both scared but they want you to know they love you.'

Peter's approach was a calculated one, aimed at bringing solace to a dying man.

'I love them too.'

Having delivered his last words, the man's eyes closed; his head relaxed.

'Shit! Shit! Shit! Shit! Shit!!'

Not only had Peter witnessed a heartbreaking moment, his fear for the safety of his own family was suddenly increased tenfold.

'Christ, I hope Tess and Em haven't been out in the car.'

This thought alone caused Peter to perform a short but tortured dance, rooted to the spot, but then he became still, bracing his body under the control of clenched fists; a position he held until he felt back in control of his mind.

Fighting a renewed sense of panic, Peter quicken his pace. Thankfully, the pain in his knee had subsided, replaced by the warmth of inflammation. It mattered not whether this was a good or a bad sign, as long as it meant he could cover more ground.

After another mile, Peter reached the familiar landmark of a concrete bridge that spanned both carriageways. It served no other purpose than to allow the farmer access to both halves of his farm; a vast area of land that had been cleaved in two by the road on which Peter strode home. It was only a short walk to the other side, but the structure was in a poor state. The heavy duty reinforcing steel mesh, set within the concrete, had rusted, occupying a greater space than it had when solid. Consequently, the erstwhile smooth external surface of the bridge had shed great scabs, large enough and of sufficient number to jeopardise the integrity of the whole. Hence, Peter opted to take a detour, up the embankment, across solid ground and back down to the road on the other side. The slope was steeper and the grass was longer than he could have imagined from the comfort of his speeding car. Up close, the deck was uninviting; covered in a thick layer of dried cow manure. It was also a great deal less safe, the safety rails on each side having vanished, almost without trace. It did, however, provide a vantage point from which to survey the surrounding area.

Suddenly, Peter's attention was drawn to the twinkle of a light in the distance; the first of its or any other kind he had seen since the collapse of the prison. Until the moment that his chair had collapsed beneath him, the sight of an incandescent bulb had held no interest, unless it caused him to lose sleep, or spoiled his enjoyment of the night sky, but the phenomenon had changed everything.

As Peter looked on, the strength of the lamp became steadily brighter; the noise of a highly stressed engine providing unmistakable evidence of a powerful motorbike heading in his direction. This, Peter hoped, was the first of many plots on a map defining the outer reaches of destruction. As such, the rider had to be stopped and questioned.

Whoever sat astride the bike was clearly in a hurry, paying no regard to the speed limit, or the condition of the road. Peter wanted desperately to flag the man down, not only to pump him for valuable information, seeking reassurance he was not witnessing the end of the world, but to warn him of the dangers he faced ahead.

Grabbing his travel pack, Peter headed down the embankment as quickly as he could, being careful not to trip in the long, tangled grass. In the time it took him to reach even ground, the motorbike had closed the distance to no more than one hundred metres. Peter raised his wooden pole in the air and began waving it from side to side, in a wide arc, sure the bulging white carrier bag at its end would attract attention. Seconds later, his eyes widened on realising the machine was heading straight for a dense patch of wreckage, sure to dismount the rider. One hand let go of the pole, palm thrusting forward as a warning sign. As it transpired, Peter's instinctive gesture played no part in the rider altering his course. Nevertheless, the motorcycle suddenly veered to one side to avoid what non-metallic remnants lay in its path. Surprisingly, the engine note hardly varied, indicating the rider had no intention of slowing; evidence perhaps of skill and ability, or else an indication he had experienced and overcome similar encounters along the way and was confident of doing so again. Whatever the case, there was no time to determine either as fact. What neither Peter nor the rider had spotted was a slick - a glint of light reflecting off an oil and water emulsion, spread evenly across the width of both lanes. The bike went down heavily and bounced, the rider and the machine performing an elaborate dance that ended with the human element impacting the bridge with a sickening thud, sandwiched between concrete and the twisted remains of the motorcycle. Only then did the machine succumb to the phenomenon, leaving the crumpled body surrounded by, and covered in, plastic components and the residue of a vanished engine and frame.

Peter hurried across to see if the rider was still alive and, if so, whether there was anything he could do to prevent the most likely outcome.

On his arrival, it became immediately apparent Peter had been wrong in his assumption. The leather clad rider was in fact a woman, and given her perfect figure, he wondered how he might have thought otherwise.

She had come to rest, laying on her side, almost in the recovery position.

Conscious of the need to keep her head immobile, Peter lifted the helmet's flip front, revealing the face of an attractive blonde, young enough to have perfect skin. Her whitened teeth brightened the blood that oozed and dripped down from the corner of her mouth. Her breathing was laboured and rasping.

Peter took her hand in his, giving it a gentle squeeze, not knowing what else he could do.

'My name's Peter. What's yours?'

'Elle.'

The reply came as a whisper.

'Okay, Elle. Don't worry, you'll be fine.'

The patient did not look convinced.

'Where have you come from?' Peter asked, leaning down to look directly into the young woman's semi-glazed eyes, speaking slowly and with purpose.

There was a delay before Elle replied as she fought to access her memory.

'Banton.'

To form the word, the patient's lips came together briefly, their parting causing a mixture of spittle and blood to spatter the road surface.

Within his grip, Peter could feel the life force draining from the rider. Holding back tears, he forced a reassuring smile and squeezed her hand a little tighter, hoping it would prolong her life.

'Elle, tell me, has the metal been affected there?'

With great effort, Elle spoke her last word.

'Everywhere.'

The rider's eyes fixed, Peter understanding in an instant there was no amount of stimulation that would ever make them move again.

Banton lay far beyond where Peter lived; this was not good news.

'What have they done?'

He spoke solemnly, sharing his immediate thought with the deceased.

Before leaving the body of Elle – a woman with no surname - Peter closed the visor to protect her face and made her as comfortable as possible. His final act was to use a sharp stone to scratch her name into the side of her helmet; the crudest of grave markings.

With nothing more to be done, Peter took up his stick and bundle, turned his back on the still warm body, and walked on, expecting the worst.

A major roundabout lay three miles from the prison, a concrete bridge carrying a dual carriageway above. The aluminium sign, depicting the layout, lay face down on the grass verge, the steel posts that had supported it having been eaten away. Concrete scabs broke from the bridge's face with unnerving regularity, prompting Peter to adopt the same plan that had seen him safely to the far side of the farmer's cattle bridge.

On reaching the top, Peter looked in both directions, along a road that never normally slept, even on a Sunday evening. Indeed, the evidence left behind indicated this particular evening had been no exception. Twisted and broken bodies lay all about as far as the fading light would allow him to see, and there were no signs of rescue. The air was filled with an overpowering smell of petrol fumes; the result of a bulk tanker having dumped its load. It was possible that forensic analysis would reveal how each traveller had died, but that assumed anyone with the necessary skills had survived, and Peter had no time to care. Nevertheless, he was not immune to the plight of others and so it was with a heavy heart that he descended the embankment on the far side to continue his journey.

The road he took was far smaller – one lane in either direction - continuing through open countryside. A mile on, Peter reached an isolated house and there he stopped. As anxious as he was to be reunited with Tess and Em – to know they were all right and to protect and comfort them - his body, and some part of his mind, urged him to rest. He was still wet, growing wearier by the minute, and his knee troubled him more than he cared to admit. He had no torch or lamp by which to navigate, and although the moon was full, scudding, broken cloud periodically plunged him into darkness.

If there was doubt in his mind he should continue, it was dispelled when a final push onwards resulted in him tripping over the wreckage of yet another vehicle, a moulded piece of plastic narrowly missing his eye, but still causing a painful scratch across his temple. In an instant, his mind was made up. It was simply too dangerous to continue.

The house was set well back from the road, hidden from view behind a neatly trimmed hedge. Already in need of modernisation, the phenomenon had done nothing to improve its appeal, the building's silhouette revealing it too had shed its roof.

Two questions sprang immediately to mind. Would he encounter the occupants of the house? If so, would they be welcoming, or hostile?

Peter had driven past the property twice a day, five days a week, for more than seven years, but in all that time he had never paid it any attention, other than to acknowledge its existence. A driveway of five metres led to the remains of a pre-cast concrete garage that had fallen down when the bolts holding the sections together rusted through. The corrugated asbestos roofing had fallen simultaneously, shattering as the individual sheets landed on the car below. The vehicle itself remained in remarkably good condition, the body having been fabricated from moulded fibreglass. The three doors were off, owing to the sudden lack of hinges, but the laminated windscreen was still in place, held there by a thick rubber strip.

146

Beyond was the house. Although it had fared better than the garage, it was in a poor state, the structure having been so affected, Peter considered it unsafe to venture across the threshold. Rather, he stood at the front entrance - surrounded by fallen tiles, timber and roofing felt – and called to anyone who might be trapped or sheltering inside. There was no reply.

The narrow hallway was substantially darker than outside, forcing Peter to reach into his pocket for a box of matches. Given that he had been drenched when the bridge collapsed into the river, it was miraculous they remained dry enough to strike. The brief flare served only to confirm entry was impossible, the ceiling and stairs having collapsed, the internal doors no longer able to swing. Taking in some detail, Peter noted a potted plant had survived, destined to die through neglect, and the receiver of an old fashioned phone that poked out from beneath a broken sheet of plasterboard. Then the light was gone. Sacrificing a second match proved worthwhile, it surviving long enough to reveal a raincoat, intact and within reach. Although small and slightly musty, it fitted reasonably well and served to sooth the sting of cool air against bare skin.

There being no sign of life and nothing to be gained by lighting further matches simply to confirm the extent of the destruction, Peter's thoughts turned to taking shelter for the night and to the relative safety of the fibreglass van. The matches had given him a coat, but in return had robbed his night vision. His first steps were tentative, any attempt at lighting his way being snuffed out by an intermittent breeze. However, that same breeze hurried a patch of cloud on, bringing moonlight to guide him to the remains of the garage and its content. Having reached the vehicle, Peter shuffled along one side towards the opening from which its rear door had fallen. In doing so, his foot caught in something laying on the floor; some kind of tarpaulin that had been draped across the bodywork to keep it pristine. A collapsing concrete panel must have caught it, dragging it to the ground. Seeing its potential, Peter groped and pulled and lifted until the sheeting was free and then cast it over the vehicle, pinning it in place with segments of the garage walls. All this was done in near darkness, the moon having disappeared once more. Having finished the task, Peter lifted a flap and crawled inside.

Seat runners, springs and frames having reduced to dust, the interior was surprisingly spacious, but moulded ridges denied him an uninterrupted flat surface on which to lie. However, the vinyl and foam remnants of the seats, once carefully repositioned, provided a bed of sorts. The process was slow, requiring the use of several matches, but Peter was under no time constraints. Untying the travelling pack was achieved in the dark as it required the dexterity of both hands, the knot having tightened under the pull of the bag's contents. Once open, Peter chose his supper by touch alone, then sat back to satiate his hunger and thirst, both of which had become apparent for the first time. Then it was time to sleep. Peter fashioned a pillow of sorts from his travel pack, moving cans to the bottom; softer items, such as packets of crisps, to the top. He lay down, drawing his knees up towards his chest. His body was ready, despite the discomfort afforded him, but his mind was not. Every attempt to slip away was an opportunity for his brain to bombard him with images of things he had seen and of things he feared he might see. Changing the subject, focusing on positive memories, failed to temper his anxiety, each recollection destroyed in an instant to be replaced by vivid scenes of death and destruction; of people dying in his arms; of pools of freshly spilled blood; of men on fire; of everything familiar to him collapsing, near and far; of conversation that denied hope. Making matters worse, he was cold, damp, and uncomfortable and he yearned for a mug of hot tea, to polish his teeth with an electric toothbrush and then to feel the sting of mouthwash.

Trying to ignore what had happened, trying to disregard the concern he had for his family, Peter made efforts to concentrate on making detailed plans for the morning. It worked to a degree. Fearing he would not sleep at all, he was comforted in that he was at least able to shut his eyes and rest them.

Many hours passed, or it could have been minutes; either way, the lone survivor eventually succumbed to his fatigue and fell into a fitful sleep.

15

'It all makes perfect sense now.'

'Joe, what are you talking about? What makes sense?'

'Why they have kept us here all this time; why they've been conducting so many tests; why they were so afraid to let the dog escape; why they felt the need to murder my entire stock. This explains everything.'

Ann looked about her, aware that someone might be listening. She then spoke in whispered tones.

'I know what they've done, but how can you say that any of this makes sense? How could anyone make sense of what's happened to the metal?'

'Don't you see woman? They knew something was up long before any of this happened. They knew and they wanted to keep it to themselves; probably some weapon that's gone wrong.'

'You think so? I've heard people say it was the meteor shower.'

'People; what do they know? Just a coincidence, I say. This has all the hallmarks of military. Just think what it would do to tanks and guns.'

The farmer was angry. More than that, he was deeply bitter: bitter at having had his livelihood snatched away from him; bitter that a way of life that stretched back over generations had so suddenly and decisively come to an end, on his watch; bitter that nobody had felt able to confide in him something that was so obviously relevant.

Joseph wanted someone to blame. If it *was* the work of the military - seeking the ultimate weapon - then somebody should be held accountable for what they had done, but then, who would that be? It was less than twenty-four hours since disaster had struck and already society, or what he could see of it, had collapsed. The guards had disappeared and the police had failed to make an appearance. So what chance was there that a Member of Parliament might show his face to answer awkward questions put by his constituents?

'If only one of those soldiers had had the bottle to stick around, I'd have rung his bloody neck. Someone should pay!'

'Joseph, I know how you feel right now, but we can't be sure this has got anything to do with the military.'

Ann had never seen her husband so fired up. Not even when the rest of Europe had seemed hell bent on ruining his business; or when the head teacher of the local school had told him his son was not making an effort; not even when a group of teenagers had broken into the bottom field on scrambling bikes, almost frightening the herd to an early death.

'Let's look at the facts shall we? When was that meteor thing?' Peter said, setting out to prove his theory.

'Ooh, I don't know – it started about the end of May, beginning of June, didn't it? And it went on for about four weeks.'

'Exactly, so it was all done and dusted nearly two months ago. If an earthquake struck and two months later a building fell down you wouldn't say the earthquake had caused it would you?'

'Well, actually, I would probably suspect the two were related in some way. Maybe the earthquake had weakened the foundations and over time small cracks had become big cracks.'

Joseph chose not to answer. He had never been good at winning arguments, even if his gut feeling told him he was right. Instead, he sat on his haunches staring at the ground between his feet, uprooting tufts of grass and throwing them idly through his heels. Ann moved to sit beside him and placed her arm around his shoulders. She did not speak; judging that to do so might upset her husband still further.

Their moment of silence was interrupted all too soon as the children came bounding back into view.

'Mum, Dad, we've been over the whole camp with the others. You were right; the soldiers have all gone. There are people all over the place fighting over what food's left and all the water bowsers have gone too.'

Joseph gazed up at his son who stood before him looking like a dog that had retrieved a stick for its master's pleasure. Next to him stood Alice, silent but as much a part of the announcement as if she had spoken the words herself. By the expression on their faces, they both sought approval, but how could he thank his children for bringing such adverse news? In the end, the best he could do was to force a smile and say 'thank you' in a tone normally associated with the clinically depressed.

Their mother shared her husband's concern, but did not wish to pass her fear on to the children. 'Never mind eh, kids; we've still got enough food and water to be getting on with and your father will come up with something before we run out.'

She looked to her husband for support.

He offered none.

'Never mind your father, where are the others?' she asked, changing the subject.

This time it was Alice who spoke.

'They're right behind us. Should be here any minute.'

As if on cue, the rest of the party made their appearance, none of whom showed the same enthusiasm as had the Dugdale children. They had basically the same news to tell, but the emphasis was weighted more on the gravity of their situation.

'I don't know how, but your kids don't seem to have been affected by any of this,' George said, directing his words at both Ann and Joseph.

Joseph responded, feeling he had to defend their seemingly untroubled attitude.

'They're good kids. They've done nothing wrong.'

'No, I wasn't saying they had. I just meant...'

George was lost for words.

Ann felt she could offer a better explanation, and at the same time detract from her husband's strange behaviour.

'I think it's because they're young and have already had these past two weeks to come to terms with some pretty strange circumstances.'

'My boy's much the same,' Graham said, reinforcing her view. 'It's like water off a duck's back to him.'

'I wish I could say the same for our two,' Tom added, shielding his children, one under each arm.

The four holidaying families and the farmer's family had been acquainted with each other for no more than ten days, but in that short space of time the intensity of their existence had brought them closer together than might otherwise have been achieved in a lifetime. Like most extended families, they did not necessarily like each other. Nevertheless, there existed the deep rooted bond between them that one might have for a rarely visited relative; a bond born out of a common experience. They had survived the plane crash together; they had survived the intolerable living conditions of the camp together; they had survived the disappearance of normality itself - together. They would face the immediate future together.

'What do we do now?' Ann asked, addressing the group as a whole.

Joseph looked about them. He saw no fences; no barbed wire; no soldiers with guns.

'Nothing to keep us here.'

'Where then?'

'Let's go home.'

16

A line of inmates filed silently down the cast iron staircase from the upper landings of the segregation unit to the ground floor, each holding a blue plastic bowl and matching plate in his hand. These were no run-of-the-mill prisoners; these were on 'the rule'; a euphemism for those kept apart from the rest of the residents for their own protection, owing to the nature of their offences. Many wore the same light blue tee shirts, ill-fitting tracksuit bottoms, and gym shoes of the very poorest quality. Peter found himself among them, wearing the same attire as the others, but with the addition of a belt fabricated from the hem of a prison-issue bed sheet.

He was puzzled and at the same time concerned for his safety.

A pecking order existed within every jail. Sex offenders were very near the bottom, but even they looked down upon police and prison officers who found themselves on the wrong side of the bars. Together with informers, and prisoners who failed to pay for drugs purchased or phones borrowed, they lived in fear they might someday discover the depths to which man's inhumanity to man could go. On a number of occasions, Peter had witnessed inmates being 'jugged'; another word reserved for use within the penal system. It referred to the practice of filling a jug with freshly boiled water, adding a quantity of sugar to make it nice and sticky, and tipping the solution over the head of an unsuspecting 'grass' of perhaps a 'nonce' - that is to say, informers and sex offenders respectively.

On reaching the bottom of the stairs, the other inmates weaved their way into the servery to collect their meals. One of Peter's former colleagues saw him, bidding him good morning as though nothing were out of the ordinary.

'Are you going to help us get this lot fed?'

'No', Peter replied, pinching his tee shirt and pulling it towards his friend to demonstrate that his status had changed. 'I'm one of them now.'

He accepted he was now an inmate, but for the life of him could not remember how it had come about.

At that moment, the Governor entered the wing. He too bid Peter a good morning.

'Governor, can I have a quick word with you?'

They entered an office that led off the main part of the wing.

'I don't understand what's happening,' Peter said, incredulously. 'What have I done to be put in here?'

'You have been accused of encouraging an inmate to commit suicide', the Governor replied sternly.

Peter remembered speaking to a prisoner on those lines, but he was not sure his actions warranted imprisonment, or whether a charge could be proven. He was almost certain no one else had witnessed his conversation and even if they had, was it really so wrong?

'This can't be right,' he said to himself. 'None of it makes any sense.'

The figure of the Governor melted away, Peter finding himself no longer within the narrow confines of a prison wing, but instead on the shores of a shallow lake at the heart of a wood The change of scenery was seamless and appeared quite natural. It was peaceful; a far nicer place to be than locked up in jail. The sun penetrated the leafy canopy above, bathing Peter's body from head to foot in a pleasing dappled light. Before him, moored to the bank, were a number of cars left over from the 1950s, floating half submerged in the water. Sun glinted off the chromed bright work. Although there seemed to be nothing intrinsically wrong with what he was seeing, neither did it make any sense.

The woodland faded, again seamlessly, leaving Peter standing on a rocky outcrop atop a windswept hill. In his hands he gripped an old wooden kitchen chair and had with him for company an adult male lion. The beast approached and commenced pawing Peter playfully, claws retracted.

'Get off', Peter said, wearily pushing the creature away with the legs of the chair.

The lion continued with an irritating series of nudges using one of its massive paws. Exasperated, Peter dropped the chair.

'Get off', he said again.

The lion continued unabated.

'GET OFF!' Peter reiterated through gritted teeth, simultaneously punching the lion as hard as he could on the jaw.

The lion was gone and in its place was Peter's family, Tessa and Emma sitting on edges of a checked picnic blanket. He knew these figures were his wife and his daughter, despite being unable to make out their features.

It began to rain. The infrequent drops quickly became a downpour, but still Tessa and Emma sat there, oblivious to the weather. Peter studied the food on offer. None of it appealed to his taste. He opened one corner of a sandwich.

'I don't like pickle, you know that,' he complained, raising his head to confront his wife.

To his horror, he found her dissolving in the rain; Emma too. The water that trickled from their bodies formed rivulets, carrying the remains of the rapidly-disappearing family with it. Peter leapt forward, frantically trying to scoop the slurry into a plastic sandwich box. Neither Tessa nor Emma seemed bothered by what was happening to them. Instead, they continued to select their favourite morsels from the many open containers that lay spread across the blanket, slowly filling with rainwater.

'No! This can't be happening,' Peter cried, waking with a jolt, utterly disorientated, his heart pounding with such vigour it threatened to break through his breast bone.

Rain was beating heavily on the roof of the van.

Prior to the extraordinary events of the previous day, the sounds of an overnight summer downpour had ranked highly as one of Peter's most pleasurable experiences. From the comfort of his bed he had enjoyed hearing the power of the rain, open windows protected by an overhanging roof. He particularly enjoyed it when the noise became suddenly louder and he would lie there wondering just how heavy the deluge could get. He had enjoyed the experience because it heightened his sense of safety. Whatever Mother Nature could throw at him, he and his family were protected by wood and brick, plastic and concrete, glass and metal. The phenomenon had changed all that, replacing sense of security with sense of fear; an irrational fear that grew with the sound of the rain. He thought of all his worldly possessions trapped within the walls of his home; a building that had probably suffered in much the same way as had the structure standing in the darkness only metres from where he lay. The thought of water damage lasted but a second, replaced by self-hatred for considering material things before the safety of his wife and daughter whose survival might have been chosen by the flip of a coin.

Peter felt helpless and panic. There would be no more sleep; no further respite from the terrifying thoughts that threatened to devour his soul.

Eventually the rain began to ease and then stopped altogether, just as daylight began to return. Without a watch there was no telling how early it was, but it mattered not. It was time to get up. Forcing stiff and aching limbs to work, Peter sat up and rummaged through his carrier bag for breakfast. His mouth was grateful for a gulp of mineral water to relieve his thirst. A packet of crisps helped contain the pangs of hunger.

The sun had not yet risen above the horizon. Nevertheless, there was sufficient light for Peter to free himself from the cramped conditions of the Reliant and to move about safely.

Although he was keen to set off for home, it seemed right to have another look around the property, hoping to find the occupier or occupiers alive, somehow holed up and making do. Having already experienced the impenetrable front entrance, Peter opted to make his second attempt at the rear.

Giving the building a wide berth, Peter pushed his way through a hedge in preference to using the path, thus avoiding trampling on the piles of broken roof slates that threatened to pitch him to the ground like a novice ice skater.

The kitchen door – or the hole where the door had once hung – seemed to offer the most likely route to the interior, but progress beyond the first metre quickly proved no more feasible than at the front of the house, both areas being blocked by similar quantities of fallen debris. Not prepared to give up so easily, having grabbed a chunk of collapsed ceiling, Peter turned to throw it clear of the house. It was only then he saw the man – in all likelihood the owner of the property - lying face down on the lawn, approximately ten metres from his position. Casting the section of plasterboard lazily to one side, Peter hastened to where the man had fallen.

A quick examination determined the man was elderly and dead. His blood, having first pooled on the ground beneath his head, had then been partially washed away by the rain, evidenced by multiple tracks, stained red, reaching from the source out across the concrete garden path. Oddly, his body lay outside the influence of falling tiles and lengths of roof timbers, ruling out a direct hit, unless he had first managed to stagger some distance before succumbing to his injuries. Against this hypothesis was a lack of dust or debris adhering to his tartan dressing gown. It was feasible the rain might have washed away most of it but no doubt traces would remain. More likely, the man, well into his eighties, had tripped over the concrete ornamental tortoise that lay, disturbed, at his feet, and in doing so had struck his head on the brightly painted garden gnome that lay close by, its face smiling, its teeth spattered with congealed blood.

The scene described an instantaneous death and the moments leading to it. The deceased still held a plastic bottle of milk in his right hand, a saucer in his left. Before retiring to bed, he had set off down the garden path to feed an animal; probably a regular nocturnal visitor - a badger perhaps, or a hedgehog. He had tripped, died and no one had come looking for him. Peter surmised the man had lived alone. If he had a wife, surely she would have been by his side when the accident happened, or discovered him soon after. It was unthinkable she would not have left him to bleed to death from a blunt force trauma – unless she was on the telephone to the emergency services when disaster struck. However, Peter had seen the remains of a hard wired phone in the hall - just as he would expect of an older person's home - but there had been no sign of a body.

This was a snap shot of an anonymous man's life and an indication of his nature. Peter felt he knew him in some small way and it was this that caused him to remain kneeling for a while, lost in thought.

The thing that eventually broke his concentration was a sudden gurgling, emanating from the supposedly deceased body. Peter startled and then quickly but carefully turned the old man over onto one side to reveal his face. The man's eyes flicked back and forth a couple of times.

'My coat', he said weakly.

'Don't worry mate, you'll be all right. I'll just fetch you something to make you more comfortable', Peter spoke loudly as one would to a foreigner when trying to make them comprehend English.

Peter ran back to the house. The French doors were off, enabling him to quickly grab a pair of heavy curtains and a floral scatter cushion. He was not absent from the old man for more than a few minutes but on his return, Peter found the man's eyes fixed and lifeless. The man was going to die anyway - that was obvious - but Peter had wanted to make his last moments on Earth as comfortable as possible. Instead, the anonymous man had seen his world collapse, had spent his last night cold and in pain, and had passed believing a complete stranger had stolen his coat.

Peter placed the cushion beneath the dead man's head and spread the curtains across his body, making him as comfortable as possible for his journey to the afterlife.

Although unable to venture into the house, Peter peered in from as many openings as possible until he saw what he had hoped for – an addressed envelope. Something a little more personal than a utilities bill would have been nice, but at least the deceased could be remembered by his name; Mr. D. Rogers.

Unable to dig any form of grave, having neither the time nor the equipment to do so, Peter instead covered the deceased with the largest fragment of corrugated asbestos sheeting he could find, first tucking the envelope beneath the curtain shroud.

Being an atheist, Peter had no prayers to say. Instead, he chose to stand for a few minutes, watching over the makeshift tomb, silently respecting the passing of a man who he had never known.

'You're probably one of the lucky ones,' he said thoughtfully, before turning back towards the kitchen.

At first sight, ingress had seemed impossible, but perseverance determined it was merely very difficult. The work entailed in clearing a path was rewarded with some dividends, the honest looter recovering a number of items of food: a sealed pack of cheddar cheese; half a loaf of bread; and a partly used tub of margarine. The rest was spoiled. Mr. Rogers seemed to have survived mainly on tinned kippers, tinned soup and tinned condensed milk, all of which had spilled their contents, and combined to make a foul smelling mess on the floor.

Without further ado, Peter collected his bag and replenished its contents before setting off in the direction of home.

The sky was much lighter, not only because the Sun had followed its usual track upwards, but because the clouds of the previous evening had moved on, to dampen someone else's day.

It was almost another mile to a small hamlet, the name of which was to be found on another aluminium sign that gave the appearance of having been tossed aside by vandals.

Raven Green - or just Raven to the locals - consisted of two short rows of bungalows, one on either side of the road. At the far end had stood a traditional red telephone box – hardly used since the advent of the mobile phone - and an independent petrol station. The box had been reduced to window panes and red paint; the garage had lost its pumps, the remains of which lay beneath the enormous canopy that before had given some protection to forecourt customers from the rain, as long as the wind had not blown it sideways.

For the most part, Raven was an entirely forgettable place. In fact, if asked, the only two comments Peter would be able to make about it were that the speed limit there had been capped at fifty miles per hour, and it appeared to have been a haven for amateur car salesmen. The second statement would be provoked by the fact he could not recall even a single occasion on his way to or from work when there had not been at least one car parked on a driveway with a cardboard price tag lodged beneath its wiper blades.

Not a single building remained intact; not the bungalows themselves; not their associated outbuildings – garages, sheds, greenhouses or lean-tos.

Despite perhaps twelve hours having elapsed since the phenomenon struck, a group of residents was to be found, gathered on the South side of the road, busily comforting one another. It being inconceivable they would have sat out in the rain all night, Peter concluded they must have put their emotional trauma on hold, found temporary shelter before dark set in, and then reconvened at daybreak to continue mourning their loss. Moving towards their position, Peter heard cries of grief and despair emanating from the rear of other properties as he passed by, but none caused him to deviate from his course. It was not long before the group noticed his approach; a young man wearing an old man's coat; a man with a stick and a bag slung over his shoulder; an outsider. Warily, men were pushed forward from the group to intercept. Peter felt suddenly exposed – vulnerable - wishing he had made efforts to avoid the situation by diverting his path through the fields. His mistake had brought him face to face with a group of desperate men and women who would have seen their food stocks spoil before their eyes; who would have quickly realised replenishing them was not going to be easy; who could see the stranger before them had food and water. Suddenly, Peter feared his stick might have to become a weapon. However, he need not have worried. All the scouts wanted was news, good or bad. Relieved, Peter was more than happy to tell them what he knew. After all, they were the first survivors he had properly interacted with since leaving the prison.

Peter gave the strangers a concise report, as if it were to the governing Governor herself. He then answered their questions candidly, explained why he could not stay a moment longer, and moved on, wishing the best of luck as he left. What he did not do was draw attention to his pack and what it contained, or offer to search, or help the group in any way. Of course he felt guilty for not doing so, but he had heard the evidence of the other survivors who would no doubt draw together to provide mutual aid. Peter had his family to think of.

Rounding the bend, and still well within the boundaries of the hamlet, Peter's eyes met the chilling sight of four bodies, laid out in a row on a front lawn, their clothes soaked in blood, its crimson colour toned down by the dust that adhered to it. An adult male, an adult female, and two children – a boy and a girl. Someone had thought to cover their faces; someone who was not there; perhaps the sole survivor of a family devastated, or a kindly neighbour who had moved on to another collapsed property, praying for a better outcome.

As if this were not enough, past a thick hedge, a grieving woman knelt over the prostrate figure of a man, trying to coax him back to life. It was clear this was her husband, or at least her partner. They had been a normal elderly couple, more than likely enjoying their retirement together. Now she was alone, and at a time when she needed the support of her soulmate more than ever.

One hundred metres further on, a young lady in her early twenties stood rocking from side to side. She cradled the limp body of a small child in her arms and was mumbling to herself as tears dripped from her cheeks. An older man was attempting to reason with her and had his arms outstretched, trying to persuade her to give up the body of her daughter. He was not making headway.

The final memory Peter would carry from this place was that of seeing a lone man standing silently in his front garden. He wore a blank expression on his face. Having locked his eyes upon Peter, his head panned silently to the right, keeping pace with the stranger's progress. When his head could turn no further, it slowly turned back to face the front, the episode having elicited very little, or no interest.

Peter was only too glad to reach the second discarded sign for Raven Green; to be leaving such a pocket of disaster behind.

From experience, the lone traveller knew there were still eight miles to go.

Thick, lush hedges lay on either side of the road for the majority of the next mile. It was quiet; the most prolonged silence Peter could recall ever having experienced. The occasional chorus of birdsong reached his ears, disguised slightly by the interaction of a gentle breeze, but there was not a man-made noise to be heard anywhere. Even when standing on an isolated hilltop, while on holiday near the Welsh borders, there had been the sounds of a distant car navigating a narrow road, a tractor ploughing a field, an aeroplane passing overhead; but the new world produced none of these.

Putting the lack of noise to one side, everything else seemed normal. Along this section of the journey, street furniture had been sparse. A missing farm gate did not appear unusual as not all access to the fields beyond required one. More obvious to the frequent traveller would be the lack of electricity pylons that previously appeared as giants marching across the landscape. Although enormous, their absence was not obvious, simply because they had been erased entirely, leaving no stumps of non-metallic structure to mark their positions. However, the high voltage cables were not of steel, but aluminium and a dozen lay across Peter's path. Logic decreed they no longer carried power, but he had seen the advertisements warning children to stay clear because electricity had a nasty habit of arcing across to anyone who got too close, whether by climbing, or by flying a kite. Potentially, the dropped cables presented a continuous barrier that stretched for many miles in either direction; a barrier that could not be skirted. Peter was sure that if they were still live, they would be buzzing, and they were not. The fact that several of the cables were touching would surely have caused breakers to trip.

Selecting a fallen branch, lost in the hedgerow, Peter moved forward with caution, half expecting the hairs on his arms to rise. Thankfully they did not. Then, having reached what he judged to be the minimum safe distance, he lobbed the stick in the air, to follow an untidy arc, landing across three of the twelve cables. Nothing. Nevertheless, when he walked forward and crossed the danger zone, he did so being very careful not to come into contact with any of the fallen cables, just in case they held residual current, though he was not sure that was even scientifically possible.

There was not another building until the end of the sixth mile. It had been a public house and was still standing, although it bore the now familiar hallmark of a caved-in roof. There was evidence the patrons had been using the car park when the phenomenon struck, but there was nothing to suggest any of them remained. Peter could only assume the pub's customers, like him, were making their way home on foot as quickly as possible.

Deciding against further investigation, Peter moved on swiftly, bearing no remorse for not having stopped to look for survivors. Logic dictated the only people likely to have remained in the building were the landlord and his wife, both of whom lived upstairs. If they had sustained injury, there would have been plenty of people around at the time to tend to them before they left for home. The stark truth was that one or both of the proprietors would be making their own plans, or they were dead. Either way, pub landlords and their clientele were of less concern to Peter than was the welfare of Tess and Em.

Soon after, Peter reached a T-junction. Although minor in terms of the national road network, it represented something far greater - the midpoint in his journey home.

From there, the carriageway rose steeply, more steeply than Peter could have imagined from the comfort of his driving seat.

Plodding to the brow of the hill, he reached another familiar landmark.

The iron gates had vanished. No longer was the estate a fortress. The triple layered barrier of a panelled fence, high wall and dense hedge - designed to isolate the undesireables from the world of the haves – had been only as good as its weakest part. With no way of plugging the breach, there was nothing to stop the working classes wandering in as though they had a right to. Peering through the gap, Peter decided the residents did not need his help. Their beautiful, expensive cars had fared no better than his own daily runabout; their home had proven no less susceptible to the accelerated rust than any other structure he had seen since the nightmare began. Perhaps uncharitably, he was pleased their elevated position had not brought them favours when it really mattered.

He moved on.

The road dived back down the hill. Cars would normally have used the gradient to pick up speed for the section of dual carriageway that constituted nearly the whole length of the subsequent mile. At the midpoint stood the last vestiges of a business Peter suspected would have taken a lifetime to build. A forecourt, full of small 'previously owned' commercial vehicles, representing thousands of pounds worth of stock. All of it had vanished and no amount of insurance cover was going to bring them back. The dead were not the only victims.

The road returned to a single lane in either direction and climbed up another steep hill into a small village. The state of the buildings was as he had come to expect. The small school, one he normally paid little attention to, had not been spared. Thankfully, the children had been enjoying the long summer holidays so the premises would have been devoid of pupils when the roofs fell in. His stomach tightened as he thought how different things might have been if it had happened during a normal school day. A host of images and thoughts entered his head. A shudder ran down his spine.

Studying the wreckage of the building as he walked past, Peter suddenly noticed another body. It had come to rest in the middle of the playground. At first glance, the man appeared to be just another driver who had found himself without a car. The school railings had not offered any resistance as he had passed through them. However, there was something familiar about this body, dressed as it was in black trousers and wearing a white, short-sleeved shirt. Peter moved closer, confirming his worst fears. It was his friend and colleague, Brian, and he was very dead; mutilated; grated; stiff; distorted - cold.

The emotions Peter had been trying to suppress since he first paused for breath outside the prison walls rushed to the surface. Feelings of helplessness engulfed him; waves of sorrow broke over him. Gently slumping to the ground, Peter sat with his head in his hands. His mind was numb, no longer aware of his surroundings. Minutes passed as his tormented brain tried to cope with the trauma it had experienced. Not just Brian but his own narrow escapes, the motor cyclist, the road littered with human wreckage, the dead child, the old man and all the other horrors he had seen. He had suffered alone for many hours now and desperately needed to share his experiences with someone else, somebody close to him.

The need to cry rose from deep within his body, but he had not cried since his childhood and found it impossible to do so, despite the justification. Then, as quickly as his emotions had been overrun, order returned. Feeling sorry for himself would never bring relief. The only thing that might would be the warm embrace of Tessa and Emma. Knowing they were all right was essential to his wellbeing; being able to discuss with Tessa what had happened and what they should do next would help both of them in equal measure; and Emma would not stop worrying until both her parents were safely by her side.

Slowly, Peter rose to his feet, gave one last mournful look at his late friend and colleague, and resumed walking.

A large roundabout, serving five main roads, lay at the bottom of the hill, just to the east of the village. Arriving at it, only four more miles of his journey remained; he would be home within an hour.

The desire to see his wife and child consumed ninety eight percent of his thoughts, but there was still room to imagine what else being home might have to offer: the facilities of a bathroom; a change of clothes; a sit down in a comfortable arm chair; a large mug of tea in his hand; a biscuit barrel by his side. There was no harm in dreaming.

He wondered what Tessa would be doing while she waited for her husband's return, and concluded she would be spending her time calmly and productively saving what she could. No sooner had the thought occurred to him did he realise how ridiculous that scenario was. For one thing, Tessa would have no idea what the fate of her husband had been, and for another, she would have to deal with a distraught daughter who would be asking awkward questions about what was happening and where her daddy was. She, Emma, would be inconsolable until Peter's arms were squeezing tightly around her.

He remembered what she had been like when he had stayed in hospital for two days in the August of the previous year. On that occasion, Emma had cried almost continually until she had seen him, bandages and all, sitting on the bench outside reception, waiting to be collected.

These thoughts carried him to the far side of the roundabout and to the outskirts of his hometown. At first, the buildings were far and few between but soon became more and more frequent.

This was his stomping ground and it was the same story: the houses had no roofs or doors; television aerials, lamp posts, street signs and drain covers had gone; cars had been reduced to piles of rubber, plastics and other man-made materials. In fact, everything fashioned from steel, or anything using steel for strength had been affected.

Dozens of people could be seen searching through the ruins for anything of use to them. On the one hand, this was encouraging as it meant there were survivors, but on the other, it meant that gone were all hopes Peter had that his family had been spared the ordeal.

Three miles from home, a large oak tree stood tall and defiant among the chaos that surrounded it on all sides.

Peter continued on his way, refusing to be distracted by the activity around him.

However, his determination faltered on rounding the next bend. Approximately two hundred metres ahead, looters were targetting a small jeweller's at one end of the High Street. A heavily built man, dressed in tracksuit bottoms, a tee-shirt, and trainers, stood outside, armed with a baseball bat. A second man emerged from the damaged building, clutching a collection of gold chains to his chest. On seeing him, the first man promptly took up a firm stance and swung his bat as hard as he could. Peter saw the second man's head pivot round violently with the force of the blow and could hear the sound of his skull shattering. The lifeless body slumped to the ground. The first man then calmly wiped his bat clean on the second man's clothing, gathered up the gold, and strolled off.

Clearly, continuing towards the High Street would be too dangerous.

Instead, Peter decided upon a detour through the municipal park that lay to his left; a decision he should have made regardless of the circumstances as the pedestrian route cut at least a mile from his journey, bringing him fifteen minutes closer to his family.

The walk through the park was a peaceful one. It was a haven from all that was happening on the other side of the boundary hedge. The trees were untouched, as was the well-tended grass, and the long, winding, tarmac path. The only indication this tranquil oasis had not been immune to the ravages of the phenomenon was the total lack of a children's play area. In fact, all that remained were a few tractor tyres and some isolated patches of tree bark, used to provide a safe surface.

The electricity pylons that had stretched across the fields adjacent to the park had gone too, leaving an unblemished skyline; a definite improvement. So tranquil was the passage through the park, it felt almost a shame to leave it and return to the real world. Spurring him on, though, was the thought of being reunited with his loved ones, and by the realisation he could not see himself living out the rest of his life among the remains of the abandoned crazy golf course.

Back among the ruins, Peter could see the dim glow of the light at the end of the tunnel; a light that grew in intensity with every step. Burdened by his weighted broom handle, Peter could not run, but his pace nevertheless increased substantially. A steady plod became a long stride. Determination of purpose cast his gaze to the ground, straying neither left not right. Finally, having travelled many torturous miles, he turned the corner into his road.

Five hundred metres ahead stood his house, or rather, what was left of it. Suddenly he did not want to be there. This was the place that would either reunite him with his family, or break his heart forever. Clearing his mind of all thoughts, Peter walked slowly, shaking, terrified of what he might find. As he neared his goal, his eyes fixed upon the house, searching for any sign of life; taking in the extent of the damage – the missing roof; the collapsed fence. He was almost level with the garage, but still there were no signs to ease his anxiety.

Nothing.

17

Tessa woke again, confused by her surroundings. Reality, penetrating her sleep, had roused her several times already. The sound of rain upon the roof had woken her too. Jumbled dreams, interspersed with bouts of insomnia, had vied, one against the other, all night. Awake in the dark, she had lain, cuddling her daughter, wishing for nothing but the start of a new day. And when she woke again, she was grateful for having snatched moments of sleep, but instantly yearned again for the night to be over. Her final sleep had been the longest. She had woken from the deepest phase of unconsciousness, her eyes wide open, but her brain lagging behind.

Staring into the middle distance, she waited to receive an interpretation of the sights that met her eyes: the pattern of a bare brick wall where a waxed pine wardrobe ought to have stood; the bright blue of a nylon tarpaulin in place of the pastel shades of a soft duvet cover.

Then it all came flooding back.

So, this was not just a bad dream. Without the slightest forewarning, or the opportunity for preparation, she, along with everyone else about her, had been dropped into the centre of a uniquely hostile alien environment. Such a sudden and total upheaval would have been bad enough faced by a complete family unit, but they were not complete. Until Peter returned home, she had to cope alone.

Tears welled in her eyes.

Emma was still asleep, cuddled up tightly beside her mother. At intervals she let out a whimper, took a shallow, shuddering breath, or tossed her head from one side to the other. It upset Tessa immensely to see her daughter's sleep disturbed in this way and for a moment she contemplated waking her. But what would that achieve? Reality could be no better than her worst nightmare. Besides, the longer she remained asleep, the greater the chance her father would be home before she woke, being one less trauma she would have to face.

It was becoming lighter. Tessa began to hear noises outside. Other residents were stirring from their makeshift homes. She felt suddenly exposed and vulnerable. In her mind was the thought that at any moment a stranger might appear and see her in bed; nothing between them - no doors, no windows, no locks, and no privacy.

Tessa's eyes peered out from beneath the cover, just in time to see a middle-aged, dazed ghost of a man walk by, only three or four metres from the garage entrance. His hair, his face and his clothing were an even grey, coated with a fine dust, trapped in the fibres and stuck by sweat to every square centimetre of skin. A line of red ran down from his hairline; the only colour to be seen. This was a man who had been buried, or who had be searching for someone who was. It would be hard to recognise her own father if her were in such a state. Nevertheless, Tessa was sure she did not know him. This was not surprising as she knew hardly anyone in the neighbourhood to the extent she would smile at them in passing; even fewer with whom she would engage in any sort of meaningful conversation. Indeed, she would have been more able to associate pictures of cars with the right property than she would the residents of those properties. After the events of the previous evening, even that connection had gone.

The ashen man seemingly had no purpose; not so the younger man who passed by in the same direction some time later, holding a length of wood in one hand and a look upon his face that dared anyone to cross him. Whether he sought only to protect himself, or had set out to forage – using violence if necessary – Tessa could not tell. Taking no risks, she lay on her back beneath the sheeting, spreading her limbs wide to present as flat a profile as possible. Her movement woke Emma who immediately tried to relate to her mother the terrible dreams she had suffered, babbling as any five year old would, lacking sufficient vocabulary to express herself. Thankfully, her words did not draw the attention of the second stranger, but Tessa felt it had been a close call.

With daylight it had become far easier to properly survey the inside of the garage; to pile cardboard and plastic into some form of barrier. If unable to prevent looters entering the garage, is was at least able to disguise the interior from the outside. To this end, Tessa ensured the least interesting items formed the outer skin. Having done so, she moved her daughter and their salvaged property behind it, before preparing breakfast from the same menu as the night before – another crisp sandwich, washed down with lemonade.

Not yet ready to venture out, Tessa kept her daughter distracted by retrieving a bag of garden toys. An oversized tower of stacking wooden bricks found an alternative use as a construction kit; an old newspaper, put aside for decorating the house, became experimental hats and paper aeroplanes. As much as Emma enjoyed the activities, she could not help but ask where Daddy was and why they could only speak in whispers. There was no easy answer to either question.

Suddenly Tessa heard the sound of more footsteps. They neared and stopped, just out of sight of the main entrance to the garage. Her first thought was the man with the stick had returned, or someone like him. Holding Emma close, Tessa dared not breathe.

Whispering instructions for her daughter to keep quite still, Tessa grabbed the wooden handle of an erstwhile rake. Not knowing quite how she intended to use it, she moved closer to the large opening at the far end of the garage.

Peeping round the brick pier that formed one side of the entrance, she could see the figure of a man dressed in an old raincoat. Although he was partially obscured by a sizeable shrub, she noted his appearance as that of a dishevelled tramp; one who was currently staring directly at their house. She flattened herself against the wall and held her breath. Emma, frightened by her mother's behaviour, could no longer remain inactive.

'Mummy, I don't like it', she said, in a frightened tone.

The stranger's stare was instantly broken and his head spun round towards the source of the voice.

'Emma?'

It was Peter.

'Oh! Thank God you're home', Tessa cried as the reunited trio converged upon each other. 'It was just awful.'

'Are you both all right?'

'Yes, we're not hurt. I made up some beds and we've had something to eat', Tessa answered, embracing her husband, her voice trembling.

'I must say, you've both done very well', Peter said, reassuringly, looking at their makeshift home. 'You can't imagine how relieved I am to see you both. I've been walking for hours not knowing if you were even still alive.'

Emma was squeezing Peter's legs as hard as she could.

'Hello my sweetheart. I hope you've been looking after Mummy for me', he said, bending down, holding her tight. 'Come on, take me to see your bed.'

The three survivors stepped back into the garage, Emma taking the lead.

Physically, Peter and his wife were desperately tired, but their minds would not - could not - rest. At least, with Peter's return to the fold, each had someone with whom they could share their thoughts.

'Pete, what's happened? What are we going to do?'

Peter took his wife's fingers in his and looked down at her face, finding it tense with anxiety. His mouth managed a weak smile, hoping it would reflect in hers. It did not.

'Tess, I know you want me to have all the answers, but really I know nothing more than you. I can tell you what's happened, but I have no idea why. I'm not sure anyone does. All we can say for sure is that whatever this is, it's only affected ferrous metal. Unfortunately, that's used pretty much everywhere and this here phenomenon doesn't seem to care whether it's been painted, or buried in concrete. Thinking about it, it doesn't seem to matter whether the metal's wet or dry; old or new. I don't know. The prison's collapsed and there's devastation all the way home. I kept hoping I'd find the edge of the disaster area, but there doesn't seem to be any. What's worse, I met someone who'd come from Banton and she told me the same thing was happening there. That's at least another ten miles north of here. Until we hear otherwise, we have to assume it's happening all over.'

'All over? What, everywhere? The whole of England?!'

Peter did not give a verbal response but his eyes suggested she might not be thinking on a large enough scale.

'The World?!'

'Look, Tess, I don't know, but yes, maybe the whole damn planet.'

'Jesus, Pete.'

'I know, love. For the time being, all we can do is salvage what we can from the house and take it from there. God, I could murder a cup of tea.'

For Emma's sake, Tessa took hold of her own emotions, realising her fear would otherwise rub off on their daughter.

'Sorry, all I have is half a bottle of lemonade. I hope that'll do.'

Tessa's comment triggered Peter to think of the pack he had shouldered for the best part of thirteen miles. Having retrieved it and untied the handles, he deposited his treasure as a small pile on the floor.

'Feel free to tuck into anything you fancy, but go easy. I suspect coming by something to eat is going to be tricky over the next few days. I hope there is a rescue plan and that they get to us before that happens.'

Peter and Tessa shared a chocolate bar. Emma was given one of her own, albeit a smaller one.

Between nibbled bites, Tessa turned to her husband, mistaking him for the fountain of all knowledge he was clearly not.

'Do you think there will be a rescue party?'

In responding, Peter used the opportunity to test what he believed.

'Well, I've not heard any sirens, or seen any traffic on the roads. I haven't seen anyone wearing a police, or army uniform. I haven't seen any planes in the sky. I haven't heard any megaphones. In fact, I've seen nothing to suggest our salvation is imminent. It doesn't look good, but that's not to say this whole thing isn't contained within what we've seen and a few miles beyond. For all we know, at this very minute, the Government might be looking through their contingency plans, but the phone and radio networks are down so they can't broadcast advice. If they are poised to mobilise, I don't suppose they'll act until they know it's going to be safe for the people they want to send in – most probably the army.'

'So, you think there's a chance we'll be okay?'

'How the fuck do I know.'

'Peter, language!'

Tessa's eyes shot downwards to where Emma sat making a series of small houses from wooden blocks.

'Sorry, I'm a bit stressed. Assuming there is an end to this madness, whoever lies outside the affected area will have declared a state of emergency. If it's only the UK, the rest of the world are duty bound to help us. If it is contained within the coastline of Britain, I reckon we should see someone within a couple of days, tops.'

'And if it's not just Britain?'

There was a noticeable pause while Peter massaged his lips with his teeth.

'I don't know. I guess we just have to hope it is.'

As much as the couple hoped for the best, Pandora's Box had been opened; the thought that the whole world had spontaneously been robbed of all its steel had been put out there. Further considering the evidence did nothing but ensure its continued freedom.

Whatever the phenomenon was, nothing like it had occurred on Earth before. And it could not be overlooked that another phenomenon – never before witnessed by mankind – had coloured the skies just months before. Two unique events of such magnitude, taking place almost one on top of the other, could not be dismissed as coincidence. What was known as fact was that the meteor shower had been visible from every point on the planet. If the first event was in some way responsible for the second, it was likely both would have global consequences.

'Right, let's hope for the best and plan for the worst.'

In general terms, Tessa hated inspirational quotes, having developed a particular dislike for them since they had come to litter social media feeds. Nevertheless, she agreed with her husband's sentiment.

'Okay. Where do we start?'

'Well, rather than thinking what we don't have, let's concentrate on what remains. I mean, we still have plastics and various other metals, so it's not all bad.'

'No, I guess you're right,' his wife answered, trying hard to sound upbeat, but failing miserably.

Peter was determined not to become disheartened.

'Right, so we search the house and gather together anything that's useful and store it in here.'

Despite her nodding in agreement, Peter could sense his wife lacked his enthusiasm.

'Spit it out. What's wrong?'

Tears collected in Tessa's eyes, but no sound accompanied them, for the sake of their daughter who continued to play, seemingly oblivious to the change of circumstances.

'What about tomorrow, and the day after that? What sort of life will there be for Emma?'

Tessa was becoming morose.

'Whatever happens, we've got each other and we still have our health', Peter replied, trying to keep her negative thoughts in check. 'Besides, whatever this thing is, they'll have the brightest brains in the world working on a solution. With the technology we have nowadays, I'm absolutely sure this problem won't be around forever. It's bound to take time but we're going to get our metal back and rebuild. Christ, if you saw the state of London after the war, you'd never imagine it could become the city it is.'

Tessa responded without a hint of the former vibrancy with which she had spoken prior to the disaster.

'Maybe, but the only reason we've become so clever is that we have computers and none of those will work now, will they?'

'Right, enough of that. We've got lots to do. Short term we need to improve this shelter and salvage what we can. Medium term we need to get out of town.'

Tessa's head tilted slightly, querying her husband's last statement.

'Not in front of Emma.'

Tessa turned to her daughter.

'Em, darling, are you going to be all right playing while Daddy and I go just over there to fetch something?'

She pointed to the patio across the lawn, no more than fifteen metres away.

Emma said nothing but nodded, her fingers continuing to place uniform blocks to form rudimentary structures.

As her parents stepped from the garage, Emma's hand swept across the floor in front of her, bringing down every one of buildings. She then lay down, selecting individual blocks to represent people to whom she gave a voice.

'My bedroom is all broken and I can't find Kittums...'

Across the lawn, Tessa spoke in whispers.

'Well?'

'Look, there were looters in town and they've done things – killed people for a useless piece of jewellery. What's it going to be like when food becomes more valuable than gold? And regardless of the murders, there will be bodies everywhere going unburied and that will bring disease. If there is no medium term solution, long term we'll have to start a new life in the countryside – form communities and survive as best we can until this whole giant mess is sorted out.'

Tessa was horrified as much by the prognosis as by her husband's willingness to accept it as inevitable. Suddenly, making themselves comfortable while they rode out the storm had become a whole new life – a primitive life of violence, hunger and disease.'

'This is not what we brought Em into the world for. There's got to be something better to hope for.'

'I'm merely trying to tailor your expectations. There may not be anything better.'

'How can you be so damned cold about this?'

'I'm just trying to be practical.'

'And where do our families fit into all this?'

Peter looked at his wife as though he did not understand.

'Mothers, fathers, brothers, sisters, aunts, uncles,' Tessa prompted, delivering the list ever more rapidly before slowing again to pose her next question. 'What are we going to do about them?'

'Hmm,' Peter responded solemnly, casting his eyes at the floor.

This simple interjection, although delivered quietly, produced a disproportionate reaction, restoring animation to his wife.

'Hmm? Is that all you have to say? Hmm's not even a word. I have to confess, I was hoping for a little more.'

She produced a false chuckle and continued.

'The entire world's on its knees and there you go, calmly talking about how we're to move to the countryside and start an idyllic new life with a group of hippy friends we haven't even met yet. Have you even given any of our relatives a single thought?'

There was no hidden message to be decrypted. Tessa viewed his words and his proposed actions as those of a man whose veins ran with ice water – heartless and uncaring.

Peter paused before responding, hurt but understanding that her words were distorted by fear and anxiety.

'Actually, I've given them a great deal of thought and you're not going to like what I have to say.'

'Go on,' Tessa said, bracing herself for an argument. 'Let's hear it then.'

'Okay, let's start with Abby, shall we? She lives the best part of three hundred miles away. Even covering ten miles a day, which is all we could manage carrying all our things, it would take a month to get down there. We can't phone her, or send a letter to tell her to stay put. She'll probably be thinking of moving into the countryside herself, if she has any sense. We could get all that way down there and still never find her. That's assuming she's still alive.'

'You're not suggesting that we just forget about your sister are you?' Tessa said, amazed at her husband's callousness.

'Unfortunately, I am,' he said, without raising his head.

'All right, but what about Faye and her husband?' Tessa asked, 'or are you going to abandon both your sisters?'

'I'm not being funny, but they live fifty miles away. That's five days slog carrying all our possessions, and it would take us through some heavily populated areas with looters who wouldn't think twice about killing us all. Don't forget, I've already seen it. What's more, it's a dual carriageway most of the way, so the roads will be littered with dead bodies. By the time we would be ready to make the journey, those bodies will be decaying, which means disease and, as far as we know, there is no health service to come to our rescue if we do catch something. And, if we did manage to get there in one piece, there's no guarantee she or her Darren would be there. I don't like

173

it either, but we have to face the facts.'

'There must be something we can do.'

Voices were becoming raised. Peter took a deep breath. When he spoke again, he did so keeping his volume deliberately low.

'Yes, I could go alone. I could travel light and fast but, best case scenario, it would still take me four or five days there and back…if I made it back.'

'Well, you can't do that. It was bad enough waiting for you to get home from work. We couldn't cope with you being gone all that time. Couldn't we just wait here and hope that they come to us?'

'And how long would we wait? Things here are going to get worse by the day and all that time we wouldn't know their intentions, or whether they're already dead. What if they were driving at the time and their car disintegrated with the rest of them? I've seen what happened to those who were. As we speak, Faye and Darren might both be lying on a road, suffering multiple fractures, their skin grated by the tarmac, and what if they are? They could be God only knows where.'

'But we don't know that!'

'Precisely! We don't know anything other than what is in front of our eyes. Face the facts; we have to think only of ourselves from now on.'

Silence fell, broken eventually by Tessa who could bring herself only partially to accept her husband was right.

'My mother's only eight miles from here,' she said, testing to see just how ruthless her husband had become.

'Your mother has a heart problem. She has trouble walking to the shops. What if she is all right? What if we do take her with us? What then? We have no transport; no medication. She wouldn't last a week.'

'We can't just leave her.'

'I know. I'm just thinking out loud. I'll go tomorrow. It should only take a couple of hours to get to her place. How I'll get her back here I do not know. Maybe I can leave her there for the time being and pick her up on the way through.'

'You're going to leave her there until tomorrow? We can't begin to imagine what state she must be in.'

'While I agree and while I would love to leave this very minute, if she is alive you would hope her neighbours would look in on her and that she'll be okay until tomorrow. In the meantime we have to improve our shelter, find food and water and start putting in place an exit plan, or we're all going to die anyway. Give me today to get things sorted here and see if Frank and his family are okay and I promise I'll set out for your mother first light tomorrow.'

'Frank and his family? So you're not prepared to put yourself out for family but you're quite happy to go swanning off in search of a mate. Is that it?'

'Don't talk bollocks,' Peter snapped, his patience pushed to its limit. 'Firstly, you know as well as I do I can run over to Frank's house in something under five minutes. Secondly, if we are to leave town, I'd rather do it in the company of someone as handy as Frank. In fact, I'd go as far as saying that if he's not there, or if he won't go with us, I don't know what we're going to do.'

'And your grandad?'

Until then, Peter had deliberately avoided the subject of his grandfather, burying his head in the sand, content to believe the problem did not exist unless he gave it thought. The truth was he loved his grandfather more dearly than anyone else outside his wife and children, and while he could ease his conscience by telling himself the rest of his family could survive without his help, it was a certainty his grandad could not.

'It may sound callous,' Peter said, solemnly, 'but I hope for his sake he hasn't made it. He's eighty four years old. He's deaf and I bet his hearing aid doesn't work anymore. He's near blind and I can't see the prospects of him getting that cataract operation being very good right now. He's confined to a wheelchair that has probably gone the same way as all the other metal around here and he goes to the toilet in a bag. I can't see how we could possibly take him with us. If I go and see him, what can I do? How can I look into his eyes and tell him I'm abandoning him?'

Tessa could not provide an answer.

'I'll look in on him as soon as I've found Frank. With any luck it'll take less than an hour to get to the home and back, dependent on what I find there and who I run into on the way.'

Suddenly, Tessa could see her husband was as vulnerable as she was.

'I'm sorry.'

Peter looked at his wife through reddened eyes and forced a weak smile, accepting her apology. To speak would have revealed he was crying and he knew it was his duty to maintain the illusion he was strong; that he was a man who had no chinks in his armour; for the sake of both his wife and his daughter. Tessa could see through the illusion as if it was not there at all, but she too knew its importance and of her role in maintaining it for all their sakes. Changing the subject, Tessa invited her husband to take in the sights of the surrounding area.

Through the shrubs that remained, bordering his neighbours' gardens, they could see how the Cunninghams and the Oxfoots had spent their night.

One of the families had managed to retrieve a tent from somewhere, and had slung the canvas across two of a dozen two metre high wooden fence posts that still marked the boundary between neighbouring gardens. Their shelter was secured to the ground using string and makeshift wooden tent pegs.

The other family had followed suit. Theirs was of a similar construction, but instead of canvas they had utilised a sheet of clear thousand-gauge polythene, weighted down along the bottom edge using a number of ornamental bricks and a garden gnome. Condensation on the underside of the plastic sheeting prevented Peter and his wife from determining which of the families where in which shelter. Neither had yet risen.

'Right, I'll just say goodbye to Em and then I'm going to pop round to Frank's. Once I'm back, I'll go and find Poppy. Then tomorrow I'll hot foot it over to your mum's. Maybe when we leave – if we leave – we could swing by Faye's, although where she lives is a bit of a peninsular, so if we do land up there we'll have to retrace our steps a bit – we'll just have to play it by ear.'

The plan was simply drawn up but harder to put into action, Emma being reluctant to let her father out of her sight for more than a second.

'Please don't go Daddy', she implored, wrapping herself around her father's leg, restricting his movement, by pinning him to the spot.

Peter, grimacing, raised his flattened hands above his head as though he were miming a gabled roof, and growled. Then, having taken a deep breath, he exhaled, pushing his shaking hands down in front of him towards the floor, his arms under constant tension. He then spoke as would any man who was trying to sound calm and in control, but who was clearly neither.

'Now don't be silly sweetheart. You know where Uncle Frank, Aunty Joyce and Danny live. It's only a ten minute walk through the small park; I could run there in five minutes. I just want to see if they're okay and find out what they plan to do. Frank and Joyce are very practical people. We'd do well to team up with them. Besides, Frank is my best man for Christ's sake.'

'Don't swear Daddy.'

'That's right, Em, you tell him he's being naughty.'

Racked with guilt, for a few moments, Peter felt unable to respond. Emma had every right to be clingy; he had absolutely no right to lose his temper with her. His arms loosened, allowing his hands to rest gently on his daughter's shoulders.

Emma stood in silence, her ear pressed to her father's thigh, her arms linked behind him, her water-filled eyes staring dreamily into her mother's face. Peter's head faced downwards as though he had not the strength in his neck to keep it raised.

It was Tessa who broke the silence.

'Of course Daddy should go. Emma and I will be all right on our own for half an hour, won't we?'

She cocked her head to one side, attempting to illicit a nod of agreement from her daughter. However, Emma responded by issuing a small, disapproving sound from the back of her throat and then whipped her head through one hundred and eighty degrees, to stare instead at the brick wall of the garage.

Tessa leant forward, placed her arms around her daughter, and pried her free from Peter's legs. Emma wriggled and issued another disapproving sound from the back of her throat, but then turned and applied herself to her mother, cuddling her as only a small child could.

Peter saw his opportunity.

'No time like the present then,' he said. 'The sooner I'm off; the sooner I'll be back. Then I'll see to Poppy and then we'll make a start on searching the house.'

With that, he kissed his wife and daughter, gave a gentle wave at waist height, exited the garage, turned, and jogged away at a steady pace.

18

As soon as Peter was out of sight, Emma highlighted a new problem.

'I want to go to the toilet,' she said, her voice small and whining.

Her statement severed Tessa's line of thought. Neither of them had drunk much since the disastrous events of the previous evening, so the question as to where and how they were supposed to go to the toilet had not yet arisen. Emma having raised the issue, Tessa realised that she too was in need.

It was a problem. The bathroom upstairs was totally inaccessible. In any event, it and the downstairs cloakroom were both out of order. Emma could squat in the flower bed if need be, but this was not a long term solution and was not even a short term solution as far as Tessa's needs were concerned. To avoid having to bare herself to the world, she needed to dig a latrine and screen it off in some way, but therein lay another problem – they had nothing with which to dig even the shallowest of holes.

Emma stood with her legs crossed, wriggling uncomfortably. Looking about the garden for the best spot to designate as 'The Loo', her mum's eyes fell upon the perfect solution.

The property was serviced by a number of underground sewage pipes that in normal circumstances carried away the waste from the toilets, sinks, bath and shower. There were a number of access pits, facilitating the unblocking of the pipes as necessary: two in the front garden; one in the patio to the side of the house; one right in the middle of the lawn. For the most part they went unnoticed, but having lost their cast iron access covers, they had become hard to ignore.

The rectangular, brick-sided pit in the back lawn measured approximately a metre deep. At the bottom was a gully. It was ideal, although a little dangerous in the form it presented itself. To remedy this, Tessa found some gutter board that had fallen from the eaves and placed the sections over the hole to reduce the size of the opening. Emma was understandably nervous despite the planks. Nevertheless, being desperate, and having the encouragement of her mother who held her firmly throughout the ordeal, she managed to evacuate her bowels successfully. The paper towel Tessa had found in the garage made an acceptable substitute for toilet tissue.

The added beauty of this open air toilet was that it could be flushed. Emma's paddling pool was still two-thirds full of water, and her luminous green plastic seaside bucket provided the means for pouring some of it down the hole. Despite its ease of use, its practicality, and her daughter's successful trial run, the facility was still not ideal. Although Tessa was in growing need of it, she was not yet ready to drop her trousers in public, being unable to imagine a more exposed location. The phenomenon had robbed her of almost all her material possessions but it had not taken her dignity.

The garage provided a number of long wooden handles – all that remained of a variety of garden tools; a headless hoe and a headless rake among them. These she hammered into the soft lawn surrounding the inspection pit, using a brick, left over from when her husband had built them an all-singing, all-dancing barbeque, several years before. All that remained for her to do was to tie a blue nylon tarpaulin to the stakes. For this she used a weak, easily broken garden twine that could be readily snapped with the hands. With the construction complete, Tessa was only too keen to try out her handy work, it proving to be a triumph in the face of adversity. Through her own ingenuity she had given her spirits a much needed lift.

***

Jogging through the estate, Peter met with very few people, and those he did see eyed him with the utmost suspicion. The small park, nowhere near as big as the one he had passed through earlier that same morning, appeared as an oasis among the devastation. The grass was still short, the paths were still neat, and the trees still paid host to birds which could be heard, rustling the leaves as they hopped about among the branches, their lives hardly affected, save for the loss of a few man-made perches.

Once through the park, it was only a short distance to Peter's destination - the house of Frank Venner and his family. Peter had known Frank since their schooldays together. He had known Joyce ever since she and Frank had started dating, and Danny, their son, from the day after he was born, seven years previously.

The Venner property was in much the same condition as his own; if not, slightly worse. Having reached it, Peter's first task was to find the occupants, hoping none of them were still inside, buried. Recognising that to spend the night in such an unstable structure would be foolhardy, and in the knowledge neither Frank nor his wife could be described in such a way, Peter chose to begin his search in garden at the rear. His hunch proved to be correct, quickly discovering his friend had constructed a lean-to against the two metre high boundary wall at the bottom of the garden.

'Frank? Joyce?' Peter called at a respectable distance, not wishing to startle anyone.

Almost immediately, a head popped out through the plastic flap at the side.

'Boy, am I glad to see you?' Frank said, rushing forward to grip his hand.

It was a relief to see his friend so animated, doubting he would have displayed the same demeanour if he had lost either his wife or son.

'Are you all okay?' Peter asked, looking directly into his friend's eyes.

'Yes, only a few scratches and bruises,' Frank replied, pushing his arms out in front of him, rotating his wrists to show the full extent of his thankfully minor injuries.

'That's good to hear.'

Peter peered over his friend's shoulders, looking for the best view of the lean-to.

'Joyce and Danny?'

Frank looked back towards his hastily constructed shelter.

'There trying to rest. It's been exhausting for all of us.'

Having confirmed the Venners were in one piece, Peter was keen to get to business and then return to his own family as soon as possible.

He began by sharing his views as to the extent of the devastation, and concluded they should all leave town within the next three days, before things started getting really ugly. He suggested the two families spend the interim period preparing for the move, and that they then join forces in order to maximize their chances of survival. It was an unnecessary sales pitch, Frank being more than willing to join his friend. During the night, a long conversation had brought him and his wife to much the same conclusion and so he spoke for the rest of his family, without the need for further consultation. However, there remained one reservation, the Venners being reluctant to leave Hexley without first determining the fate of some of their relatives. Peter sympathised, explaining he and Tess were in the same position. Both men provided a precis of their own situation which in essence were different but the same. Distances, directions and numbers of relatives varied, but whether one hundred or two hundred miles away, the fundamental problems matched – lack of communication and infirmity.

It was an awkward subject to address and was not for either man to furnish the other with a definitive answer, but one for which each family would need to make their own decision.

'I told Emma I would only be gone half an hour; whatever that is,' Peter joked, indicating the absence of a watch on his wrist. 'Let me know what you intend to do. You know where we live. I do hope you decide to come with us. You know we'd value your company, and your skills.'

'You'll still be around for the next three days, right? I've got some things to talk over with Joyce, but I'm sure we'll see you before then,' Frank responded, trying to brave a smile.

There being no more to be said, Peter shook his friend's hand and walked from the property, raising his arm in a wave as he went. A short while later, having jogged back to the ruins of his own home, Peter was welcomed by his wife and daughter who were clearly relieved to witness his safe return.

Peter was quick to notice the new, hastily erected structure in the middle of the lawn and was immediately impressed at his wife's ingenuity in providing such a practical facility, demonstrating his admiration for her by becoming the toilet's third customer. Having finished, realising water would swiftly become a scarce resource, he declined her offer of passing him a bucket with which to flush the inspection pit. He considered her argument that if he did not, the hole would soon fill and become a health hazard, not to mention the smell, but concluded they would be gone from the place before any blockage had risen above the gully at the bottom. As for the odour, he promised to find something with which to cover the pit until it was needed. Tessa was not in agreement but let the matter go, there being more pressing things to think about, namely Peter's promised trip to the old people's home.

So as not to leave Emma believing her daddy was going to be absent more than he was around, Peter decided to delay his departure.

'I think the first thing to do is to make the garage more secure. It'll give us some privacy, provide a better night's sleep and give us somewhere safe to store whatever we can salvage from the house.'

Peter had three more tarpaulins like the one his wife had used for the toilet surround, any one of which was large enough to fill the hole left by the garage's missing up-and-over door, but the question arose as to how it could be held in place. Garden twine was not strong enough. A more practical alternative was the plentiful supply of luminous bright orange nylon rope that Peter had hoarded in the garage for years. It being the waste product of the cable-laying industry, a workman had been more than happy to leave it with Peter rather than haul it back to base. It did not hold knots well, but still Peter had kept it, hoping one day he might find a use for it. Soon his critics would be silenced, if only he could find some way of cutting it to length.

Even if that could be achieved, Peter wondered what he might then tie it to, all the nails and screws having disappeared, as had the drill and the hammer he would need to drive them into the wall.

'We could burn through the rope.' Tessa suggested, helpfully. 'I recovered a box of matches last night.'

Hers was a neat and practical solution. Not only could they reduce the rope to more manageable lengths, the technique had the added bonus of sealing the ends, preventing fraying. However, Peter had reservations.

'Good idea. That would definitely work, but I think we should save our matches – treat them like gold dust. They'll be hard to replace and I want to hold off having to start a fire by rubbing sticks together for as long as possible.'

'A length of aluminium then. We could sharpen an edge on the concrete. Or we could use a piece of glass? There's plenty of it about – wall mirrors and all sorts.'

Her husband liked both ideas.

'Yes, I could find a bit of glass and wrap a bit of sticky tape around it for a handle. That would probably do it. Then, when I've got a bit more time, we could use a road sign, or something. We could cut it down to size by bending it backwards and forwards until it snaps and then give it an edge. Nice one Tess.'

The fallen summer house provided a suitable shard of glass; the garage gave up a roll of masking tape. Tessa gathered a number of spare shards and placed them safely in a sealable plastic box, keeping one aside for immediate use. It had the curve of an Arabic dagger and once the wide end had been wrapped in corrugated cardboard and bound with tape, the similarity became even greater.

Having the capability of cutting the rope to whatever length the task required, the next problem to overcome was one of how to tie the rope to the tarpaulin without tearing holes in it. The manufactured holes had lost their metal grommets. Without them, if rope was passed through and then pulled tight, placing the material under tension, the flat, blue weave would simply part. Thankfully, Peter knew the solution.

Selecting a small, smooth stone from a flower bed, he pushed it into the polypropylene, forming a polyp on the other side, and then tied the rope tightly around its base. The trial knot held firm and proved to be a complete success, allowing the couple to move onto their next problem - finding an anchor point around which to tie the other end of the rope.

To fix the top of the sheet, Peter would have liked to have slung the rope over the roof joists, but with it being a flat roof, the boards lay directly against them, requiring an alternative solution. He realised the most obvious answer would be to pass the rope through the gap between the top of the garage wall and the bottom of the roof deck, were it not for the fascia boards, still attached to the ends of the joists. This begged the question, why they remained in situ when the nails driven through them had disintegrated? On investigation, Peter discovered the pitch used to seal the roof was acting as a glue, securing the boards to the roofing felt. In effect, they were hinged along their entire length.

With the help of his wife pushing on the inside of the fascia with a long stick, Peter was afforded access to the ends of one of the joists, enabling him to loop the rope around it at one end, then the other. Unfortunately, there were no corresponding fixtures at the base of the wall, but there were plenty of broken concrete roof tiles which could be stacked along its entire length, pinning it to the floor. To complete the job, Peter positioned two lengths of wood diagonally across the opening to brace the tarpaulin, tying it off in several places.

With a little ingenuity, the garage was soon ready to receive salvage from the house and provide them temporary accommodation until it came time to move on.

'Right, now that's done, I'm going to nip down town to see if Poppy is all right.'

Tessa appeared uneasy.

'Pete, I know I gave you a hard time about rescuing our families, but now you're going, I really don't like it.'

'Me neither, but I've got to go. We both know that,' he replied, pushing two black plastic dustbin sacks into his pocket, just in case he found anything during his trip worth salvaging.

'But what if you come across someone with a baseball bat? You told me yourself you had seen people killing each other down there.'

Her husband paused for thought.

'Don't worry. Two can play at that game.'

With that, he rummaged through a pile of unsorted detritus in one corner of the garage, quickly retrieving an inherited bat; one he had kept on the off chance he and Emma ever wanted to play French cricket in the park.

'Where on Earth did that come from? You don't even play the game. You hate sport.'

'It was my Dad's. Anyway, if anyone jumps out at me, I'll knock them for six,' Peter said, playfully swinging the bat at shoulder height in the direction of deep square leg.

Peter could see his wife was in no mood for humour.

'It's okay Tess. Twenty minutes there. Find Poppy. Figure out what to do with him. Twenty minutes back again. Bosh. I won't even need this,' he said calmly, swinging his father's bat idly at his side. 'Believe me, I intend to do everything I can not to meet anyone; mugger or otherwise.'

Seeing her mother wrap her arms around her father, Emma followed suit, clinging tightly to both parents' thighs. After a few moments, Peter pulled away sufficiently to be able to look into his wife's eyes.

'To be honest, I'm more concerned about leaving the two of you here alone. I want you to remain in the garage and keep the glass knife with you at all times. You never know.'

'That's hardly practical. I'll cut myself.'

'Then I'll do something about it before I go.'

Within only a short time, Peter had fashioned a scabbard from the flap of a cardboard box and most of the remaining roll of masking tape. It included a belt loop through which he passed a length of orange rope, and a piece of garden twine attached to the base of the scabbard to secure it to Tessa's thigh and thus stop it flapping about; a technique adopted from the gunslingers of the Wild West.

As though she was incapable of performing the task, Peter then tied the orange belt about his wife's waist and the twine thong about her leg.

It was then time to leave.

19

Peter's departure was met with resistance, but Emma, having seen her father keep to his promise once already - returning from Frank's house as quickly as he had said he would - was quicker to let him go a second time. It helped that he was going to see Poppy – Emma's pet name for her great-grandfather. She loved him dearly, especially because he had a pet mouse which he would pull from his jacket pocket on demand and keep from running off by holding it between the palms of his hands. She had never actually seen it - despite being invited to peer into the hole in his grasp, framed by his crooked thumbs – but she had heard it many times. Peter had heard it too when he was a young boy, it having taken many years before he realised the mouse was merely the product of an old man's hands, liberally coated with moisturising cream, being squeezed together, expelling trapped air with a squeak; that and a child's imagination. Under normal circumstances, Emma would have wished to accompany her father, but that was when they had a car. When she heard the visit involved walking into town, she soon experienced a change of heart. Peter used his daughter's reluctance to his advantage, but feared, in the days to come, they would be walking an awful lot further than Emma had the ability to comprehend.

***

The old age pensioners' home lay only two miles from the Allerton's ruined property, at one end of the High Street. This is where the major shops were to be found and, in all likelihood, the worst of the looting. For Peter, there was no avoiding the area, but there were steps he could take to reduce the possibility of confrontation along the way.

Adjoining the housing estate was a large industrial site, accessible to pedestrians via a road, common to both areas. For many years, four concrete bollards had denied vehicles passage along it, placed there by the council at the residents' behest, to stop the large volumes of commercial traffic that once thundered through. To provide access for emergency vehicles, a locked metal gate spanned the gap between the inner two bollards, the key to the padlock being in the possession of the professionals who might need to open it. The gate, the padlock and, no doubt, the key were gone, but there were no longer any vehicles to take advantage of the situation.

The road beyond the bollards avoided the residential homes that lined the main road down to the centre of town and would lead Peter to within a quarter of a mile of his grandfather's lodgings without having to pass even a single domestic property.

To describe this area of once thriving small-to-medium sized businesses as having been devastated was to make an understatement of biblical proportions. It suggested the site had merely been laid to waste. In truth, many of the buildings had relied so heavily on the use of steel in their fabrication, they were better described as having been obliterated. In many cases, no trace remained to prove they ever existed at all, other than the foundations upon which they had stood. This was particularly true in the case of the breaker's yard that had been home to hundreds of neatly stacked cars, awaiting dismantling and the crusher. Even the concrete floor was undetectable, buried as it was beneath a liberal application of sludge, thanks to the effect of rain on the heaps of fine rust particles.

Overall, it looked as though contractors had done a very good job in meeting their obligation to clear several square miles for redevelopment. However, the area was not entirely bereft of features.

A large area at the far end of the industrial site belonged to the district council and was home to one of their many recycling centres. The daily collections had been brought there in refuse lorries, together with a steady stream of public vehicles, dumping unwanted recyclables that were too big to be left at the roadside.

All the skips were gone, and in the case of the one reserved for metal, so too had its contents. The discarded wood survived, but it had spilled across an area twice its original size. Likewise, the clothes bank now resembled an oversized jumble sale, one that had experienced a herd of bargain hunting women rifling through the garments with gay abandon. Many hundreds of newspapers, having been set free, had blown across the site in all directions, until the downpour had brought them to the ground and glued them there. Huge vehicleless tyres remained in sets, the disappearance of the dumpsters and tractors having, in some cases, been so swift their tyres remained upright, standing on their tread. Fences, gates and refuse collection vehicles may have gone, but there remained a mountain of glass; another of garden vegetation; a third of pink sacks, containing plastics and paper and the residue of tin cans that had not survived. Most importantly, the pink sacks still contained plastic bottles; some with lids; many without. Those with caps in place were the most desirable, being ready to fill with water without the need for Peter having to rummage for a screw top that fitted. Undoubtedly, these were items to be harvested, but that was best left to the return journey, or perhaps a dedicated second trip. Peter had not yet decided how he would transport his grandfather back home, but whatever method he chose, or was forced to adopt, it was unlikely his hands would be free.

Just as Peter had hoped, not another person moved among this wasteland, allowing for swift progress, confident he was safe.

A tract of land, belonging to the railway companies, marked the border between industrial site and the centre of town. It appeared as though a scheme to lay track along its length had run out of money before the job reached completion. Here, Peter could see, for half a mile in either direction, a neat bed of ballast supporting moulded concrete sleepers, nestled into the stone chippings at regular intervals. The only clue to the fact there had been a fully operational, main-line railway running along this section was the presence of two unbroken parallel shadowy lines.

Logically, the inherent dangers normally associated with crossing railway lines no longer existed, but having had the lesson drummed into him from an early age, Peter could not help but look both ways for oncoming trains. He felt foolish when he realised what he was doing, but he was prey to the same forces that caused him to use the indicators at every junction, even if he were in the middle of nowhere and it was three o'clock in the morning.

The road on the far side of the track skirted round one end of a large, modern housing estate. There was no contact to be made with other survivors at this point as the developers had surrounded the entire area with a two metre high, brick-built wall, breached every so often by narrow roads, leading inwards. The wall had given those within a sense of superiority, helping them overlook the fact they had paid exorbitant prices to live in undersized boxes, with paper-thin internal walls, built on plots so small they struggled to achieve the status of having 'pocket handkerchief' gardens. The residents of these boxes were the type of people Peter judged would have suffered the most, having measured their quality of life in terms of how many material possessions they owned. What, Peter thought, had all these years of snobbery achieved? And how would these people manage without their status symbols? As enthusiasts of executive cars, the sights that must have befallen the residents would have been heartbreaking – BMW, Mercedes,

Lexus; the choice of the up and coming, and the arrived; all gone.

Walking towards the large roundabout that formed the hub of the town's road network, voices could be heard emanating from the other side of the wall. For the most part Peter could not make out what was being said, although it was clear it was not relaxed conversation. Only one phrase was decipherable, it being spoken with urgency and at greater volume than the voices of the rest of the party.

'Shh! Footsteps.'

The voices fell silent.

The roundabout not only fed the road to the housing estate, but also served the main road to Billingford - his mother-in-law's home town - the entrance to the car park for Hexley's main supermarket, and a dual carriageway which continued both north and south.

The roundabout had not always been there. Within Peter's memory, its predecessor, a junction on the edge of town, fed roads half as wide as these and through open fields.

Since then, the sleepy town of his childhood had expanded year on year, consuming every centimetre of undeveloped land. Where once there had been a small bungalow resting in the middle of a large garden, there now stood a dozen houses. It was a necessary evil. The population had increased nearly nine fold over the past two hundred years; a statistic Peter was only too well aware of, it having been his view for some time that the Earth was home to too many people. Perhaps the disaster was God's way of stemming the expansion – at least nature's way, the disaster not having changed Peter's views as to the existence of a God one bit.

The four lanes of the dual carriageway had cut a swathe through the town. Not only had they eaten up acres of unspoilt land and divided the community in two, they were unsightly; crash barriers, signposts daubed with graffiti, and towering lampposts doing nothing to enhance the appearance of the local environment. The road being a no-go area for pedestrians, planners had thoughtfully provided an underpass. Few used it though, fearing the muggers and drug addicts who patrolled the area after dark.

The alternative to the tunnel had been an unattractive steel footbridge, painted in battleship grey, which carried the residents of Hexley safely above the roar of the traffic. It too had its drawbacks. To rise to such heights meant climbing a flight of steps on one side and negotiating a slope on the other, the gradients of which had been made as shallow as possible to enable mothers with prams to use them. This meant that a crossing of only twenty metres or so had been increased to one of several hundred, and required more energy than most pensioners were able to muster.

In one evening, the phenomenon had rendered the planning decisions of the local council entirely inconsequential, the footbridge having been swept away; the cars that had passed beneath it having been utterly destroyed.

Peter crossed the carriageway to be faced by an embankment, thickly planted with trees and shrubbery, its intended purpose having been to dampen the ever present noise of the cars and other motorised vehicles which had, until recently, thundered past. For this purpose, the thicket barrier had proven most effective. However, its sound deadening properties were incapable of containing the babble produced by a multitude of raised voices, penetrating the foliage from the far side.

Peering through the undergrowth, Peter could see clearly the town's largest car park and the remains of the supermarket it had served. Vast crowds had gathered on the tarmac, busily looting. Food was already scarce and these people had plainly decided to procure the dwindling supplies for themselves. The scene was anarchic. Half their number were scrabbling through the remains of the store, salvaging anything that was vaguely edible. The other half were hell bent on robbing the successful ones of their pickings, no holds barred. Repeatedly, in the space of only a few minutes, Peter was witness to one callous murder after another. Normal, everyday members of society had armed themselves with anything they could lay their hands on. A variety of sports equipment: cricket bats; baseball bats; snooker cues. Others relied on lengths of timber, pulled from the wreckage of their homes. All were capable of staving in a man's skull.

The acts of violence did not stop with the men. Women and children fell beneath the weight of the blows. Babies were torn from their mother's arms, to be tossed to the floor like sacks of rotten vegetables, so that food hidden within their shawls could be harvested. One woman, apparently coming to the aid of her husband, had mounted the back of an assailant and was busy gouging out his eyes with her long finger nails. The man screamed in agony as blood began to trickle in rivulets down both his cheeks. His cries brought no leniency.

Peter was not unaccustomed to scenes of rioting and looting, but they had been on the television, via news broadcasts from other countries, rarely his own. Prison uprisings, of which he had seen a few – large and small - were a different matter, offenders usually being more concerned with damaging as much government property as possible, than with injuring anyone, unless they were members of staff trying to quell the riot. This was the first time he had seen civil unrest in the flesh. He stood still for a moment, wondering what these people must have been like before disaster removed any reference to normality, and failed to reach a conclusion. Just two days previously they would have offered each other the unused portion of their car parking tickets. Seemingly, the phenomenon had taken their metal, but replaced it with a licence to kill one another. The two aspects were wholly irreconcilable.

Although there were probably still pickings to be had, it was obvious there was nothing to be gained by securing further supplies if it was at the expense of putting his life in the hands of one of the many self-appointed executioners. Instead, keeping under cover, Peter gave the area as wide a berth as possible.

Thankfully, the buildings that stood along his revised route were of no interest to the looters: a car showroom; a church; and a washing machine repairer.

The home in which Peter hoped to find his grandfather stood just off the main High Street. Peter and his family had battled long and hard with the authorities to get a placement there. It had been the perfect choice - convenient for visiting and the shops were within easy reach for those reliant on wheelchairs.

In the end, to the relief of all concerned, the council had capitulated. As it transpired, the Allerton's insistence had made very little difference. Whether Poppy had been housed in Hexley, or been forced into a home nearer to the terraced two up, two down house he had lived in for the previous forty-seven years, it would have mattered not. The two homes were only five miles apart, which made little or no difference to Peter who undertook the journey only once a week, and by car. As for the proximity to the shops, Peter's grandfather had never plucked up the courage to leave the confines of the home, the noise of the traffic being overwhelming; the unevenness of the pavements threatening to jar his back. In retrospect, the decision to fight had resulted in no tangible benefit during the two years prior to the disaster. It had, in fact, led to an unanticipated disadvantage, the close proximity to the shops placing the home in close proximity to the looters.

Like every other building in the vicinity, Glendale Lodge had failed to escape the devastating effects brought about by the accelerated rusting process and was in a very poor state of disrepair.

The best part of a day had elapsed since the event and still residents were to be seen shuffling round the small car park in their dressing gowns and slippers, their addled minds unable to comprehend what was happening to them. Others, those who retained their mental faculties, but little else, sat with blankets drawn up around them, grouped together on mattresses at one end of the car park, well away from the building. The members of staff had clearly done what they could for these ageing refugees, but many were noticeable by their absence. They too had families and could not be blamed for putting their spouses and children first.

The home had catered for a variety of customers, ranging from those who were simply no longer able to look after themselves in their own houses, to those in the advanced stages of dementia. The latter never ceased to unnerve Peter on his weekly visit with his wife and daughter, that being under normal circumstances. One particular old lady would often wander into his grandfather's room asking if it was the right stop for the number thirty-two; always the same number. Peter had always tried to be kind, suggesting she might like to try further up the corridor, but his grandfather would have nothing of it, swearing at her profusely, annoyed that he was forced to spend his twilight days locked up with a bunch of mad people. He had a point.

Without the constant care and supervision they were used to, all the survivors of Glendale would be dead within a day or two. It was inevitable. For some, this would present a welcome release, freeing them at last from an unending series of waking nightmares. Until then, at least they were suffering no more than they had been already. Not so those who still possessed a keen mind, imprisoned in a worn out body. They looked pitiful; wasted; forgotten.

A glance at the faces of the survivors told Peter his grandfather was not among them and that a search of the two-storey building would be necessary – a daunting prospect. To reach the entrance, he had first to negotiate a crowd of fragile men and women whose unnatural stares would make the bravest man experience second thoughts.

Peter looked for a clear passage and caught the eye of an old woman with badly stooped shoulders.

'Hello Billy, I've been wondering where you got to.'

Peter smiled and sidestepped round behind her. She did not think his actions rude. In fact, she had already forgotten the encounter.

Just then, a care assistant emerged from within the building, as surprised to see him as he was her.

'Boy, am I glad to see you? I could do with some help.'

'Look love, I don't mean to be rude, but I came to see if my grandfather's all right. That's all. I've got to get back home. My wife and kid need me.'

The woman was disappointed - that much was obvious - but she also understood.

'What's his name?'

'Henry Allerton, room number seventeen, upstairs.'

The mention of his name brought an instant change in her expression. She could no longer maintain eye contact and began fumbling for words.

'It's okay, you can tell me. I can handle it.'

'I'm sorry Mr Allerton, Henry didn't make it.'

At first, Peter did not say anything. He felt numb, but then, to his surprise, relieved. What would he have done with an eighty-four year old wheelchair-bound man who had no wheelchair? A man that had cataracts, was stone deaf in one ear, was partially deaf in the other, and relied on a plastic bag for going to the toilet.

'Where is he? I want to see him.'

The carer guided the visitor through the space where the security-controlled double doors had hung, across the foyer to the lift where she stopped at the edge of the exposed shaft, and looked down. Peter followed suit and saw immediately what had become of his grandfather.

Henry Allerton, a week short of his eighty-fifth birthday, lay in a crumpled heap alongside another of the care assistants, at the bottom of the shaft which formed a pit, a metre or two deep. Both were very much dead.

'The lift must have been at the top when it happened,' the carer said helpfully. 'I checked to see if they were still alive, but there was nothing I could do.'

'That's okay, I'm sure you did your best.'

The pair stood in silent reflection for a moment.

'I feel I should bury him.'

'How?'

'I know it's not possible, but I still feel that I should.'

'Have you seen my Billy, I know he's around here somewhere?'

It was that damn woman again.

'Why don't you hurry up and die,' Peter thought, angrily.

The carer guided the old woman back outside, one hand placed gently behind her shoulder.

'Come on Mabel. I'll look for Billy. You stay out here with your friends.'

When the carer returned, she found Peter apparently searching for something. Without saying a word he walked off purposefully, reappearing a few minutes later bearing two bed throws, a small plank of wood – probably the front of a drawer – and a small lipstick.

'I'm sorry, I forgot to ask your name.'

'Rita.'

'Hello Rita. My name's Peter. Pleased to meet you.'

She smiled sheepishly.

'Rita, would you hold these for me?' he asked, passing her the coverlets and other items.

She took them from him.

Peter then carefully lowered himself down into the pit where he immediately set about attending to the corpses. First, he straightened them out, crossing their arms upon their chests. He then removed anything from beneath the bodies that looked uncomfortable to lie on. He then checked their dress, fastening the odd button here and there, smoothing out creases, neatening their clothes and tidying their hair. Finally, he took the bedding from Rita's outstretched arms and placed them, one over each of the bodies.

'What was her name?' Peter enquired, indicating his grandfather's companion.

'Beverly.'

Peter took the piece of wood and having written a short memorial inscription upon it, placed it with reverence in such a way that it lay on both the deceased at once.

Back on ground level, Peter said a prayer directed towards his grandfather, but one that also encompassed all those who had suffered, and those who continued to suffer. He spoke awkwardly. As an atheist he had not spoken a prayer in many years, but his grandfather was a believer and he spoke the words for him.

'Sorry Grandad, that's the best I can do.'

20

With her husband away determining the fate of his grandfather, Tessa's nesting instinct encouraged her to tidy the interior of the garage. Having discovered a dustpan and brush that Peter had kept beneath his workbench, she set about sweeping up patches of powdery rust, broken glass and the cobwebs of spiders that had not the faintest idea anything untoward had happened.

Anything that had survived, but which was no longer of use, was added to a growing pile of discarded items, dumped beneath the lilac tree in one corner of the Allerton's garden: the plastic handles of several tools; the casing of a now defunct electric heater; the arms from a set of deckchairs, to name but a few. A plastic box containing a number of old toys kept Emma distracted for a while, but only a while. Soon she began to whine and then sniffle. At first, Tessa continued her work unabated, blocking out the noise as best she could, but as her daughter's emotional state deteriorated, Emma's noises became too invasive to ignore. The temptation was to shout. If it had been her husband who complained she might well have done, but this was not an adult who would understand the actions of a woman under stress, later to forgive her for her outburst. This was a child who had every right to be upset and deserved her mother's compassion.

'Come on,' Tessa said brightly, lifting Emma to her feet. 'Let's surprise Daddy.'

The hastily devised plan was for both of them to re-enter the house, on the understanding that if it became too dangerous they would have to abandon their salvage operation until Peter's return.

Mother and daughter re-entered the kitchen from the patio.

In the hunt for something to eat the previous evening, Tessa had already partially cleared the downed plasterboard ceiling, working with failing light, her eyes operating beyond their normal limits. In re-entering the house, she thought she knew what to expect, but daylight revealed something far worse than her memory and imagination had prepared her for.

Without a roof for protection, overnight rain had permeated down through the house to the smallest recesses of the ground floor and, in seeking the lowest point, had saturated everything standing in its path. Water dripped steadily from the exposed floor joists overhead; every surface was cold and wet to the touch.

The 'white goods' - the washing machine, the dishwasher, et cetera - had been reduced to small piles of plastic and rubber, lying on the floor beneath worktops which remained in place, supported by the base units which themselves remained wedged in position. The doors of the units had fallen off, but internal shelves remained supported on plastic pegs at each corner.

The wall units were a different matter, the individual panels and pelmets having fallen and scattered in all directions, adding to the chaos.

Keeping her daughter close by, Tessa worked methodically, sifting through the clutter, ensuring nothing that might prove useful was missed. The tall cupboard that had stood next to the fridge-freezer had fallen apart, as had the fridge-freezer itself. Tessa swiftly ejected the composite sheets onto the patio, revealing a treasure trove of sealable plastic storage boxes beneath, enough to fill two black plastic bin liners, torn from a virgin roll, about fifty in number.

Most of the contents of the freezer were still edible but would not remain so for long, everything having defrosted. Although the cardboard outer packaging was soft, dirty, water logged and coated in melted ice cream, the food itself - breaded fish, chicken nuggets and beef burgers – had been individually sealed in plastic and remained fresh. So too were the many varieties of vegetables, stored in opened plastic bags but sealed with clips. Two loaves of sliced white bread had been squashed out of shape, but otherwise remained edible.

Mixed with the contents of the freezer were the contents of the fridge. Packets of ham, bacon and cheese, tubs of sauces and spreads had survived, but the eggs, jars of jam and honey, and most of the fresh vegetables had become fallen casualties.

Tessa suspended her search in order to place as many of the salvaged items as possible in the cool box she had found in the garage the previous evening. Although there were no ice blocks to chill the interior, nevertheless she hoped to prolong the life of the recovered food by shielding it from the heat of the sun.

Back in the kitchen, Tessa found a variety of fruit, crushed and spoiled, beneath a fallen cupboard. More useful was the discovery of two unopened bottles, one of orange cordial, the other of lemonade; a roll of cling film; and a box of matches. Emma remained close, helpfully holding open carrier bag after carrier bag while her mother filled them. Every so often the search would pause while Tessa removed full bags to the patio, creating more space in which to scavenge.

Tessa retrieved more storage boxes, this time containing food - six varieties of breakfast cereal. There was milk too, but without refrigeration she doubted the three of them would get through all sixteen pints before it curdled, even if they were joined by her mother and Peter's grandfather. Thankfully, there were also two cartons of UHT milk to be found, both having a very long shelf life. Tessa had bought them in case of emergencies, but had never envisaged the circumstances under which they would finally be used.

Peter had always thought his wife's obsession with stackable storage boxes an expensive indulgence. However, being able to retrieve so much food because it had been stored safely, she felt vindicated; something her husband would hear of on his return.

Mother and daughter ferried another haul out onto the patio. The inventory continued to grow: one medium sack of potatoes; one packet of sultanas; one squeezy bottle of tomato ketchup; one tub of multi-vitamins; one bag of dry pasta shapes; one bag of spaghetti; one packet of lasagna sheets.

Then there were more of Tessa's life-saving boxes, containing numerous things with which to make drinks with and to eat: instant coffee; cocoa powder; milk shake flavouring; custard powder; flour (three types); sugar (three types); and rice (white and brown).

Although productive, the search was nevertheless unpleasant, one area standing out from the rest as being particularly disgusting, every surface covered with slime – akin to rummaging through the contents of a slop bucket, spilled into a child's toy box. The cupboard had been stacked full of tinned goods, the protective metal casings having disappeared in the same moment. Gravity then pulled the varieties of content downwards, mixing one with another and the whole. Rain had then diluted the lumpy mess, ensuring the cocktail spread further than would otherwise have seemed possible.

The Allertons had kept the first aid kit in the kitchen and some of it had survived: a tub of antiseptic cream; a roll of surgical tape; a robust plastic bottle containing cough mixture; another containing children's liquid analgesic; sticky plasters; a tub of headache tablets; a variety of sterile bandages; and a sling. None of it would be much use for mending broken legs, or treating a burst appendix, but they were prized all the same.

A bottle of cooking oil remained intact, and a box of tea bags had escaped rain damage, sealed as it was in cellophane. Amazingly, a large plastic bag of table salt lay in a puddle, the contents remaining dry.

Tessa retrieved a number of plastic plates and beakers that had belonged to Emma, now commandeered for use by the whole family, all the normal crockery and glassware having smashed into hundreds of pieces - all but a pair of glass ovenware dishes, complete with lids.

A bottle of washing up liquid remained on the window sill, alongside another of anti-bacterial hand cleaner, a pair of rubber gloves and a large vase, still stuffed with fake plastic flowers. The spring of the pump dispenser had vanished, but the contents had escaped unaffected.

All that remained of Tessa's professional set of steel saucepans were the wooden handles and the copper bases. Her extensive collection of baking tins and trays had all but disappeared, flakes of non-stick material mixing with dust, mixing with rainwater.

From beneath the gaping hole where the sink had been, she retrieved a wide variety of cleaning fluids, disinfectant and washing tablets. Some of these, she thought, might be particularly useful in combating infection.

Some utensils - four wooden spoons of differing sizes, a silicone spatula and a plastic potato masher – were still perfectly useable. However, nothing remained of the six-setting steel cutlery set, meaning the family would have to rely on the plastic ones Tessa had already salvaged.

Half buried beneath a mound of recipe books, Tessa found a bulk pack of a dozen half-litre bottles of spring water and three two-litre bottles of soda – lemonade and cola. Of the recipe books, even if the pages had not been stuck together, their content had been rendered useless by the phenomenon. References to oven temperatures, weights, measures and cooking times had become irrelevant.

The final items given up by the kitchen were a plastic mixing bowl, another multi-pack of crisps, a box of freezer bags, a funnel, a wooden chopping board and a ball of string – tougher than the garden twine.

'Right, Em, that's the kitchen done.'

For each carrier bag that Tessa hauled to the relative safety of the garage, Emma carried just one item, clutched in folded arms, the occasional grunt indicating the enormity of her effort. Although this helped her mother in only a very small way, the job provided Emma both purpose and a welcome distraction.

Witnessing her mummy place the last of the goods inside, Emma adopted the stance of a workman - legs spread apart, elbows pushed out, and knuckles resting on her hips. All she needed to complete the picture was a child-sized hard hat.

Her mother could not help but smile.

'Thanks Em. Daddy's going to be so proud of you when he gets to hear how hard you've worked.'

Having felt vulnerable to robbery at the hands of passing looters, with the removal of the last salvaged item from the patio, Tessa felt more at ease. Being an organised woman, her priority was then to unpack each bag, sort the contents and tidy each item away. In this way she knew what she had, what had to be eaten first and where she could lay her hands on each item. The task requiring her focus, it made sense to allow Emma to amuse herself outside – to allow her to grow in confidence and adjust – as long as she did not stray from the lawn.

Having bagged the last of the thawed freezer goods and squeezed them into the cool box, Tessa's decision to allow Emma to disappear from sight was suddenly put into question.

Her daughter must have been close by as her words were spoken in a normal voice and clearly audible.

'Mummy, who's that man?'

Sitting on her haunches, Tessa sprang to her feet, her limbs launching her through the side door, hands ready to pull her daughter out of harm's way.

Her eyes fell upon the features of a complete stranger – perhaps a neighbour of many years, but one she had no recollection of ever having seen before. Something in his demeanour caused her concern to escalate.

Instinctively, Tessa reached to her side with her right hand, and with her left, pushed Emma behind her back. Having unsheathed the glass blade, she raised it to shoulder height, the tip pointing downwards. The stranger's reaction was unexpected. Clearly he did not think a woman would use such a weapon, or maybe he doubted its effectiveness.

'Put that down. Just give me what I want and I won't hurt you – either of you.'

Tessa stood her ground as the man cautiously took several steps forward, his outstretched hand cautioning her not to do anything she might regret.

'It's okay, I won't take everything.'

Tessa's features strengthened, but still the man doubted her resolve.

'Now, I know you want to avoid any unpleasantness, especially in front of the little'un.'

His eyes briefly diverted towards Emma who peered back from behind her mother's waist, the fear written across the five year old's face doing nothing to alter the assailant's intention.

The man's eyes flicked back to Tessa, silently urging her to reconsider her position, but seeing no hint of capitulation he lunged forward, aiming to disarm his victim and claim the rewards.

The man was a poor judge of human nature; of the capability of a woman protecting her family.

Without a single word having been spoken in return, Tessa - scared and enraged - brought the weapon down, accompanying the blow with the grunt of a tennis pro.

The shard's tip pierced the back of the man's hand. Tessa withdrew the blade, bringing her clenched fist back to her shoulder, prepared to strike again as necessary. It was not. The injured man screamed, cursed, clutched his wrist, and ran off, his body stooped forward.

Satisfied the danger had passed, the warrior mother lowered her arm and immediately sank to the ground, adrenalin causing her whole body to tremble. Seeing Emma's renewed trauma, Tessa's outstretched free arm wrapped about her daughter's waist, pulling her downwards so that each might be soothed by a comforting embrace.

At that same moment, Peter drew level with the garage, two dustbin sacks - each full of plastic drinking bottles - knotted together and slung over one shoulder. Hearing the scream, he ran the last metres, only to see a man scurrying from the scene, leaving a trail of blood in his wake.

Unsure whether to give chase, his instinct was to first check on his wife and daughter.

He found both in a state of shock, crumpled on the ground, arms entwined.

'You okay? What's happened?'

'Some man tried to steal our stuff.'

Tessa sounded breathless, her voice shaking.

'Pete, I stabbed him,' she added, incredulous.

'Badly?'

'In the back of his hand.'

She raised her right hand to inspect the state of the weapon. The tip of the glass shard was missing, the remaining portion smeared with blood –

thankfully not her own.

'I was so scared, especially when he just kept on walking towards me. I couldn't help myself. I just reacted. Pete, what am I going to do?'

Peter lowered himself to the ground, shuffling between his wife and daughter so that his arms could gather both of them to him. His arms squeezing them tightly, his hands then had sufficient reach to remove the improvised knife from his wife's grasp, casting it away to one side.

'What do you mean?' he asked, smoothly.

'Are you not listening to me? I stabbed him! That's grievous bodily harm, or even attempted murder. I could go to prison.'

Peter's expression became confused. His hand turned his wife's head towards his, drawing it forward so that his nose rested on hers.

'Tess, you're not going prison. For a start, what you did was self-defence. There's not a jury in the land who would find you guilty. Besides, what you did was pretty minor in comparison with what I've been seeing. I don't want to say too much in front of Em, but I've just witnessed things you wouldn't believe normal humans are capable of.'

For all her husband's words, Tessa still seemed unsure.'

'Look, Tess, the guy underestimated you and got what he deserved. That's the end of it.'

In the brief lull that followed, Tessa realised her husband had returned with a bunch of empty bottles, but without his grandfather.

'So, how did you get on in town?'

Peter could not answer directly, aware how the news might further impact their daughter.

'Em, why don't you take us inside and show me what you've both been up to.'

Pride and keenness to impress her daddy proved the perfect antidote to Emma's latest upset. Wriggling free from Peter's embrace, she leapt to her feet and grabbed his hand, eager to pull him into the garage.

There was just time for an exchange of knowing glances between parents and a whispered sentence.

'Tess, my grandad; he didn't make it.'

His wife reacted with a multi-facetted expression; one that demonstrated shock, enquiry and sadness, all at the same time.

Yanked to his feet by a hand many times smaller than his own, Peter lifted his free index finger, indicating to his wife they would talk again on the subject, at a more appropriate time.

Peter was given the opportunity to admire the fruits of Tessa and Emma's hard work and responded with appropriate praise. Subsequent conversation was then directed by Emma asking a simple but inevitable question.

'Daddy, where's Poppy?'

Peter closed his eyes and thought for the briefest of moments. When they opened again, his face bore a kindly smile.

'Poppy's going to stay at the home. The nurses there are looking after him. He's too old to come with us. He said he would like to but his legs are not strong enough. He said you can tell him all about it someday.'

'Daddy, why's Mummy crying?'

'It's nothing darling. Grownups just do that sometimes.'

In the hope of avoiding the conversation deepening, Peter returned to the subject of the morning scavenge.

'You've done well. The sight of all this food makes me realise I'm hungry. How about I knock something up for us before we see what else we can find?'

'I'll do it,' Tessa responded. 'I know what we have and what needs to be used up first. Besides, you're a hopeless cook.'

Peter smiled and said nothing in his defence, accepting she was right.

Emma looked withdrawn. Peter thought for a moment.

'I know what I can do while we're waiting,' he said brightly, turning towards his daughter. 'Wait here with Mummy. I won't be a minute.'

With that, Peter stepped outside the garage, walked across the lawn and into the ruins of the Allerton's house. He returned a few minutes later, laden with a plastic storage box.

'Here you are; your favourite toys. Okay, some of them have suffered a bit and they're all a bit wet, but we can soon dry them out.'

Emma took no time reacquainting herself with the selection, hugging sodden plush toys, pleased to see them; mourning the fallen.

It was not long before lunch was ready – buttered bread and cold meats. The defrosted food would have to wait until later when they had built a fire. Once they had eaten, Peter guided his wife into the garden.

'I know it makes me sound heartless, but it's okay about my granddad. With the way things are, it's probably best he was put out of his misery then and there, rather than deteriorate over days and weeks because we can't look after him. Saying that, coming face to face with what happened to him, and the state of the other residents at the home, it made me realise how I've been letting logic rule my decisions. When I was there, all I wanted to do was rush over to Billingford to see if your mum's okay, but I couldn't. It would have taken me three hours just to get there and back. Even if I sorted her out and reassured her that we're going to pick her up on the way through, I'd have been gone for at least four hours and there was no way of telling you. I had to come home but with each step I took, the guiltier I felt. Thoughts have been filling my head how she might be there all alone, waiting for someone to come to her. So, do I set off for Billingford now, or do we spend the rest of the day salvaging what we can and I go tomorrow?'

Tessa replied with a question of her own.

'How bad was it?'

Peter looked at his wife for clarification, but quickly turned away again, as though it was too painful for him to see the sadness her face portrayed. Tessa's hands cupped her husband's cheeks, gently twisting his head, re-establishing eye contact. She would not speak until he answered.

'Pretty bad,' he said, solemnly.

'Then you still think we should leave town?'

'I'm sure of it. There are bodies everywhere and no one has the means to bury them, or the inclination to try. There's going to be disease, the food's going to run out and that can only mean desperate people doing things they wouldn't previously have imagine doing, just to stay alive. We have to go.'

'Then our priority must be to finish making our preparations. If Mum's okay now, she should be okay for another twelve hours. If she's not, it's probably too late anyway.'

Tessa fell silent. Soon after, fresh tears could be seen rolling down her cheeks.

Peter moved closer to place a comforting arm around her shoulders.

'What is it? Your mum; stabbing that man; this whole crazy, God awful affair?'

'Not really. It's just that I found this in the kitchen.'

She held up the remains of her calendar, rain soaked and bereft of its coiled wire spine. Picking up one of the loose leafs, she eyed it wistfully.

'We're supposed to be going over to Karen and Dan's for tea next Saturday. I guess we won't be doing that now.'

Peter did not know how to react, finding it difficult to understand why his wife attached so much significance to such a trivial event, and chose to remain silent, squeezing her tighter; the only means to comfort her he had at his disposal. Tessa was not content to upset herself just the once, choosing to look at other entries, penned on subsequent pages.

'Stop it will you,' Peter snapped. 'That life is over. Don't you get it? You're just making it harder on all of us.'

Tessa dropped the flaccid pages at her feet, freeing her hands to catch her head as it fell forward. Her cries took on a renewed vigour. Emma, hearing them, forgot her toys in an instant, dropping them to the floor, her urge to rush outside and throw herself at her mummy - to grip her tightly - being suddenly far more important than keeping herself amused. Her bottom lip began to quiver.

'Mummy, please don't cry anymore.'

Peter altered his position to hold both his wife and daughter.

'I'm sorry. I shouldn't have spoken to you like that.'

He remained hugging them for a few moments until their tears subsided.

'Right, Em, there's no time to waste. Can you fetch me the bags. I'm going to have another look round inside.'

Emma was pleased she knew exactly where to find the carrier bags and disappeared inside the garage, leaving time enough for her father to speak as few words in private, albeit in hushed tones.

'Okay, tomorrow it is. I just hope your mum's okay, or I'll never forgive myself.'

It was Peter's turn to venture inside the house. Save for a brief foray into the lounge to retrieve his daughter's toy box, this was the first time he had seen the extent of the devastation within. His eyes fixed upon the smallest details, one after the other, each resulting in a sigh and a shake of his head.

Tessa and Emma looked on from the relative safety of the patio. The living room offered little that had not previously been salvaged by his wife: a few sodden cushions; Emma's fibre tipped pens; a handful of pencils; and a pair of curtains which, although damp, would serve well as blankets, if they were given time to dry. However, the display cabinet was in a sorry state, the shelves having collapsed, taking with them the family's collection of expensive ornaments. The DVD player, the cable TV box, the television, the stereo, the lamps and the mirror, were all beyond repair. A ruined box of tissues rested in a pool of water.

Seemingly forgetting her daughter was in earshot, Tessa shared her thoughts across the room.

'Do you know, the worst part of all this is that you hope to see your children grow up, get married to an accountant and settle down happily ever after. You want them to have more that you did. What can Emma look forward to now? Instead of giving her a fine china dinner service on her wedding day, we'll be pushed to find a full set of plastic cutlery.'

For the sake of their daughter, Peter responded light heartedly.

'An accountant? I always hoped for someone with a personality.'

'You know what I mean. What about Emma's future? Her education?'

His attempt at humour having failed, Peter changed tack.

'Firstly, we don't even know that this is permanent. If it is, it will be up to us to teach her to read and write. We'll gather together a library of books. She'll be okay.

'Look on the bright side. At least we won't have any money worries anymore.'

From the living room, Peter ducked out of sight beneath the lean-to in the hall, formed by the collapsed floorboards of the bedroom above. In the darkness, his wife had been unable to open the doors of the built-in cupboard, but with the advantage of light and brute force, he found a way inside. It was a worthwhile effort, Peter retrieving further useful items: a pair of training shoes each; three nylon bags; several hats; gloves; newspapers, useful for lighting fires; and an assortment of coats.

Alone with his thoughts, Peter's mind was struck with a harsh reality - how hard everything was going to be in future. Simply finding something to drink would be an everyday problem. The water might be contaminated. Cats and dogs would become feral and could prove a real danger. They might even become food. The thought of someone feasting on poor old Podge did not bear thinking. That brought him to realise he had not seen the family pet since he had left for work the previous morning. That begged the question, why had Emma not mentioned him? Was the fact she had not done so a measure of how deeply she had been affected? On the subject of animals, Peter presumed the bars and cages within zoos must have disappeared, releasing all manner of beasts into the public arena, and there would be no dart guns to subdue them. Then there was the subject of infection. A simple bite, or a scratch might prove fatal.

Overwhelmed, Peter spoke aloud but for the ears of no one.

'I just want this thing never to have happened.'

The immediacy of getting home to his family, the scavenging, and thinking about what needed to be done - it had all taken his mind off the situation. But what had been a series of crises to overcome had already become the norm – the way things would always be.

Tessa could see no movement; could hear no sound.

'You all right?' she called.

Her words made Peter realise he had given up – that he was standing motionless, in a daze. If it had not been for his wife and daughter relying on him, he felt he would have remained that way until eventually he was absorbed by the ruins.

His purpose restored, Peter pushed though into the dining room from the hall. Most of its contents were either ruined, or of no practical use: the dining table and chairs; an extensive collection of unplayable DVDs; a second television.

It did, however, give up some medical books that had survived undamaged, having miraculously remained dry. Peter flicked through pages that described the signs and symptoms of countless illnesses, together with causes and treatments. He could see the value in keeping it, but doubted many of the suggested treatments would still be available, not with the loss of so many hospitals, scalpels and doctors.

Many of the family photo albums had escaped too, but Peter knew there would not be room to carry them all – probably very few. He also knew that thinning them out would cause agonising decisions to be made, but comforted himself in the thought the task would be low on their list of priorities; a can to be kicked down the road.

It was time to tackle the rooms upstairs and that meant finding and using a ladder. Placing it where the stairs had been seemed the natural choice, but with the collapse of one of the bedroom floors, it was not possible to find a suitably flat area of ground on which to place the ladder's feet. Nor did the first floor offer a safe edge on which to lean one. The alternative was to gain entry through one of the upstairs windows, preferably to the master bedroom as it boasted the largest opening.

The aluminium two-piece ladder had been secured to the exterior wall of the house by means of two sturdy steel brackets and two corresponding steel padlocks and chains. It now lay on the patio, small plugged holes in the brickwork being the only evidence that one had ever been attached to the other.

Having positioned the ladder against the house, with the aid of his wife, Peter made his ascent.

The non-opening sections of the double glazed window remained intact, but the opening casements had fallen outwards to the ground, offering easy access to the bedroom.

Peter stepped gingerly into the wreckage while his wife and daughter waited patiently on the lawn.

Every so often he appeared at the broken window through which he cast a bulging pillow case, or a bag, preceded by a warning to stand clear. The contents of these varied: toiletries; clothing; stationery; Emma's most beloved toys; carefully selected reference books; and bedding. Each time, Emma ran to retrieve the salvage and helped store it safely in the garage, out of sight of potential looters who might otherwise be tempted to kill for it. With the experience of the morning fresh in her mind, Tessa had already strapped a replacement glass knife to her side and was fully prepared to use it.

Peter reappeared at the window.

'This will come in handy when the matches run out,' he called down, holding aloft the lens from a magnifying glass, before burying it at the centre of yet another bulging pillow case which he then dropped onto the lawn.

'That's probably going to be the last, but I'm going to try to reach the boxes that were stored in the attic.'

Wriggling up between the joists, the forager entered the roof space, although such an area no longer existed. Tiles and timbers had fallen, partially burying the numerous storage boxes that Peter had hidden there out of sight. The majority had suffered damage but were still in situ, thanks to the flooring he had laid over the top of the insulation. For Tessa and Emma, it was worrying to see Peter working on such a high, unstable platform, but at the same time comforting that by standing back, they could follow his progress as he grubbed through the remains.

Several times he could be seen moving roof parts to one side, only to be rewarded with access to useless items such as Christmas decorations and school work dating back to his childhood.

Peter could be seen placing items into a bag, none of which excited him, but then something triggered a profound change in mood.

'I've found it!' he shouted, triumphantly holding up a large book for his wife and daughter to see.

Waiting until he had climbed back down to the bedroom window, Peter wrapped the last of his finds before casting them to the ground. Next through the window was Peter himself, committing his right foot to a conveniently placed step situated just below the level of the sill. It felt secure. With both hands holding the tops of the two ladder rails, he then swung his other leg out of the bedroom, placing his left foot on the next rung down. This should have felt equally secure. However, the transfer of his body weight was sufficient to sheer the rung flush with the rails on either side. The unexpected failure jarred Peter's muscles, causing his heart to leap into his mouth. Then, without a moment to recover, his right foot lost its support too, dumping him unceremoniously on the ground next to his precious book.

Miraculously, despite a fall of four or five metres, Peter escaped serious injury, although he faced the prospect of aching limbs in the morning. Given he was able to walk, if not hobble away, his only concern was how it had happened. The answer presented as a fresh dusting of powder, whitish in colour. Evidently, although not a ferrous metal, aluminium had fallen victim to a second phase of the phenomenon.

Tessa rushed to her husband's side, only to be wafted away by a man who was less interested in the pain he suffered than the wider implications of the event.

As if she could not have noticed the missing ladder herself, Peter pointed a flattened hand at the spot where it had stood, moving his arm up and down, drawing attention to the fact it was not only absent at its base, but all the way to the top.

'Damn!'

'What does it mean?' Tessa asked, her voice trembling.

'It means, my dear, that by the end of this thing, we cannot count on having any metal left at all. So much for using the street sign as a blade.'

'Oh, dear God. What'll we do if it all goes?'

'I guess it'll be a matter of forgetting the Bronze Age and bracing ourselves for a return to the Stone Age. We have no choice.'

'How can you be so calm about it? I know our ancestors did all right, otherwise we wouldn't be here, but they learned the skills they needed from the day they were born. What the hell do we know about working with stone, or hunting, or making clothes out of skins? I mean, who knows any of that stuff these days?"

'I'll tell you who knows at least some of that stuff, and that's Frank.'

'What are you on about? He doesn't knap flint, or tan leather.'

'No, but he is an expert with the longbow and they haven't been standard issue since the Norman times. If he doesn't know how to make stone tools, he's the sort of person who'll pick it up pretty quick.'

'We don't even know if he's coming with us.'

'Don't worry, he will, and even if he doesn't, we have this.'

Peter unwrapped the book he had held aloft from the remains of the attic, just minutes earlier. It was a guide to survival techniques, written by an ex member of the Special Air Service - the SAS – Britain's military elite. Peter's mother had bought it for him in his early teens; a time in his life when he did little else but daydream about being marooned on a desert island. Back then, he had tried out some of the shelters in his mother's back garden and had put together a survival kit just in case the worst ever happened. It never had of course - until now – and even if one of his kits were still in his possession, it had consisted of an old flip-top tin, containing, among other things, safety pins, a needle, a craft blade and a miniature metal-cased torch. None of these would have survived. Nevertheless, much of the text and the illustrations remained relevant, with or without metal – of any kind.

'This will be our Bible. It could prove to be the most valuable thing we own. Some of the references mention knives and corrugated iron, fishing hooks and the like, which are clearly no longer relevant, but it also shows ways around it when you don't have them.'

With that, the brass garden tap, and the copper pipe that supplied it, both fell from the exterior wall of the house, degrading to nothing more than a powdery residue even before the detached parts had reached the ground.

'Damn. Sometimes I wish I was wrong to think the worst.'

Trying to concentrate on what they had, not what they had lost, back inside the shelter of the garage, Tessa began to take stock of the day's pickings while Peter sat down to read his all-important survival guide.

'Here's something...,' he said, pawing at the pages. 'It says we should allow four pints of water per person per day, for say ten days, by which time we should have found a new source. That works out at least fifteen gallons per family. More if your mother comes with us. Whichever way, it's more than I thought. Lucky we've still got the paddling pool.'

'You must be joking. Emma and her friends have been playing in that for the past three days. It's got bits in it.'

'It'll be fine. We'll just have to strain out the grass and insects and be careful not to disturb the sediment on the bottom.'

'I think you'll find we have to boil it too.'

'Have you been taking a sneaky peek at my book? That's like the very next sentence. It says here we have to boil it for eight minutes, but as we don't have a watch anymore, we'll just have to guess. Once it's cooled, we can put it in those bottles I brought back from the recycling centre.'

'And just how do we intend to boil it?'

'I don't, that's your job tomorrow, while I'm fetching your mother.'

'Cheers.'

'I see you managed to save your Pyrex casserole dishes, although I don't know how they'll stand up to direct heat. I wish the aluminium had held out just a little longer. I'm sure we could have found an aluminium saucepan somewhere.'

'Okay, I'll give it a go, but I'll need you to help me get started.'

'Of course I will. I'll build some sort of hearth and we'll use the charcoal from the barbeque as fuel. I don't suppose we'll have enough, but perhaps Frank has got some.'

Tessa, attentive to her husband's spoken thoughts, proffered her own.

'If he hasn't, we can always burn wood. There's plenty of it lying about – the remains of the fence panels and the summer house for a start.'

'Good thinking.'

Peter found himself suddenly in awe of his wife, realising what a tower of strength she had been right from the beginning. She had sheltered their daughter through the night; she had provided meals for them; she had built an improvised toilet; had fought off an assailant; and she was willing to drink water from a paddling pool, boiled on an open fire. All this from a house proud mum with interests in cinema and sewing.

Tessa noticed her husband staring at her.

'What?'

'I've underestimated you.'

Peter did not expand in what way, but by the tone of his voice, it was meant as a complement.

Without a further word being said, Peter returned his attention to the book.

'It also says here that we should add bleach.'

Tessa grimaced at the thought, but her husband continued without reaction.

'Tomorrow, remind me to hunt out a plastic teaspoon so we can measure it out properly. I don't want to kill us.'

By evening, the garage had been transformed into a reasonably comfortable apartment. Thanks to their decision to buy cheap patio furniture, fabricated entirely from moulded plastic, they had a table and chairs at which to eat their evening meal.

Wood from the shed provided fuel for the fire that cooked the burgers for tea, which were sandwiched between slices of bread that it was judged should be eaten quickly, before they went mouldy.

The act of gathering wood for the fire brought about a couple of last minute finds. Firstly, a reel of fishing line, sadly without hooks – useful for both its intended purpose and perhaps also for setting snares. Secondly, a dozen individually plastic-wrapped firelighters which could each be broken into multiple pieces to eke out the supply.

Emma was the first to succumb to sleep. As she snored quietly, Peter and Tessa lay exhausted beneath their improvised bedding.

Peter could hear his wife sniffing like a blood hound.

'What the hell are you doing?' he whispered, jovially.

'Jesus, we stink.'

'That's something you're going to have to get used to.'

Tessa did not respond, but inwardly doubted whether she ever would.

After a pause, Peter withdrew his arms from beneath the covers and held his left hand close to the improvised candle lamp.

'My ring!' he exclaimed.

Where, for many years, there had been an immovable gold wedding band, there was now only a white indentation encircling his finger.

Tessa sat up, confused and angry.

'Gold too?' But gold doesn't rust. Everyone knows that. It's a fucking element. It stays in the ground for millions of years and still comes out shiny.'

Despite all that had happened since the phenomenon first made an appearance, Peter was still shocked to hear his wife swear so strongly.

'You've still got yours,' he said.

Tessa looked panicked.

'Quick, pass me some tape. Anything as long as it's sticky.'

'I've got some gaffer tape.'

'Perfect. Tear me off a small strip and hurry.'

Peter knew what she intended it for.

'It won't protect it. You're wasting your time, and the tape.'

'Just give me the damned stuff.'

Peter obliged. His wife then quickly wrapped it round her finger, over the gold band, smoothing the adhesive against the metal.

'It's no use. It won't make any difference. A thick layer of concrete did nothing to save the steel, so what chance have you got with a piece of sticky tape?'

Tessa said nothing, but her expression changed suddenly. Almost immediately, the index finger and thumb of her right hand began massaging the tape that encircled the ring finger of her left.

'It's gone, hasn't it?'

Tessa nodded.

'I need to cut this off.'

Peter looked confused. His wife, on the other hand, appeared to know exactly what she was doing and quickly found the box of glass fragments. She picked one out at random and broke it further, pinching the smaller piece between her fingertips. Carefully, she then began cutting across the width of tape, eventually peeling it away to reveal a line of residue stuck to it. Laying it carefully to one side, she took up the roll, cut a small strip from it and pressed it against the contaminated length, overlapping fresh tape at both ends. Having done so, she folded the laminated strip, bringing the ends together to reform the ring. This she place in the plastic box with all the reverence of closing the lid of a coffin. Despite having achieved her goal, she still looked sad.

Peter reached out and held his wife's finger tips. Neither he nor his wife spoke for a moment.

'At least I have something,' she said finally.

'It's a shame mine is gone completely, but I still have you and Emma and that's what counts, and believe me when I say, I am never going to let any harm come to either of you.'

Lifting the blankets, Peter encouraged his wife to lie down close by his side. Beneath the covers, he could not resist feeling the indentation caused by the missing ring. Thoughts ran through his head leading, quite unexpectedly, to him letting out a satisfied laugh.

'What's so funny?' Tessa asked, confused.

'Oh, I was just remembering the looters, killing each other for a few gold trinkets, none of which will exist by now.'

21

Driven by a sense of guilt, Peter was keen to make an early start for his mother-in-law's house, there being some distance to travel and no telling what condition she might be in when he got there. A day and a half had elapsed since disaster struck and in that time Eileen had suffered two nights with perhaps only her dog, Freddie, for company; if, indeed, either of them had survived.

Despite the growing urgency for his departure, Peter had two matters to attend to before setting off. The first was to feed his hunger, to sustain him over a journey of approximately sixteen miles. He estimated the round trip would take five or six hours, but knew it might take considerably longer, depending on Eileen's state of health and how she coped with the relatively long distance on foot – eight times further than a round trip to her local parade of shops. If all went well, their next journey would be in search of Peter's sister, Faye, and her husband, who lived more than fifty miles away. The awkward truth was that Eileen was nowhere near as spritely as she had been only a few years previously, and had come to rely on a growing menu of medication to keep her alive, stocks of which Peter anticipated would be exhausted within a matter of days; weeks at the most. Unless the Allertons could fabricate some form of transport, Peter knew the journey to his sister's would be agonisingly slow and the constant effort would, in all likelihood, be the final nail in his mother-in-law's coffin. Unfortunately, Eileen and Faye lived in completely opposite directions, ruling out the possibility of collecting Tessa's mother on the way through, saving time and unnecessary stress on Eileen's legs and heart. And when they reached Faye's house, whether or not they were successful in finding her, the journey was destined not to end there, the area being far too populated for it to be considered any safer than it would be to remain in Hexley.

The second task was to set Tessa up with the means to boil, and thus sterilise, their stock of water; enough to sustain two families during their journey to the countryside. Being aware how susceptible the human body is to dehydration – lasting only three to five days without it - both Peter and his wife agreed that securing a good supply of potable water should take precedence over everything else for the entire duration of his absence.

Breakfast took no time at all, consisting as it did a bowl of cereal each, making use of the dwindling supply of milk before it soured. Peter kept back a dribble though, hoping for a cup of tea before his departure.

No longer hungry, all three members of the Allerton family gathered together sufficient concrete roof tiles to form a crude hearth. The first batch of paddling pool water was to be boiled in one of Tessa's oven-proof glass dishes, resting directly on a bed of recovered charcoal briquettes. Although the fuel was easy to ignite - the family having matches and firelighters to hand – it was clear from the outset the process was going to take a considerable amount of time.

'Let's think about this,' Tessa said, candidly. 'The charcoal will take about half an hour to ash over. Then we need to bring the water to the boil. Then we need to keep it boiling for eight minutes. Even if the Pyrex dishes hold out, we can't fill them more than half way or they'll boil over – say about three pints. How many did you say we need?'

'About thirty gallons.'

Already Peter was sounding worried and his wife had not yet finished.

'That's about eighty batches at about an hour each. That's more than two working weeks. The charcoal's not going to get us very far. I know we've got plenty of wood to burn, but still... By the time you get back from Mum's, I'll be lucky if I've processed a couple of gallons at most.'

'Hmm, I've thought of another problem,' Peter added, glumly. 'Your dishes sit nicely on the charcoal, but we can't very well balance them on a pile of burning wood. I'll have to reconfigure the bricks so the edge of the glass sits on them. Best I hang around until you've finished the first batch to see how you get on.'

The charcoal having developed a film of grey ash over its surface, Tessa gently lowered one of her two surviving glass dishes onto the tiles, arranged so that only the edge of the vessel was supported. This exposed the vast majority of its bottom to the considerable heat. Disappointingly, the water seemed to take forever to come to the boil, and when it did, the job was still only half done.

'Now what do we do? I've got to time eight minutes. We've got no clocks and I can't very well count four-hundred-and-eighty elephants, can I?'

'Just guess.'

Tessa shrugged her shoulders and fixed her eyes upon the turbulent surface of the water, her lips silently forming words, their movements becoming more and more pronounced as the estimated minutes passed. Finally, she broke her stare and lifted the dish of thoroughly boiled water from the coals, wearing salvaged oven gloves to protect her fingers. Before she had even attempted to pour the first batch into bottles, she immediately placed her second salvaged dish over the heat.

Peter offered to test the processed water for purity. Without waiting for his wife's response to his suggestion, he dipped a clean mug beneath the surface, brought it level and pushed a teabag into the scalding hot liquid. Meanwhile, Tessa used a second mug to scoop up some of the remaining processed water, her intention being to pour it into one of the empty plastic bottles her husband had scavenged from the remains of the recycling centre. In the absence a clean funnel, the task was made more difficult, but Tessa showed a steady hand and swiftly filled the container half way, managing not to burn herself in the process.

'Bugger!'

'What's the matter, Hun?'

'The damned bottle's melted.'

Peter put his mug of tea to one side in order to give the developing situation his full attention.

'Poo,' he said, seeing the now concertinaed plastic. 'I guess, in future, you're gonna have to let it cool a bit before you pour.'

'No shit, Sherlock.'

Peter did not react well.

'I don't need your sarcasm. In fact, I don't need any of this shit. I was only trying to help.'

'Look, Pete, we're both on a short fuse. Maybe you should get going and leave me to work this out by myself.'

'Sorry, you're right.'

With that, Peter took up his cricket bat - now sheathed in cardboard, daubed with boot polish to waterproof it - and fixed it diagonally across his back, the handle protruding high above his shoulder, affording rapid access should he need it.

'What about your tea?'

Peter added the last dribble of milk – set aside for the purpose – before setting it to one side to cool a little while he made final preparations, slipping his arms through the loops of his bag.

Emma could see her daddy was about to abandon her again and ran over to cling to his legs, making it clear she was not happy to see him go. Placing a free hand across her shoulders, Peter maintained contact with his daughter until the contents of his mug were gone.

'Right, my little darling, can you look after this for me?'

The request caused Emma to release her grip.

Having handed her the empty mug, Peter dropped to his haunches, the recent injury to his knee making him wince. Having accepted the pain, he placed his hands on his daughter's upper arms and looked directly into her eyes, forcing a smile.

'You look after Mummy while I'm gone. I'll try not to be long. I'm just going to see how Nanny is.'

Emma's head drooped, but she accepted one final hug without resistance. Peter rose to full height, gave Tessa a kiss, turned and began to walk away, issuing a wave as he stepped from the garden onto the pavement. However, before he had taken another step, a familiar voice stopped him in his tracks.

'Where're you off to?'

It was Frank and he was alone.

'Very fetching,' Tessa said, commenting on Frank's glasses, the original hinges and screws of which had been replaced by coloured electrical tape.

'What do you expect me to do?' Frank snapped, indignantly. 'I can hardly wear my contact lenses any more, can I? There's no way I can keep them clean and I don't fancy going blind thank you very much.'

Twice in a short space of time, Tessa's sarcasm had unintentionally caused upset among those she loved and liked the most. The comments and attitudes she had provoked filled her with guilt and confusion, bringing her close to tears.

'Frank, she didn't mean it nastily,' Peter said, coming to his wife's defence. 'We're all a bit highly strung at the moment and that can make us say the wrong thing.'

'Sorry,' Frank said, placing a friendly hand across Tessa's shoulder blade. 'I guess I am a bit sensitive at the moment.'

Peter could not help but notice that his friend had in his free hand a selection of longbows. Frank had been a part-time archer for many years and took great pleasure in loosing an arrow from any type of bow. Compound and recurve both had their merits, but it was the traditional English longbow that he held in greatest esteem. Not only did he enjoy using them, he also enjoyed making them. It was a skill at which he had become adept. So much so, that until recent events changed everything, it had provided a useful second income, offering medieval experiences to the public at the weekends.

'In reply to your original question, I'm just popping over to Billingford to check up on Tess' mum,' Peter said, adding a directed nod, enquiring after Frank's personal arsenal. 'Is one of those for me?'

'Ultimately, yes, but I think you should stick with your cricket bat for now. Might be better at close quarters, especially with you being a novice and all.'

'You're probably right.'

There followed a momentary lull in the conversation.

'So, are you coming with us?' Peter asked, producing the most pitiful of expressions.

It was an unplanned tactic and one that was not needed.

'Of course we are,' Frank replied, drawing a smile from his friend.

Peter relaxed visibly.

'Excellent.'

That determined, other conversation could continue.

'I see you have the bows, but what about the arrows? More specifically, the arrow heads. They're metal aren't they?'

'They were. My entire stock is fucked.'

A look and a nod from Tessa reminded her friend that a child was present.

'Sorry. Yes, all the arrows have lost their tips, but I can assure you they're still quite deadly over shorter distances. I was thinking about fashioning new ones out of flint, but the idea raises a couple of problems. Firstly, I have no idea where to find the raw material - it's not part of the natural geology around here. Secondly, I've never napped flint in my life.'

'Funny, that. I was only saying to Tess a little while ago that if we're force to live in the Stone Age, the person most likely to possess the skills we need would be you. You may not have done it up to now, but I'm pretty sure you'll pick up flint napping in no time.'

'Well, it's nice to hear you have so much faith in me, but it doesn't alter the fact I have nothing to practice with.'

Tessa had an idea.

'Couldn't we attach pieces of glass to the shafts with strong glue?'

'I suppose we could if I knew where to find some – glue that it; there's plenty of broken glass around. Besides, I think most strong glues come in metal tubes don't they?'

'We'll find something – mastic maybe; that comes in plastic tubes. We could break them open with bricks if needs be.'

Frank nodded in agreement.

'You're right; we'll find something, even if it's chewing gum.'

The subject having reached a natural conclusion, there followed an awkward silence. Peter looked as though there was something he needed to say, but was reluctant to do so. In truth, he needed a favour.

Stealing himself in readiness for rejection, he spoke.

'Frank, I know it's a lot to ask, and I know you have your own family to think of, but would you look after Tess and Em while I'm gone – it would mean staying here as we're busy sterilising water as best we can for the journey.'

Frank was quick to put his friend at ease.

'No problem. I'll fetch my two here – safety in numbers and all that. Anyway, I'm sure Danny would benefit from playing with Emma, and Joyce and I can help Tess with the chores. You don't want me to come with you then?'

'No, I'll be fine on my own. You're far more use staying here ensuring no one comes to harm. Tess's already had a close shave. I'm sure she'll tell you all about it when I'm gone.'

Peter's request explained his side of the awkward silence, but the reason for Frank acting similarly was yet to come.

'Look,' he said, 'I'm sorry if I couldn't give you a firm answer the other morning. We had a few difficult decisions to make. It's hard to simply write off whole swathes of your family. We had to be sure we're doing the right thing.'

Despite Peter issuing assurances he fully understood his friend's position, Frank felt compelled to elaborate.

'It's just that it couldn't have come at a worse time. Joyce's father retired last month, so her parents decided they'd go on a once-in-a-lifetime cruise around the world.'

'I remember you saying.'

'Her parents and my parents have always got on well together, so they decided to make up a foursome. Then Joyce's sister got to hear about it and decided she and her husband should tag along. Her husband's loaded and they don't have any children. We didn't want to miss out, but there is no way we could have come up with that sort of money.

'The cost of the cruise was bad enough, but then there was the spending money, and you have to fork out a fortune on clothes. They expect you to change for dinner and have the right dress for the dances and everything.'

'You don't mean they're on the cruise right now do you?'

'Yes, that's just it. Joyce is terribly upset by it all.'

'Where are they?' Tessa asked, genuinely concerned.

'I can't find their itinerary. All I know is they were flying out to meet the ship. Then they were sailing off, stopping for two days here, two days there, for the best part of a month. I've got no way of contacting them you see. I don't know where they are, or if they're even alive. They may have been lost at sea, or they may have been on land when all this happened. Not knowing is the worst part. You can't imagine what it's doing to us.'

'Shit, that's awful. Mind you, I guess we've all lost someone. One of my sisters lives hundreds of miles away. I don't suppose we'll ever see her again, or find out whether she lived or died. My other sister, Faye, only lives about fifty miles from here, but that might as well be five hundred miles. I keep thinking we should try to find her, but her house is in completely the wrong direction. The only good thing is that she has her husband, Darren, so with any luck she's not having to manage alone. Anyway, knowing her, they'd have been out when it all went tits up. She could be anywhere. If only I'd had the chance to check social media beforehand, I might have had a better idea. I couldn't though because you're not allowed mobiles at work.'

Frank could see he and his family were not the only ones to have suffered loss. Whether virtual or genuine, the outcome was the same.

As if the declared reason for Peter's upset were not enough, he felt the need to share another piece of news. For this, his entire stance changed, leaning forward slightly, his head held to one side.

'I've already found out the fate of one of my family.'

Frank's ears pricked.

'Oh?'

Peter mouthed the words 'My granddad. He didn't make it. We haven't told Em.'

The exchange left all parties looking sad, leading Tessa to take control.

'Right, Peter, you'd better be off. Looks like the next batch is coming to the boil.

'Emma, come and say bye to Daddy again and then show Uncle Frank where you've been sleeping.'

Peter felt the need to interject, halting his wife's flow.

'Tess, just a thought. Store the bottles in the garage as you fill them. We don't want any prying eyes seeing that we have fresh water.'

'Don't worry. I've got it all in hand.'

Peter realised these were not empty words

'I know you have, but still…be super careful, won't you.'

'Bye then, Emma. Love you,' Peter said, waving to his daughter as she led Uncle Frank towards the garage door. 'Tess, Frank, see you soon.'

22

Peter had chosen to travel light for three reasons: it would enable him to move more swiftly; he would present less of a target should he encounter attackers; and he needed to maintain spare capacity in order to transport his mother-in-law's possessions from Billingford to Hexley, if she was in a fit state to make the journey. With this in mind, he had with him: a rucksack; four small bottles of mineral water - left over from his journey home from work; his father's trusty cricket bat; and a sheathed glass blade, similar to that used by Tessa to great effect.

The first leg of his journey took him close to Glendale Lodge, the mere proximity of which evoked strong memories of his recently deceased grandfather and of the surviving former residents whom Peter had abandoned. Saddened at his loss and upset by the way he had been forced to think only of himself, his wife and his daughter, he consoled himself with the thought that Rita - the caring carer - had remained at her post to look after them, and that if he, his family, and the Venners were to survive, it was necessary for Peter to become calculating, strong and ruthless.

As was the case the previous day, the journey into the centre of town, via its now extinct industrial area, brought very little contact with other survivors. In contrast, the passage from the town centre to the countryside on the far side, through one mile of densely packed residential development, could not have been more different. There were swarms of people everywhere, each one, Peter thought, a potential enemy.

A constant two-way stream of pedestrians passed each other on the Hexley to Billingford road. Wounded front-line troops returning from the trenches, heading in one direction, fresh replacements ready to do battle for whatever food and water remained within the ruins of the shops, heading in the other. Peter followed the wounded.

Strangely, those heading for the front seemed not the least bit discouraged by the sight of the bloodstained, empty-handed veterans hobbling painfully back towards their homes. More importantly, they paid no attention to Peter as he weaved in and out against the flow, trying not to be a hindrance in case it sparked a hostile response. As for the walking wounded, they were too badly dazed to care what he did.

The numbers dwindled towards the clearly defined edge of town. Beyond lay two miles of green belt land, offering nothing but cropped fields, hedgerows and uninterrupted skies, and beyond that, the small picturesque village of Clitch End, perched atop a steep and leafy hill.

The population of the village was small, as was the lone store that served them. All activity now centred upon it as the residents set about plundering the stock, despite vehement protestations from the ageing couple whose life it had been running it. The looting there was carried out in a far more civilised manner than had been evident in nearby Hexley. The premises were being picked clean, but not a single punch was thrown, or even hinted at. Some of the locals seemed apologetic towards the victims of their crime, having known them as friends of the family for many years. It was a shame to see the small community forced to abandon its integrity, but at the same time, reassuring that not everyone in the world had become a psychopath overnight.

More countryside, a farm shop under attack, and then the beginning of a ribbon development leading towards the heart of Billingford.

If the town were likened to a clock face, Peter entered it at three o'clock, while Eileen resided on the outskirts at a quarter past six. The pattern of movement among the residents was the same here as it had been in his own town, so there was no reason to believe Billingford's High Street would be any less violent a place. The detours that steered him clear of any possible trouble added vital minutes and extra distance to his journey, but he considered it a wise precaution.

The affluent, tree-lined avenue in which Eileen's bungalow stood had become a shadow of its former self. True, it had the appearance of being much broader and more spacious than usual, this owing to the lack of vehicles parked along both kerbsides, but it was no longer the fastidiously manicured street that Peter had helped maintain ever since his father-in-law died.

The pavements on both sides of the road were for the most part clear, the garden walls and well-kept hedges having contained the majority of the debris that had rained down from the rooftops. Walking along the path adjacent to the odd numbered houses, stepping over the occasional fallen gate as he went, Peter could see the lawns were still neatly trimmed and the flower beds were devoid of weeds; at least those that were not buried beneath piles of roofing tiles, felt, and timbers. This had been a neighbourhood that had openly demonstrated a sense of civic pride. The garden gates alone were proof of that. The paint that coated their surfaces was fresh, as was the paintwork wherever it was to be found. All that hard work had served its purpose when the world was normal, but had become irrelevant at a stroke, given the population's newly enforced way of life.

There was an analogy to be made here with the sending of men into battle. Their parents brought them up as best they could, gave them a good education, and taught them right from wrong. Then the army would get hold of them as raw recruits, moulding them into well-polished soldiers. They would teach them to drill, to fight, and even to shave. Then they would equip them with the latest technology before, finally, they would dump them on a beach, only for them to be shot dead before completing a single step. What purpose did that serve?

It was not uncommon for Peter to have such thoughts. In fact, the purpose of him being placed upon the Earth puzzled him to such a degree he had already decided upon his own epitaph. His memorial inscription would read simply, 'What was all that about then?' He imagined that it would bring a smile to later generations, but at the same time, realised that no authority would ever let him engrave such a flippant remark on a tombstone. In the new world, though, there would be no tombstone; no authority to have a say. In all likelihood, if he died before the world had recovered, his body would remain unburied, picked clean by carrion crows, foxes and flies, each pleased to find such a ready source of food.

General fatigue had steadily shortened Peter's stride over the course of the day and with his mother-in-law's gate in sight, his pace became slower still, his subconscious battling with the desire to know Eileen's fate, but being afraid to find out.

Her bungalow was set well back from the road, affording Peter passage up a garden path, free from debris. The property itself was in a bad way, the front entrance being impassable. The driveway ran down the side to a single width garage set into the back garden. If she was alive and if she was still on the property, this was the only building offering any sort of shelter.

Where Eileen's garage differed from Peter's was in the construction of the main doors. The Allerton's had been a modern, all-metal up-and-over affair that had vanished with the wind. Being of an older design – originally hung in the 1950s or 60s - Eileen's consisted of two wooden doors with frames for obscured glass panes at the top of each. Glue and carpentry joints of various types – tongue and groove; mortice and tenon – ensured both doors remained intact. The hinges, being metal, had decayed, allowing the doors to fall to the ground, smashing the glass, fragments of which could be seen on the drive. The fact Peter found the doors propped into their frame with the aid of a few additional lengths of timber - presumably scavenged from the bungalow - meant that someone had attempted to weatherproof the building; someone with more strength than Eileen. Whoever that person was had even gone to the trouble of replacing the glass panes with torn corrugated cardboard panels.

There was hope. Nevertheless, as Peter moved stealthily round to the side door, he did so, expecting the worst. Ignoring logic, his mind filled with images of flies swarming above his mother-in-law's decomposing body. If he had stopped for a moment to give thought to the plausibility of that scenario, he would have realised insufficient time had elapsed since the disaster struck for flies to make much progress.

The first indication that all was not as he feared was the absence of the smells normally associated with death.

'Hello? Eileen? Are you in there?'

There being no reply, Peter drew his glass knife and prepared to enter, trying first to survey the interior without poking his head through the door, recognising anyone might be in there – frightened, or simply guarding precious supplies. Just because this was Eileen's garage, did not mean other survivors had not commandeered it if their own property could not afford them shelter. That someone might possess a cricket bat, just like his own, and be waiting to strike the first person that stepped across the threshold. From what Peter could see in the dim light, there was an unmoving body on the floor, hidden beneath a pile of bedding, and no one else.

Peter stepped inside, twisting at the waist to face anyone who might be standing flattened against the wall. His precaution was unnecessary.

'Hello? Eileen?'

This time he spoke louder.

The body reacted, rolling over lazily to face him.

On closer inspection, the makeshift bed looked comfortable - fashioned from foam-filled seat cushions, Eileen's head resting on several pillows, her body buried beneath an extra thick continental duvet, sufficient to keep out the colds of Antarctica.

'Oh, hello dear. What do you think of all this then? I told you no good would come of that meteor shower.'

Peter could not remember having heard such a reference before, but then

223

her I-told-you-so attitude was well documented, as was her ability to talk seemingly endlessly without pausing for breath.

He had obviously woken her from a deep slumber as her mouth had kicked into gear before her eyes had begun to focus properly. She blinked slowly.

'What time is it?' she continued with a yawn.

'I've no idea.'

'No, of course not. I was forgetting.'

She pulled back the bedding to reveal Freddie curled up next to her.

'I see the dog's all right,' Peter said, disappointedly.

'Oh yes, Freddie's my hot water bottle,' she replied, failing to register the note of sarcasm.

'Well, I'm afraid he can't come with us.'

'What! Don't be so ridiculous.'

'Look, we don't have enough food for ourselves, never mind that thing.'

'Thing! Well, I'm not leaving without him and that's my final say on the matter.'

Peter was sorely tempted to take the woman's offer, but knew it was not a viable proposition.

'Okay, you win.'

Eileen seemed pleased with herself and shared her satisfaction with the dog, whispering in his ear.

'You've managed pretty well as far as I can see,' Peter said, changing the subject.

'I'm not entirely useless you know,' Eileen replied. 'I have been through this type of thing before.'

'What?'

'I remember the power cuts in the nineteen-seventies. My generation is used to dealing with this sort of crisis.'

'Eileen, I think the complete breakdown of society is a bit more serious than having no electricity for a couple of hours due to a bunch of union members going on strike.'

'Nonsense! Hitler flattened London during the war and look at it now. This isn't a complete breakdown of society. It's an upset.'

It was all Peter could do to stop himself pointing out that she may have been conceived during the final phase of the war, but she certainly was not in a position to claim she had lived through it. Anyway, maybe he had misjudged the old cow. The fact she was alive proved that.

'Have you got everything you want to take with you? We can't take much as we've got to carry it all. No transport you see.'

Eileen had already carried out her own salvage operation with the aid of a surviving neighbour; a man several decades her junior who had popped round to make sure she was all right and to plug up the main entrance of the garage. She had made quite sensible choices as to what she should keep. Being impressed by his mother-in-law twice in one day was almost too much for Peter to bear.

The final tally filled only four carrier bags, Peter having decided a lot of what she had put aside – bedding, for example – could be replaced at the other end of their journey. Every morsel of food, on the other hand, was placed in his rucksack for safe keeping.

'Right, before we go, have you got everything?'

'Yes.'

'Are you sure? What about your medicine?'

Peter was most particular on this point as Eileen had a history of forgetting to take her medication with her on days out, leading to some rather sticky moments in the past.

The question had been entirely necessary. Nevertheless, Peter instantly regretted asking it, fearing it would prompt his mother-in-law to start talking about her medication and ailments as others would discuss the British weather. Such monologues were always long, extremely dull and totally unstoppable.

'Yes, I think so but I can't help wondering what I'm going to do when my current supply runs out,' she said, checking her stock.

'How many do you have to take anyway?'

'Well…'

Peter realised what he had done. Pandora's Box had been opened.

His shoulders slumped visibly.

'… the Metformin and the Glyclazide are for my diabetes. I've got a good month's supply of those.'

'It's lucky you don't use a needle, or you'd be really stuffed,' Peter interjected, trying desperately to break her stride, but his efforts proved futile.

'The Thyroxine is for me thyroid of course. I've got plenty of those for now. The Simvastatin, Amiodarone, Bisoprolol and Isosorbide Mononitrate are for my heart. I'm running low on all of those by the looks of it.'

While regretting having raised the subject, Peter was simultaneously amazed how the old girl rattled off the names of her medication, and she was not finished yet.

'The Aspirin thins my blood. I've got five hundred of them, and then there's the GTN for my angina, but I don't use that very often.'

'How do you remember all that lot?'

'Well dear, I take do them every day you know.'

All of a sudden, Peter felt pity for his mother-in-law.

'Don't worry Mum.'

'Mum' was an expression he had never before used in connection with this terrible woman. His change of attitude was enough to unnerve anyone who knew them. Perhaps the events of the past few days had softened his heart.

Eileen looked startled, but said nothing.

Peter felt embarrassed.

'I'll see if I can liberate whatever it is you need from the pharmacy if you give me the list. If I can't get any, then I'm sure you'll be okay if we keep an eye on your diet and you take it easy.'

Eileen could not help but shed a tear as she bade farewell to the place that had been the source of so many of her fondest memories. She and her husband had brought up the children there and had spent many happy years together under that, now unrecognisable, roof.

In addition to the four plastic carrier bags, bulging with her belongings, Eileen insisted on taking her handbag. The clasp had given way but she had not left the house in more than thirty years without one and she would not change her ways just because of some minor catastrophe. Likewise, she was not about to go anywhere without her headscarf which she tied securely beneath her chin.

Peter took control of the carrier bags, mindful of his mother-in-law's condition. Three of these he tied to a broom handle in much the same way as he had travelled back from the prison, the technique having proven so successful. The fourth he held in his free hand. Now fully laden, the journey ahead promised to be long and extremely arduous.

Progress was slow from the outset, but otherwise everything went smoothly. The first mile passed without Eileen exhibiting any undue discomfort or difficulty, and her dog kept faithfully to heel without once providing Peter with a single excuse for hating it more than he already did.

The second mile began, as had the first, with Eileen talking incessantly on every subject known to mankind. It was as though she had discovered the Encyclopedia Britannica for the very first time and had an overwhelming desire to share what she had read with whoever was prepared to listen. Strangely, so Peter thought, the one subject upon which she did not touch was that of the predicament they faced.

It was a well-documented fact that this lonely old widow could talk for England, but even by her standards, her current display was unnatural. For the sake of self-preservation, Peter's mind shut itself off from the bombardment, managing sporadically to conjure up a few words of acknowledgement, designed to limit any offence he might otherwise cause. His timing being hit and miss, his words were often spoken out of context. Nevertheless, despite her son-in-law's obvious lack of interest, Eileen's onslaught continued unabated.

Peter amused himself with the notion that if the officiators from the Guinness Book of World Records could be present, Eileen would be sure to warrant a special mention.

The third mile began to take its toll. Eileen's incessant noise ebbed and finally stopped altogether. Her resting features winced.

'You all right Mum?'

'It's this damn leg of mine. It's been ballooned you know?'

'Would you like to stop for a while?'

She did, the pause being the first of many to come, the distance between each becoming shorter and shorter.

Four miles covered and Peter was left wondering if they would ever make it home, and if they did, how they would cope with the planned journey to the countryside?

The pair stopped for refreshments and to give Eileen an opportunity to deplete her reserves of medication. They sat quietly together at the side of the road, atop a low grass embankment, while Freddie explored their immediate surroundings, every so often discovering odours quite unacceptable to man, but intensely pleasurable to a dog.

'This reminds me of the war.'

Peter's heart sank on hearing his mother-in-law's foreword to what promised to be one of her set piece tales of yore. They were all very, very long and he had been subjected to them all a thousand times before.

'Mum, you weren't even in the war.'

'No, but my mother was and she used to tell me all about it.'

Peter, having failed miserably to prevent the retelling of another familiar story, dedicated a small portion of his mind to what Eileen was saying and let the rest wander wherever it chose to take him. It was wise not to ignore her entirely as, in the past, she had been known to slip the odd question in to test whether or not he had been paying attention. Her plan to expose him rarely succeeded though as his brain had become subconsciously attuned to hearing key words which told him, to within a paragraph, the point in the saga she had reached.

As Eileen droned on, Peter's attention became less and less focused on her voice. He began instead to notice, in greater depth, details of his surroundings that he had long since taken for granted. It brought serenity – normally associated with a visit to an empty church - to the chaos that had befallen the world. The only movement was that of the dog snuffling about; the only noise – other than Eileen's soliloquy - the breeze rustling the leaves of some nearby silver birches. Peter's wandering thoughts sought silence. At first this proved an impossible task, but after a while he realised his mother-in-law's unstoppable chatter no longer challenged his desire. The period between this realisation and Eileen's next utterance could be measured in fractions of a second, affording Peter insufficient time to turn his head from his fixed gaze across the fields by so much as one degree.

'Oh dear!' she said with a matter-of-fact air.

As she did so, Eileen slumped against her son-in-law's shoulder, her head sliding down his chest, landing motionless in his lap.

Peter had no intention of giving in without a fight. Following a momentary pause, both the first aid training he had received at work and his moral obligation to try to save her, kicked in.

A quick examination gave little hope. No pulse; no signs of breathing; the patient totally unresponsive to a range of stimuli. Despite the facts, Peter nevertheless began administering rescue breaths, mouth-to-mouth, and chest compressions, delivered to the beat of Nelly the Elephant, providing the correct cadence. Within only a few minutes he was sweating profusely and exhausted. Continuing the cycle of breaths, compressions and checks for vital signs for what felt like an eternity, the first aider began reluctantly to accept the truth. Despite his best efforts he could detect no improvement and knew there would be none unless professional help arrived; professional help he also knew would not arrive. After a further minute, his actions decreased and then stopped. However, the thought of his wife's reaction to the loss of her mother prompted him to deliver two more breaths and another set of rib-breaking compressions, until reality overtook emotion. At that point his mind and body knew they could do no more.

Peter lay back on the embankment, eyes closed, giving his body a chance to recover physically; his mind a chance to find inspiration. There was nothing more to be done than bury the deceased. He owed it to Eileen and to his wife, while proving to himself he had not yet become a savage. Peter had known this woman since before he was married and had disliked her for almost as long. Nevertheless, she was family and did not deserve to be abandoned in the middle of nowhere without a proper Christian burial. Ideally, her body would be placed in the same grave as her husband, her name chiseled in the stone beneath his, but the cemetery in which Bob lay was many miles away; an impossible distance without transport.

Thankfully, the soil in the adjacent field was well broken, which made digging relatively easy with the aid of a short length of plank, salvaged from the remains of the farmer's fence. Peter toiled without displaying or feeling emotion; digging was a process to which he was accustomed. However, once finished, no longer able to disassociate the task of digging from the task of interment, his tempered attitude began to soften.

There was no way to get Eileen to the shallow grave other than to drag her there; an action that afforded the deceased little respect. Kneeling beside her, he raised his mother-in-law's arms above her head. She gave no resistance. He then stood, took her cold, lifeless hands in his, formed a grip and began pulling, all the while averting his eyes from her body, especially from her head that hung at the end of a flaccid neck.

Peter walked in a wide arc, lining the body up with the shallow grave in order to pull his mother-in-law into her final resting place from the feet end. She fitted well. He placed her arms gently by her sides and tidied her clothing, sensing that someone was looking down upon him; judging his every action.

Everything seemed rushed: they had walked; they had sat; Eileen had died; Peter had dragged his mother-in-law into a shallow hole with the intention of performing her burial without ceremony or discussion. It felt wrong. It felt matter-of-fact. Tessa had not had the chance to say goodbye to her mum, or to grieve. The police had not had a chance to make a report. The medical services had not had a chance to save her, or even provide an opinion. Peter was alone, without anyone to tell him it was all right.

He sat for a while, half expecting Eileen to open her eyes, as she had done in her garage, and say, bleary eyed, 'Oh, hello dear.'

Having checked for any sign of a pulse at her wrist and at her neck, and found none, Peter emptied Eileen's belongings onto the ground, taking the spilled clothing and placing each item one by one across her body, shielding it from direct contact with the soil; delaying the act of back-filling the grave, affording her one last opportunity to wake up before it was too late. He left her face uncovered.

It proved easiest for Peter to sit on the ground and push the soil back into the hole with the soles of his shoes, before finishing the job using the section of fencing. All the while, Freddie sat at Peter's side, looking confused. Eileen made no complaint. There remained only to place a cotton blouse gently across her face and cover it with soil.

Freddie stood and looked on as Peter drove the plank into the ground, on it the briefest of memorial inscriptions, spelled out in wax crayon.

The grave having been suitably marked, Freddie took up position, lying along the length of the freshly disturbed earth.

'Sorry boy, that's the best I can do.'

Peter was touched by the show of devotion, but at the same time, was pleased the dog would no longer be his concern. For that matter, he felt ashamed to admit to himself that a part of him was relieved Eileen would no longer factor in the family's evacuation plans. Had she survived, they would have managed, but her health might have been their downfall.

Thinning out her belongings to leave only what he could make use of, Peter moved off towards home, this time at a much quicker pace.

23

No sooner had Peter set out for Billingford to determine Eileen's fate, Frank had returned to his own house to pack the Venner's belongings and bring the rest of his family to the Allerton's property. Tessa, meanwhile, continued with her efforts to sterilise enough water for their journey. Alone, save for the company of her young daughter, she was then able to review the viability of the operation she was trying to perform. So sure was she in her conclusion that the completion of the task was impossible, she immediately abandoned the fire, choosing instead to look for inspiration and advice in the survival book her husband had retrieved from the wreckage of the roof space. She quickly found what appeared to be a sensible alternative – a filter. Unlike her husband, Tessa was happy to read instructions and soon set about looking for the necessary materials with which to build one.

The plastic gutter downpipe at the corner of the house had been fashioned from two pieces: one full length; one cut down. The sections were easily separated and had survived without being punctured by falling tiles. Conveniently, the smaller section was of just the right length, both in terms of effectiveness and ease of transport.

Adapting the written advice to her circumstances, Tessa cut a piece of cotton material to size and held it in position over one end of the pipe, using first an elastic band and then a trio of interlinked cable ties - recovered from the area of her husband's work bench - to fix it permanently in place. Then, with Emma's help, Tessa crushed into small pieces a portion of their remaining supply of charcoal. This they poured into the tube. On top, Tessa placed a second piece of cloth, preventing the different strata from mixing at their boundaries. A layer of Emma's play sand; a third piece of cloth; ornamental gravel retrieved from the tops of many garden flower pots; and a final piece of cloth to cap the pipe, keeping the contents from spilling.

'I think we're ready to try it out,' Tessa said, brightly, pleased with the end result.

Having balanced the newly completed filter over a collecting bowl, she began pouring contaminated water into the top of the pipe. The process was not a swift as she might have hoped, but the steady trickle exceeded the rate at which it could be processed by fire alone. Within a short time she had collected the first gallon – enough to fill the glass kitchen measuring jug eight times. The water looked clear, but there was no guarantee it had been stripped of microscopic organisms that might still make them ill. To ensure it was safe to drink, she then carefully added two drops of bleach, mixing them in thoroughly, just as the text directed. The tip of her finger transferred the smallest quantity of fully treated water to the tip of her tongue.

'Nasty. That's going to take some getting used to. Maybe it won't be so bad if I add some orange.'

The only person to hear Tessa's words was Emma, but they were not meant for her ears; rather they were an outward expression of a mental note being hastily scribbled.

It was at this point the Venner's arrived, all three members of the family laden down with their most precious possessions – sentimental, useful and easily transportable being the criteria by which each item had been chosen. Joyce and Danny walked at least three paces in front of Frank.

'Hello Tess,' Joyce called, sounding more cheerful than the circumstances warranted – it was an effort. 'What you doin'?'

Tessa placed the filter to one side and ran over to embrace her friend before she could even set her bags down. Joyce made no effort to extricate herself from the bear hug, grateful for the warm reception. The children were pleased to see each other too, immediately breaking off to enter their own world of make believe, playing together as though nothing was out of the ordinary.

The water was quickly forgotten as both women exchanged experiences while busying themselves in storing the Venner's bags out of sight in the garage.

Concerned that his own property was now abandoned and open to plunder, Frank made his apologies and left to fetch more of their salvage. Joyce did not appear as worried to see her husband leave as Tessa had been to let her own husband go, leading the latter to believe her best friend in the whole world was of much stronger character. Each time he returned, he found Tess and his wife locked in animated conversation, delivered at twice the normal rate – so much had to be said.

Eventually, Frank returned for the last time and declared their old house clear.

'Let's celebrate with a glass of water,' Tessa suggested.

Their picnic cups charged, Tessa, Joyce and Frank toasted each other's health and good fortune before taking a much needed mouthful. A grimace appeared simultaneously on each of their faces.

'Tastes a bit funny, doesn't it. A bit like a swimming pool,' Frank commented, his tongue and lips working as if trying to dislodge a length of sticky tape, or a stray hair from his mouth.

'That'll be the bleach,' Tessa confessed. 'You're going to have to get used to it. It's either that or some very nasty stomach bug.'

'Oh well, maybe I'll get used to it in time,' Frank responded, placing his empty cup carefully to one side. 'Besides, when we reach our destination – wherever that may be – we can stick to boiling the water rather than adding something from a chemistry set.'

His smile assured his audience he was only joking.

Tessa took the criticism as it was intended, and smiled. Joyce's expression, however, revealed quiet irritation.

'Anyway, enough talking. Let's get your beds made up. Then I can do some more filtering. There a whole paddling pool of the stuff to get through.'

The adults moved inside and immediately set about rearranging their belongings so as to free up sufficient floor space for six temporary beds.

'How on Earth are we going to shift all this stuff?' Tessa asked. 'We haven't got any transport and we certainly can't carry it. I mean, you've just been back to your place at least half a dozen times. Even if Joyce carries some of it, you won't have enough arms, and even if you did, you'd still need to stop for a rest every few metres. And it's not just you. We're in exactly the same boat.'

'I've been thinking about that,' Frank replied, clearly pleased with himself. 'Bearing in mind we no longer have the luxury of such things as wheels or tools, whatever we do, we'll have to be inventive. When I was a little boy, I had some plastic cowboys-and-Indians figures. One of my favourite was a squaw with a papoose strapped to her back, leading a horse which was dragging behind a kind of A-frame affair, and all her belongings were strapped to it. I reckon we could make our own versions – one for each family. I know we don't have a horse, but I'm sure Pete and I could make some sort of harness and drag them – at least across hard surfaces.'

Something had been developing in Joyce's mind. Even she could not say with any certainty how long it had been festering, but the roots most certainly coincided with the collapse of her house, the destruction of most of her possessions and the end of civilization as she had known it. Why it manifested as anger towards her husband was a mystery too, but probably had something to do with feeling he had accepted their circumstances too easily; had not expressed loss in the same way as she felt it.

Her eyes bore into her husband's skull, the pressure behind her words building until her lips were no longer strong enough to contain them.

'You mean to say that you're basing our salvation – everything - around an idea inspired by a tiny plastic toy that you owned when you were still in shorts? I don't believe what I'm hearing! I mean, most of our family and friends may be dead, our house is in ruins, our future couldn't be more uncertain, and you're not phased by any of it. You think it's some great big adventure, don't you. Well, maybe you'll think differently in a few days when we don't have anything to eat and we're forced to drink from puddles, or water flavoured with toilet bleach. Are you fucking crazy?'

She spoke slowly and precisely, rising sharply to a crescendo.

Frank, puzzled by his wife's reaction – having no previous experience of her swearing, at all - defended his position vigorously, his voice raised, his tone bordering on aggressive.

Tessa had known both Joyce and Frank for many years and in all that time she had never heard one raise an uncivil word against the other.

'Look!' Frank began. 'There are lengths of timber lying all over the place. It's just a matter of finding the right bits. We have string and the means to cut it, and although it was the memory of a toy that sparked the idea, the method of transport has been tried and tested by a culture that has lasted for thousands of years. So what's your problem?'

Caught in the middle, Tessa felt awkward. Not only that, she worried what the adults shouting at each other might do to further increase the trauma the children had already suffered.

'If it's of any help, Pete retrieved a survival book from the attic. It's got an entire section on how to tie knots.'

Tessa's delivery was deliberately friendly, her hope being that it would seed a more level headed conversation.

'There you go. Tess thinks my idea will work.'

Her words had not been chosen as carefully as she thought, Frank drawing her skillfully towards his team.

'Well, I...I mean...'

Tessa stuttered. She had no desire to be used as ammunition by either side, or to offend them. Hers was an impossible position, it requiring a presidential speech writer to avoid either scenario. As her only prior involvement in politics had been to pencil an X in a box once every four years, her remaining option was to change the subject entirely.

'How about I make use of our fire pit to cook the rest of the defrosted food? We can eat some now and save some for Pete and Mum, when they get back. I don't think it'll last until tomorrow.'

Joyce would not be distracted so easily, her gaze remaining fixed upon her husband, as though her friend had not uttered a sound.

'Oh, I see. So you think Tessa's opinion trumps mine, do you? Well, isn't that lovely. Why don't all of you just drag your stuff into the countryside without me? I'm sure I'll be okay living in what remains of my lovey house.'

'What is your problem?'

Frank's question was clearly not designed to get to the root of the matter, so he could then support his wife more effectively. To Tessa's ears, it sounded more like he was offering to step outside the pub with a drunkard who had just spilled his pint.

'What's my problem? My problem is that until a few days ago we had a life. It's all gone – never to return - and you don't seem to care. It's just an adventure to you. To hell with my feelings.'

Her words became progressively broken, the last of them morphing into tears. The fire had been extinguished by rivulets that sprang from the inner corners of her eyes. Her body shrank.

Frank had failed to read the signs, but was quick to react to the consequences of his shortcomings.

'Oh God, Joyce. I had no idea. I'm so sorry. I didn't mean to…'

His arms engulfed his wife's shoulders, his face buried in her neck, dampening her skin with his own tears. This was the final straw for Toby who threw himself at his mother's waste, his sobbing equal to that of both parents, multiplied by a factor of ten. Not knowing why the Venners cried so, it nonetheless triggered Emma to join in their emotional pile up. Miraculously, Tessa's eyes remain dry, her fortitude blazing an example for the rest of the party to follow.

'Okay, enough of this. We're all upset, but there's no point crying. It's not going to solve anything. Let's get the fire stoked up and see what kind of meal we can cobble together. When the time comes, we can talk about Frank's ideas and any others anyone else cares to put forward.'

Tessa had suddenly become the teacher who makes light of a grazed knee by telling her pupil to stop making so much fuss and dab the wound with a wet tissue.

This time, her words took effect.

By the time the meal had been prepared, cooked and eaten, Frank had found paper and a crayon and had produced a sketch of his proposed design – a letter 'A', formed of three sturdy lengths of wood, the widest part – the feet - still narrow enough to fit between driveway gates and other similar obstacles. Wood batons of increasing length spanned the void between the diagonal sides, providing a flat area to which the cargo could be attached.

Without waiting for final approval, Frank began scouting for suitable materials and quickly discovered a new technique of rubbing architrave up and down the corner of the brickwork in order to wear a groove. Placing each piece of prepared timber on the edge of the fire pit in turn, the applied pressure of his foot then snapped the batons to near exact length. The same technique did not work so well for the three main elements and so pieces that were already of the right dimensions had to be sourced. Nevertheless, it was not long before all the components were laid together on the lawn, by which time Joyce's faith in her husband had been fully restored. She did not speak an apology, but instead placed her hand softly on Frank's head as he knelt down, carefully placing the individual pieces to form two complete frames.

'Now all we've got to do is bind everything together.'

***

As the adults stood in the middle of the lawn, admiring Frank's work, Emma, who had been balancing on one of the foot-high gravel boards that remained trapped between the surviving concrete fence posts, caught their attention with a single word.

'Daddy.'

Tessa's head whipped round to see her daughter was now looking down the road. All five survivors gathered quickly on the pavement from where they could see Peter, alone, head bent forward, eyes fixed on the ground, walking without purpose towards their position.

'Where's Nanny?' Tessa asked aloud, she being used to referring to her mother from Emma's point of view.

Not waiting for a reply, she set off at speed towards her husband, her arms flailing as though she was running in heels.

Peter, aware of his wife's approach, stopped dead in his tracks, lifted his head briefly and set the end of the broom handle down on the pavement, using it for support. Tessa pulled up in front of him.

'Where's Mum?'

Peter's already sad expression sunk still further.

'I'm sorry sweetheart, she didn't make it. Her heart gave out on the way over. It was very peaceful.'

The words were delivered just as he had practiced, over and over again, mile after mile. He had considered lying to her, telling his wife her mother had been rescued and cared for by her neighbours, but had subsequently died in her sleep. The idea had been dismissed as he knew the truth would fight to be known, or cause him unbearable pain for as long as he suppressed it.

From two hundred metres distance, Frank and Joyce could not hear what had been said, but knew instantly by Tessa's body language that the news was not good. Peter could be seen placing his arm round his wife's waist before encouraging her to walk back up the road to their property. He could be seen offering her a tissue from his pocket and seemed to be providing words of consolation.

On their arrival, the adults retired to the privacy of the garage, while the children were permitted to play in the garden under strict instructions they were neither to cross the boundary fence, nor attempt to enter the ruined house.

Once seated, Peter recounted, in minute detail, what had happened. He explained that Eileen had died peacefully. He told how he had tried to revive her. He related how he had buried her in a marked grave so she would not be forgotten and wildlife would be prevented from reaching her remains.

'Honestly Tess, she didn't suffer in the slightest.'

Tessa stopped crying for a moment.

'Perhaps it was for the best,' she said weakly, trying to put on a brave face. 'She would eventually have run out of pills anyway and that could have led to a slow, painful death. Who knows, in a few weeks' time, we may be wishing we had gone the same way.'

It spoke to the underlying feeling that no one sought to contradict her.

Taking her own advice, Tessa ceased crying altogether, save for the occasional sniffle. However, she was clearly not all right, remaining as she did seated, silently staring into the middle distance.

It was Joyce's turn to set the mood onto a new and better path.

'Here, we've saved you some food. Why don't you take it outside and eat it in the fresh air. Frank, you can keep Pete company…talk about your ideas for carrying all our stuff out of here.'

Frank's body language asked what should be done about Tess.

'Go on. Off you go. I'm going to stay in here with Tess for a while. It'll be good for both of us.'

Peter took a plate of food from Joyce and got up to leave, torn between his natural instinct to be there for his wife and the realisation her friend was probably better able to manage the situation.

Frank noted his friend's hesitation.

'Come on, I'll show you what your wife's been up to while you've been gone. Clever woman you have there.'

'Okay, and what's this about us carrying all our stuff?'

'Don't worry, I'll show you that too. It has to be said, Tess isn't the only genius around here.'

Whatever Joyce said, it clearly worked as Tessa joined the men outside while they were still admiring the filter. So advanced was her recovery she managed to explain its construction and operation.

As impressed as he was, Peter could not help but become distracted at seeing Frank's handywork, set out as it was on the lawn. He listened to - but did not need to hear - his friend's sales pitch, realising immediately that these pieces of wood represented an effective solution to what would otherwise have been a major problem. In fact, his vision was more advanced than that of the designer.

'Those batons will be perfect. I think we should tie numerous water bottles to both frames and cover them over before adding the rest of the supplies. For one thing, it should help prevent the growth of algae by keeping them out of the sunlight. It also keeps them hidden from prying eyes. We can keep one or two bottles to hand for use as we walk.'

'I agree,' Frank replied. 'I think we should split everything equally between the two frames. That way, if we lose one we still have everything we need, just less of it.'

'Agreed.'

Joyce suddenly looked concerned.

'What do you mean, if we lose one?'

Reluctant to admit to his wife his fears that they might come under attack along the way, Frank chose not to answer.

Without the need for previous discussion, Peter shared his friend's fears, but could see a response was necessary, if they were to move on.

'Oh, you know, the bindings might snap, or something. I mean, they have been thrown together from scraps, haven't they.'

To Frank's surprise, Joyce accepted Peter's hastily fabricated explanation without further comment, tutting in recognition she had been stupid in missing the obvious.

'Thinking about it, I'd be amazed if they don't break with all the weight we're going to put on them. Mind you, I have faith in my husband. If anyone can turn a childhood toy into the real thing, it's him.'

Frank gave a genuine smile and quickly seized upon her response to maneuver the conversation still further from the truth.

'On the subject of weight, Pete, I notice you've amassed a pretty hefty pile of books in the garage. You don't intend to take them with you do you?'

Peter thought it a strange question.

'Of course I do.'

Frank thought the confidence of his friend's response equally strange.

'It's just that we're taking a ton of water with us. Shouldn't we be trying to keep the weight down in other ways? I mean, we've got to drag these things for miles – they haven't got wheels you know.'

'Maybe, but these books are our future. We've got to preserve what we can of our knowledge; otherwise, how else are we going to rebuild our society?'

Not wishing to get into another argument, Frank steered another tack, hoping his friend would reconsider when he pulled on the harness for the first time.

'Okay, this is the plan as I see it. It's a clear sky, so it should stay light for another three or four hours. I say we bind these frames together and test them with our body weight alone. Then we use up the last of the cooked food and get straight to bed. In the morning, we get up at sunrise and load the frames. Then we get the hell out of here.'

24

Thanks to one wall of the garage being little more than a semi-opaque sheet of polyester tarpaulin, light flooded the interior long before the sun had risen above the horizon. Peter had stolen no more than four hours sleep, stubborn thoughts on the subject of the big day having kept his mind active long after the rest of the party had drifted off. At intervals, Peter had sat up, cleared his mind, lain back down, got comfortable, and thought of sheep, only to find his mind still wished to practice the arrangements for the following day, over and over. Only when he resorted to using breathing exercises that he had forgotten he knew, did his mind finally agree to let him doze.

On waking, residual tiredness was immediately overruled by the realisation of how much more there was yet to be done. Thankfully, the A-frames had been completed to schedule, long before the light had faded. The harnesses too, although it had taken considerably longer than anticipated, requiring Frank and Peter to remain awake late into the evening, working by nothing more than candlelight. However, the construction phase formed only the first section of a lengthy to-do list. Everything the families owned – everything they wanted to take with them – had now to be carried outside, bound in some way to the two primitive sleds, harnessed to the men, and tested.

Peter exited the garage as quietly as possible, but Frank, being in much the same mental state as his friend, woke at the slightest of noises and soon followed Peter into the open. It was quickly and quietly deemed unfair to wake the rest, bearing in mind the nature of the day ahead. Having taken this decision, it was not possible to make a start on loading the frames. However, it was still possible to conduct a road test. Peter volunteered to step into the harness of one of the sleds, carrying it first to the road in front of the property, away from the sleeping wives and children. Frank stepped on board, simulating at least a partial load.

As his friend began to haul, it became all too evident just how noisy dragging two wooden legs across a rough concrete surface could be. Nevertheless, Peter continued to pull until he had covered two hundred metres. On the positive side, it worked. On the negative, the nylon rope harness bit into his muscles and would require padding if they were to be able to drag their belongings over any longer distance, especially when taking into account that the fully laden weight would be substantially more than Frank, even though he was normally considered quite a lump. It was also noted that the wooden feet had worn down alarmingly quickly for such a comparatively short distance. This the two men dismissed, it being suspected that when the cornered ends of the frame eventually became flattened - increasing the footprint - the erosion would be slowed. In any case, there being no other materials to hand which might offer greater durability, there was little point in worrying about it.

Unable to sit around idly for any length of time, Peter re-entered the garage to fetch a makeshift knife and some tape, moving with the grace of a Shaolin monk. Hence, the sleeping occupants remained undisturbed. Meanwhile, Frank retrieved a sofa cushion from the Allerton's living room, after which the two men returned to the driveway at the front of the property, upon which the test rig had temporarily been abandoned. There they made themselves comfortable before beginning work to improve the Mark I harness. Having first sliced and teased the foam cushion filling into lengths, they then carefully wrapped the strips around key sections of the nylon rope. The wadding was then covered in off-cuts of clear, heavy-gauge polythene and bound with insulating tape to finish the job.

The second road test proved infinitely more satisfactory than the first, promoting confidence that a journey of a hundred miles would not be too much to ask.

Returning to the rear of the property, to make the same improvements to the second harness, the men were in time to witness Tessa emerging from her cleverly constructed toilet facilities, while Joyce was standing on the lawn, busily brushing her teeth.

'We could hear you, you know,' Joyce said, mumbling, trying not to empty the contents of her mouth before she was finished.

Joyce had spoken. It was only right then that *her* husband should respond.

'At least that explains why you don't seem that bothered, waking up to find us both missing.'

'Missing? It was hardly a secret where you were. I'm surprised you didn't wake the entire neighbourhood with all that scraping up and down the road and whispered talk — you need a volume control.'

'Sorry,' Frank said, sheepishly.

Peter had an observation to make.

'You mentioning the neighbours makes me realise, I haven't see any of them – not a sign. For a start, both the Cuthberts and the Parkinsons seem to have disappeared.'

His thumb indicated the temporary shelters still standing on the boundary lines between their neighbour's and their next-door-but-one neighbour's gardens.

'Come to think of it, I haven't seen them since I got home.'

'They must have snuck out,' Tessa suggested. 'Either left for the countryside, or maybe they've got relatives who live near here.'

The wives made breakfast, not because they felt subordinate to their husbands, but because Frank and Peter were naturally stronger; more suited to loading the frames. The children lay in, playing with their toys from the comfort of their beds, Danny flying a small aeroplane at arm's length, Emma repeatedly undressing and dressing her favourite doll. All the while, the men carried belongings from the garage, dividing everything between the two A-frames to which the bags, boxes and bottles were fastened. Water, being the most valuable of all commodities, formed the bottom most layer. Bedding and tarpaulins went on top, the latter providing protection against adverse weather; both items being the first they would need when making camp for the night.

In all, Frank had brought four longbows from home: two to be buried within the cargo; one each for the men to have close to hand, strung for immediate use. In addition, Frank also supplied two quivers, largely unaffected by the rust. A missing rivet had parted the shoulder strap from the bag, but was easily repaired with twine. The arrows themselves bore a variety of heads: ancient flint, worked by a hunter and bought from an antiques shop; small glass shards; and shattered plastic, easily blunted but sharp. All had been set in place with twine and bitumen, torn from the edge of the Venner's garage roof and melted over a flame.

'Have you ever used a bow?' Frank asked.

'Once or twice,' Peter replied. 'I had a little go when we took Emma to an event at a castle somewhere. I didn't fire too many arrows because they were charging quite a lot, but to be honest, I think I did pretty well.'

'That's good. I was going to suggest we have a quick practice, but if you don't need to, I'd rather not as I don't know how the tips would fair if we keep loosing them at targets.'

242

Other than bows and arrows, each of the adult members of the party wore a glass knife around their waists, and Peter's cricket bat was also easily to hand, its sheath pushed between the outer tarpaulin of his A-frame and the rope that bound it there.

Finally, it was time to leave.

Despite the garage having been home for only four days, nevertheless it had become more familiar to its transient inhabitants than the ruined house that stood, ravaged, a short distance across the lawn. With the temporary end wall removed and stowed, the interior looked vulnerable yet clean and well ordered, the non-essential belongings that were too many to be carried remaining stacked neatly to one side. Peter and Tessa bade their shattered homes a silent farewell while Emma crouched on the path watching a snail leave a pearlescent trail.

'Come on,' Peter said. 'Let's get out of here.'

'Which way?' Frank asked.

'That way,' Peter replied, waving a nonchalant hand. 'It's the shortest route out of town and doesn't go anywhere near the High Street.'

'What about Fay?'

His wife's question drew yet more anxiety from Peter's wounded psyche.

'I'm afraid we can't do anything for her. She lives in the wrong direction and a long way away. It's just too dangerous. Let's just concentrate on what we have and be grateful.'

The group gave no judgement.

'Ok, that way it is then,' Frank said.

Emma took her mother's hand. Danny, being seven, was too old and wise to be guided and instead flew his plane beside him, walking next to his dad.

Reaching the main road, the Allerton-Venner party discovered that a number of the other local residents, weighed down with bags of all descriptions, had chosen that same moment to head out of town. Many of them looked on with interest and with more than a touch of envy, seeing that they had fabricated for themselves a mode of transport.

No one felt able to speak. Instead they walked in solitude amid the herd, concentrating on the rhythmic sound produced by the frames scraping along the road.

Every so often a thought needed to be shared.

'Let's stick to the main roads. Everyone else will probably be doing the same, but there's safety in numbers. Who knows what might be lurking in some of the back lanes.'

'Perhaps after a few miles, we'll find the end to all this,' Joyce offered, grasping at straws.

There was nothing to be gained by dashing her hopes.

'How many people do you think are doing the same as us?' Joyce asked.

'All of them, by the looks of it,' Frank responded, sardonically.

A look from his wife recalibrated instantly the boundaries of what Frank was and was not allowed to say, and the tone he was permitted to take. He tried again, being careful not to upset his wife and not say anything that might upset the children, knowing that minds of that age had a tendency to soak up idle conversation.

'Well, there must be a lot of people who didn't make it – you know, when it first happened – the collapsing and accidents and all. Then there will be a lot of people caught up in tussles over the surviving groceries. And, as we know, lack of medicine and fitness are probably preventing a few making the journey. Then you have to wonder how many would like to, but feel they can't leave infirm relatives behind. Then, I suppose, there will be a cohort of people who think it's safer to stay put and await rescue.'

'There you go again with your fancy words. Cohort!? Where did you get that one?'

Peter's friendly snipe was easily dealt with.

'I read.'

He smiled at his friend before turning his laboured gaze to Joyce.

'To answer your original question, we could be talking a quarter of the population on the move. If my estimate is correct, I reckon there'll be fifteen thousand refugees from every medium sized town in the country, forty thousand from the bigger ones and who knows how many from the conurbations.'

Frank looked to his friend to see if he would pick up on the use of another big word, but Peter had fallen back a few paces, seemingly beginning to struggle.

Frank stopped.

'You OK?'

'Knee's giving me a bit of jip. I'll be fine. Besides, there's not really enough room for us to drag these things side by side.'

'Fair point, but let us know if you need a rest.'

The unscheduled stop gave Joyce time to consider her husband's hypothesis. She found it sobering.

'So, mass migration is inevitable. Is that what you're saying?'

'Yep. Unless we're wrong and there is an end to all this, I can't imagine another logical scenario.'

The party fell silent, returning to their inner thoughts.

Although it was still relatively early, the pedestrian train managed to cover less than a mile before it became patently obvious they had failed to beat the rush. To the already substantial number who had accompanied them from the housing estate, bands of fleeing townsfolk joined them, their numbers increasing wildly as roads merged.

Everyone was leaving via the main road. From kerbstone to kerbstone, not a single centimetre of tarmac went untrodden. The rate at which the stream flowed, being determined by the pace of the slowest member, was merely a trickle, but even the hardiest would confess to feeling a sense of claustrophobia, and of fear the human traffic was so dense it might cause them to become separated from a loved one. Keeping an eye on the children became so fraught, Tessa considered attaching them to her wrist via a lead. However, as both began to whine and complain that their feet hurt, Peter suggested they would be better off allowing them to step onto the frames. Although the added burden this placed on the husbands was unwelcome, it nevertheless had the effect of solving both problems.

As the miles passed slowly, the refugees began to need the toilet. Every tree and sturdy hedge became a screen for somebody emptying their bowels, until it became impossible to find a suitable patch of earth unsoiled by someone else. Nobody possessed the means to bury what they had done, nor did they have the inclination. Consequently, after only a few more hours, the smell of human waste permeated the air along the entire length of the route.

Being trapped in the middle of the pack, the Allerton and Venner families plodded on, mile after mile, deprived of any view other than that of the other refugees. It was a pitiful sight: belongings crammed into plastic carrier bags, held in hands and in bunches over their shoulders; weary mothers and children sagging under the weight; other's bearing the burden of homemade yokes, the ends jabbing fellow travellers about the head and shoulders; other's bearing crude stretchers, piled high with their precious belongings.

The day lasted an eternity until the light at last began to fade, forcing the refugees from the roads into adjacent fields where they could set up camp for the night. Exhausted, Peter's group followed suit, grateful for a chance to sit down, although their pitch was so small it reminded Tessa of the beaches of Spain in high summer. As tired as they were, it was too early to rest. No sooner had the multitude of groups dropped their bags and posted guard, members of each were sent out, foraging for fuel with which to make fire.

Large men in heavy boots kicked at fence posts until they were dislodged, or broke under the attack. Smaller men resorted to uprooting the woody hedgerows. Those close enough, began ravaging the trees of a small copse. Others found it easier to liberate the timber from an abandoned, isolated, house. Wherever it came from, most families were able to find enough combustible material to see them into the night, if not, until morning.

Despite the suspicions each held for the other, there was still the community spirit of people pulling together in the face of adversity. Anxious to save matches, settlers could freely borrow tapers from their temporary neighbours, who for the most part, were willing to help.

With a good fire lit, Frank and Peter turned to the task of creating shelter. This was achieved by tying the two A-frames together to form an arch, then using two of their tarpaulins to simultaneously cover their belongings and form a tented canopy. Having secured the bottom edges with pegs, beaten into the soft soil with a wooden mallet, the job was complete. By the time they were done and the evening meal had been prepared and eaten, the only light that remained was provided by the hundreds of small fires that speckled the fields for as far as the eye could see.

The two children succumbed to the allure of the soft duvets at the first opportunity, but their parents, although fit to drop, needed time to wind down before they could hope to sleep.

Under different circumstances this would have been an idyllic setting: the children asleep; the adults sitting round an open campfire, Peter with his arm round his wife, Frank cuddling Joyce; staring into the flames, lost in thought.

His mind suddenly interrupted, Peter's gaze turned skywards.

'I wonder what happened to them.'

Frank looked up, expecting to see the something that had triggered his friend to speak.

'Who?'

'The astronauts in the International Space Station; I wonder if they know what's been going on. They may be up there right now having simply lost contact with mission control and be wondering what to do. Scary.'

'Oh, I'm sure they do. In fact, they'd be some of the first to know something was up. I mean, they orbit the Earth every ninety minutes or so. If we're right and this thing's planet-wide, they can't have helped but notice all the lights have gone out.'

'True. Just think, if you were up there and you had been informed of the problem, what would you do? You couldn't stay up there forever, but on the other hand, you wouldn't want to risk a re-entry, not knowing if you'd break up as soon as you entered the atmosphere. One minute you'd be doing twenty-thousand miles an hour inside a space ship, the next you'd be doing twenty-thousand miles an hour in your underwear – metaphorically speaking.'

'Simple, if they stay up there, they'll die. No question about it.'

'I guess they'd probably get back to Earth no problem. If the meteor shower was to blame, there must have been an incubation period and if that's the case, the capsule could safely re-enter, land and have a good few weeks before disintegrating.'

'Pete, you're rambling.'

Tessa's observation returned the group to another period of quiet contemplation. However, Peter was unable to keep his thoughts to himself for very long.

'I wonder if submarines have been affected. Some of those nuclear subs will have been submerged since long before the meteor shower started and may still be down there now. They may not yet have come into contact with whatever is causing the rust.'

'Nothing seems to have stopped the rust so far,' Tessa replied. 'Not paint, not concrete. Either they have already exploded…'

'Imploded,' Frank said, correcting her.

'Whatever. Anyway, either they have already *imploded,* or the thing will become infected when they surface, and I'm sure they have to do that to use the radio.'

'Oh, so now you're an expert on nuclear submarines are you?' Frank said, playfully.

'Very funny.'

'Now here's a thought,' Peter said, changing the subject.

'Go on,' Tessa asked.

'Both our gold wedding bands have gone the same way as all the other metal, haven't they?'

'Yes,' Tessa replied, soulfully.

'Well, it makes you think about what might have happened to the likes of

Fort Knox?'

'Christ yes!'

This thought caught Frank's imagination.

'I would love to see the face on the man who was guarding that lot at the time.'

'I can just imagine what his bosses must have said when he told them,' Joyce added with a smile. 'What, *all* of it?!'

The silence returned, interspersed with the occasional snigger as the image of the poor guard kept invading their thoughts.

Then it was Joyce's turn to break silence.

'I think, at times like this, one should concentrate on the good points.'

'Times like this? How often have you known the world brought to its knees then?'

Frank was being pedantic.

'You know full well what I mean.'

'Go on then, what good has come out of it?'

'Well, think of Africa. They always seem to be shooting each other, or hacking each other to pieces with machetes. Without guns and knives there'll be no more wars.'

'Yes,' Frank responded, 'except that now normally-civilized people have taken to caving each other's heads in with whatever comes to hand, and your argument is a bit of a double-edged sword isn't it? True, some African nations have been fighting civil wars for years, resulting in many thousands of innocent people starving to death, and true, the very organisations that have tried to help them have been hampered by gun-wielding guerillas who will now find themselves without so much as two rifles to rub together, but on the other hand, the aid agencies will have been left without food to distribute, or the means to do it if they had any. Death will hit Africa on a whole new scale. I guess the Sudanese and other people like them were just destined to have a really shitty life.'

'Very eloquently put,' Peter said. 'Mind you, all this might be some consolation to them, knowing that at least now they won't be the only ones up shit creek without a paddle.'

'I cannot believe this has been a catastrophe for every single person on the planet,' Tessa said. 'What about those lost tribes of the rain forest? I doubt they had any metal in the first place. They probably haven't even noticed.'

Joyce sided with Tessa.

'Well, I say good luck to them. They've always lived in harmony with nature so they deserve to get something back.'

Peter was quick to change the subject.

'I saw a programme once about the Statute of Liberty.'

This was another opportunity for Frank to be playfully cruel.

'Is there anything you haven't seen a programme on?'

'Ha, ha, very funny. Anyway, in this programme they were saying how many times the Statue of Liberty has been used over the years to demonstrate just how catastrophic a disaster is. For example, in one of the 'Planet of the Apes' films, the hero finds out he isn't on another planet after all, he's in the future, and he knows that because, at the end of the film, comes across the statue half buried in the sand.

'A lot of sci-fi magazines, from the fifties I think, regularly showed it being zapped by aliens on their front covers.'

'Is there any point to all this?' Frank said, feigning disinterest.

'Don't you see the irony? Now, when a disaster of monumental proportions does actually strike, the Statue of Liberty, being made of copper sheeting over an iron framework, will have disappeared completely. Not a filmmaker's dream, I'm sure you'll agree.'

'I thought it was made of stone,' said Frank.

'No.'

'I guess it's time to hit the sack,' Joyce intervened, herself tired and wishing to avoid a continuation of this kind of meaningless conversation.

One by one, the parents squeezed into the cramped shelter, trying not to wake the children. Peter, the last in line, stood at the entrance while the other's found a space. Not far away, a man sat by his fire cuddling his son to his side. Even though they spoke softly, the night air allowed for crystal clear transmission of sound over great distances.

'Dad, I don't want to go camping any more. Can we go home now?'

The boy's innocent remark cut through Peter like a knife of finest Sheffield steel. There was no question of anyone being able to go home, or of things becoming better merely because the refugees were fed up with their situation. Any improvement would be gradual and all the signs were that the rest of their lives were going to be nothing less than a day to day, hand to mouth struggle, fraught with hardship and danger.

Peter dipped beneath the tarpaulin with a heavy heart.

25

The following morning, the majority of the refugees rose at the same time, ate at the same time and got under way at the same time. Peter surmised it was a herding instinct, left over from prehistoric times. As much as he scoffed at the masses for believing they were free-willed when, in reality, they were sheep, he had to accept he was just as bad, falling into step with the rest.

Day two of the journey passed in much the same way as the first, although many people lacked the energy of the previous day, and blistered feet were becoming a problem, especially for those who had managed only to salvage ill-fitting, inappropriate footwear.

Food was beginning to become scarce, causing swarms of ravenously hungry people to descend upon the fields to grub out every last root vegetable. Then, as the choicest pickings dwindled, fights broke out with increasing frequency, some of which were to the death. Each fatality represented another source of disease, but one less mouth for the natural resources of the countryside to feed.

The seemingly endless ribbon of men, women and children moved ever slower. The old and the frail simply collapsed by the roadside, ignored by passers-by who sidestepped them. Pleas from desperate relatives fell on deaf ears. The sanctity of life no longer held the same meaning.

A few black-marketeers worked their way up the line, offering plastic goods in exchange for food and water, the only things left of true value.

Days passed as a monotonous living hell: the lack of food; the constant fear of sudden attack from all quarters; the pain brought on from hauling belongings; the relentless toll of feet pounding nameless roads.

As the populated areas migrated to the unpopulated, the line of refugees began to peter out. Roads met and divided with a corresponding doubling and halving of the number of travellers that ebbed and flowed without pattern.

It was a case of the blind leading the blind. Nobody knew where they were. Few had maps and those who did found them next to useless, all the signs having been washed into the soil.

After ten days on the road, it was time for the Allerton's and the Venner's to make a decision; to continue following the pack indefinitely, or to stop and build a permanent camp. Peter took the vote.

'Frank?'

'We see more dying with every day that passes. It's becoming more frequent. I say that if we carry on, it won't be long until we're next.'

'Okay. Joyce?'

'I agree. The kids can't take much more of this. We need proper shelters where we can get a proper night's sleep. We need to be able to store what little food we have left, out of sight, and we need to find a regular source of clean water.'

'Tessa?'

'Never mind the kids; I don't think I can go on much longer. Anything has got to be better than this.'

'Okay, that just leaves me. I agree, we must find somewhere today, or at least by tomorrow. It means getting off the beaten track. We must avoid areas where there are a lot of unburied dead and where people might find us and try to take what we have. Besides, if we continue, we'll probably find ourselves going too far, and heading back towards a built up area. That would be disastrous.'

It was settled. At the very next junction, Peter's party chose the route least liked by the rest of the refugees. Then, at the next junction, he did the same. By the evening, this policy had paid off and the last of the fellow survivors had been shaken off.

It was not practical to drag the A-frames across rough terrain, through long grass. Instead, they chose to follow a long, winding farmer's track of compressed, crushed, stone; one that led to a series of similar tracks, skirting a number of fields. The choice that Peter made at each turn was not entirely random. He had his eyes set on a wood, lying at the base of a moderately sized hill. It promised ample wood for the fire and raw materials for the camp. In addition, he had never been in a wood that did not have at least a small brook running through it, or a rabbit warren.

Nearing the trees, Peter secretly felt it unlikely that nobody else had already discovered this same spot, but it was worth a try, and if there were anyone else, it might be possible to persuade them that the woods could support another half dozen people. Frank was having similar thoughts. The women and children, however, were not thinking of anything else but their fatigue, and their pain, and their griping hunger.

The group stopped, at which point Peter instructed Frank to guard the women, children, and supplies, while he entered the woods to reconnoitre, armed with his cricket bat and glass dagger. There were no complaints from his wife who was too far-gone to care, as were Joyce and the children.

It was not long before Peter could be seen on the other side of a small ditch, his thumb raised as an indication their journey was finally at an end. The realisation brought the group to life. Reinvigorated, they quickly traversed the ditch with the heavy frames in tow.

'Nobody else here,' Peter announced. 'It's all ours. There's a stream over there. I don't know how safe it is to drink the water, but it's a good flow and we can boil it, or use the filter. I just hope there are no bodies floating in it up stream.'

Plans were formulating in his head as he spoke.

'We'll make camp tonight as usual. Then tomorrow, we'll set about constructing something more permanent, set well back so we can't be spotted from the fields. Then, maybe we can set some traps and eat properly.'

The A-frames were bound together in record time. Fallen wood was abundant and easily gathered, but Frank could see that in the long term a store would be needed if they were to avoid being troubled by the rain.

'Pete, it's all very well building back from the edge of the wood, but it's not going to stop people spotting our smoke is it?'

Tessa was, as ever, concerned about attack.

'There's nothing we can do about that. All we can do is to keep as low profile as possible and be well armed. Maybe in the long term we could build defences – a ditch and a palisade. Anyway, enough of that. Let's get some sleep.'

As the group settled down, feelings were mixed. They had all needed a place they could call home and the isolated wood looked to be ideal, but there remained the ever-present threat of attack and the question of where the next meal was coming from. Nevertheless, fatigue overrode anxiety and within a short time, all were asleep.

The following morning, the children were allowed to stay in bed as long as they wanted. Breakfast, although sparse, was served to them there. The women paired up to gather firewood, armed with their glass knives and taking it in turns to keep a look out. The men, meanwhile, set about building the new shelters.

Peter had once visited an open-air museum that had gathered together a collection of buildings from throughout the ages, one of which had been a

charcoal burner's cottage. It was this design the two friends s(
emulate. There would be two - one for each family - built next to ea(
to afford added protection. They would be constructed with the doors
towards the fields, making it easier to spot incoming strangers.

The design was simple. Two rectangular holes, each large enough to
three, dug into a raised bank of clay soil. Branches would then be b(
together forming apex structures over the holes. These would then
covered with the nylon tarpaulins and finally covered in layers of soil a
bracken to help retain heat.

The design may have been simple, but the construction was a differen
matter. Firstly, the holes had to be dug without the use of spades. This, the
two men achieved by pounding the ground with broken branches. The loose
soil could then be scooped out with the aid of Emma's plastic seaside bucket
and spade. Next, enough branches of suitable length had to be collected, but
without a saw or an axe, this task was easier said than done. Even binding
together the branches to form the roofs was troublesome. They had ample
kite string with which to complete the task, but cutting it with glass was a
slow process and burning through the string was not an option as any slight
breeze would extinguish the flame, and matches were too precious to waste.
All things considered, the two men were lucky to complete the first of the
shelters by the end of the second day, and the second, two days later.

Gathered round the fire for another sparse meal, Peter was pleased with
their progress 'Well, we've got decent shelter, ample water and endless
supplies of firewood. Now, all we need to do is sort out is some food, and I
think the good book can help us there. Tomorrow we set some traps.'

ught to
h other
facing

leep
und
be
id

oserved, her arms and shoulders bearing the weight
ρ bowl, piled high with hand wrung laundry. 'I hope
ıl need the extra layers.'

.pect?' Joyce responded. 'By my reckoning, today is the
:ptember. Well into autumn.'

.irst,' Tessa repeated, wistfully. 'Emma should have started at
. by now. She'd have loved it. I'll have to home school her now,
ɔ I teach? I feel as though she should experience the full range of
out what relevance are they. History? How's that going to help?
phy? She'll likely never see another town, never mind another
.ry. You can't even talk about other cultures. There aren't any. Just
ple living hand to mouth, struggling to survive.'

Γess, you're thinking too much. Just be thankful for what we have. We've
got shelter, water and each other. Okay we could do with a bit more food,
but in the spring we can grow crops, pick berries and make preserves – who
knows what else.'

'If we make it until spring.'

Tessa's downward spiral into melancholia was checked, almost before it had
begun, with the return of Frank and Peter to the encampment, each proudly
holding a brace of rabbit aloft.

'Get the fire stoked. We're having a feast.'

'I've been thinking,' Peter said, idly, repeatedly drawing his glass blade
down the centreline of a rabbit's belly. 'I'm sure there must be a cure.'

'For what?' Frank asked.

'The rust of course. The way I see it, we are not talking about just an
acceleration of the normal rusting process. If we were, only iron and steel
would have been affected. No, when even gold is consumed, you know that
something quite different is happening.

'I've been convinced from day one that it was too much of a coincidence
this all started only a short time after the meteor shower. The two events
have to be linked. Cause and effect.

'Although nothing collided with the planet, a lot of material entered our
atmosphere and, if the meteors were carrying an infection, it could have been

passed on.'

'You could well be right, but how does that help us,' his wife ei
imagine quite a few people have come up with the same idea, but
how it was caused doesn't help us, does it?'

'Of course it does,' Peter replied, amazed by her lack of foresight.
whatever it is that has infected our planet has a life cycle. It might d.
it has finished attacking all the metal we have to offer. If so, it may be po
to re-smelt the residue. We have to experiment.'

'Even if you're right, how can we hope to smelt metal when we
difficulty in doing something as apparently simple as cooking a rabbit?' Fr
interjected, referring to the four mutilated carcasses, clearly unimpressed.

'I used to melt aluminium in my back garden as a boy. I built my ow
bellows then and I'm sure I can do it again now. We can make a furnac
using clay. I'll need to gather a few bits and pieces together so I'll probably
have to go into town, and I'll have to find a reasonable sample of rust to work
with, but it's all doable.'

'Are you mad?' Frank responded, incredulous. 'You said yourself, built up
areas are dangerous places; full of disease and God knows what else.'

'I know there are risks, but without solving the problem through
experimentation, what future is there for our children?'

'If you bring disease back into camp, there is no future,' Joyce said,
solemnly.

'Then I take it, you're all against me.'

Tessa could see her husband was hurt.

'It's not that we're against you; it's just that what you are proposing seems
rather dangerous.'

Without saying another word, Peter stood, turned and walked slowly away.
At a distance of about a hundred metres he sat down with his back against an
ancient oak, his knees drawn to his chest, his forearms resting on them, a twig
held loosely between his fingers.

Sometime later, it appeared he had decided to swallow his pride and to re-
join the group, unable to resist the aroma of cooking meat. However, his
refusal to speak with anyone demonstrated he was still sulking, as did the fact
he returned to the group, not for meat, but only to gather his hunting
equipment before walking off into the woods.

Later still, he could be seen near the banks of the stream, fashioning a
collection of saplings into what looked like a loosely woven, upside down

.1en proceeded to fetch handfuls of soft
.1 daub them over the whole surface of the
.1ving a largish opening at one end and a

and when he was all but finished.

, and some rust,' he said, making no reference to his

.1gh with it aren't you,' Tessa responded, her voice
.ppointment and concern.
.1d that portrayed determination, but he was willing to

must be abandoned houses around here. If there are, I should
.1d what I'm looking for without going into town which has got
.he risk of me catching something.'
.e did not look convinced.
, you know I wouldn't do anything to put us in danger and I'm not
.5 this just for me. Quite the opposite. I'm doing this for us. You're
ays telling Emma that Daddy will make it better. Well, just because this
.1ing may be a bit out of my league, I've still got to try. Otherwise, how am
I ever going to be able to look her in the face again?'

'Pete, you're only mortal, like the rest of us.'

'I know that, but she doesn't.'

Tessa paused to consider her position.

'Okay, we need to know the area anyway and there may be something out
there we can eat. You can go, but you've got to be careful.'

A smile grew across Peter's face.

'Thanks, sweetheart. I'll be careful. Don't you worry.'

'Come on. You must be starving. I've saved you some rabbit.'

Tessa took her husband's hand and together they walked back to camp as
though sharing a romantic stroll through the park.

Peter had always found it difficult to issue an apology. Frank, on the other
hand, had never been one to hold a grudge.

'So, Pete, I'm sorry I dismissed your ideas out of hand. It's just that we've
got so much on our plate already.'

'That's okay. I know my ideas must seem a bit mad, but you've got to agree,
restoring metal would be a huge deal and make the chances of our long term

survival that much greater.'

'Do you really think you can do it? No disrespect, but you're not a scientist. You're just a screw.'

'Correction, I *was* a screw. Now I'm just someone who doesn't have any answers, but is willing to try and find some. As you always kept on telling me, I used to watch an awful lot of TV – mostly documentaries – so I know a little bit about a lot of things. I've also read a lot of books and I used to carry out some pretty scary experiments as a boy.'

'That's an understatement,' Frank agreed. 'How you never killed yourself, I do not know.'

'It's not just about what I know. I've always had the confidence to have a go, whether it was tinkering with the car, or climbing on top of the roof to fix the aerial. These days, all that makes me just as qualified as a university lecturer.'

'All right, I agree that you're pretty handy to know and I know you used to melt aluminium as a boy, but melting steel is a different kettle of fish. How can you hope to achieve the kind of temperatures you'll need?'

'It may take longer, and I may need charcoal instead of twigs, and it may take a greater and more sustained effort than I have ever given before, but I am sure it can be done. Besides, who said anything about smelting steel?'

'But I thought...'

'No, Frank. My first goal is to melt some metal. It's probably too much to hope that it will work first time. I may have to develop a new technique, or find additives to cancel out the infection. It could take countless firings. Ultimately, I want to find a cure for all metals, but using steel would take too long. At best, I would only be able to conduct one experiment a day and the effort needed would probably kill me. I intend to stick to what I know best - aluminium.'

Tessa had remained silent, listening to the two men's discussions.

'Excuse me, but haven't you missed something? If you do find deposits of rust collected somewhere, how are you going to tell what metal they were?'

All eyes turned to Peter.

'I haven't worked that one out yet. I'm sure that there's plenty of rust out there, but you're right, I've no idea how to tell the difference between one pile of dust and another.'

'If you find any at all,' Tessa responded, driving another nail into his coffin. 'We've had some nasty weather since this thing happened. Most of it has probably been blown away by the wind, or washed away by the rain.'

She had a valid point. Just as Peter was beginning to convince the others that his ideas held some merit, his wife had sent him right back to square one.

'I don't know what's the matter with you lot. The whole world would benefit from a cure. You should all be helping me come up with some ideas, or at the very least, give me moral support.'

The children had no idea what their parents were talking about, but Tessa, Frank and Joyce could see he was right.

'Greenhouses are made of aluminium. If you could find where one stood you might be able to recover some residue,' Joyce suggested.

'No good. As Tess said, there's been a lot of rain since the phenomenon. Greenhouses would have all been washed away,' Peter responded, ever the realist.

The conversation continued for a while, but eventually concluded without a solution to Peter's problem. However, he had resolved to go on an expedition the following morning and he had at least secured the agreement of the others.

Peter had a restless night. He could not wait to get under way, knowing the cure might be within reach. Before leaving, he made a point of wrapping his arms around Emma and giving her an enormous hug. He wanted her to know he still loved her more than anything else in the universe. Sadly, she no longer responded as she used to in the days before the disaster. It was understandable she should be traumatised by what had happened, but Peter feared the change in their relationship had more to do with her blaming him for their current situation.

Tessa watched her husband leave camp. She knew the dangers he might face and hated that he was prepared to put her through so much anguish. She hated herself even more for secretly urging him on, hopeful he might find something they could eat. At least he was well armed: a glass knife at his side; the sheathed cricket bat, and a quiver worn on his back; a bow slung across one shoulder.

The purpose of the expedition was twofold. Firstly, Peter had a specific shopping list: a good source of rust deposits - preferably aluminium, or perhaps lead - which he would attempt to re-smelt; and some materials out of which he intended fabricating bellows. Secondly, it was an opportunity to explore the surrounding area, about which none of the party knew anything.

To this end, Peter had with him a folded A3 sheet paper and a sharpened crayon with which to sketch a map. Knowing the sun rises in the east and sets in the west, he orientated the virgin piece of paper by adding an arrow in the top left-hand corner, indicating north. Everything he then drew would be relative to this line. Counting his paces gave his map a measurement of distance, so a scale was added at the bottom right. Finally before setting off, two small shelters, drawn at the very centre of the page, indicated the Allerton-Venner encampment.

His meticulous recording of features and distance made progress slower than it would otherwise have been, and Peter was well aware that time was limited. He had given himself until noon to find what he was looking for, or turn back, allowing sufficient time for him to make the return journey before nightfall. Slowing him down still further was Peter's decision to stop every two hundred paces to tie a piece of rag to a convenient branch, or narrow tree trunk, carefully positioning the knot in the direction of the previous rag. In this way he would be able to re-trace his steps without becoming lost, the prospect of which worried the lone explorer even more than being set upon by bandits. It was a genuine concern as he lacked a natural sense of direction, a trait inherited from his mother.

Over the years, Peter and his mother had found themselves lost in the most unlikely places, once having to escape a nature reserve through somebody's garden, unable to find their way back to the car park. Even navigating the gardens of stately homes had caused a few problems.

Unlike his mother, Peter's father had possessed the navigational skills of a homing pigeon. If only he were there to lead the way, but of course, he was not, and without knowing the area, Peter knew he might wander for days without ever seeing his family again. A sensible precaution would have been for the group to have agreed that if anyone became separated from the party, they should all meet up again at a prominent landmark. Unfortunately, there were none. Nor could they agree to meet up in a particular village because they had not the faintest idea where they were.

Where possible, Peter tried to stick to a linear route, running from south to north. Inevitably there were a number of obstacles to negotiate: a wide, shallow, stagnant pond; a ditch; undergrowth that was too dense to penetrate; a tree that had been blown apart by lightning. He noted these on his map, and moved on.

Eventually, Peter emerged from the trees to find a lane running across his path, east to west. It curved sharply to the north after a few hundred metres in either direction.

Having tied another strip of cloth at the entrance to the wood, Peter took the arbitrary decision to follow the lane to the west. However, in rounding the bend, he discovered the road continued north in a straight line for at least a mile - maybe two - holding very little promise for a quick discovery. The sun was now almost directly overhead, indicating he would soon have to return to camp. Being reluctant to go back empty handed, and knowing his progress home would undoubtedly be quicker, Peter calculated he still had enough time to reconnoitre the lane to the east. At least to determine what was round the corner.

Having amended his map to show the disappointing western route, Peter retraced his steps and continued east, a sense of anticipation growing with every step.

What he found merely frustrated him. The lane immediately curved round to the right and then, after another fifty metres, to the left. Seven times Peter thought the next bend must be the last. Seven times was he forced to overcome fresh disappointment and carry on, but then, rounding the eighth, perseverance was at last rewarded, an isolated row of three detached dwellings coming into view, hidden behind a thick hedge, less than half a mile in the distance.

It was a relief to discover they were uninhabited.

Entering through the front door of the first house, Peter pushed forwards to where the stairs had once been, hoping to find the remains of a cupboard beneath. His luck was in.

Visible beneath the wreckage were the remains of a vacuum cleaner; the source of a plastic pipe ideally suited to the fabrication of the bellows he would need in order to raise the temperature of his furnace to a critical level. Then, all that he needed was some suitable residue, the biggest concentration of which was likely to be in the garage. However, before leaving the premises, Peter decided to sweep the interior, looking for anything of use. He quickly deemed that accessing the upper floor was too dangerous, especially for one travelling alone, and it was established quickly that the ground floor had already been thoroughly ransacked.

The occupiers must have had a comfortable income. All the rooms were of a good size and the layout included a study and a library. Desiring to build up and preserve a comprehensive reference collection, Peter found the latter of particular interest, he being unable to sit back and watch the accumulated knowledge of thousands of years lost in just one generation. There were some inventions, such as the internal combustion engine, that he considered best forgotten, but key books such as an encyclopaedia would form the heart of his repository.

Peter would have liked to bring his entire library with him from home, but weight and space had been limited. Now was an opportunity to restore some of what he had lost. The rain had irreparably damaged a lot of material, but good quality, solid wooden bookshelves had saved many more. In fact, there were too many to carry back to camp and would have to be retrieved at a later date. For time being, Peter settled on three volumes: a brief chronological history of the world; a single-volume encyclopaedia; and a world atlas. He carefully wrapped each in their own carrier bag before inserting them into his rucksack. He then placed other books of importance in a black plastic dustbin sack and tucked this under a fallen bookshelf for protection.

The only other discovery was a single, heavy duty, plastic carrier bag. It was large, rectangular, opened along the long edge, and was perfect for making bellows. With the pipe and the bag secured, all that was needed for completion were two pieces of wood with which to form the mouth. These he found outside – two pieces of baton of roughly equally length, about the same as the opening of the carrier bag.

The remains of the garage were to be found set into the large back garden. The building, probably dating back to the nineteen-fifties, had been constructed from corrugated asbestos, bolted to a steel frame. The broken sheets now lay in a flattened pile and had clearly not been home to any kind of vehicle at the time of collapse.

As Peter searched, he became aware of a rather unpleasant smell wafting towards him on the breeze. Unfortunately, it appeared to be emanating from the direction of the other hitherto unexplored properties.

Pushing through the chest-height box hedge between the first two gardens, Peter entered the second ruined house through the back – albeit with great difficulty. Again, very little had been missed by the looters; all except for a single cellophane-wrapped packet of long grained rice that remained perfectly preserved and ready for the taking.

Having exited the building through the front, Peter next explored its associated garage; a detached structure that stood at the end of a gravel driveway, adjacent to the house. The slates, which had formed its roof, had fallen outwards, away from the walls. These, being constructed of brick, remained standing, protecting a thin, rain-washed layer of sediment, coating the entire floor, and a seemingly random collection of plastic and rubber, indicating this had once been a high end car. Peter set about shovelling the deposits into a canvas bag that he had brought with him specifically for the purpose. It was almost certainly steel residue, but in the absence of anything else, it would have to do.

The last house, entered via the front door, gave up four items: an ordnance survey map – seemingly of the local area - showing rivers, roads, towns and landmarks; a book of street maps for the entire county; a road atlas for the entire country; and perhaps most useful of all, a utilities bill upon which was typed the address of the building Peter found it in – Pump Lane, Banton-Harbury. Armed with this piece of information and a full range of maps, the group would now know where they had chosen to settle and what was to be found in their locale.

Buoyed by his success, Peter stepped from the kitchen into the garden intending to make a quick search of any outbuildings before hastening back to camp to show the others his discoveries. Tessa would be particularly grateful to see the rice. Frank would be more interested to know where they were as it would inform future sorties.

Even before stepping from the kitchen, Peter noticed that the smell, which had first offended his nostrils from the garden of the first house, had become noticeably more pungent, and wondered what might be causing it.

The property's detached garage stood well back from the road, accessed via a long driveway that ran to the side of the front lawn, along the side of the house, and alongside the first ten metres of lawn at the back. It was similar in construction to his own garage back home in Hexley, being built of brick with a flat roof of bituminous felt laid over timbers. Save for the lack of doors, it remained a perfectly serviceable building.

The garage was no great distance from the back door, but judging by the ever increasing potency of the smell as Peter walked across to it, it stood close to the source. By the time he reached the entrance, the smell had become so abhorrent that, had it not been the discovery he made there - his most significant yet - he would undoubtedly have turned away.

There, on the concrete floor, was the shadow of a ladder, outlined in powder. He knew instantly that it must be aluminium. No one made ladders out of steel these days. It must have been slung on steel brackets beneath the roof joists. When the brackets had disappeared the ladder would have fallen to the floor and would have lain there until the next day when the lightweight succumbed to the phenomenon.

Peter stood in silence. Tears began to well in his eyes.

'Thank you.'

He then set about the task of collecting the aluminium residue. There was nearly the whole ladder's worth. A small portion had been lost where it had lain next to the door opening. However, sufficient residue remained to enable him to conduct dozens of experiments, imbuing Peter with a sense he would ultimately be successful.

Having completed harvesting the garage floor, and with his thoughts no longer distracted, Peter stood up only to receive another waft of the breath-catching smell that continued to pervade the entire area, indoors and out. Just as a piece of music can trigger vivid recollections from many years in the past, so too could the merest hint of a scent, and this was much more than a hint. Memories of a specific incident - one that had occurred shortly after his father's death - came flooding back into Peter's mind.

Only two weeks had elapsed from the diagnosis of his father's throat cancer to his last rattling breaths. The suddenness of his passing had sent the entire family reeling. It had been a very sad and painful time and, what with the funeral arrangements to be made and the tidying up of his affairs, some things were given higher priority than others. His mother's lawn was way down the list and had remained uncut for the best part of a month. When one of the neighbourhood cats killed a mole and decided not to eat it, the corpse had lain unnoticed in the long grass, decomposing a little more each day. When Peter finally got round to mowing her lawn, he inadvertently ran over the mole's body. The fast moving rotary blades shredded the creature, spreading it in all directions, releasing a stench so foul that Peter had found himself incapable of drawing breath.

All these years later, a similar stench caused Peter to cover his mouth and nose with his hand. The smell was not only unpleasant, it had attached to it an association with his father's passing and served to rekindle feelings of sadness that caused Peter to hurt anew, every bit as much as he had back then.

However unpleasant, Peter felt compelled to investigate the source. He had no idea what he might find, but one thing was for sure, it was not a dead mole.

Cautiously, Peter walked down the side of the garage and round a large rhododendron bush which obscured his view of the lion's share of the garden. There he found his answer.

Both the woman and the man appeared to have died as a consequence of receiving massive blows to their heads. The man lay of his side, his hands bound to his feet with rope, his skull hardly recognisable as such. The ragged clothes he wore did nothing to conceal the army of maggots that were busy devouring his badly decayed flesh. The woman, on the other hand, was naked and had been pegged out on the lawn. Her distorted head lay at an unnatural angle to her shoulders. Peter could only surmise the deceased man had been forced to watch his wife as she had been subjected to a horrific sexual assault before their attackers executed them both.

Peter turned, staggered back down the side of the garage, and vomited violently.

The bodies had obviously lain there for some time, but in the chronological history of the world since the phenomenon, this was recent. What really bothered Peter, more than the odour, or the sight of the bodies themselves, was that they had not died as a result of the disaster; nor had they had been killed for food, or in self-defence. They appeared instead to have been murdered purely for pleasure. As an ex-prison officer, Peter knew what sort of terrible atrocities man was capable of inflicting on man, but never before had he seen it at such close quarters.

He could not leave soon enough. Having gathered together his belongings, Peter hurried off in the direction of camp.

The journey back passed in a blur, the subconscious portion of his mind navigating the route, relying on the knotted rags to bring him home. All the while, the conscious part of his mind sought to deny access to images of the tortured couple, that rose, unwanted, from the depths of his long term memory, concentrating instead on the successes of the expedition – finding food; finding materials with which to finish the kiln; finding maps of the area; finding ample deposits of rust with which to experiment. However hard he tried, though, the disturbing images persisted in doing just that; disturbing his train of thought; disturbing his psyche.

Met by his wife, it was immediately obvious something was troubling him, but Peter stubbornly refused to admit anything was wrong. How could he tell Tessa that club-wielding maniacs were roaming the countryside, raping, torturing and murdering? How could he risk adding to the children's trauma?

Still, his reports of success did not chime with his mood; with his body language – the ninety-three percent of communication he could not hide.

'Look, love, it was a great success. I got what I want and a bit of rice to vary our diet. Let's just leave it at that.'

Tessa considered prying further, but accepted it was futile and could only lead to argument.

The evening meal was frugal, the traps having produced only one small rabbit. The rice promised to swell in the survivors' bellies, but it had been cooked sparingly so as to eke out their rations, the adults being fully aware the traps were prone to be empty. The small portions suited Peter as he had no appetite, despite having fasted all day. Unable to finish the meagre meal, he divided the left overs equally between Emma and Danny, and fell into silence.

Darkness descended soon afterwards, forcing the two families to retire to bed. It was cold and in the fading light their breath was visible. Winter was still some months away, but it was a stark reminder they only had colder weather to look forward to. Keeping warm was not really an issue. There was plenty of wood to burn, but food was already scarce and that situation could only get worse.

Emma lay between her parents. The size of the shelter did not allow for much variation in the sleeping arrangements, but it served to keep her warm. For Peter, images of decaying bodies haunted the darkness, keeping him awake. Emma could not sleep either and asked her mummy for a story. Prior to the disaster, this had been her daddy's duty, Tessa being called upon only if he had to work late. Faced with evidence the special bond between father and daughter had suffered more than he had imagined, the demons inside Peter's head were suddenly dampened with sadness, exchanging one state for another, equally unpleasant.

Tessa had a good imagination and was always able to conjure up a tale from thin air; perfect for the interior of a shelter that had no lighting by which to read a book. It was obvious what was at the forefront of her mind, the story centring on a magic box that produced endless supplies of their favourite food. She painted such a delightful picture, that when finished, her and her daughter's mouths were salivating. With the story told, reality seemed that much bleaker. Tessa had learned a valuable lesson and would be more careful about the subject in future. Peter, on the other hand, was unaffected by his wife's graphic descriptions, mostly because his mind had wandered to other matters, shortly after the first mention of food.

Lying on his back, his eyes wide open, Peter stared into the darkness, in much the same way he used to try and steady the room when it swirled as a result of drinking too much alcohol. Suddenly he became overwhelmed with a powerful desire to do something tangible – something that might help smooth the vortex. Without feeling the need to explain himself, he sat up and began groping about for a box of matches and for one of Tessa's patent candle-lamps. The initial flare died down, leaving sufficient light for him to locate the crayon map he had produced earlier that day. His eyes fixed upon the marks annotating the position of the three isolated houses. Using the same wax crayon, he added a large skull and cross bones beneath them, accompanied by the word BEWARE!

He felt instantly more at ease and able to settle down. His wife saw that he made to extinguish the candle.

'I know they're in short supply, but can we leave it burning? I don't want to be in darkness. Not tonight.'

'Sure.'

Peter pulled the bedding over his shoulders, put his arm around his daughter and turned his mind to thoughts of experimentation and to finding the cure that would restore metal to the world and the love that his daughter had once shown him.

Slowly he found sleep.

As dawn broke, Peter emerged from the shelter feeling light headed; hardly surprising for one who had neither slept well nor eaten a great deal in the past twenty-four hours. Nevertheless, he decided to wait until the others had risen so as not to eat alone. Throughout history, sharing mealtimes had been a social event. Eating in the company of the entire group gave them all a chance to spend some quality time with each other. In the meantime, the half-finished kiln called to him. It made sense to use his time effectively, working to completion while waiting for his friends and family to greet the day. Water and enthusiasm would keep hunger at bay.

Taking the large carrier bag he had retrieved from one of the houses in Banton-Harbury, he made an incision in one corner. Into this he pushed the first five centimetres of the vacuum cleaner extension tube before sealing the joint with tape. Next, he took the two lengths of sawn timber, held them together inside the opening of the bag and pierced small holes through the plastic along the entire length, just beneath the wood. Taking them one at a time, he proceeded to lace the pieces of wood to the bag with kite string, reinforcing his work with more sticky tape. The bellows were complete.

The next job was to incorporate them into the wall of the furnace. This was the purpose of the smaller of the two holes which Peter had left in the clay wall during construction. Being plastic, the pipe could not be pushed all the way through to the interior of the furnace as it would melt as soon as a fire was lit. Instead, the wall at the point of entry had been made thicker, enabling the tube to feed air into the furnace while remaining fifteen to twenty centimetres from the fire itself. Once the pipe had been sealed in place using more wet clay, it was time to test the effectiveness of the installation.

Peter knelt down, took hold of one of the pieces of wood in each hand, opened the bag to its greatest capacity, closed the handles together, and pushed down. This motion met some resistance as the sides of the bag ballooned out like the cheeks of a trumpeter. Continuing the application of pressure caused the bag to deflate, ejecting a strong flow of air through the pipe, into the furnace. He tried it for a second and third time. The seams of the bag remained intact and proved to be working every bit as well as the bellows he had made as a child.

To complete the construction, Peter made a loose fitting clay plug with which to stopper the large opening. All that was then needed was to light a fire inside to harden off the clay. All this he achieved before the other five members of the small community began to surface.

Frank crawled into the open and raised himself to his feet slowly, his body stiff after an uncomfortable night's sleep.

'It's getting cold,' he said. 'Soon we'll have to start thinking about keeping a fire going throughout the night.'

'I've been reading about that,' Peter responded, wishing to reaffirm their long friendship, fully aware how the effort it had taken merely to continue their survival had tested their relationship to the limit. 'If we build two fires, one just outside the entrance to each of the shelters and then a crude screen on the other side of the fire, it will have the effect of reflecting heat inside. Perhaps we should make that our task for the day. It may get even colder tonight.'

Frank was pleased and relieved to discover his friend thinking of things other than dreams of becoming the saviour of the world.

'The easiest form of construction would be to sink two branches vertically into holes in the ground, then tie more branches horizontally between the two. Although I'm not sure how effective it would be, or how they might stand up to the elements.'

Frank listened to Peter's suggestion before putting forward one of his own.

'There is an alternative. It would take more time, but the extra effort might pay dividends in the long run. We make a double skinned screen and fill the space between the two with mud. What do you think?'

'Neither's going to be easy as we've got nothing to chop the wood with. We'll have to break it or burn it in two. How about we see how we get on making the single screen. If that goes okay, then we can add a second and the soil.'

'Okay. It's a plan. We'll get started after we've had a bite to eat, and while we're collecting wood we can check the traps.'

'Perhaps we could use some of it to light a small fire inside the kiln...just to dry it out.'

'I don't see why not. I'll be interested to see how this things works.'

27

The party rose and ate together, just as Peter had planned. Frank explained how he and Peter were going to improve the camp. Everyone appreciated the idea of being warmer. The two men then went foraging for wood. The women and children formed their own party, carrying a bowl in the hope of finding the last blackberries of the season, or a patch of mushrooms they could be sure were not poisonous. The construction of the first screen took place at a steady pace, the two men working together to great effect. Such was their progress that Frank was more than content for his friend to sporadically divert his attention to tend a small fire, lit within the interior of the virgin kiln. Quid pro quo, Peter suggested they did not build the lesser structures and then review, but adopt Frank's plan for a double-skinned wall from the outset. If the project was worth doing, it was worth doing well.

'This is going so well, I think we should go with your design. I don't think we can finish them both today though, so I say we complete your one first, including packing it with earth, and then start on ours tomorrow.'

The offer was a generous one, favouring one family over the other – the Venners over the Allertons; *his* family over Peter's. Frank could see the sense in it. Completing one sturdy structure - fit for purpose - would give them the satisfaction of making a definitive tick against their to-do list. Two half-finished screens would be just that – half-finished – and besides, they would be at the mercy of any strong wind that came their way, threatening to undo all their hard work.

By the time the first structure was complete, and the last of the earth had been tamped down within the willow lattice frame, the light was beginning to fade. It was then that Peter made a further suggestion - rather than start the second wall, that he instead put the kiln to the test. For that purpose, the failing light was no hindrance as Peter felt he could work by the glow of the furnace alone. And it did not matter if the ambient temperature dropped to an uncomfortable level as the kiln's operator would be kept warm by the heat radiating off the clay walls and by the exertions of working the bellows.

Again, Frank was in agreement, but as interested as he was in the process, nevertheless he opted to spend the evening with the rest of the group – Tessa and Emma included.

The crucible was fashioned from clay. Once charged with aluminium residue and placed in the core, Peter worked the bellows rhythmically, stopping every so often to cast more fuel into the red-hot interior. After a while, Frank re-joined him, seeking an update.

'How's it going?'

'As it happens, I'm just about ready to pour.'

The pumping stopped and the clay plug was removed. Peter shifted his position, kneeling down so that his chin almost touched the floor.

'This is the tricky bit. When I did this as a boy, I had pliers to grab the crucible. I used an old tin which I bent over at the top to give me something to grab hold of. Now all I've got is a forked stick and a hand-made clay pot.'

Peter's eyes fixed upon the splayed end of his stick, guiding it forward, his free hand shielding his face from the savage heat.

Frank squatted on his haunches, his head positioned at an awkward angle, desperately trying to catch a glimpse of the crucible and its contents.

Peter stabbed, grunted and cursed.

Despite having spent the previous hour soaking in a bath of water, the stick caught light quickly and would need to be replaced before any future firing. Nevertheless, it held out long enough for its operator to rescue the blackened, crudely fashioned clay vessel from the inferno. Embers filled the pot to the brim, requiring Peter to reach for a second stick and flick them to one side, but still the surface was masked by a layer of ash.

Anticipation grew as Peter quickly repositioned the crucible to a clear patch of dark ground, and there attempted to tip it on its side.

'Okay, next time I'm adding a lip on either side of the bowl. It's got to make this part of the process easier.'

Instinctively, Frank came to his friend's aid, using another stick to tip the crucible from the burning forked branch. To their delight, from beneath a dull layer of impurities, a small quantity of immensely shiny material trickled onto the bare earth. It was the first metal of any description that either man had seen since the morning after the disaster; the first metal that anyone in their group had seen in nearly a month.

Their reactions were similar, but different.

Peter was restrained and merely uttered a decisive, 'Yes'.

Frank, on the other hand, reacted with an Americanised whoop that Peter would normally have found most annoying, but on this occasion let pass without comment.

Both men shared identical smiles that were larger than their faces, their eyes remaining transfixed on the small pool of cooling metal as it dulled. However, their expressions soon faded as the material continued to become increasingly drab, the edges of the ingot beginning to fall away from the central mass.

In less than a minute, the small, grey lump that had briefly been identifiable as a quantity of semi-liquid aluminium was once more nothing than a miscellaneous patch of dust.

Frank laid a firm hand upon his friend's shoulder and squeezed.

'I don't know what to say.'

'It's okay. There's no denying I'm disappointed, but I really didn't expect to have complete success at my first attempt. At least this proves my equipment works.'

'True. Remarkably well, in fact. What will you do now?'

'Well, it was silly of me to think heat alone would provide the answer. If the infection did come to Earth with that meteor shower then it had already been exposed to incredible temperatures as they burnt up in the atmosphere. What I need to do now is find an additive that will kill the infection.'

'Additive?'

'Yeh. I think I might try acids and alkalis to start with.'

'Okay, and where on Earth do you intend to find those?'

'Oh, I don't know; foodstuffs maybe.'

Peter's limited success prevented his friend from speaking too harshly. Nevertheless he felt the need to say something.

'Mate, what you've done is great and I'm all for you doing it again, but don't forget our priorities. We've got your wall to build, wood to collect and we really need to go hunting.'

'Yeh, yeh. We can do all that between firings.'

'Hmm, I think it should be doing the firings between the other stuff, don't you? I mean, as important as your experiments are, you wouldn't be able to carry them out if we froze to death or starved, would you?'

'Yeh, yeh, whatever. That's just semantics. Now, I need to find a notebook so I can write down my results and ideas.'

Frank left his friend in the darkness.

'If you won't accept any other advice, at least do this. Go to bed. Tess and Emma need you and you won't be good for anything if you don't get some sleep.'

Having failed to heed his friend's advice, staying up long after the rest of his family had cocooned themselves for the night, Peter was nevertheless the first to rise the following morning, so driven was he in his quest to discover the ultimate solution.

Aluminium having a relatively low melting point, it was a simple but laborious task to turn a second sample of residue into its molten state, but there were only limited ingredients to hand that he could then add to the mix. It seemed logical to start with extremes on the pH scale and according to the salvaged encyclopaedia some examples might be hydrochloric acid and drain cleaner; more readily available, battery acid and bleach. Any one of the many thousands of scattered car remains promised a supply of strong acid, if the battery casing remained upright, but bleach was already on site. However, as pungent as it was, the addition of toilet cleaner to the crucible made no difference to the final outcome. Undeterred, influenced by the teachings of his school days' science lessons, Peter shrugged his shoulders and updated his notes - aim, method and conclusion.

Tessa approached and sat next to her husband who, at first, did not notice her presence, his mind being so focussed on his work.

'Oh, hello darling. I didn't see you there.'

Tessa chose not to make a point of it that she had been sitting there for some time, there being other things she wished to say.

'So, Frank tells me you have quite a list of experiments to carry out.'

'That's right. I'm probably going to have to conduct dozens of experiments before I'm finished – perhaps even hundreds. Why's that?'

'Pete, don't get me wrong, I think it's great what you've done. I don't know many men who could have built a furnace, made bellows and melted metal - especially all on their own - but right now we need food more than we need a lump of aluminium. Winter's not far off so we need to think about finding enough to eat now and to be able to put something by for the cold months ahead. So, how about you forget all your fun and games for a while and go foraging with Frank? You can carry on where you left off in the spring. There's no hurry. What do you say?'

Tessa's techniques – the laying on of a gentle hand and the use of her most practiced non-offensive tone - did nothing to mitigate her husband's reaction, which was delivered swiftly and at full volume, startling Emma who remained at some distance, still within the confines of the shelter.

'Fun and games! Is that what you think of my work? Christ, woman, what

I'm trying to do could be the salvation of mankind.'

Tessa took the fingers of her husband's free hand in her own, holding them gently, hoping to calm him sufficiently that he would begin to see reason.

'I understand you want to save the world – we all do - but first we have to save ourselves.'

Peter looked pityingly upon his wife.

'Clearly you don't understand. If you did, you would know that this is bigger than you, me and Emma. It's bigger than all of us. I have a destiny to fulfil.'

He paused for a moment as if to consider whether he should reveal his hand fully.

'Go on. You're obviously dying to say something.'

'It's nothing.'

'No, I want to hear it.'

'Okay, if you must know, I have been chosen by God. There, I've said it.'

Tessa uttered an involuntary chuckle.

'God? When did you start believing in *him*? You're always telling everyone you're a devout atheist. I've heard it a million times.'

Tessa could see in her husband's expression he did not consider it a laughing matter.

'I know what I said, but that doesn't mean I was right. Every believer must have a moment when they see the truth. For me it was being confronted with the remains of that ladder. You wouldn't be doubting me if you'd been there. I mean, residue, kept dry so I could find and harvest it; still holding its form in the shape of a ladder so it couldn't be anything other than aluminium. I mean, I ask you, what are the chances of that happening? I said I needed aluminium. We all agreed how difficult it would be to find it. Then, lo and behold, the very first time I'm out on a recce, there it is, waiting for me – not anyone else – waiting for *me*. You can't tell me there wasn't a greater hand at play.

'Then, when I began to think about it, I saw everything for what it really was – like I had been trusted to know the meaning of life. It was suddenly so obvious. I realised how my ignorance had made me blind and I found myself crying for those lost years of not knowing.'

Peter noted the way his wife looked at him.

'You won't understand. You're like I was.'

In truth, Tessa was not angry; rather she was worried that she was witnessing her husband succumbing to overwhelming stress, lunging towards mental breakdown.

'Try me.'

'Okay. Firstly you must see that we were put on this Earth merely to procreate. Everything else is incidental. We know that the Sun's fuel will run out one day, millions of years from now, and that to continue to procreate we will need to leave this planet. God knows that because he made it that way. Therefore, it must be right that we send rockets into space despite the impact they have on the planet. All those years I worried about pollution, I needn't have bothered. The planet is expendable. It's just a tool for us to use, and when it's broken, we can discard it. God's okay with that. This is a test to see if we're worthy. We must overcome this, the ultimate obstacle to us leaving this planet. The dinosaurs had their chance and they blew it. I was put here to make sure we don't blow our chance too. I have the job of restoring metal to our world, to pass the test, and put mankind back on track to reaching the stars. The good news is that if this is a test, God has provided a solution. I just need to find it.

'Tess, you may find this difficult to swallow, bit I am God's chosen one.'

His voice petered out, becoming distant, but then it returned with an afterthought.

'Deep down, I always knew I was different.'

The ensuing exchange of words was ugly, resulting in Tessa producing tears; the sign for Peter to stop the onslaught. He still cared for his wife deeply and wished to make amends.

'I'm sorry.'

His arm reached around her shoulders and pulled her tight. His warmth was comforting, shutting off the tears; a kiss on her head brought forgiveness.

'Right, this is what I'm going to do. Frank and I are going to go hunting for as long as it takes. When it gets dark I'm going to fire up the beast again, but only if it doesn't stop us doing what we have to do to survive. How does that sound?'

'That sounds great.'

'It will give me an opportunity to reflect on my results and help me plan my next step. With any luck I'll find some willow bark. Barks from many trees are medicinal. Willow produces aspirin for example. And who knows, we might find something to eat. If nothing else, the fleshy part of a pine tree is edible. Did you know that? Just like a vegetable.'

A gentle squeeze elicited a smile from his wife.

'No, I didn't know that. So now we're going to be eating Christmas trees are we?'

'Yep. Including the baubles. They're plastic and haven't been affected.'

It was nice to see a hint of the man she had loved these past ten years, his humour being the thing that had first drawn her to him. Nevertheless, it was impossible to delete her husband's revelation from her mind, fearing he was on the brink of total collapse.

Tessa and Joyce hoped their husbands' trip would be fruitful, but were equally looking forward to having the men out from under their feet. There was a great deal to be done around camp; one of the first things being to give the children some errands to keep them out of mischief.

'Danny, take Emma into the woods and collect as much firewood as you can. We're getting through it like nobody's business, but don't go too far. I want to be able to hear you.'

Joyce issued her instruction and was relieved to find that neither child put up a fight.

In fact, for the two young friends, it was not a chore; rather it was an adventure to be out alone, away from the discipline of their parents.

With the men and children absent, the women were left to power on uninterrupted. Both became unaware of the day passing and it was not until mid-afternoon that Joyce realised she had seen little of Danny and Emma for some time. They had been back many times – the pile of sticks and branches paid testament to that – but not for a while; not for an uncomfortably long while. Nor had she heard them.

She stopped to listen but failed to detect the sound of shrill voices near or far.

'Tess, have you seen the kids?'

'No.'

Tessa put down what she was doing and began to scan their field of view.

'I hope they're all right.'

Joyce was about to add something when her friend interrupted her, tapping the back of her hand on Tessa's upper arm, the same hand then being used to point towards the tree line.

'There's Danny now.'

Joyce turned to confirm the sighting. It was a relief to see her son, but a shock to see that a strange man accompanied him. A few moments later,

Emma came into view. She too was being escorted by a stranger. Danny appeared to be walking awkwardly and then it became apparent why. His hands were bound behind his back and he was held on a lead, tied around his neck. Emma was bound in a similar fashion. The two men were armed with wooden clubs; crude but effective.

A bolt of fear struck both women simultaneously. The temptation was to run towards their children, but even in their panic stricken state they realised independently and instinctively that this would only serve to place their children in greater danger. Besides, Emma and Danny were being guided towards their parents, on a direct route towards the heart of the camp. Whatever these men wanted, the mothers would soon find out.

'Good afternoon ladies.'

The words were not meant to be pleasant; they were meant to be menacing and in that they succeeded.

'What do you want?' Tessa responded, her voice trembling.

The same man spoke again.

'The two little'uns tell me that your men are away, so we thought we'd pay you a visit and keep you company for a while.'

'Cut the crap,' Joyce said, unable to contain her rage. 'Untie our children and tell us what the hell it is you want.'

'The children remain tied. That way we're sure to get what we want. If you co-operate, you all live. If you don't, you die. It's as simple as that.'

At this Emma began to cry uncontrollably, but stopped short as the second man gave a sharp tug on her lead.

'All right, what do you want?'

Tessa struggled to hold back her own tears.

'First, I want you to get your clothes off - all of them.'

Joyce began to protest, but was stopped by Tessa who, by her expression alone, made it clear she felt that resistance was futile. Joyce could not help but conclude the same.

Both women stood with their heads hung low as they slowly and reluctantly removed their clothing until they stood naked and humiliated before their children and the two assailants.

The dominant male handed Danny's lead to his accomplice.

'Down on the ground - both of you.'

The women took this to mean for them to sit on the ground with their knees drawn close to their chest and ankles crossed. Their interpretation served to anger their assailant further.

He approached Joyce first, this time barking his order.

'Lie back.'

His instruction was accompanied by a hard shove to her shoulder.

Joyce complied; she could hardly refuse. She lay, rigid but shaking, her hands down by her sides, her legs firmly clamped together. The man unshouldered a bag and took from it a number of wooden stakes, a wooden mallet and some short lengths of yachting rope, frayed at either end. Placing his foot between her ankles, the man spread her legs. Having pegged them in place, he moved up towards her arms. Joyce was breathing heavily, even more so as he knelt beside her head. She flinched as he gripped her wrists tightly; first one, then the other. She turned her head away, her eyes shut tight.

Everyone with the exception of Tessa had their sights fixed firmly upon Joyce. All saw the trickle of water running from under her body. Tessa was not aware because she had chosen instead to stare at the man who was holding the children like a pair of attack dogs.

When it came to Tessa's turn, unlike her friend - who lay pegged out beside her, spread eagled - she forced herself to watch.

Satisfied at his handiwork, the dominant male stood up and without taking his eyes off his prey, spoke to his partner.

'Which one do you want?'

'The one on the right. I like water sports,' he replied excitedly.

'Okay, but I go first.'

With that, the first male, who stood at Tessa's feet, dropped his trousers around his ankles. There was no doubting how excited he was. He remained where he was, manipulating himself slowly and gently, relishing the sight of Tessa's body, taking in every minute detail – every contour. His mouth was watering, his tongue licking his lips every so often, his entire body shaking with anticipation. Tessa's body was shaking too, but for entirely different reasons. Instinctively, she closed her eyes, attempting to blot out the world, but her action served only to focus her attention on the disgusting noises that her captor made – groaning and squelching. Her eyes reopened, her pupils immediately fixing upon the man's hand and groin.

A smile developed across his face, indicating he was ready. Tessa tensed still further, her breathing becoming shallow and fast, sufficient to make her feel light headed. But then, quite without warning, the attacker's smile turned in an instant to a grimace that took hold and distorted his entire face. Almost immediately, he fell to the floor, grabbing at an arrow, lodged deeply in his left buttock. Peter rushed forward and kicked the assailant in the head, several times, rendering him unconscious. Frank had simultaneously planted an arrow of his own in the neck of the other assailant who immediately dropped both leads and fell to the ground, gasping for air. His fate was sealed moments later by Frank who bludgeoned the man about the head with the attacker's own club.

Frank ran to untie the women and children while Peter bound the surviving assailant's hands, securing him to a tree with a length of the man's own rope.

'Oh God Frank, I was so scared,' Joyce said, tears rolling down her cheeks.

Tessa was equally grateful to be free.

Helped to their feet, both women gathered their clothing and dressed while hastening to their children's side, engulfing them with a comforting hug only a mother could give. The men's arms and bodies then added a second layer of protection.

Peter was the first to break away, so he could address both wives and the children.

'You'll be all right here. Frank and I have got to deal with these two. We'll bury this one and come back for the other. He won't trouble you.'

Joyce and Tessa nodded, but said nothing. Neither Emma nor Danny raised their faces from their mothers' necks.

Frank was reluctant to release his grip, but felt obliged to help his friend attend to the unfinished business.

In silence, Frank and Peter each took hold of one of the dead man's arms and dragged him away towards the fields where it was easier to dig a shallow grave; deep enough not to be disturbed by ravenous foxes.

Minutes passed before the surviving assailant returned to consciousness. Groaning, he tried to stand, but the pain in his buttock caused him to crumple back to the ground. Tessa maintained her grip on her daughter, but lifted her head to study the wounded wretch. He was naked from the waist down and flaccid; an ugly, dirty piece of meat. The precious arrow had been pulled from him flesh, causing blood to flow in a steady rivulet. His face was badly swollen and Tessa suspected his teeth had loosened, or flown from his mouth. His nose had moved across his face.

Tessa felt no pity.

As the injured man tried to speak, blood spattered over his chin.

'Please don't let them kill me. I wasn't going to hurt you.'

He sounded stupid; his plea pathetic.

Tessa rose to her feet and approached the captive.

'Is that the best you can do?' she sneered, driving her foot into his groin; the air from her lungs and his.

Having experienced some satisfaction – received some recompense - she turned away, gathered together her friend and the children and guided them towards the stream in which to cleanse themselves.

Nearly an hour passed before the men returned, or so Joyce guessed. They said nothing to either woman as they untied their captive from the tree and lifted him unceremoniously to his feet. The man was in no fit state to walk. Blood continued to trickle down his leg. His trousers, which remain about his ankles, restricted his movements still further.

'Here's the score,' Peter said. 'We might be persuaded to go easy on you if you take us to your camp, where we will help ourselves to anything we want.'

'I don't have anything,' the man replied defiantly, through gritted teeth and gaps.

'Then you're going to die. It's as simple as that.'

'All right, all right. We don't have a camp. Everything we have is in bags. They're stashed back there in the woods.'

A nod from Peter was all that was needed. Supporting the would-be rapist, one under each arm, Peter and Frank dragged their captive away into the trees, in the direction of the stockpile.

Surprisingly, their prisoner turned out to be a man of his word; at least a man who told partial truths. The bags – numbering two - lay camouflaged beneath some bracken near a large oak tree which was easily identifiable by a scar running down the length of its trunk. Simultaneously, the two friends allowed their prisoner to slump to the ground, at the base of the tree. Landing heavily, the man let out a single yelp, but was otherwise grateful he could rest, rocking the weight of his body to one side, easing the pressure on his wound.

Peter turned the contents of the bags onto the woodland floor. The items that tumbled from them were a cause for disappointment - a few snacks, water bottles, extra items of clothing, some plastic carrier bags and a roll of sticky tape. These were the possessions of a forager, not a nomad.

'Where's the rest? Where's your camp?' Peter asked, angrily.

'Fuck you.'

Peter said nothing in response, but ducked his head to unshoulder the bag he had been carrying since leaving camp with Frank earlier that morning. Having some idea what his friend might to do, Frank gave their prisoner a second chance to cooperate.

'Look fella, you know this isn't everything you've got. We know this isn't everything you've got. Tell us where it is and we'll take it by way of recompense. That's it. Then we'll let you go and as long as we never see your face again, that'll be the end of the story. What do you say?'

The man spat as best as a dry mouth could hope to.

'Go fuck yourself.'

His narrowed eyes noted movement and flicked from his inquisitor to Peter.

The captive's anxiety spiked on seeing the latter pull a length of rope from his own bag, but then waned on discovering it was to be knotted, not about his neck, but round the bindings that secured his wrists. Suffering a rollercoaster of fear and pain, the next peak brought renewed, severe discomfort. The free end of the rope having been cast over a protruding branch, the prisoner was then hoisted until his feet barely touched the ground, making him adopt the stance of a fully trained ballerina on pointe.

'What are you going to do with me?' the man pleaded with difficulty.

Peter was calm in his response.

'What's your name?'

'Mike.'

The man saw an opportunity to appeal to his captor's good nature.

'I've got two young children. They'll be wondering where I am. My wife, she's pregnant. She hasn't let me have sex for six months. That does things to a man. You must know that. I wouldn't have hurt your kids…or your missus. I know it's sick, but I just wanted to wank over them. Nothing else. Then I'd have let them go.

'Look what you've done to me.'

Mike's swollen eye indicated in the direction of his wounded buttock.

'And you killed my brother. Haven't I been punished enough?'

Peter could not help but be annoyed by the mixture of blood and spittle that flew from Mike's damaged mouth, thankful it fell short; equally by the creature's worthless and overlong mitigation.

'Poor Mike. I really think you could have come up with something a little better than that. I mean, one of those children you had tied up like a dog was my precious daughter. The other was my God son. One of the women you pegged out on the ground was my wife, and do you know, five years ago, she was pregnant, just like yours. I confess, I wasn't getting much at the time – they tend to go off it a bit when then can't breathe – but I don't remember staking out my mate here's missus and knocking one out over her, or trying to shag her. As for the idea there are kids out there who actually care about whether you live or die, I very much doubt it.'

Mike sensed the worst.

'What are you going to do with me?'

Peter remain impassive.

'There are no authorities to deal with you now, and I can't just let you go, can I? You're far too dangerous. I've seen what you're capable of. I found two other victims of yours in the garden of a deserted house nearby. I'm left with only one option; I'm going to have to kill you.'

'Well fuck you,' Mike cried, defiantly, his desperate movements aggravating his wound, causing him to wince.

Further outbursts were prevented by the application of a long sock tied in a large knot at the back of the rapist's head.

'Sorry, that's all I have. I would rather I didn't have to gag you at all, but I don't want to upset the women and children any more than they have been already.'

Peter spoke with as much passion as a delivery driver informing the customer of a substitution.

If it was possible, the restrained man's eyes became even wilder with terror – something that did nothing to divert his captor from the task he had in mind.

Without further delay, Peter unsheathed his knife and turned his attentions to the flaccid, bruised flesh that hung down between the prisoner's legs. He stared at it for a moment, wondering how it was that such a proportionately small part of a man's anatomy could have the power to devastate a person's life in the way it did.

The captive may have been battered, but he was not blind. He could see his captors' intentions and began thrashing about violently.

'Do hold still,' Peter said impatiently, taking a firm hold of the man's phallus, stretching it in order to reveal its base, buried in an uncontrolled, unwashed bush of pubic hair.

As he did so, a small quantity of pre-cum oozed into the palm of his hand, an instant reminder of the events that had so narrowly been avoided.

'You really got turned on by the prospect of raping our wives didn't you? Well, I'm one of those people who believe that the punishment should fit the crime.'

The man's muffled pleas for leniency turned to muted screams of agony as Peter sawed at the flesh with the shard of glass. Peter had never seen so much blood. Not even from the wrist of inmates who had slashed themselves with razor blades.

It was several minutes before Mike lapsed into unconsciousness at which time his body stopped convulsing and his chin dropped to his chest. All this time Peter and Frank looked on, the former fascinated by the death throes. Peter realised he still had the man's severed organ in his hand and saw a fitting last resting place for it. The sock was no longer necessary and was removed. A gag of a different description took its place.

'That's the damnedest tongue I ever did see,' he joked, much to the disgust of his friend.

Frank's reaction did not go unnoticed.

'What are you looking at? If we hadn't got back when we did, the women would have been raped, they would have all been dead and these two would have been roaming the countryside looking for their next victims.'

Frank could not argue with his friend's point of view. He too had wanted revenge. It was just the form of retribution he felt uneasy with.

'Hadn't we at least bury him?'

'Not yet. We're not even sure he's dead. It would be sick burying someone who might still be alive. God, imagine how terrifying that would be,' Peter responded, seemingly genuine in what he was saying. 'We'll come back tomorrow and do it. Now, help me carry these the bags back to camp. Oh, and it's probably best if we don't mention any of this to the others.'

Frank agreed readily, but wondered how they might cover up his friend's deeds when he was crimson from head to foot with the blood of another man.

'Pete?'

'Yes.'

'Just before you killed him, you said you had seen their handy work before…when you went on that expedition on your own.'

'That's right.'

'Pete, why didn't you mention it before? We could have taken precautions.'

Peter inhaled deeply through his nose.

'I wish I had. At the time I didn't want to cause alarm. Everyone's been through so much already. All that time we were dragging him to the woods, I kept asking myself if it was all my fault. And the answer is that I think it was. So I could find my way back to base, I tied rags to the trees. Looking at it now, I gave them a path to follow all the way into our camp. Please don't hate me because I already hate myself enough for both of us.'

Frank detected genuine remorse.

'I don't blame, or hate you. The only people to blame are both dead and good riddance to them. Now, let's get the worst of that off you before the women and children see you.'

28

A new day brought a noticeable change in Peter's mood – a willingness to co-operate; to be part of a team; to think of things other than smelting rust and watch its inevitable return to dust.

'Frank, if you're up for it, I think we should go on another expedition.'

'Of course I'm up for it, but what about your fire screen. It's a bit unfair that ours is finished and we haven't even gathered the materials for yours.'

'We can manage without that for a while. I've been thinking about what Tess said to me. Our top priority is to find food. The rest can wait.'

'Well, let's do it then. Any ideas where we should head?'

'As a matter of fact, I have. I've been studying the ordnance survey map I picked up on my solo expedition, cross referencing it with the book of street maps I found. There are no road signs, but I found a letter with an address on it. The long and short of it is I think I know where we are.'

Peter held the first of these maps forward, stabbing the poorly folded sheet with his index finger.

'Here, on the edge of this patch of green.'

Frank studied the area.

'Certainly handy to know, but it's a shame it doesn't show buildings in any great detail.'

'No, but it does show roads, and their size.'

'And?'

'Well, to my way of thinking, we should avoid the main roads if we want to steer clear of other people. Besides, if there were any pickings, they'd have been robbed by the thousands of refugees like us, making their way to fresh pastures. If we stick to the back roads, we may find something among the wreckage of vehicles that could be of use. Obviously, on our way we'd be on the lookout for the normal stuff too – rabbits and berries and the like. What do you say?'

'I think it's a great idea. We could all do with some food right now and we can show Joyce, Tess and the kids where we've been and where we're heading. It might make them feel more at ease, us being gone – especially after yesterday.'

'Ok, I just need to add a few bits to my bag and then we can be off.'

Despite the ordeal the women and children had suffered during Frank and

Pete's previous absence, Joyce was more than happy for her husband to get under way and that Peter was going with him, there being safety in numbers.

Just a Frank was keen to assuage any fears his wife might be harbouring, she was equally keen to remind him of her capabilities and for him not to worry unduly.

'We'll be fine.'

She spoke with confidence.

'We'll keep the kids close until you get back and Tess and I will keep weapons at the ready. Please try your best to find something to eat. We've already exhausted all the snacks we got from those animals yesterday.'

Frank could not help but smile and plant a kiss on his wife's cheek. She had come so very far since her breakdown in the back garden of the Allerton's crumbled property, back in Hexley. Every day since she had demonstrated new strengths and his love for her had grown ever stronger.

'We won't return empty handed, I promise.'

Given the limited success of previous expeditions, this was a bold statement to make, but Frank knew his wife would not hold him to it if they returned empty handed. Clearly she would be disappointed, but no more than the hunters.

'You're wise to take extra precautions, but I doubt that there are any more like those two in the local vicinity, so try not to worry.'

This was another questionable statement and Frank knew it. It was true the chances of there being multiple pairs of rapists loose in the area was slim, but as resources became ever more scarce, there was every chance other survivors would be out to steal whatever they could, and by whatever means.

Since settling, excursions from camp had mostly been confined to skirting the edges of the woods, or penetrating the dappled shadows of the trees, accepting their cover as protection from potentially hostile survivors. This was the first time Frank and Peter had deliberately chosen a path into open countryside, potentially exposing themselves to spotters, sentries and other foragers.

Whatever the risk, the benefit of scouting new ground became quickly apparent. The timbers of five-bar gates formed small piles of building materials in each breach of the hedgerows; rabbit scat proved commonplace, strewn across patches of closely harvested grass, indicating a potential source of meat; and then there were the wild animals, foxes seen trotting across fields in the distance.

Frank could see an opportunity to maximise their chances of gathering food, while minimising the effort required to catch it.

Having sat on his haunches to examine the droppings as might a tracker, Frank raised himself to full height before presenting a suggestion.

'We haven't come far and already this is looking promising. Why don't we lay up here and see if we can pick off one or two rabbits. I mean, given the amount of pellets we're treading in, there must be dozens of them around here.'

Peter had other ideas.

'No. Firstly, I think you're overestimating our chances of success. We'd be better off coming back at a later date and setting some traps. Secondly, it's not what we set out to find. Thirdly, I see this trip as being as much about determining what's out here as bringing home the bacon – metaphorically speaking.'

Seeing the merit in his friend's counter-argument, Frank shouldered his bow, sure that if it looked as though they would return to camp empty-handed, there would be an opportunity to find a rabbit or two on the way back.

Having walked across several interconnecting fields, the foraging party eventually reached a junction where two lanes merged. There, the remains of two cars told a story. The surviving components lay in two confined piles, close to where they had fallen. Neither vehicle had been moving when the phenomenon rendered them useless for travel. Rain had since washed away all traces of metal deposits, dispersing them into the grass and wild flower verges. The fine sediment there was flecked with red and blue – vestiges of the paint that had attracted the original buyers.

All that was left in the road were two neat jumbles of plastic, glass, rubber and woven synthetic materials. Atop the front pile was a peculiar rectangular fibreglass lid which Peter recognised as the housing for a wheelchair that would have been affixed to the roof of a disabled person's car. He had seen one in action. The disabled driver had activated a mechanism by remote control from the comfort of her driving seat. The lid of the box had opened. An arm had swung outwards, a wheelchair attached to its end. A winch had lowered the wheelchair to the ground where it was easily extended and its frame locked into placed. The old lady had then transferred from her seat to the chair. It was a time-consuming process, but nonetheless an excellent bit of kit.

Sure enough, on clearing the grey moulding from the wreckage, Peter discovered the remains of a wheelchair, but also those of the driver, much mauled and decomposed, having made many a meal for rats, foxes and maggots. So advanced was the deterioration of the corpse, there was, in fact, little odour to offend Peter's nostrils; so advanced, her gender was only recognisable by the tattered remnants of her clothing.

'What a thoroughly unpleasant way to go,' Peter said. 'I mean, she wouldn't have died straight away. In which case, why was she left like this? I mean, surely the other driver would have checked to see if she was all right. Even if they couldn't do anything, surely they could have made her comfortable; not just left her alone and helpless beneath a fucking fibreglass box.'

Frank shrugged his shoulders.

'Who can guess what happened here, or what was going through anyone's mind. You've seen how normally civilised people have suddenly found the strength to murder their neighbours for a box of cornflakes. How is this any different?'

The matter was forgotten.

While Peter's focus remained with the non-metallic vestiges of the disabled woman's vehicle, Frank's turned to the car behind. There he found no evidence of a driver, or any passengers, other than a weather damaged handbag, stripped of zips, buckles and studs. It was more palatable to believe the owner of the handbag had gone for help than to think she had panicked and run off, but the second option seemed the more plausible. The additional discovery of a pair of women's shoes, discarded further up the road, gave weight to the notion the wearer had simply run away, discarding her low heals so as not to impede her escape.

Peter cared nothing for his friend's sleuthing, or conjecture, being more interested in the leading car; more specifically, its battery. The black plastic box had landed and remained upright, covered and protected from the elements by the laminated windscreen that had slid from its frame, moving forward before coming to a rest among a cloud of powdered rust. If Peter had been a statistician he would have wondered at the odds of this happening. As it was, he was simply grateful and excited in equal measure.

Having wasted enough time as an amateur detective, Frank expanded his search from the area of the front and rear seats to the boot, covered by the rear window and the parcel shelf beneath.

Whatever had caused the previous occupant, or occupants, to flee the scene, and however much they appeared to lack morals, the fact she or they had acted so quickly and without thought had ultimately benefitted the Allerton and Venner families to the tune of one weekly shop, left abandoned.

The items, picked from the supermarket shelves a month before, were still bunched together within half a dozen plastic carrier bags. At first sight, Frank discovered congealed pools of unpleasantness: not-so-fresh fruit and vegetables; lidless jars of pasta sauce; contents of tinned foods; disintegrated paper bags of flour and sugar; and dairy products, sealed in plastic and their shells, but long past their sell-by dates.

More than half of the find had spoiled. Nevertheless, much remained usable and edible: sultanas; mixed nuts; seeds; the inner packaging from a box of cereal, the processed wheaten contents sealed fresh within; cleaning products; rice; pasta; fruit tea bags; a glass jar of instant coffee with a plastic lid; a sealed packet of biscuits; several jars of spices, also with plastic lids; ketchup in a squeezy bottle; a tub of multi-vitamins; a bottle of dandelion and burdock fizzy drink; and a variety of health food snack bars. Whatever had eaten the disabled woman had spared the shopping. Why that was, Frank did not have an answer, but was very thankful all the same.

'Pete, I think we've hit the jackpot,' he said, holding up a sample of the goods he had recovered, hastily wiped clean on his trouser leg. 'Whoever she was, she liked the healthy option. Bless her.'

'Bless her? You've changed your tune. All of a sudden she's a saint.'

'Anyone who provides a starving man a meal is ok in my books.'

Peter was pleased to hear his friend's news for two reasons – the families would eat and Frank was happy enough not to realise that the reason for the trip had not been primarily about finding food, but was rather a lucky happenstance.

Clearing aside unwanted detritus, Peter lowered his head to the marooned battery, its lead terminal posts missing. Positioning himself on his knees, he peered into the two holes left in the plastic casing, detecting a reflection, bouncing off the surface of a liquid within. Given the battery had been sheltered from the rain, it could only be sulphuric acid. Perfect. And yet there was something else; something that caused Peter's excitement to grow so quickly and so monumentally he found it almost impossible to contain.

'Here, Frank, what do you make of this?'

If his friend had been closer, he would have detected a shaking in Peter's voice.

Temporarily abandoning his task, Frank walked over and took up position on his knees next to his friend.

'What am I looking at?'

'I'm not sure. Have a look inside this here battery and tell me what you see. Don't stick your fingers in though. I'm pretty sure that's acid in there. The good stuff.'

Frank leant forward and looked, repositioned his head and looked again, shifting his head from side to side, hardly able to believe what he thought he saw.

'Oh for a bloody torch right now.'

'Don't I know it? Still, what do you see?'

'Well, it looks like a car battery full of acid. You can see the surface a centimetre or two down.'

'And?'

Frank seemed reluctant to answer truthfully, fearing he would make a fool of himself. A look from his friend gave Frank the courage to finish his report.

'Well, it looks like the plates are still intact, but that can't be; they're made of lead – or at least I think they are. Whatever, they're metal of some kind.'

Having received confirmation, Peter sat back on his heels and grabbed his foraging bag. From within he produced and unexpected item – a turkey baster – which he fed through one of the terminal holes into the acid. His eyes were placed closer to the battery than common sense would allow, especially given that he had no safety goggles and the liquid he sought to extract had the potential to blind him in an instant. As unwise as it was, at least it allowed him to witness the sudden disappearance of the lead matrix which proved only to have been a ghost of the electrodes, suspended within.

'Bugger.'

'What's wrong? You got it in your eyes? You need to wash it out immediately. Here, I've got some water.'

'No, it's worse than that.'

'What then?'

'The plates. The disturbance of the turkey baster in the acid has caused them to disappear – to disperse.'

Frank's face startled.

'Fuck, Pete. I'm so sorry.'

As much as his own excitement had been dampened, Frank knew how much Peter's discovery had meant to him; how it had boosted his hope for finding a cure to all mankind's problems.

'You all right?'

'Yep, I'm fine. This thing is big. If it was that easy to fix, someone with more brains than me would have already done it, wouldn't they. Even though the acid didn't prevent rust, it did preserve it to an extent. Sulphuric acid must be at least a part of the cure. From now on, every experiment is going to have a measure of this stuff in it, and if I run out, I don't care if I have to check a thousand more cars, I'll find as much as I need.'

'That's the spirit.

'Come on, suck out as much as you can and then let's get back to the others.'

Pete nodded.

'Ok.'

In addition to the salvaged shopping, Frank could not help but take the car's rear window too, hoping he might incorporate it into the Allerton's shelter.

The rabbits of whom the foragers had seen evidence on their outward journey were clearly visible on their return.

'Looks like they live to hop another day,' Frank commented, feeling the weight of the hoard pulling down on his shoulder.

The wives saw their husbands returning from a distance and tried between them to determine whether the expedition had been successful or not.

'Any luck?' Joyce asked as soon as she judged Frank was in earshot.

'I'll say. Pete's suggestion really paid off.'

The salvaged groceries were presented as proof of the luck they had experienced.

As always, the food was rationed, but it tasted good. The vitamin pills were kept aside for the days when they had nothing to eat.

Eating together promoted conversation.

'Do you know what I miss?' Joyce said.

'Where shall we start?' Tess replied.

'Well, yes, there's a whole tonne of things I miss, but right now I really miss not being able to shave.'

'I agree on that one,' Frank said, running his fingers through his tousled beard.

'You think you've got problems. I hate being all hairy - armpits, legs…and the other bits,' his wife responded.

'Don't I know it? It's like an Angora rabbit that's had a wash and blow dry down there. As for the legs, it reminds me of our dear old dog.'

'Charming.'

'Don't worry, darling, I still would.'

'In your dreams.'

'Believe me, it's been so long, that's the only thing in my dreams these days.'

'Well, as you've been so clever in bringing back all this lovely food, maybe I need to do something about that.'

'Don't get too excited though, I'm only talking about lending you a hand.'

Joyce spoke in code, aware that younger ears were listening.

Later, alone with his wife, Peter could not help but reopen a previous conversation.

'I can't help but remember the look on your face when I told you I am God's chosen one. Well, today's events are further proof.'

Peter described in some detail what he had found and under what circumstances, pointing out how very unlikely it was that he had gone out with the sole intention of finding acid and had found it perfectly preserved at the very first vehicle they stumbled across.

'I mean, what are the chances of me finding a battery that had fallen to the ground in the upright position, protected from the rain which would otherwise have diluted the acid and ruined it?'

Tessa did not want an argument to spoil an otherwise positive day.

'I have to say, that is quite a coincidence.'

'Damned right it is.'

'Fancy a fruit tea?'

'Please.'

'Well, you go do whatever you have to with your experiments and I'll bring it over.'

Grateful for the offer, Peter took his newly acquired bottle of acid over to his open air laboratory, already stocked with samples of bleach and whatever other active fluids he had found to hand.

The mug of tea was presented together with a lone chocolate biscuit, such treats being strictly rationed, a packet providing no more than two or three servings per group member.

Tessa felt obliged to keep her husband company – at least for a while.

Peter was more talkative than usual, acknowledging her presence, but still his mind tended not to stray from the thing he held closest to his heart.

'Imagine, if we can find a car park near here, it might prove to be a gold mine.'

Tessa wondered how fanatical he had become, wondering whether he was still capable of conversation on other matters.

'Why don't you tell me a bit more about you expedition today. We've been stuck here so long it feels like you've been travelling the world, experiencing all sorts of wonders we can only dream about.'

To her surprise, Peter spoke poetically of the countryside, describing the endless sky, the waving grass and the serenity of a landscape devoid of people. Somewhere inside him was the man she had married.

'I was thinking. Why don't you stand up for a minute? After today, it's only fair that you get the same rations as Frank.'

After a very short while, Peter found himself alone once again, his stress level dialed down several notches, the memory of a recent goodnight kiss still lingering.

His smile did not leave him in an instant, but faded gradually, even as he turned his thoughts to his next experiment.

29

Peter was making preparations for yet another firing: scraping out the ash from the furnace; checking the crucible for cracks; measuring out precise quantities of aluminium residue; preparing additives; replenishing the woodpile; ensuring his meticulous notes were up to date.

In the days since sourcing the sulphuric acid, Peter had once again lost interest in anything else.

Frank looked on in despair.

'Pete, stop what you're doing and come hunting with me.'

'I'm busy. Besides, you know where the rabbits hang out.'

'I do but that's beside the point. We need to talk.'

Frank stood in silence, patiently awaiting his friend's reply. Peter, however, continued writing up his experiments, seemingly in no hurry to provide one; but then, just as Frank's willpower was about to break, Peter finished writing his sentence, gathered together his papers, and stood up.

'I'll just drop these off in the shelter and get my things.'

There was no explanation for his sudden change of heart.

Frank was left dumfounded and a little suspicious, having expected his friend to have offered greater resistance.

Tessa was glad to see that her husband had acceded to Frank's request. Someone needed to put Peter's work into perspective. She understood his experiments were valid, but not if it meant the families had to go hungry as a consequence. The food items recovered from the wreckage of the car had been welcomed, but were limited and could only be considered as a one-off, unexpected bonus, not a new source to be tapped whenever the larder became bare.

Something of what Frank had said must have got through to his oldest friend; godfather to his son. Peter prepared for the foraging expedition with enthusiasm, equipping himself with shoulder bag, a freshly made glass knife, his bow and a quiver full of arrows.

'I don't know how long we'll be,' he said, turning to his wife. 'You'll be all right won't you?'

Tessa was surprised. It was the first time her husband had shown any real concern for any of them in a very long time.

'Yes,' she said, simply.

'Good.'

A kiss would have meant everything to Tessa, but Peter – once a passionate lover – had become a man of few emotions and turned away without giving even a hint of a smile.

Peter and Frank, walking side by side, moved away from camp in silence.

They had covered a considerable distance before either of them uttered a single word. Frank had been biding his time, waiting for the right moment to speak, searching for the precise words with which to express exactly what was on his mind.

'Pete, I'm worried about what's happening to you.'

'Why, what is happening to me?'

'You've changed.'

'Is that it?' Peter said, stopping in his tracks to face his accuser. He looked directly into Frank's eyes, his head tilted slightly to one side, indicating a sense of disbelief.

'Is that all that's been bothering you? Is it? Of course I've changed. If you hadn't noticed, we're currently experiencing the greatest threat to mankind since our forebears stood up on two legs for the first time; our lives have been turned upside down and we struggle daily just to stay alive. I think you should be more worried if I hadn't changed.'

Peter had become animated. Frank, seeing this, spoke to qualify his statement, hoping this would calm the situation.

'Look, I agree with you. We've all changed as a result of what's happened. It's just the way you have changed. Take for instance that man you killed.'

Before he could continue, Peter butted in with a few choice words of his own.

He spoke slowly and deliberately, as if he were talking to an imbecile.

'That man was about to rape our wives and murder our families. What else could we have done with him? Let him go? There are no police to turn to now you know; or had you forgotten?'

When Frank had asked his friend to abandon what he was doing so they might talk, he knew he was facing an uphill struggle, trying to get Peter to listen to what he had to say, never mind take notice. As it turned out, the task proved far more difficult than he had anticipated. Peter had become defensive, resentful of anyone who questioned his integrity; especially when it was the best man at his wedding, who should have known better; should have shown loyalty.

Despite his friend's unwillingness to engage in debate, Frank knew he had no alternative than to persevere.

He continued walking, this time at a much slower pace. Peter matched his step.

As they walked, Frank directed his gaze downwards, focusing his mind. He took a deep breath, filling his lungs with fresh country air, subconsciously honing his mind.

'I agree with you that he had to die, but did you really need to slice his dick off and stuff it in his mouth?'

'It seemed the right thing to do at the time,' Peter replied, casually. 'Besides, he did look funny didn't he?'

'That's just what I'm getting at. You found the whole thing amusing.'

'Well, I'm sorry you don't like my sense of humour. You always used to like my jokes.'

Frank came to a halt, turned to stare at his friend of many years, and slowly shook his head in disbelief. Peter looked back at him, wearing a puzzled expression.

'What you did to that man isn't the only problem. I get it you feel you must find a way of restoring metal to the world, and that's an honourable thing to do, but it shouldn't be at the expense of all else. Fine, take your time and find the cure, but what we need now is food and we need to prepare for winter.'

Peter did not like what he was hearing. He paid no attention to the merits of Frank's argument, seeing the words as blasphemy. Peter had been chosen by God to save humanity. Any suggestion that he should desist in doing God's work was utterly unforgivable.

Not realising the extent to which his friend had taken offence, Frank continued.

'In all the time I've known you, you've only ever been to church for one reason, and that was to marry Tess. So what's all this about you having been chosen by God as the saviour of mankind? Tell me you're having us on.'

'That's disappointing. I told Tess in confidence. Never mind, I'm not embarrassed by what I said and I stick by it.'

'Pete, you're not the bloody Messiah. You're not even a disciple.'

In questioning Peter's beliefs and motives, Frank had most definitely overstepped the mark.

Peter calmly unshouldered his bag and bow and lowered them gently to the ground. He then stood almost motionless, his lips pursed, his eyes slowly scanning the ground about him. Frank was slow to read his friend's body language. Perhaps his words, harsh as they were, had finally got through. Feeling this must be the case, he relaxed his posture and offered a smile as a sign of friendship; a virtual olive branch by way of reconciliation. Peter said nothing. His hands slid up his thighs towards the belt around his waist. Then, in a flash, he unsheathed his knife, and with both hands, lunged towards Frank's stomach. Frank blocked the thrust, taking hold of both of Peter's wrists, pushing them downwards, both men grunting with the effort. Peter had chosen a particularly vicious shard as his weapon, the wide end, bound with masking tape, tapering away in a curve to a fine point. The long edges were sharp, the tip was fine, but the whole was brittle. Frank brought up one knee, striking the blade across its broad edge. The instrument snapped easily, leaving the assailant holding only the grip. Effectively disarmed, Peter came to his senses as quickly as he had lost them. The struggle for life and death ceased. The men stepped apart and looked at each other, neither speaking a word. Frank's face portrayed shock, betrayal, disappointment and confusion. Peter's face was blank.

'I'm sorry Frank. You made me do it.'

His voice was weak; distant.

Frank raised both hands, his palms facing his erstwhile friend at shoulder height, angled slightly inwards. He took a breath as if to speak, his lips rolled together, the muscles about his eyes tensed and relaxed, his head twisted almost imperceptibly, but there were not the words in his vocabulary to express the myriad things running through his mind. In the end, he managed only one short sentence.

'I pity you.'

With that, Frank dropped his hands, gathered his things, turned and walked back towards camp. Impassively, Peter watched him go, letting him walk twenty metres before he chose how to react. Bending forward, he picked up his bow with his left hand. He then drew an arrow over his right shoulder, the notched end of the shaft pinched between his right thumb and forefinger. In one movement the notch engaged the string, the other end of the shaft coming to rest in a groove formed by his gripped left hand.

Frank continued to walk.

Peter adopted a side-on stance, pushed the bow forwards, withdrawing the string and the arrow as he did so. His right eye looked down the length of the shaft, lining up the glass tip of the arrow with his target – the broad area between Frank's shoulder blades. Peter could feel the enormous power stored in the bow; and the enormous power that it gave him, having within his hands the means to dispatch the ultimate punishment.

Suddenly, there was a distraction. Joyce had wandered from camp, coming in search of her husband. Seeing Peter moments from losing and arrow into her husband's back, she stopped dead in her tracks, her eyes flitting between both men. Without another thought, she let out a scream, pushed into the world from the pit of her stomach.

'Frank! Look out!'

Frank's face turned towards his wife, and then quickly in the direction indicated by her outstretched arm. His body, tensed for action, spun round to face the threat. His reaction to discovering that the threat was an arrow, aimed directly at his heart, was not what Joyce expected. She saw her husband relax, then his head drop so that his gaze fell upon the floor, at which point he pursed his lips and gently shook his head from side to side. His right hand rose to shoulder level and then flopped back to his side. Then, ignoring the gravity of the situation, he turned back to resume his original course, reaching his wife in a dozen paces. Frank placed his hand on his wife's upper arm, turned her to face camp, and then, with his arm round her waist, walked off, ignoring her demands for an explanation, her arm gesticulating angrily back in the direction of Peter's position.

Peter remained stationary until his arms began to shake and he was no longer able to maintain tension in the bow, at which point he allowed it to relax, and then drop to his side.

Alone, he began to cry in a way he had not done so since childhood. Tears rolled down his cheeks; mucus bubbled from his nostrils; strings of saliva sewed his upper lip to his lower lip which parted to allow the passing of sounds of utter despair.

It was getting dark before Peter eventually returned to camp, his eyes turned to the ground just in front of his feet. Tessa was waiting, worried, and with a thousand questions on her lips.

'Pete, what happened?'

He looked up at her, but said nothing.

'Frank and Joyce came back hours ago. Frank immediately started packing their things and when I asked what had happened, he wouldn't give me an answer.'

Peter shrugged his shoulders.

'Joyce was the only one who would say anything. She told me you were mad and I was welcome to go with them. Why would she say that, Pete?'

'We voiced a difference of opinion, that's all.'

'That's all? It must have been a pretty big difference. Pete, they've gone and they're not coming back. The kids were crying. It was horrible.'

'Hmm. We're probably better off without them anyway. It's times like this when you discover who your friends really are. This was the first real test and they failed.'

'Shouldn't we go after them? Joyce told me they have somewhere better in mind. Perhaps we should follow them.'

Peter had no desire to move anywhere. It would mean disrupting his experiments.

'No, we'll be all right. Everything we have is here.'

'But, Pete?'

Peter picked up his hunting gear, and made to stow it.

'From now on, you keep Emma in the shelter with you; I'll sleep in the one vacated by the Venners. That way I won't disturb you.'

'Disturb me?'

'Yes, I intend to continue my experiments tomorrow morning, at first light. I've lost enough time as it is.'

True to his word, Peter resumed his experiments, just where he had left off. Having risen long before his wife and daughter, it did not enter his head to have breakfast before he started. Indeed, when Tessa approached him to say she was taking Emma foraging for food, he barely acknowledged her presence, never mind suggesting she bring him something to eat.

With sadness in her heart, Tessa turned to walk away, but then to her surprise, Peter began to speak.

Her head turned to find that the words were meant for her, but the face that delivered them was more interested in whatever task her husband had to hand.

'You do that dear. You know where the fields are, don't you? I've got to tell you, I think I may be on to something. I remember seeing a programme which said something about rust being caused by a chemical reaction with a particular kind of oxygen. Somewhere along the line, free radicals, or radicals, or something, are formed. Anyway, the scientists were saying these free

298

whatsits land up in our bodies and might be the cause of aging. We get them from exposure to the sun, from smoke and from meat cooked on the barbecue. Luckily for us there are anti-something's in fresh vegetables and red wine which reduce their numbers. It's a shame I don't remember more, but that can't be helped.

'What if this rust phenomenon were caused by a particularly virulent strain of these things, or something like them? The answer to our problems could lie with fresh vegetables. They might provide an anti-dote. Wouldn't that be something? The scientist were always going on about the importance of eating your five a day.'

'Look Pete, I have no idea what you are talking about.'

Peter's head turned to his wife.

'No, of course you don't. That's why I've been chosen and not you.'

Their brief conversation was terminated, and for all the good it did, it might as well never have taken place. Tessa was about to turn away again when she noticed the remains of a potato. Peter saw it as another possible antidote. Tessa saw it as the waste of a precious meal. She dearly wanted to say something, but found herself too frightened of what her husband's reaction might be.

Peter established a pattern that morning. Tessa would take Emma in search of food every day, providing Peter with sustenance whenever she could. He did notice that the portions were becoming smaller and less frequent.

Several mornings passed. Tessa approached her husband as normal.

'Pete, we need food. Emma's not well.'

'She'll be all right once I've found what I'm looking for. I'm nearly there. I can feel it.'

'You should see yourself. You look terrible.'

'You don't look so hot yourself.'

'I know, and who have I got to thank for that?'

Her sharp words were lost on her husband as he doggedly continued preparing for the next firing.

Two days elapsed before another word passed between them. Peter was once again carrying out his experiments. Tessa approached with the intention of persuading her husband to suspend his activities for just a few days in order that they could more effectively search for food. It was a pointless exercise. Tessa knew that, but she had to try.

She spoke quietly and with some effort.

'Pete, Emma is really not well.'

'Give her plenty of fluids and let her rest.'

As she had anticipated, her husband dismissed her request out of hand, sure in the knowledge she and his daughter could manage if only they would make the effort, and that the hardship would be worth it in the end. Tessa went to leave, but unusually Peter wanted to say something himself.

'I've been meaning to bring this up for ages, but I've been so busy.'

'What?'

'I think it's time we started doing stuff again.'

'What!?'

'I know we've been under a lot of pressure, but I have my needs. We've done nothing since the day I brought back the acid and even then it only took the edge of it. Seriously, how am I meant to concentrate on my work while I'm constantly distracted by this aching in the pit of my stomach? We've got the two shelters now so we can have our privacy. What do you say?'

'You must be mad.'

'Why?'

'We've got no contraception for a start.'

'I'll pull out.'

'That's not good enough. What happens if I get pregnant? We can't find enough food as it is!'

'You won't get pregnant, I promise.'

'Pete, I don't have either the energy, or the inclination, and even if I did, I'm not prepared to risk falling pregnant when all we can rely on for contraception is a promise from a man who, just lately can't be relied upon for anything.'

'As I said, I have my needs.'

'Well, go and see to them, but don't involve me and don't do it in front of Emma.'

'Look Tessa, I'll take you with or without your permission if I have to. Just remember that.'

Tessa could not believe what she was hearing.

'You're no better than those rapists you killed.'

She would have stormed off at this point, but found it quite impossible. Instead, she walked slowly away without uttering another word.

Her reaction came as a surprise. It annoyed Peter sufficiently that he found it impossible to return to his work. Venting his frustration, he snatched up the journal in which he recorded every aspect of his experimentation, and made a personal entry:

Today asked T for sex - refused. Will allow 3 days for her to come to her senses.

The entry was short but had the desired effect, diffusing pent up feelings of anger and frustration that would otherwise have been harmful to his progress. Now that his wife's unpleasantness had been put behind him, and inspired by the weight of the book that sat in his hands, Peter turned his thoughts towards his next steps. The interruption had been unwelcome, but he could see how it might be put to his advantage, forcing him to take time out to re-evaluate his position.

Turning to a virgin page of lined paper, Peter selected a different colour of crayon, taking care to sharpen it to a point using the edge of a glass shard - a fresh crayon for fresh ideas.

Making himself comfortable against a tree trunk, he began.

My thoughts on the infection.

<u>Source:</u> almost certainly the meteor shower. An unprecedented event. So too was the loss of all metal. Two such unusual phenomena, so close to each other, too great to be a coincidence.

<u>Method:</u> meteor entered atmosphere. No material reached ground. Therefore spread via atmosphere - Incubation period - effect.

<u>Extent:</u> almost certainly worldwide. Meteor shower was global. Therefore, rust is global. Also, no signs of external aid.

All metals appear to have been affected. Not an accelerated form of normal rusting - even gold reduced to dust.

<u>Possible cures:</u> Extreme heat - meteors entering atmosphere experienced temperatures far higher than furnace, but survived. Conclusion - heat not the answer.

Extreme cold - infection would have experienced the cold of space, but survived. Conclusion - cold not the answer.

Anything in nature that might provide a cure would have to store it within its structure. Otherwise, infection would have died on contact. Or, effect might be real but localised.

Already tried: salt; acids; alkalis; fresh vegetables; greens; potato skins; medicines; tea tree oil.

Why did samples re-rust? What is contaminated - sample or environment? Heating the sample drives out oxygen. Does heating suspend infection or make it vulnerable? If heating makes vulnerable, extended exposure to relatively low temperatures might weaken it more. Does it need oxygen? It would not have got it in space, but perhaps survives in hibernation until finds it. Is infection more vulnerable while suspended? Does heating drive out the infection only to be re-infected from the environment?

Methods: Is it better to add potential cures to samples while cold or once molten? If infection more vulnerable when heated, cure should be added when molten. Might be necessary to duplicate each experiment, adding cure to samples before and after. Adding when molten might cause cure to vapourise before it has any effect. Adding from cold might cause cure to be cooked out as are vitamins from veg when overcooked, but does ensure even distribution throughout sample. Perhaps I already have the cure but have not been using enough.

Peter stopped writing, having had a rather unpleasant thought. If the infection was airborne, or in the environment, he would never be able to solve the problem. He might be successful in finding a way to rid a sample of the infection, but he could never hope to treat the entire planet, in which case, the metal would always become re-infected. Such thoughts were defeatist and would not be permitted to flourish.

Having taken a moment to re-sharpen the crayon, the amateur scientist continued setting his thoughts down on paper.

Does infection need a host, i.e. metal, or can it lie dormant? If it does, infection might have moved from environment to metal. Cured metal could stay healthy unless comes in contact with infected metal.

Questions brought possibilities and avenues for exploration, but they also brought more questions.

Had any molten sample taken longer to revert to rust than any other?

Of this he could not be sure. He had made no observations as to timing during his experimentation. After all, he did not possess a watch. On reflection, this factor might be of great importance. He would have to construct a timepiece and re-do all his previous work. It was a daunting task, but until he had re-tested every potential antidote he had tried so far, none could be discounted. From then on his operation would have to be conducted under much stricter scientific conditions.

His final entries laid down the methods by which further experiments would be carried out.

1) Weigh out equal quantities of aluminium residue.

For this he would need to construct some crude scales.

2) Weigh out equal quantities of potential cure.

3) Once molten, continue heating for a timed period.

4) Once poured, visually gauge the quantity of slag produced. Note the texture. Note the colour.

The infection might be contained within the impurities. More slag might indicate more infection having been driven out. Changes in texture and colour might indicate a potential cure had brought about an effect.

5) Time how long molten sample takes to revert to rust.

The time piece that Peter envisaged building would not tell the time of day, but a simple water clock would give a relative indication of how effective one additive had been when compared with another.

Peter was happy with his work. It had used up a substantial quantity of precious paper, but it had been worth it. Lacking anyone who was willing to discuss the problem with him, putting it in writing had allowed him to air and challenge his own views, potentially bringing him one step closer to discovering a cure.

The day was almost at an end. Peter decided to retire early in order to design the clock in his head. Going to bed with a problem usually meant waking with an answer.

From the solitude of the Venner's abandoned shelter, Peter could hear the sounds of his daughter whimpering nearby, and the muffled tones of his wife who tried to placate her. Shielding himself from the psychological affect her cries would otherwise have had on him, he imagined how they would all feel when he at last restored metal to their lives. The smiles in his head blocked reality and he soon found salvation in sleep.

At first light, Peter was keen to get going once again. It was unfortunate his body did not share his enthusiasm.

'Don't fail me now,' he said aloud, annoyed that his strength was beginning to fade, just as he was beginning to feel that the solution was in sight.

Tessa was also up at first light, keen to prepare whatever food she could find, not so much for herself, but for her daughter. She was hungry, Emma was ill, and despite the way her relationship with her husband had suffered, especially since the departure of the Venners, Tessa still felt it her duty to care for Peter too. To this end, she divided up the Spartan provisions, giving equal portions to Emma and her husband, leaving herself short by almost a half. She took the meal to Peter who was both grateful and amiable, apparently having forgotten their previous exchange. He spoke of nothing but his experiments and showed his wife his notebook, failing to cover the entry that recorded the ultimatum he had set down. Tessa was too weary to notice; too focused on her hunger pangs to care. Seeing that there would be nothing gained in provoking him by suggesting he leave his work, she listened for a while before slipping away in a daze in search of another meal.

It took the morning to complete the water clock, but having finished it, Peter was pleased to see it worked very well. It seemed consistent, although there were no other timepieces to compare it with, and it 'ran' for an appropriate length of time; long enough to measure the extended firing time, and accurate enough to measure how long it took for the metal to re-rust.

The scales were easier to construct, being a simple balance that compared the weight of a quantity of aluminium powder to the weight of a medium sized stone.

With his new methodology firmly in place, Peter began his experiments afresh. Not only did he have to try each previous potential cure again, but he now had to carry out the same experiment twice. He was further hampered by the need for firings of extended length, costing more time, energy and fuel. In addition, the furnace had a life span and required constant repair. Eventually, patching the damaged walls was no longer enough. A new furnace was required, built several hundred metres into the trees, closer to untapped areas of readily available wood.

The bellows, too, needed repair. Large carrier bags were scarce, forcing Peter to make do with adhesive tape, the layers of which were becoming thicker with every passing day. Then there was the plastic vacuum cleaner pipe which, although set back from the interior of the kiln, still suffered during each firing, causing it to grow shorter and shorter, necessitating its reseating many times. Thankfully Peter had a spare.

Days went by, but for Peter, time stood still. Hunger pangs went unnoticed. Tessa continued to bring him food, but often now it amounted to little more than a plate of stewed nettles. Sometimes they would have a half-hearted argument, but Tessa never seemed to have the stomach for anything more.

Invariably, she would eventually wander away, nothing gained, just as she had expected.

Then, one morning, having just witnessed his latest batch of molten metal stubbornly revert back to powder, Peter stopped for a moment, and in that moment realised he had not seen his wife in what seemed like an unusually long time. It must have been a while as he felt even more hungry than usual. In his mind, there could be only two explanations. Either she was out foraging, or she was sulking. Whichever it was, he still had a job to do and, if necessary, he would just have to get on without her.

Peter's new way of working had brought some progress. His first task had been to establish a benchmark. To do this, he had fired a measured quantity of powder for a measured length of time. He had used no additives. The sample had become molten and, as expected, rusted immediately upon cooling. He had repeated the procedure, this time increasing the length of firing to see if time in the furnace had any bearing. This sample also melted and reverted to powder on cooling. However, the latter slowed down the reversion considerably. Several more firings followed to determine the optimum length of time the sample should remain in the furnace. With this established, Peter started adding substances which he felt might have an effect. Most produced an almost identical result. Equal amounts of slag. The molten samples were the same colour and consistency and reverted at the same rate. There were others that showed more promise. Specifically, the samples which had been treated with tea-tree oil - a preciously rare antiseptic taken from the first aid box - potato skins, cut thick to retain the layer of goodness, and the bark of the silver birch. All performed noticeably better than the rest; all but the acid which appeared to have by far the greatest potency.

Peter was growing more excited with every partial success, sure that his quest was nearly at an end. It just needed one more leap of imagination, but thinking clearly was becoming increasingly more difficult. He had been surviving on water, very little, or no food, and almost no sleep. His skin seemed looser; so did his teeth.

'The sooner I finish here the better. Then we can all get back to normal,' he whispered hoarsely, the quality of his voice taking him by surprise.

Trying to focus his mind on his work, Peter thought hard about what the results were telling him to do next.

The firing was weakening the infection. He was sure of that. The oil, skins and bark were each producing more slag. Why? Did the slag contain dead infection? Perhaps attacking the infection with one substance was not enough. Combining the two or three most promising additives when the infection had already been weakened by the heating process...

Peter stopped his mind in its tracks, afraid to let any new ideas enter his head in case they dislodged the fledgling thought that was trying so desperately to emerge from its shell.

It hatched.

Peter needed to make fresh preparations. He had to know the answer. Darkness was a long way off, but he knew that it was his enemy and would be upon him before he knew it. The clouds looming overhead were his enemy too. Grey and foreboding, they threatened rain. There was fuel to be gathered and he would need fresh supplies of potato skins. Then there was the firing itself. That was by no means a quick process.

What to do first?

Peter scampered back to the heart of the encampment where he found his wife and daughter lying inside their shelter.

'I see you took my advice. Plenty of water and bed rest.'

Tessa gave him a contemptuous look.

'Have we got any potatoes? I'm nearly there.'

'No, Peter, we haven't got any potatoes.'

She spoke with a resigned tone.

'Okay, you rest. I'll go and find one.'

Then, as an afterthought, he added, 'Have you thought any more about what I said?'

Tessa half closed her eyes, sleepily, and slowly shook her head from side to side.

'Perhaps now's not the best time, eh?'

Having found new energy reserves from deep within, Peter set off in a hurry for the fields.

It was a sorry sight when he got there. The crop had been lifted by a thousand or more passing refugees, leaving only the odd stray potato here and there to be unearthed. Tessa had returned to this same patch of ground many times before, and on each visit had found it harder to locate one of the dwindling number of remaining vegetables – ones that were not entirely rotten.

Peter grubbed about in the soil with a stick for several hours until perseverance finally paid dividends, providing him with two partially preserved specimens. Although definitely past their prime, they still appeared fit for purpose. Nonetheless, Peter harboured a concern their condition might affect their potency, but he had no choice.

Peter ran, as best he could, back to the site of his furnace.

Emma's plastic knives were not much good at cutting most things, but they made swift work of paring the skins into an awaiting container. Once crushed with a stone, they, along with a dozen drops of tea tree oil and a quantity of finely shredded bark, were added to a sample of the aluminium residue, and rolled in to a ball of paste. This was then dropped into a freshly formed crucible and placed inside the furnace where it would be safe. All that remained to be done was to restock the fuel supplies. Peter had used all the twigs and branches that lay on the floor of the wood for several hundred metres around. Nevertheless, no more than an hour passed before he was ready. This was not time wasted. Peter hoped that by letting the mixture of powder, oil, skin and bark stand for this length of time, the additives would have a chance to marinate, working on the invisible infection. The last ingredient to be added to the mix was a portion of acid, delivered to the crucible by means of the turkey baster, dripped into a hole pressed into the ball of paste with his thumb. Once applied, a stick was used to fold in the corrosive liquid.

Pumping on the bellows, stopping every now and again to stoke the fire, time should have flown by, but this time it was different. Perhaps it was the anticipation. Perhaps it was his body letting him know it had had enough. Whatever the case, the rate at which the water clock emptied now seemed to have slowed to an idle.

Finally, the clock indicated the end of the firing process.

The clay plug was removed from the mouth of the furnace, after which the crucible was carefully maneuvered out, balanced on a forked stick, a second branch clamping down upon it to keep it steady. Once safely on the ground, a metre from the fierce heat of the furnace, Peter scrapped the slag to one side and watched as the mirrored surface dulled as the molten metal cooled. It dulled, but it did not appear to be crumbling as it had inevitably done in the past.

The clock was still dripping and it continued to do so, surpassing all previous records. Eventually, the clock was dry and still the metal remained solid, defying the laws of the new world. Peter had to be sure. The sample had to be cooled to see if it remained stable. First he poured water into the crucible, and when the metal had stopped hissing, he took it to the stream to immerse it completely until his fingers were numb with the cold. The nugget was still there.

Shaking with excitement, Peter hobbled back towards the shelters, weakness of limbs causing him to stumble clumsily through the undergrowth. He called his family from as far away as the stream – a distance too great for a town crier to make himself heard; impossible for a man whose larynx had been exposed to unfiltered smoke for days on end – and yet still he called the names Tessa and Emma, over and over again.

Breaking through the trees into the clearing, Peter came to an abrupt halt. The centre of camp appeared devoid of activity; uninhabited.

'Where the fuck is everyone?' Peter whispered, his throat strained from overuse.

A breeze rustled the flap of the shelter that, since the departure of the Venner family, had been given over for the sole use of his wife and daughter. It drew Peter's attention.

'The lazy bitch,' he snapped, aggrieved that while he had been toiling steadily since first light, the rest of the family had chosen to spend the day in bed.

Had this been just another day, like any other since the disaster, Peter's grievance would have grown and grown until it was nothing short of a fiery rage, but today was not just another day. There could be no comparison, for this was the beginning of a new dawn. The beginning of the salvation of mankind, and he was the instrument of the Lord who had made it all possible.

Holding the small, unblemished nugget of solid aluminium between the finger and thumb of his right hand, Peter could not contain the news of his triumph as he flung back the tarpaulin entrance flap.

'I've done it...' he rasped, the rawness in his throat causing him to finish with a cough and a splutter.

His words seemed to lose their impact almost before they had been fully formed; certainly before Peter recovered from his coughing fit.

Something was very wrong. The appalling smell alone told him that.

Peter's heart pounded as he reached with his left hand into the darkened confines of the shelter in order to throw back the heavily soiled bedding, but then he hesitated, fearful of what he was about to uncover. Having taken a moment to brace himself, and to inhale a lung full of fresh air, filtered through the fingers of his right hand that still held the aluminium nugget, he yanked - nothing. The shelter was bare. Then he noticed a note, written in crayon, tucked into the fabric of the roof. The note was not written in his wife's hand, but was definitely the handwriting of a woman.

We've taken Tessa and Emma. They're safe and in good hands.

It could only be the work of Joyce.

There was no point trying to call out. They would be far away by now and Peter doubted his current voice would carry to the next shelter, let alone out of the encampment.

Placing the nugget in his pocket, Peter sat down to think; something that was not easy these days, given the near starvation diet he had been forced to adopt. He studied the note, hoping it might reveal clues to their whereabouts. It did.

The paper had been taken from his personal supply; one that he kept dry, sealed in a Tupperware box. He quickly retrieved the tub, opened it, rifled through the remaining papers, and confirmed what he had suspected. The crude map that he had drawn of their surrounding area had gone; the crude map that bore the word 'BEWARE!' It might have been taken weeks ago, but it most certainly had been taken - not mislaid - and this he knew would lead him to his family and to the Venners.

30

There was not an hour of light left in the day; the amount of time Peter believed he would need to reach his intended destination, even by the most direct route, given his current weakened state. His body had been worked hard: pumping the bellows; fetching water for the clock; gathering wood with which to fuel the furnace. At the same time, Peter had not eaten in days, his lungs had been exposed to unfiltered smoke for hours on end, and insomnia continued to plague him, despite his crippling fatigue. There was nothing else for him to do than spend one last night in the Venners' shelter and mentally prepare for the morning.

With day break, there was nothing to detain Peter any longer. He had no breakfast to consume; no last minute preparations to make.

By normal standards, the distance to travel was not so great, but the push that had ultimately restored metal to the world had taken its toll, making every step a hardship; a personal mountain to conquer. His reserves were spent. All he had left was an inner strength, generated by a desperate yearning to be reunited with his family. He wanted them close by. He wanted to take them in his arms and to squeeze them with all the remaining might his withered body could muster. He wanted to show them that he had fulfilled his promise to his daughter in making everything better. He wanted Emma to love him again as she used to.

Peter set out on a linear route, running from south to north. En route he passed a wide, shallow, stagnant lake; stumbled across a ditch; bypassed a patch of impenetrable undergrowth; remembered a tree that had been blown apart by lightning.

Eventually, he emerged from the trees to find a lane running across his path, east to west. It curved sharply to the north after a few hundred metres in either direction. He knew to follow it to the east. As expected, the lane immediately curved round to the right then, after another fifty metres, to the left. It continued to wind this way and that a further seven times. Then, at last, Peter caught sight of the remains of an isolated and familiar row of three dwellings, hidden behind a thick, unkempt, hedge. The buildings still lay something less than half a mile ahead. His approach was slow and silent, brought on not by stealth, but by his body shutting down. He would love to have run the final distance. He would love to have been able to call to his loved ones. He could hear his rasping breath more than he could his own voice, which died in his throat. His eyes were heavy, his brain having rerouted all energy into keeping him upright and moving forward.

From the road, through deadening eyes, Peter could see no signs of life at the first house. At the second, he noticed that the remains of the brick-built garage had been cleared; that the slates that had once formed the roof had been stacked to form a neat pile. However, there were no other signs of recent habitation. The third and final residence offered greater hope, its garage, the one that had provided such a valuable crop of identifiable aluminium residue, had been closed to the elements, a blue tarpaulin hanging across the aperture where once a metal up-and-over door had sealed the opening.

Peter shuffled up the length of the driveway, anticipation building with every painful step. In less than a minute he was standing silently outside the garage, his ears straining to hear the slightest sound that might hint of what lay behind the blue, plastic wall.

He heard the faint sound of voices; familiar voices; voices that were not aware of his presence.

'Tess! Emma!' he rasped.

The voices within became instantly more excitable.

Moments later, a single arm punched past one edge of the tarpaulin and cast it aside. It was Joyce, and beyond her was a hospital, five mattresses squeezed in side by side, two being occupied by two rather sick, but clean patients, tucked beneath freshly laundered bedding. Their faces and exposed arms looked shockingly emaciated, but both seemed comfortable and well cared for.

Joyce wore a worried expression on her face. Nonetheless, she stepped aside, allowing Peter to pass. He needed no invitation. Hobbling across the cramped floor, he collapsed to the ground between his wife and his daughter, wrapping his arms around both of them as hard as his weakened muscles would allow.

Simultaneously, both patients rolled onto their sides, their arms reaching across to rest on his back.

Peter began to cry uncontrollably. When finally he stopped and was able to lift his head, he found, to his great relief that Tessa and Emma shared his tears, and they were smiling. Peter could not contain his emotions.

'I'm so sorry. I'm so sorry for everything. I'm so sorry for neglecting you.

I'm so sorry for nearly losing you. I'm so sorry for not being there when you needed me the most.'

His words were delivered at a whisper.

At that moment, Frank entered the shelter, stopping just inside the door. His and Peter's last encounter having been less than amicable, Frank surveyed the scene warily.

His best and oldest friend was unarmed, filthy, and as close to death's door as Tessa and Emma had been when they had been brought to the sanctuary. Frank could feel nothing but pity.

With effort, Peter reluctantly pulled himself from his wife and child's embrace and stood up, his body stooped, his head inclined more towards one shoulder than the other.

'Sorry, Frank.'

Frank's face became contorted.

'Looks like we'll be needing to squeeze in another bed, but first we need to clean you up; you're filthy.'

After several days of tender loving care, provided by Joyce, and latterly supplemented by Tessa and Emma, who were slightly more advanced in their recuperation, Peter was fit enough to leave the confines of the garage and discuss with Frank what had happened.

'Those bandits, they lied to us. As we thought, the items they surrendered to us were only a small fraction of the stuff they'd hoarded. The rest was here all along. It must have been here when you visited before. You just didn't see it. Joyce and I found it in the undergrowth, beneath some tarpaulins. We were lucky to find it as they'd camouflaged everything really well.

'Since then, we've been systematically stripping out everything salvageable from all three houses, sorting it and storing it. Not just the piles of tiles and timber you must have already seen, but all those things we saved from our own houses but couldn't bring with us; things to make our new home more comfortable.

'We've cleared the downstairs toilet in this one and made it waterproof and that's where we keep the majority of the food those bastards squirreled away. Here, let me show you.'

The small room was filled from floor to ceiling with plastic boxes and bags, resting on a makeshift platform and on the shelves of a salvaged solid wooden bookcase – joinery and glue keeping the individual pieces whole.

Frank was keen to list some of the foodstuffs.

'We've got cereals; oats; cooking oil; nuts; dried fruit; biscuits; crisps; not to mention toilet rolls; the list goes on.'

'Jesus, I wonder where they got all that from.'

'Well, you and I both witnessed the looting in the days immediately after the event. Those two would have thought nothing of bludgeoning someone to death to get hold of what they wanted. In a dog eat dog world, seemingly they were the Rottweilers. And they were thorough. They didn't just accumulate food. If it wasn't metal, they saved it – cookware; tools; containers; bedding; clothing; weapons; again, the list goes on and on. We're in the process of making another room watertight. Maybe you could help us…if you're feeling up to it.'

'Of course I can. Anything I can do to make up for being such an arse.'

'A psycho nutter arse, if you ask me.'

Peter smiled, pleased his friend could make light of what he had become.

'Granted, a psycho nutter arse. But not anymore.'

'Glad to hear it, otherwise I'd have to hide all the sharp objects.'

Peter smiled again.

Frank paused for a moment before changing the subject.

'Forgive me, but when we were back in camp and I wanted to know what you thought you were doing, I rifled through your papers. I came across that map you drew on your first expedition. When I walked out of camp that last day, at first I had no idea where I was taking my family, but then I thought of that map and took it. I didn't fully appreciate the meaning of the word, BEWARE! I just knew it was a definite place we could head for. We only discovered the remains of the couple when we were recovering this little lot. They were still pegged out in the back garden, hidden in the long grass – we buried them as best we could. To be honest, there wasn't much left to put in the ground. Handy because the tools we have to dig with are only good for making the shallowest of graves. Seeing them brought it home to me why you felt such hatred towards the men who nearly killed our families.

'Despite the fact you tried to kill me, I still feared that we'd lost you. I always hoped you'd return – the old you, not psycho you, of course.'

Peter was glad his friend finally knew the truth, but found difficulty accepting an apology.

'I would have killed you…had you not stopped me, and yet you feel the need to apologise for nicking a scrap of paper. It's me who needs to apologise.

'Can you forgive me? I mean, truly forgive me?'

'These are extraordinary times. Of course I forgive you.'

By their body language alone, it was clear neither man felt comfortable displaying their own emotions, nor witnessing the other's.

'Here, let me show you something else we've done.'

Frank led his friend to the garage belonging to the middle house which had been re-roofed and had once again become, for all intents and purposes, weather tight. Inside, Frank had lined the walls with more quality bookcases. Each shelf was filled with books; books carefully chosen for the information they contained; books preserving the knowledge of mankind; and many of the classics.

'There's even a Bible.'

'No need to have one on my account, but I suppose we should keep it – and maybe a Koran.'

'So, your back to being an atheist, are you?'

'I was always taught you should never discuss religion or politics. And why would you feel the need when there's so much else to talk about.

'Anyway, where did you get all these? They can't all have come from one house.'

'No, it turns out there's a small town about three miles up the road to the west. They had a library. Your design for an A-frame enabled me to bring them back; them and the foam mattresses we're now sleeping on.'

Peter approved of his friend's work, but then waited for a lull in their conversation.

Choosing the right moment, not wishing to raise concern or alarm, or to seem ungrateful, Peter put a question that had been at the forefront of his mind since being deemed fit enough to leave the sanctuary of the garage.

'Frank, the clothes I was wearing when I got here, where are they?'

His friend appeared surprised.

'They were rotten. I threw them away. Why? Didn't I do the right thing?'

'No, these are far better.'

Peter put his facial muscles through an exercise routine, his eyes fixed on nothing in particular.

'Before you threw them away,' he asked, trying to sound casual, 'did you check the pockets; did you find anything?'

'No, they were so dirty I really could have done with a pair of tongs to handle them; I wasn't about to stick my hands inside the pockets. Why, was there something valuable in them?'

Peter considered the question before answering; thought of what he had nearly lost for the sake of fanatically following his self-determined quest to the detriment of all and everyone else.

'No, nothing important.'

Printed in Great Britain
by Amazon

42847033R00189